# Queen
# in Waiting

# JEAN PLAIDY HAS ALSO WRITTEN

BEYOND THE BLUE MOUNTAINS
(A novel about early settlers in Australia)
DAUGHTER OF SATAN
(A novel about the persecution of witches and Puritans in the 16th and 17th centuries)
THE SCARLET CLOAK
(A novel of 16th century Spain, France and England)

*Stories of Victorian England*
{ IT BEGAN IN VAUXHALL GARDENS
{ LILITH
THE GOLDSMITH'S WIFE
(The story of Jane Shore)
EVERGREEN GALLANT
(The story of Henri of Navarre)

*The Medici Trilogy*
*Catherine de' Medici*
{ MADAME SERPENT
{ THE ITALIAN WOMAN } Also available in one volume
{ QUEEN JEZEBEL

*The Lucrezia Borgia Series*
MADONNA OF THE SEVEN HILLS
LIGHT ON LUCREZIA

*The Ferdinand and Isabella Trilogy*
CASTILE FOR ISABELLA
SPAIN FOR THE SOVEREIGNS
DAUGHTERS OF SPAIN

*The French Revolution Series*
LOUIS THE WELL-BELOVED
THE ROAD TO COMPIÈGNE
FLAUNTING EXTRAVAGANT QUEEN

*The Tudor Novels*
*Katherine of Aragon*
{ KATHERINE, THE VIRGIN WIDOW
{ THE SHADOW OF THE POMEGRANATE } Also available in one volume
{ THE KING'S SECRET MATTER
MURDER MOST ROYAL
(Anne Boleyn and Catherine Howard)
THE SIXTH WIFE
(Katherine Parr)
ST. THOMAS'S EVE
(Sir Thomas More)
THE SPANISH BRIDEGROOM
(Philip II and his first three wives)
GAY LORD ROBERT
(Elizabeth and Leicester)
THE THISTLE AND THE ROSE
(Margaret Tudor and James IV)
MARY, QUEEN OF FRANCE
(Queen of Louis XII)

*The Mary Queen of Scots Series*
ROYAL ROAD TO FOTHERINGAY
THE CAPTIVE QUEEN OF SCOTS

*The Stuart Saga*
THE MURDER IN THE TOWER
(Robert Carr and the Countess of Essex)

*Charles II*
{ THE WANDERING PRINCE
{ A HEALTH UNTO HIS MAJESTY
{ HERE LIES OUR SOVEREIGN LORD
THE THREE CROWNS (William of Orange)
THE HAUNTED SISTERS (Mary and Anne)
THE QUEEN'S FAVOURITES (Sarah Churchill and Abigail Hill)

*The Georgian Saga*
THE PRINCESS OF CELLE
QUEEN IN WAITING
CAROLINE, THE QUEEN
THE PRINCE AND THE QUAKERESS
THE THIRD GEORGE
PERDITA'S PRINCE
SWEET LASS OF RICHMOND HILL
INDISCRETIONS OF THE QUEEN

*General Non-Fiction*
A TRIPTYCH OF POISONERS
(Cesare Borgia, Madame de Brinvilliers and Dr. Pritchard)

*The Spanish Inquisition Series*
THE RISE OF THE SPANISH INQUISITION
THE GROWTH OF THE SPANISH INQUISITION
THE END OF THE SPANISH INQUISITION

# Queen
# in Waiting

## JEAN PLAIDY

G. P. PUTNAM'S SONS / NEW YORK

G. P. Putnam's Sons
*Publishers Since 1838*
200 Madison Avenue
New York, NY 10016

Library of Congress Cataloging in Publication Data

Plaidy, Jean, date.
  Queen in waiting.

  1. Caroline, consort of George II, King of
Great Britain, 1683–1737—Fiction.   I. Title.
PR6015.I3Q43   1985      823'.914      85-9287
ISBN 0-399-13101-9

Printed in the United States of America

1 2 3 4 5 6 7 8 9 10

# CONTENTS

# BIBLIOGRAPHY

*Lives of the Queens of England of the House of Hanover* — Dr. Doran

*The Four Georges* — Sir Charles Petrie

*Caroline of Ansbach* — R. L. Arkell

*Caroline the Illustratious* — W. H. Wilkins

*Caroline of England* — Peter Quennell

*The House of Hanover* — Alvin Redman

*A History of the Four Georges and William IV* — Justin McCarthy

*The Four Georges* — W. M. Thackeray

*British History in the Nineteenth Century* — G. M. Trevelyan

*Sir Robert Walpole* — J. H. Plumb

*George II and His Ministers* — Reginald Lucas

*Lord Hervey's Memoirs* — Edited by Romney Sedgwick

*The Dictionary of National Biography* — Edited by Sir Leslie Stephen and Sir Sidney Lee

*British History* — John Wade

*History of England* — William Hickman Smith Aubrey

*England Under the Hanoverians* — Sir Charles Grant Robertson

*The First George* — Lewis Melville

*Eighteenth Century London Life* — Rosamund Baynes Powell

*Bishop Burnett's History of His Own Time*

*A Constitutional King, George the First* — Sir H. M. Impert-Terry

*Letters of Lady Mary Wortley Montague*

*Notes on British History* — William Edwards

## The Unwilling Bridegroom

SOPHIA CHARLOTTE, Electress of Brandenburg, was discussing the possibility of a marriage for her dear but sadly impoverished friend Eleanor Erdmuthe Louisa, widowed Margravine of Ansbach.

"For you see, my dear Frederick, her position is intolerable as it stands and what will become of that poor child of hers if her mother has no position in the world?"

Frederick, Elector of Brandenburg, smiled at his wife. He rarely smiled when he was not with her for his was far from a genial nature; but since their marriage he had never ceased to be delighted with her and had been a faithful husband which was something of a miracle when the way of life among German princelings was promiscuous by habit and the coarser the more natural.

But no other German prince possessed a wife like Sophia Charlotte. She was the most beautiful Princess in Germany, so he believed: as soon as he had seen her he had been struck by this unusual beauty, so outstanding among the buxom ladies of his previous acquaintance. She had a grace and charm inherited from her Stuart ancestors for her mother was Sophia, Electress of Hanover and *her* mother had been Elizabeth of Bohemia daughter of James I of England. The Stuart charm was very noticeable in Sophia Charlotte—tempered, thought Frederick, with good sound German common sense. Charm and good sense! What a combination!

"Well, we must bring about this marriage. It would be excellent from all points of view," he said.

"It would give me great pleasure to see her happy. Poor soul, I fear she has no easy time in Ansbach with that stepson of hers. I believe he always resented his father's second marriage and now he has a chance to express his disapproval. It's no atmosphere in which to bring up children."

"Nothing could suit us better than to see a friend of ours married into Saxony. John George has been a cause of trouble since he inherited. And I believe that woman of his is in the pay of Austria."

"Then he needs marriage with a woman like Eleanor to break the association. Though I've heard that his passion for Magdalen von Röohlitz is quite violent and she has great power over him."

"Eleanor will break that."

Sophia Charlotte was dubious. Eleanor was a dear creature but meek and although pretty enough in her way, perhaps not persuasively charming or erotically skilled enough to break the hold of a sensuous woman like von Röohlitz.

Sophia Charlotte's inclination was to turn away from unpleasantness and such relationships as that between the dissolute Elector of Saxony and his mistress was in her opinion decidedly unpleasant; but she was never one to shirk the distasteful at the expense of duty; and she was deeply concerned about her friend.

Her husband looked at her a little wistfully. He would have been delighted if she had taken more interest in politics. He had often visualized an ideal relationship. She was the only woman in the world with whom he would have shared his powers—and she did not want a share in it. If she had brought that penetrating mind of hers to the study of politics, if they had worked together, what a pair they would have made! But no! She preferred literature, music, art and discussion to statescraft. She would converse learnedly with theologians on the possibility of an after-life but had little concern for the affairs of her husband's electorate.

Yet what could he do but indulge her for his greatest desire was to please her. There she sat now—serene, almost unbelievably beautiful, gravely discussing this marriage—not because the alliance would help to break friendship between Saxony and Austria and turn it towards Brandenburg where it was needed, but because her friend and protégée, poor widowed Eleanor, needed a home and settled life for her children.

Her children! That was at the root of the matter. He and Sophia Charlotte had one son, Frederick William—and the little boy was already showing signs of an ungovernable temper—and she longed for a daughter, preferably like Eleanor's who was a pretty little girl, now about eight years old, flaxen-haired, and plump with bright blue enquiring eyes. He had seen Sophia Charlotte's eyes on little Wilhelmina Caroline. And it was to provide security for the child that Sophia Charlotte wanted this match.

He went on: "When she is married into Saxony it will be easier for her to provide for her children's future."

"Poor little Caroline!" She was referring to Wilhelmina Caroline who was known by her second name. "That stepbrother who is now the Margrave resents them at Ansbach. Eleanor was delighted when I suggested she should come to us in Berlin."

"I'm not surprised, my dear. You make them very welcome and it is, as we all know, an honour to be a guest at Lützenburg which you have made comparable, so they tell me, with the Palace of Versailles."

"That is an exaggeration. Nothing on earth could compare with Versailles. We are none of us in a position to set ourselves up as little Kings of France. Nor do we wish to. Lützenburg is ours ... we have made it as it is and certainly we have not tried to imitate Louis."

"You have made it so, my dear, not I," he reminded her.

"But for your generosity I should never have had the opportunity." She smiled at him wishing she could feel more strongly towards him. But she felt no love for him nor for any man. Moreover he was middleaged and deformed, and when she had first seen him she had been horrified, but her mother had warned her years before that all Princesses must accept the marriages which were made for them and even if they must go to bed with a gorilla for the sake of the state they should not complain. Frederick was no gorilla—merely in her young eyes an unattractive, unshapely old man whom she had learned to tolerate; and his indulgence to her had touched her, for not only did he wish to please her by giving her gifts like the beautiful castle of Lützenburg, not only did he allow her to invite her own circle of friends there, even though they were of no interest to him, but he was actually in awe of her. When she considered the promiscuity of her father, the Elector of Hanover, and the crudeness of her eldest brother George Lewis with his dreadful mistresses; when she considered her dignified mother's resignation and the manner in which George Lewis treated his beautiful wife, Sophia Dorothea, she must think she was very fortunate.

"I want you to be happy," he said rising and coming nearer. She put out a hand for fear this might be an approach to some display of affection.

"You are so kind," she said coolly, and he immediately recoiled. "I have asked her to come along to see me," she went on. He saw the tender smile touch her face; she had never shown such tenderness for him. "I have asked her to bring young Caroline with her. She is such a bright little thing."

"She should be grateful to you."

"Not yet. Only if her mother marries into Saxony and through the marriage can arrange a happy future for her."

He went to her, took her hand and kissed it. As soon as he left her he was scowling, wondering why one of the most powerful Electors in Germany should be so humbly eager to please a woman who showed him little else but a kindly tolerance.

\*     \*     \*

Caroline looked out of the window over the lawns to the terraces and statues and thought how much more pleasant it was here than at Ansbach. Secretly she thought how much more beautiful, how much more stately, how much more exciting was the Electress Sophia Charlotte than her own mother—although she would admit this to no one.

Poor Mamma was so often in tears. It was a sad life when you were resented and unwanted. She knew that well enough for she shared in the resentment. William Frederick did too but he, poor child, being two years younger than herself was too young to understand. At six one understood very little, whereas at eight . . .

Well at eight one understood that Mamma was very unhappy at Ansbach, that her stepbrother George Frederick, who had been Margrave since their father's death—although, being a minor, in name only—did not want them; and that was not a very pleasant way of living. How much better to be Electress Sophia Charlotte who was so beautiful and clever and adored by everyone. There was no question of *her* being unwanted.

And this goddess had time to take notice of a little eight-year-old girl, to ask her about Ansbach. Caroline was uneasy remembering that conversation. Had she said too much? Would Mamma scold in her tearful way which was almost worse than bullying? Sophia Charlotte asked about lessons, not as a governess would, but as though she were interested because learning was so exciting. Was it? Caroline had not thought so until the Electress had made her feel it was, and now she was eager to find out, for surely the Electress could not be wrong? Electress Sophia Charlotte had selected Caroline for particular notice, had talked to her as she had never been talked to before. She had made her feel that she was *important*; and to be made to feel important by the most important person one had ever met could only mean that one *was* important.

What an exciting discovery!

Caroline could scarcely wait to be once more in the presence of this goddess and yet she feared it. Suppose by some little stupidity she forfeited her regard?

"I hope," she said aloud, "that we stay at Berlin for ever and ever."

From the window she saw a man walking with other men in the gardens. She knew who he was—someone very important because he had been pointed out to her, John George, Elector of Saxony. The most important guest in the Castle—far more than the widow of Ansbach and her young daughter.

John George was gesticulating. How angry he appeared to be! thought Caroline, and wondered what those men were saying to him to make him so.

"I don't think I like him much," she said aloud.

*        *        *

John George of Saxony was arguing with his ministers—two of whom had accompanied him on this visit to Berlin. They had even followed him out of doors to continue the discussion and would not leave him alone so that he felt as though he were going mad. Surely an Elector should not have to obey his own ministers.

"My lord Elector, this marriage is a necessity. It is for the purpose of making it that we are here. Alliance with Brandenburg is essential to us, and this marriage is their condition."

"I have no wish to marry this woman."

"She is meek."

"Insipid!"

"All the better. She will give you no trouble."

"She had better not try to."

"She will know her place. She needs the security you can give her, and she'll be grateful for it."

"I have no desire to give her anything."

"Your Highness, Brandenburg wants this marriage, and we want Brandenburg."

John George scowled. He knew what they wanted. They wanted to separate him from Magdalen. Well, they were not going to. He missed her now. There was no one like her. They could offer him other women but they couldn't satisfy him for more than an hour. He went back and back again to Magdalen. He thought of her constantly. Other women were only proxy for Magdalen. He even thought of her when making love to others. And they were offering him this dessicated widow for a wife!

State reasons! There was certainly no other reason why he would take such a creature to his bed.

The argument went on. He knew they would wear him down in the end. Ministers had great power over their rulers; and according to them Saxony needed the friendship of Brandenburg. He was prepared to let them apply themselves to matters of state if they left him in peace to apply himself to Magdalen. He smiled, remembering her. She was insatiable, that woman—and so was he. That was why they were so well matched.

The argument continued.

\* \* \*

Nervously, Eleanor, the widowed Margravine of Ansbach, awaited her suitor. Her large blue eyes showed clearly her apprehension and now and then she would lift a hand to smooth her plentiful auburn hair. She had been considered beautiful in her youth and she was not old now; she had the buxom looks so admired in Germany and her first husband had appreciated her charms. But that was some years ago; and since then she had borne two children.

She was very fearful of the future. When her husband, the Margrave, had died the peaceful life was ended; it had not been an exciting existence, but she had never been one to look for adventure; she had been well satisfied with her marriage and would have been contented to spend the rest of her days in the grand old palace which had delighted her from the moment she saw it.

As the daughter of the Duke of Saxe-Eisenach, marriage with the Margrave of Ansbach had been considered a worthy one, even though Ansbach was a very small principality when compared with those like Hanover and Celle. But the palace was as grand as anything to be found in either of those territories and Eleanor had loved it from the moment she first saw it. She liked the Bavarian countryside and the little town of Ansbach, nestling cosily close to the castle and the Hofgarten with its parterres and plantations. She had thought of it as home as soon as she had stepped into the great hall and glanced up at that magnificent ceiling, on which was depicted the glorification of the Margrave Karl the Wild, and seen the enormous statue in the centre of the hall of the Margrave embracing

Venus. And later she had grown accustomed to the flamboyant designs in the rooms, the gilded minstrels gallery in the dining hall, the marble statues and the crystal chandeliers.

She had enjoyed riding through the streets of Ansbach, the capital city of her husband's little domain. She had received the loyal cheers of the citizens for the Margrave was deeply loved and respected, largely because he, a Hohenzollern, and connected with the Brandenburgs, had not scorned to concern himself with trade, and as a result he had made a thriving community. He had brought skilled weavers from abroad; nor had that been all. He had set up metal workers in his town; and all his officials and servants were commanded to buy articles which had been produced locally. This foresight had brought prosperity to Ansbach; and the citizens made their approval of his methods known when he rode through their streets with his family.

"Long live the Margrave! Long live the Margravine!" She had basked contentedly in his popularity.

There had been minor irritations. It was often difficult for a stepmother to win the love of her predecessor's children; and George Frederick, the elder of her stepchildren, his father's heir, actively disliked and resented her. This had seemed unfortunate but not disastrous when her husband had been alive; but when on his death George Frederick had become the Margrave of Ansbach, it was a different matter.

He did not exactly tell her to go, but when he took over the apartments with their brilliant frescoes and porcelain galleries which she had inhabited with her husband he made it clear that she was not welcome in his palace.

She was a proud woman and had no wish to remain where she was not wanted, so she decided that she would leave Ansbach with her children—Caroline who was then only three years old and William Frederick who was two years younger. Her old home was in Eisenach on the border of the Thuringian Forest and here she went with the children, although she knew it would only be a temporary refuge.

Often she thought of her kindly plump husband prematurely killed by the smallpox, and longed for the old days. There was little pleasure in spending one's life visiting other people who, kind as they were, would not wish her to stay forever.

Sometimes she asked herself if she had been headstrong in leaving Ansbach. George Frederick was a minor, and not allowed to govern; and until he married and had a son, the heir presumptive to Ansbach was her own son William Frederick.

Her greatest friends in her misfortune were the Brandenburgs and at their suggestion she had sent William Frederick back to Ansbach—for after all it was his home—and had travelled to Berlin with young Caroline.

Here she had made the acquaintance of the Elector John George of Saxony, and both the Elector and Electress of Brandenburg had persuaded her that it was her duty to accept the proposal of marriage he would make to her.

It was for this reason that she was waiting for him now.

He was coming towards her—a young man with wild eyes, full sensuous lips, and an ungraciousness about his manner which was disturbing.

He bowed stiffly and she fancied avoided meeting her eyes.

He was thinking angrily: She's older than I thought. Already a matron and a mother of two!

"Madam," he said, "I believe you have some notion why I have asked for this ... er ... pleasure."

His voice was cold; he scarcely bothered to hide his dislike.

She looked alarmed and that angered him still further. There was no need for her to play the coy maiden. She knew very well what his purpose was; and she doubtless knew how vehemently he had had to be persuaded. He was not going to pretend to her now or at any time. He would make no secret to her or to anyone that if he was forced into this marriage it was under protest.

She inclined her head slightly, conveying that she was aware of the reason for his visit.

"I understand you are prepared to marry me."

Eleanor wanted to cry out: No! I must have time to think. I have allowed them to persuade me. I have been carried away by their arguments. She thought of herself growing older, Caroline becoming marriageable. What hope would she have of finding a suitable husband for her daughter if she were a wandering exile? But if Caroline's stepfather was the Elector of Saxony...

She said quietly: "Your Highness does me much honour."

Much honour indeed! He wondered what Magdalen would say when he returned to Dresden. Her mother would be furious because he knew that Madam von Röohlitz dearly desired her daughter to be his wife. An exciting project! He would be willing to marry Magdalen but his ministers would never agree of course, and he had to take this poor creature instead.

He looked at her with fresh distaste but reassured himself that a wife and a mistress need not interfere with each other.

"Then you will take me as your husband?"

"I . . . I will, Your Highness."

"Then that matter is settled."

He bowed turned on his heel and went to the door. The natural sequence to such a question and answer should have been an embrace, a confessing of admiration, a promise of enduring affection. But he had no intention of letting her think he cared sufficiently for her to pretend to hold her in any regard. She would have to understand that this was an arranged marriage. He might have to attempt to get an heir; she had two children already so was no doubt fertile, and once she was pregnant he need not see her unless it was necessary to get another child.

Left alone Eleanor stood staring at the door. She was trembling. He had seemed so strange. He was younger than she was —in his twenties and not without good looks. Uneasily she remembered having heard a rumour that he behaved oddly at times since he had had a blow on the head. She had heard too that he was dissolute, extravagant—in fact a libertine.

What will this marriage be like? she asked herself.

It will be like many other marriages of state, she told herself. Arranged. The surprising aspect was that she should have something to offer. If he had not been infatuated with a woman who was reputed to be a spy for the Austrians would the Brandenburgs have arranged this marriage? It was scarcely likely. Her duty was to influence him when she was married; she had to keep him aware that alliance with Brandenburg was preferable to that with Austria. How could *she* persuade him when he seemed to regard her with such distaste?

She could have wept with humiliation and frustration. With the passing of the years tears had come with increasing ease.

It was a bitter choice—to wander from one friend's hospitality to that of another, becoming more and more of an encumbrance as the years passed; or marriage with a man of wealth and some power who could, if he were so inclined, make a good match for her daughter.

There can be no choice, she thought. Besides, it is the wish of the Brandenburgs. But how I wish it need not be, how I wish my dear John Frederick had lived. Never had the palace of the Margraves of Ansbach seemed so inviting; never before had she longed so fervently to be back in those baroque rooms with their porcelain galleries.

Trying to hold back her tears she went to find her daughter.

\* \* \*

Caroline curtsied before the Electress Sophia Charlotte.

"Well, my dear," said the Electress. "We have some good news for you. Have you told her yet?"

"Not yet," answered Eleanor. "I thought I would consult you first."

"Come here, my child."

Sophia Charlotte stroked the auburn hair and smiled into the pink rather plump little face with the bright blue, very intelligent eyes.

"You will soon be going to a new home, my dear. I think that will please you."

"Are we coming here?" asked Caroline eagerly.

Sophia Charlotte shook her head but she looked pleased because Caroline had betrayed her desire to stay in Berlin.

"No, my dear. You are to have a father."

Caroline looked bewildered; then she saw that her mother although pretending to smile was really very frightened; but as the Electress was pleased she supposed it was a good thing.

"You will be going to live in Saxony and you will find it very agreeable to have a settled home."

"When are we going?" asked Caroline.

"You are impatient, my dear, but when you are at Dresden we must see you often. You shall visit us and we shall visit you."

"Then," said Caroline, "I am glad we are going to Dresden."

Sophia Charlotte smiled over the girl's head.

I wish, thought Eleanor, that I could feel as pleased.

\* \* \*

It was arranged that the wedding should take place at Leipzig and neither the Brandenburgs nor John George's ministers saw any reason why it should be delayed. It was only the bride and groom who wished for that.

Both had considerable misgivings. Eleanor, who had gone back to Ansbach to make preparations, spent a great deal of the time on her knees praying for a miracle, by which she meant some occurrence which would make the marriage unnecessary. Blankly she faced the future trying hard to convince herself that it was all for the best and that marriages which were made as this had been, often turned out to be the most successful.

John George in Dresden had no such illusions. The more he thought of marriage with Eleanor the more he loathed the idea; he was beginning to hate the woman they had chosen for him.

His ministers had suggested that while he was waiting for his wedding day he should not see his mistress. It would not be considered good taste and it was impossible to keep such meetings secret. If news reached the bride-elect that her husband was spending his nights with a mistress she might decide not to marry him after all.

That made John George laugh aloud. "Then for the love of God tell her."

"Your Highness is not serious."

"Never more. Never more," he cried.

But he dared not oppose his ministers. His position was too precarious. Harried on one side by them and by Magdalen's letters on the other he was frantic and when he was frantic he was furious.

"I won't go through with it!" he declared a hundred times a day.

But his ministers assured him that he must.

Magdalen's letters were smuggled in to him every day. He had betrayed her, she wrote. He had promised her marriage. He had taken her virtue ... and so on.

He laughed reading them. All written by her mother, he knew. Magdalen was too lazy to write; all Magdalen wanted to do was make love. "Very creditable, my darling," he said fondly; and he wanted her with him, no matter if she did say what her mother had taught her to; he didn't care if the old woman was taking bribes from Austria. Magdalen was worth it. With her masses of dark hair, her willowy body which was at the same time the most voluptuous in the world, how different she was from the flaxen German women he had known before! She was a perfect animal; she cared nothing for politics; she cared nothing for anything but sensual pleasure.

He wanted to be with her. He would marry her if he could—to please her mother and her too, for that ambitious woman had convinced her daughter that what she wanted was to be the Electress of Saxony.

He might defy his ministers and the Brandenburgs yet. What if he married Magdalen ... secretly? What if he summoned them all to his presence chamber and told them they could stop the preparations for the wedding in Leipzig for he was already married?

He shivered. They were powerful old men. They had the experience which he lacked and had deposed their leaders for less.

No, he must do as they wished. He must marry that woman. He would prove to them that she was a spy ... a spy for the Brandenburgs. What was the difference between spying for the Brandenburgs and spying for Austria?

To hell with the agreement they had made with the Brandenburgs and which they fondly called The Golden Bracelet!

But a pretty princeling who is young and uncertain cannot say to hell with his ministers or his ministers may say to hell with him.

He must do as they wished but it should not always be so. One day they would have to obey him. In the meantime there was nothing he could do but depart for Leipzig.

\*          \*          \*

Leaving Caroline in Ansbach with her brother, Eleanor travelled to Leipzig with her friends the Elector and Electress of Brandenburg, and with each stage of the journey grew more and more uneasy; and when she met her future husband her fears were increased. She had heard rumours of his passionate attachment to Magdalen von Röohlitz whom he had made a Countess and on whom he had bestowed rich lands, but she had not thought he would be so inconsiderate as to allow the woman to accompany him to Leipzig and attend his wedding.

In fact John George had not known it either but his satisfaction was immense when he discovered that Magdalen had been smuggled into his entourage. That was her mother's doing. He believed that indefatigable woman never gave up and had some idea that even at this late hour he might be persuaded to substitute his brides.

They were together during the journey. His ministers pretended not to see. They doubtless said to each other: Let him have a little sweetmeat before he takes his medicine.

He was determined to enjoy his sweetmeat. She railed against him at first in a half-hearted way, repeating the phrases her mother had taught her. "If you wanted a wife why should you choose her? Have you forgotten you promised me ... ?" No, he hadn't forgotten he soothed her, and he wished with all his might that it could be different. If it were possible he would marry his Magdalen and send that woman back to Ansbach or to the Brandenburgs wherever she belonged. All he wanted was his Magdalen. Nothing would be changed. She would see.

Magdalen was ready to be placated. In her opinion any time not spent in love-making was wasted time.

The days were filled with tension. It was feared that at the last moment the bridegroom would rebel. His ministers wrangled together. It had been a great mistake to allow Magdalen von Röohlitz to come. Who had been responsible for that? They blamed each other but they all realized that they would not feel safe until after the ceremony.

There had been that shocking episode when he had received his future wife with his mistress beside him. Coldly he had greeted her, plainly showing his dislike and then during the ensuing banquet had given his attention to his mistress. Fortunately the bride was of a meek disposition; fortunately the Brandenburgs were too eager for the marriage to take offence.

And to the great relief of all except the bride and groom the wedding day arrived and the marriage was solemnized without a hitch.

But at the banquet and ball which followed the bridegroom said not a word to his bride; and made it clear that he had no intention of consummating the marriage by brazenly spending the night with his mistress.

## The Shadow of Murder

DRESDEN, where Caroline joined her mother, was very opulent; it was said to be one of the most licentious courts in Germany and since the Elector's marriage had become even more so. Having obeyed the wishes of his ministers by marrying a woman he did not want, John George made it clear that as far as they were concerned that was an end of the matter. The woman they had chosen for him might live in his palace but he wanted nothing to do with her. It was only on state occasions that he saw her and then he treated her as though she were not there. At the same time he made no secret of his unflagging devotion to Magdalen von Röohlitz, and as her mother scarcely gave her daughter a moment's peace, instilling into her mind that she had been betrayed by her lover, that she should have, besides everything else her lover had given her, the supreme gift, the title of Electress—even Magdalen was beginning to grow ambitious for that one thing he could not give her, and he grew more and more resentful against his wife.

Caroline very quickly discovered that as the daughter of her mother she shared the resentment; and this knowledge made the court of Dresden an alarming place for an eight-year-old girl.

Yet it was very beautiful. The gardens were laid out in the French fashion with fountains, statues and colonnades; they and the court throughout were an imitation of Versailles; and the Elector behaved as though he were the Sun King himself. There were lavish banquets, balls, garden fêtes and entertainments in the palace. It only had to be said that this or that was done at the French court and it was done in Dresden. And everything was presided over by a dark-haired woman whom Caroline's stepfather could not bear out of his sight and whom everyone said was the Electress in all but name.

At first she had been puzzled, for her mother should have borne that title. Of course she did; and on state occasions she would be dressed in her robes and stand beside the Elector; and then immediately afterwards she would go to her apartments, take off her robes, dismiss her attendants, lie on her bed and weep. Caroline knew because she had seen her do this. No one took very much notice of the child; she was expected to remain in the small apartments assigned to her, with her nurse, her governess and one or two attendants. No one was the least bit interested in her; she was merely an appendage of the woman whom nobody wanted. She was even less significant than her mother who was at least actively resented. She might have been one of the benches in the ante room, one of the flowers in the beds about the fountains. Not so useful as the bench, not so decorative as the flower—but any of them could have been removed and cause no comment.

The Electress Sophia Charlotte had talked of Dresden as though she would be very happy there. She could certainly never have been to Dresden. But since Sophia Charlotte had thought it would be so different surely it should have been if something had not gone wrong. Caroline had an enquiring nature. Passionately she wanted to understand what was going on around her—particularly when it concerned herself. Her mother's unhappiness worried her, for although she had never been a gay woman, although she had never been brilliant like Sophia Charlotte, she had never been as sad as she was now.

B*

She had seemed older since she had come to Dresden; dark circles had appeared under her eyes; she had grown pale and thin.

It was disturbing to be so young and so defenceless; but Caroline knew that before she could do anything to strengthen her position and that of her mother she must understand what it was all about.

She had alert eyes and sharp ears so she decided to put them to use. When servants and attendants whispered together she listened and often scraps of conversation not intended for her came her way. She was secretly amused that grown up people could deceive themselves into thinking that firstly she was deaf and secondly she was stupid; for often they would glance her way, warning each other with a look that they must watch their tongues in her presence; but the desire to talk was almost always—fortunately for Caroline—irresistible.

"They say he has never yet shared her bed."

"Not he! He can't spare the time from his Magdalen."

"Well, she can't say she didn't know before. He made that clear."

"Oh yes, she knew he had no wish to marry a widow with a couple of brats."

A couple of brats! Caroline's natural dignity was offended. She wanted to confront the gossipers and demand to know how they dared refer to a Princess of Ansbach as a brat. As for her brother, he was the heir presumptive to Ansbach, for if their stepbrother had no sons he would be Margrave one day; this was the reason why he remained at Ansbach, otherwise he would be with her to help her fight her mother's battles. And the servants dared refer to him as a brat!

She was on the point of calling to them when she hesitated. What use would that be? She knew exactly how they would act. First they would swear that she had been mistaken; then they would take great care never to say anything in her hearing again which would mean that she would be completely in the dark. So how foolish it would be just for the sake of temporarily asserting her dignity, to lose an opportunity of understanding this peculiar situation.

Meanwhile the voices went on.

"I wouldn't be in Madam's shoes for all the wealth of Germany."

"Nor me, poor soul. Why it wouldn't surprise me what those two got up to ... with Mamma in the background."

"There's one I should want to watch. No, it certainly wouldn't surprise me either. She's capable of anything to get rid of Madam Eleanor and set up her darling little Magdalen in her place. If I were Madam Eleanor I'd be watchful ... very watchful indeed."

Caroline put her hand over her heart which had begun to leap uncomfortably. What did they mean? Her mother must be watchful. Could they mean that she was in danger? And if so, did she know it?

Caroline had already begun to realize that her mother was somewhat ineffectual and would never be capable of looking after herself. Someone then would have to do it for her. Who? Her eight-year-old daughter?

How could that be when she was only a child, when she was only vaguely aware of the meaning behind the intrigue which was going on about her.

How careful she would have to be! She would have to stop being a child immediately, for children could make so many mistakes. Suppose she had rushed out and protested just now, as her first impulse had directed her to do. What she would have missed! She must remember that in future. Before she did anything rash she must stop and think.

\*        \*        \*

During the months which followed Caroline learned more of the state of affairs between her mother and step-father. She knew that it was a miserable marriage, undertaken with reluctance on both sides—on his because he had been forced into it for state reasons, on hers because she had been obliged to seek position and security for herself and her daughter.

In a way, thought Caroline, I am responsible; for perhaps she would never have married him but for me.

There were lessons to be done, but no one cared very much whether she did them or not. Her mother was too much engulfed in her own misery; and why should servants care whether the little girl from Ansbach grew up an ignoramus or not. She would ride a little with her few attendants, taking care to keep well out of the way; she would walk and sit in the magnificent gardens, slinking away when she heard the approach of a party; from the window of her bedchamber she would watch the open air entertainments; she would listen to the music from the ballrooms, going as near as possible but always making sure that there was a way of escape should she need it.

She kept well out of the way of her stepfather whom she regarded as an ogre and he naturally never noticed her absence; in fact he had forgotten her existence and only remembered it when, on those rare occasions when he was in the presence of his wife, he wanted to taunt her with her uselessness; and those occasions were growing less for she bored him so much that he found no pleasure even in quarrelling with her.

Caroline found little enjoyment in her mother's company either for Eleanor was in such a state of nervous tension that she could not pay much attention to her daughter; her mind was dominated by her own depressing situation and as she did not believe she could discuss this with her daughter had nothing to say to her.

A whole year had gone by since Caroline's arrival at Dresden, but she felt more than a year older. Nine years old but very knowledgeable in the ways of men and women. She had seen her stepfather with his mistress revelling in the gardens at some féte; she had watched their crude caresses. She had to grow up quickly for there was no one else to protect her mother from a fate which was none the less horrifying because her daughter did not fully understand it.

*     *     *

There was one at the Dresden Court of whom Magdalen von Röohlitz was in awe and that was her mother. She would never forget that it was her mother who had first put her in the Elector's way and who, once the liaison had started, conducted it so cleverly from the shadows that she had made what might have been a fleeting affaire into what it was at this time.

The extremely ambitious Madam von Röohlitz was the widow of a Colonel of the Guards; not a position in which she could have had high social ambitions if she had not possessed an outstandingly beautiful daughter. She had been the first to appreciate Magdalen's charms and assess their value. She had always known that Magdalen's brains did not match her beauty; but since she had a very clever mother this was not an insurmountable difficulty—in fact, it was proving an asset. Magdalen could make full use of her erotic genius while her mother planned calmly behind the scenes.

Magdalen had little to complain of so far. She was, in fact, astonished how easily she could please her lover when all she had to do was satisfy his sexual desires, and as hers were as eager for fulfilment as his, that was no hardship. Mother arranged all the tiresome details and was very happy to do so. That seemed a pleasant enough arrangement to Magdalen; and she was surprised to discover that Mother was not pleased.

She had come to her daughter's apartment because it was time they had a little talk.

"You need not frown, daughter. If you will do exactly as I say it will be easy enough."

Magdalen nodded and stretched her limbs luxuriously.

What a magnificent creature she is! thought her mother. It would be churlish to reproach her for not being able to *think*, when she is so expert in other matters.

"That man would do a great deal for you."

"He always says so."

"Talk is one thing, actions another."

Magdalen yawned.

"You must listen to me because this is important. You are a Countess now, my dear; you are very rich, and that is as it should be. I'm delighted. But things could be so much better."

"Could they?" asked Magdalen.

"Of course. What happens when important visitors arrive? Who has to receive them? You or her? Then she is brought forward, isn't she? She is after all the Electress of Saxony and his legal wife."

"He's never with her."

"That is not my point, Magdalen. She is received. She is accepted. I wish that for you."

"Well, she's his wife."

"You should tell him how humiliated you feel."

Magdalen raised her eyebrows. "How humiliated do I feel?"

"You, whom he swears he loves as he can never love another woman are snubbed, covertly insulted by visitors from other courts."

"But I'm not, Mother."

"They say, 'Oh she's only his mistress.' And they pay Court to Madam Electress."

"Oh no, Mother . . ."

"Listen to me. You could become Electress."

"How?"

"By insisting that he marry you, of course."

"He's married already."

"You are determined to see the obstacles."

Magdalen looked puzzled. "Well, she is his wife, isn't she? They were married in Leipzig."

"Oh yes, their dear friends the Brandenburgs saw to that."

"Because you had been too busy with your dear friends the Austrians."

"Because you, my dear, were not subtle enough. I had to find money from somewhere and you betrayed the fact that we had friends in Austria who had been kind to us. But never mind. That's all behind us. Let's think of the future. How would you like to be the Electress of Saxony?"

"I shouldn't mind it. I shouldn't mind it at all."

Madam von Röohlitz gave her daughter a playful slap.

"Well, listen to me. I have an idea. Pay close attention."

"Yes, Mother."

\*　　\*　　\*

Caroline was in her mother's bedchamber reading aloud to Eleanor who lay on her bed, her nervous fingers pulling at the coverlet; Caroline knew that she was not listening. Yet if she stopped she would realize it and ask her gently to go on.

It seemed useless and ineffectual; for Caroline was not really paying attention either.

Caroline stopped reading and said: "We were happier than this in Ansbach."

"What did you say?" asked Eleanor.

Caroline said: "Mamma, couldn't we go away somewhere for a little change?"

Eleanor looked startled. Then she said: "Where could we go?"

"To Ansbach perhaps."

"We should not be welcome there."

"We are not welcome here."

"Caroline, what do you mean? This is our home?"

Home! thought Caroline. Where you were unhappy! Where no one wanted you! Where people whispered about you in corners.

"Perhaps," she said, "we could go to Berlin."

"To Berlin. I doubt whether they would want us there either."

"Mamma, how can you know? The Electress Sophia Charlotte was so kind. She talked to me about lessons and things like that."

"I hope you are getting on well with your studies, Caroline." That worried look was in her eyes. She was thinking: I neglect my daughter. She is allowed to run wild. Oh what will become of us?

"I try to work at them," answered Caroline gravely. "The Electress Sophia Charlotte said I should. Do you think she will ever come here to see us?"

"Nobody ever comes here to see us."

There was no bitterness in the tone, only a sad resignation.

Nothing will ever change, thought Caroline.

But even as the thought entered her mind one of her mother's attendants came into the room. She was agitated and showed clearly that something had happened to upset her.

She did not seem to see Caroline sitting in her chair, but went straight to the bed, and handed a paper to Eleanor. "I couldn't believe this when I read it, Your Highness. It is ... terrible."

Eleanor took up the paper in trembling hands.

"What ... Oh, I had heard ... Oh, *no*."

"They are saying that it could not have been circulated without the Elector's consent, Your Highness."

"I am sure that is so."

Caroline shrank back into her chair and watched her mother intently.

She threw the paper on to the bed. "This is the end," she said wearily. "He is determined to be rid of me."

"They will never allow such a law, Your Highness."

"If he insists . . ."

"No. It can't be. It's another plot of that von Röohlitz woman. Nothing can come of it."

"A great deal has come of her plans. I feel very faint."

"It's the shock. Lie still, Your Highness."

"Lie still," murmured Eleanor. "Yes, for what else can I do. Just be still and wait . . . for whatever they plan against me."

Caroline sitting in her chair wanted to run to her mother, shake her and cry out: It's not the way. You shouldn't allow them to hurt you. You should fight them as they fight you.

But she sat still while the woman brought an unguent from a cupboard and rubbed into her mother's forehead.

"That's comforting," said Eleanor.

The pamphlet fluttered to the floor not far from Caroline's feet. She picked it up and read it. It was obscurely phrased but the gist was that it might be advantageous for men who could afford to support more than one wife to have another.

So the Elector thought this a good idea! The reason was plain. He was able to support another wife, he was not satisfied with the one he had, and there was someone he would like to set up in her place.

Yes, she could understand why her mother was disturbed.

Eleanor was saying in a sad tired voice: "I feel so . . . alone, and I know they are determined to be rid of me by one means or another."

"Your Highness should not distress yourself."

"How can I help it? They are getting restive. They have endured me long enough."

"Your Highness, this could never be. There would be an outcry. It is against religion as well as the laws of the state."

"They're desperate," said Eleanor. "This could be a safer way ... than some."

She was aware of Caroline standing there with the pamphlet in her hand.

"Oh ... Caroline. Put that paper down. I want to rest. Go now."

Caroline laid the pamphlet on the table and went out.

They thought she understood nothing; they thought she was a child still.

\* \* \*

Magdalen told all her friends that very soon she would be the Electress. The Elector was going to marry her. He had a wife already? Oh, but the Elector believed that in certain circumstances a man should have two wives.

Madam von Röohlitz had discreetly let it be known that anyone seeking honours should come to her. Magdalen would be able to arrange anything with the Elector she considered desirable, but as she would be very busily occupied her mother would shoulder some of her daughter's responsibilities.

Madam von Röohlitz was almost delirious with the new sense of power.

Her suggestion of another marriage had worked very well. Magdalen had learned her part adequately; she had told her lover how much she desired to be his wife and he yearned to grant her wish.

She assured herself that the plot was succeeding far better than at first she had thought possible. The fact was that the Electress was such a spineless creature that no one cared to defend her. Her only friends, the Brandenburgs, were far away; but she must impress on Magdalen the need to get this matter settled as quickly as possible.

However she was soon disappointed for although the Elector would willingly have married Magdalen, his ministers had refused to consider the question.

"It strikes at the very tenets of our Faith," they declared. "It is quite impossible."

"Nothing is impossible if I decide it shall be done," shouted John George.

"Your Highness," he was told, "a man who has one wife in the eyes of God cannot have another until her death. That is the law of the Church and the State."

"I will be my own law!" he cried.

But he knew they would not allow Magdalen to be his wife and he would remain married to that woman whom he had come to loathe . . . until death parted them.

He was angry but not so deeply as Madam von Röohlitz. He still had his mistress even though he could not make her his wife. As for Madam von Röohlitz, what had become of the lucrative business she was going to build up by selling honours to those who could pay well enough for them?

She shut herself in her apartments and would see no one . . . not even Magdalen.

Till death parts them! she murmured and seemed to derive a little comfort from the thought.

*     *     *

Someone was standing by Caroline's bed.

"Wake up your mother has sent for you."

Caroline scrambled up. It was dark and the candle threw the long shadow of her nurse on the wall.

"What is it?" she asked, her teeth beginning to chatter because she was conscious of a sense of doom.

"Your mother has been taken ill and is asking for you."

"How . . . ill?"

"Don't talk so much. She's waiting."

As she was hurried into her robe she was thinking: She is going to die. She will tell me what I have to do when I am alone.

Then a feeling of desolation struck her and she knew that she had rarely been so frightened. She was so lonely. She had no friends in this alien court. Because she was her mother's daughter nobody wanted her.

"Hurry?"

"I'm ready," she said.

She was taken to her mother's bedchamber where Eleanor lay in her bed looking exhausted, her skin yellow, her eyes glassy.

"My child..." she began and Caroline ran to the bed and kneeling took her hand.

"Mamma, what has happened. You are ill."

"I have been very ill, daughter. I think I am going to die."

"No ... no ... you must not."

"I have no place in this world, child. Life has not been very kind to me. I trust it will be kinder to you."

Caroline gripped the bedclothes and thought: I will never let people treat me as they have treated you! But how prevent it. There must be a way. She was sure of it and she was going to find it.

"Mamma, you are not going to die."

"If this attempt has failed, there will be others."

"Attempt ... failed ..."

"I ramble, child."

It was a lie, of course. She was not rambling. Why would they treat her as a child? It was true she was only nine years old but the last year at the Court of Saxony had taught her more than most children learn in ten. She knew how frightening marriage could be; but she thought: Had I been Mamma, I would not have allowed it to happen. What would she have done? She was not sure. But she believed she would have found some way of avoiding a position which was degrading, wretched and had now become very sinsister indeed.

"If anything should happen to me, Caroline ... are you listening?"

"Yes, Mamma."

"You should go back to Ansbach."

"Yes, Mamma."

"You could write to the Electress of Brandenburg. She was my good friend until she persuaded me to this marriage."

Caroline spoke hotly in defence of her beloved Sophia Charlotte. "But, Mamma, you need not have married had you not wished to."

"You are a child. What do you understand? I would to God I had remained a widow ... for he will do nothing for you ... nothing for me and nothing for you. No, you had best go back to Ansbach. Your brother will help you."

"I am two years older than he is, Mamma. Perhaps I can help him."

Eleanor smiled wanly. "Go and call someone," she said. "I'm beginning to feel ill again. And don't come back till I send for you."

"Yes, Mamma."

She called the attendants and then went to sit in the ante room.

She heard her mother groaning and retching.

She thought: What will become of me when she is dead?

*       *       *

It was not now a question of trying to listen. Caroline could not escape the whispers.

"It was an attempt to poison the Electress Eleanor."

"By whom?"

"Come, are you serious? Surely you can guess."

"Well if there is to be a new law that a man can have two wives why bother to rid themselves of the first?"

"It'll never be a law. That's why. They know it. They will keep to the old ways. It's been used often enough and is the most successful."

"Poor lady. I wouldn't be in her shoes."

"Nor I. He'll have the Röohlitz ... never fear. He's set on it and so is her mother."

"Poor Electress Eleanor, she should watch who hands her her plate."

They were planning to poison her mother. They had tried once and failed. But they would try again.

She was frantic with anxiety, but to whom could she turn? She, a nine-year-old girl without a single friend in the palace— what could she do?

If only the Electress Sophia Charlotte were here, she could go to her, explain her fears, be listened to with attention; she would be told what to do and it would be the right thing she was sure. But Sophia Charlotte was miles away and there was no one to help her.

She went to her mother's apartments. Eleanor was in her bed, recovering from her attack and she looked exhausted.

Caroline threw herself into her arms and clung to her.

"Oh Mamma, Mamma, what shall we do?"

Her mother stroked her hair and signed to the attendants to leave them. When they were alone, she said: "What is it, my child?"

"They are trying to kill you, Mamma."

"Hush, my child, you must not say such things."

"But it's true. And what are we going to *do*."

"It is in God's hands," said Eleanor.

"But unless we *do* something, He won't help us."

"My child, what are you saying?"

"I know it sounds wicked, but I'm frightened."

"Where did you hear this?"

"They are all saying it. I overheard them."

"So ... they are talking!"

"Mamma, you don't seem to want to *do* anything."

Eleanor lay back on her pillows and closed her eyes. "What can I do? This is my home now ... and yours."

Caroline clenched her fists, her exasperation overcoming her fear.

"Why don't we run away?"

"Run away! To where?"

"Let us think. There must be something we can do. This is a hateful home in any case. I should be glad to leave it ... and so would you."

"My place is with my husband."

With a murderer! thought Caroline and stopped herself in time from saying the words aloud.

"We could go to Berlin. Perhaps they would let us live with them ... for a while ... until we knew what to do."

"We should have to wait to be invited. You shouldn't listen to gossip, my child. It's not ... true."

Caroline sighed wearily. It was useless to try to make her mother take action. She was well aware of the danger; but it seemed that she preferred meekly to be murdered than make any effort to avoid such a fate.

"You see, Caroline," said Eleanor, "this is where we belong."

"Can we belong where they are trying to be rid of us?"

In that moment Eleanor was as frightened for her daughter

as for herself. What would become of Caroline? The child was growing up and in what an atmosphere! Her licentious stepfather made no secret of the life he led; he would sit with his friends at the banqueting table and they would discuss their conquests—not of wars but of women—in crude detail, seeking to cap each other's stories and provoke that rollicking laughter which could be heard even in the upper rooms of the palace; he could often be seen caressing the bold Countess von Röohlitz in public; while equally publicly he insulted his wife and sought to replace her. Now he was advocating polygamy because he wished to discard his wife—if he could not have been said to have discarded her from the moment he married her—and set up another in her place. And because his plans were not proceeding fast enough it might be that he had tried to poison her.

All these things were talked of; and this young girl heard what was said.

I should never have brought her here, thought Eleanor. Better to have stayed at Ansbach—poor and without prospects. For what prospects have we now?

"My poor child," she whispered.

"But what are we going to *do*?" demanded Caroline.

"There is nothing we can do."

"So you would stay here and let them kill you?"

"That is only rumour."

"Mamma, you know it isn't. Let us go away. We mustn't stay here. It isn't safe."

Sighing, Eleanor turned her face away. "You must not listen to servants' gossip, my child. It is beneath the dignity of one in your position."

What can I do? wondered Caroline in desperation. She won't help herself!

"Go now, my dear," said Eleanor. "I want to sleep."

Caroline went away. It was no use warning her mother; it was no use planning for her. She would do nothing. Could it be that in some way she was responsible for what was happening to her? If I had a husband who was planning to murder me, I would not stay and let him do it.

What will happen to us? wondered Caroline. It seemed inevitable that her mother would be murdered, for although she knew the murderers were at her door she made no attempt to escape from them.

*  *  *

If I were older, thought Caroline, I should know what to do.

It occurred to her that she might write to the Electress Sophia Charlotte and explain what was happening. Even if it was a bold and ill-mannered thing to do, the Electress would forgive her for she was so kind.

Surely when one knew that a murder was about to be committed a breach of etiquette would be forgiven.

In any case something would have to be done. If only she were a little older, a little wiser. If only she knew what to do for the best.

She began to compose the letter in her mind. "My mother is about to be murdered. Please come and stop it...."

It sounded so incredible. They would say she was a ridiculous child, a wicked one to suggest such a thing. What if her letter went astray and was taken to the Elector or that fierce Madam von Röohlitz? Doubtless they would murder her too. There were not only murderers in the palace, there were spies too. But surely they would not spy on insignificant Caroline. Yet if she attempted to foil their plans she would not be insignificant.

If only there were someone. If her brother were here he might help. But he was such a child. Two years younger than she was and living at Ansbach he would not have learned as quickly about the wickedness of the world as she had.

I don't want to be murdered before I've had a chance to live, thought Caroline.

But something must be done. Perhaps even now they were slipping the powder or the drops into her mother's food or drink.

And her mother knew this could happen; yet she lay on her bed patiently waiting. When they offered her the poison cup she would meekly sip it and tell herself it was God's will.

The will of a wicked husband and his mistress was not God's will.

But God helped those who helped themselves, so there must be something which could be done.

"What?" cried Caroline. "Please God tell me what?"

She felt so helpless, shut in by her own youth and inexperience.

\* \* \*

That night another attempt was made to poison Eleanor. She was very ill and she knew that this time it would have been certain death if she had eaten more than a mouthful of the food which had been brought to her room.

All through her delirium she had been conscious of her daughter. She had imagined that the girl was standing at her bedside, her eyes reproachful.

"What have you done, Mamma? What have you done to me?"

"It was for your sake. . . . It was for your sake. . . ."

And the Caroline of her delirium shook her head in sorrow.

When she was a little better her thoughts clarified. Caroline was right when she had said they must go away. Perhaps if they left the Court of Dresden her husband would cease to persecute her. If she placed herself where he did not have to see her he might forget about her. Perhaps he would pass the law for which he was agitating and she would no longer be the Electress of Saxony. That would be a happy day. She would eagerly throw away the title that marriage had brought her for the sake of preserving her life. There were the children to care for. If she were dead who would care what became of them? No, she must make an attempt to fight for her life. Her little daughter had taught her that.

With a firmness which astonished her attendants she asked that her husband be brought to her.

When the message was taken to John George he was first of all surprised and then exultant. She was dying and she wanted to see him before she passed away for ever. Well, he did not object to seeing her once more since it would be the last time.

When he looked at the pallid creature in the bed his hopes

were high. She was a very sick woman. He was surprised how she clung to life, but he would soon be a widower ... though not for long. Magdalen and her mother would see to that.

"You are ill," he said, standing at the end of the bed and looking at her with distaste.

"I am much enfeebled. I had a bad attack during the night." He bowed his head lest she see the speculation in his eyes.

"I know," she went on determinedly, "that the best news you could hear of me would be that I were dead. It seems possible that that pleasure will not long be denied you. I would, however, ask your indulgence."

He looked steadily at her. "Well?"

"I would prefer to die in some place other than this palace. I should like your permission to leave."

She saw the curl of his lips and she knew he was thinking: Escape me and my murderers! Go right away ... perhaps to Berlin ... to her dear friends who would nurse her back to health, and she remain an encumbrance, though a distant one, to prevent his giving Magdalen what she so passionately desired! What a fool the woman was if she thought he would agree to that!

He was about to tell her she would remain where she was when she said: "I would not wish to go farther than the Dower House at Pretsch. I know I have not long to live ... something tells me it is only a matter of a few weeks. I could die peacefully there." Her eyes were wild and glassy. "It is, one might say, a dying request."

He shivered a little. He believed she was telling him that if he did not grant it she would haunt him after death. He was no more superstitious than most, yet the accusing eyes of a victim whom one was sending to an early grave could be alarming. Pretsch, he thought. With trusted servants to see that she had no opportunity to escape to Berlin. To see that his orders were more effectively carried out than they had been here, for if what he had commanded had been done she would not have been fixing those wild eyes on him and making this request.

It was not a bad idea. Magdalen would be happier when his wife was no longer at the Palace. Then she could act as Electress as much as she wished and would be more readily accepted when the real Electress was out of the way.

To Pretsch to die. It was not a bad idea.

He gave his permission and the next day, to Caroline's relief, she left with her mother and a few attendants for the Dower House.

* * *

Death, like a mischievous trickster, was threatening where it was least expected.

News of the death of Eleanor would have caused no surprise but, although enfeebled and ill, she continued to exist at Pretsch and it was in the palace at Dresden that tragedy struck.

Magdalen von Röohlitz kept to her apartments, seeing no one and the rumour was flying round the court and the whole of Dresden that she was suffering from the smallpox.

This was God's answer to her wickedness, said the whispers. She had planned to take the life of another and now her own was in jeopardy; she had planned to put on the robes of an Electress—instead it could well be a shroud.

And even if she survived would the Elector be so passionately devoted to her when she emerged from the sick room pitted with pox?

Madam von Röohlitz was in despair. All her ambitions lay in her daughter; she had schemed; she had dreamed; she had seen her dearest hopes about to be realized for surely even if John George's plan to bring in polygamy failed, the attempts to poison Eleanor must sooner or later succeed; and now here was everything about to be ruined.

Caroline listening to the rumours, which had reached the Pretsch Dower House, wondered whether her prayers had been answered. She had prayed that something would happen to save them. Could this really be an answer to prayer?

Life was unaccountable. A few days before her mother had seemed doomed and Magdalen von Röohlitz triumphant; now by one little stroke of fate the position had been reversed.

It seemed as though everyone was caught up in this almost unbearable suspense.

In the Dower House Eleanor no longer thought of imminent

death. In her apartments Madam von Röohlitz rallied against her ill fortune; in her bedroom Magdalen lay restless and delirious, blessedly unconscious of her plight.

John George summoned the doctors, and demanded that they tell him it was not the dreaded scourge which had attacked his mistress. They were sorry they could not obey him because there was no doubt that the Countess was suffering from smallpox. He stormed at them; he gave way to fury; then he wept. His beautiful Magdalen ravaged by the scourge which destroyed life or on those occasions when life was spared almost always destroyed beauty. This could not happen to him and his Magdalen when they had such wonderful plans for the future.

But it had happened.

"She must not die. Anything rather than that. I must see her. I must talk to her."

"Your Highness," said the doctors, "you must not go into her apartments. That would be very dangerous. You know the nature of this terrible disease."

But he would not listen to them. He went to her apartments; he took her into his arms.

"Listen to me, Magdalen," he cried. "You must get well. It will not matter if the pox disfigures you. I will not care. I want you to live. Do you understand that?"

But she only looked at him with glazed eyes; and throughout the palace they heard him shouting in his grief.

\*   \*   \*

Magdalen von Röohlitz was dead.

When the news was brought to the Dower House it was like a reprieve. Those servants who had received their orders from the Elector were stunned and did not know how to act.

Eleanor's health immediately began to improve. Caroline, alert, fully aware of the situation, waited for what would happen next.

She heard that the Court of Dresden was in mourning, that the Elector was so stricken with grief for the loss of his mistress that he kept in his apartments and would see no one.

But there was more startling news to come.

John George had caught the smallpox from his mistress and was suffering from a major attack.

A few days later he was dead.

The shadow of murder was lifted from the Dower House and Eleanor was once more a widow.

*        *        *

There was a new Elector at Dresden. Augustus Frederick had taken his brother's place and was determined to make the Court even more notorious than before. He had no time to consider his brother's widow and as long as she and her family did not make nuisances of themselves he had no objection to their continuing to take possession of the Dower House. Though just outside Dresden, this was far enough away not to bother him, so the Dowager Electress could stay there as long as she wished.

Eleanor rose from her sick bed but the treatment she had received from her late husband had left its mark and she remained an invalid.

But it was a great joy to her and her daughter not to live in perpetual fear; and as the days passed, the nightmare receded. Life at the Dower House was uneventful and peace was something which was only fully appreciated when it had been missed.

One day Eleanor said: "Your brother should join us. It is not good for families to be separated."

So William Frederick arrived at Pretsch—a charming little boy of nine. He was affectionate and happy to be reunited with his mother and sister.

How *young* he is, thought Caroline. And then the experiences at the Court of her stepfather came back more vividly to her mind.

She thought: After having lived through that, I could never really be young again.

*        *        *

She worked hard at lessons, for it was rather boring to play truant from the schoolroom and she had a fear of being ignorant.

Life was so different now that simple matters had become important. Could she find the correct answers to mathematical problems? Had she cobbled her needlework? Did she know when to speak and when not to speak, when to bow and when to curtsey?

No one cared very much whether she was in the schoolroom or playing in the gardens of the Dower House. She could have escaped and wandered off alone into the country if she cared to. But she must not neglect her lessons, she knew. One day she would meet the Electress Sophia Charlotte once more and that lady would be very shocked to find her ignorant.

She would sit over her books. Her handwriting was bad; her spelling worse.

I must improve, she told herself. I must not disappoint the Electress Sophia Charlotte.

One day there was a letter for Eleanor from the Electress Sophia Charlotte.

Eleanor showed it to her daughter.

"How kind she is!" said Caroline.

"Her conscience troubles her. But for her and her husband I should never have married."

"She thought it best for you," cried Caroline.

"It is so easy to see what is best for others."

"They could not have married you against your will."

Eleanor sighed and gave up the discussion.

"Well, she now says we must visit her at Lützenburg."

Caroline clasped her hands. "When?" she wanted to know.

"Who can say? This is no definite invitation."

"Then you must write and say we shall be happy to go. Ask them when we can come."

"My dear child, that could not be. What a lot you have to learn! I fear you run wild. Sometimes I sit here and worry about you children...."

"Don't worry about us, Mamma," said Caroline impatiently. "I can look after myself and William Frederick. But what about Lützenburg? She says we must visit her."

"It is merely a form of politeness. An invitation is not an invitation unless some date is given. Besides, I am too weak for the journey."

"Then, Mamma, write and tell her so, and perhaps she will come to see us."

Eleanor smiled wanly at her daughter, and because Caroline was so eager at last she agreed to do as she suggested. As a result the Elector and the Electress of Brandenburg paid a visit to the Dower House.

*     *     *

Caroline was rapturous. During the years of terror she had thought a great deal about Sophia Charlotte and had taken great comfort from the fact that she existed. Often when she had felt particularly lost and lonely she had promised herself: I will write to Sophia Charlotte. Or even more wildly, I will run away and go to Sophia Charlotte.

And when Sophia Charlotte arrived she was not disappointed. Her goddess was more beautiful, more dignified and more *kind* than she remembered. Her adoration shone in her eyes and the Electress was aware of it.

She was all the more beautiful because the Elector her husband was a little man, whose head seemed to rest on his body without a neck to support it; he was pale and small. But how different from the wicked John George, and how he doted on Sophia Charlotte, which was natural for all the world must love her.

When Sophia Charlotte embraced Caroline she told her she had often thought of her during the past and that she hoped they would always be friends.

Always be friends! Caroline would be her slave!

She said with emotion: "I should always wish to serve you, Madam."

A reply which enchanted Sophia Charlotte.

*     *     *

Sophia Charlotte's conscience did worry her. In the private apartments assigned to them in the Dower House she discussed this with her husband.

"Eleanor has become an invalid," she said.

"At least she's still alive," replied the Elector.

"She might so easily have been murdered and we are in a way to blame."

"My dear, you must not think like that."

"But I do. We arranged the marriage. We persuaded her to it. And that poor child, what she must have suffered."

"And you like the child?"

"I like both children but the girl is enchanting. She attracts me because although she is only a child she has an air of wisdom. I tremble to think that before long she may be an orphan. Frederick, what will become of those children if their mother dies?"

"The boy will go to Ansbach, I daresay. He's the heir presumptive."

"And Caroline?"

"Doubtless she will make her home there too."

"And if the boy does not become Margrave? Oh, it is an uneasy future. In a way we *are* responsible. My conscience would never let me rest unless . . ."

He was smiling at her indulgently understanding what she was about to say. She knew this and smiled at him ruefully. It was one of those occasions when she wished she could have given him a deeper affection.

"Go on, my dear."

"Something would have to be done for Caroline."

"I know what is in your mind."

"And you would raise no objection?"

"If it were your wish I daresay it would be mine."

"You are so good to me." There were tears of emotion in her eyes. He took her hand and kissed it. "Thank you," she added.

She was warm in her gratitude and he in his turn was grateful to have kindled that warmth.

\*    \*    \*

To no one else had Caroline ever talked as she did to Sophia Charlotte. They would walk in the gardens of Pretsch and while they talked look down on the valley of the Elbe and beyond to the towers of Wittenburg, once the home of Martin Luther.

Sophia Charlotte talked to Caroline of that great man; she spoke animatedly of how he had defied the Pope and publicly burned the Papal Bull. At the same time she talked judicially for as she pointed out to Caroline one must never be fanatical because as soon as one did the vision became blurred and the judgement impaired. At the same time one could applaud bold men who struck blows at tyranny. She talked earnestly of tolerance, for she thought it necessary to men's dignity that they should have freedom to form their own opinions.

It was fascinating talk and Caroline was glad she had disciplined herself to study because in doing so she had prepared herself for such conversation; and her reward was the approval of Sophia Charlotte.

Everyday the Electress would look for her.

"I shall sadly miss our talks when I leave Pretsch," she said.

And Caroline was torn between the sorrow parting must bring and the joy that the great Electress Sophia Charlotte— beautiful, brilliant and courted—should really want to share the company of an eleven-year-old girl.

\* \* \*

Everyone at Pretsch was talking about the scandal of Hanover. Caroline listened and even asked questions of the servants.

She discovered that it concerned the Electoral Prince George Lewis, his wife Sophia Dorothea and a dashing adventurer named Count Königsmarck. Caroline had seen the Count for when he had visited Dresden she had been there. Very handsome, popular, gay, reckless, everyone at the Dresden Court had been aware of him—even the young girl who had had to keep out of sight.

Königsmarck had at one time been a favourite of John George; but when he had left Dresden he had talked very indiscreetly about the shocking way in which John George treated his wife. After that Königsmarck had not been welcome at Dresden; but when John George had died so suddenly the Count had returned to Dresden to stay awhile with his old friend Augustus the new Elector and there once more he had talked indiscreetly—this time of the notorious Countess von Platen who was the mistress of the Elector of Hanover; he had

joked about her and her lover as well as George Lewis, the
Electoral Prince, and his mistress. He had boasted rather senti-
mentally too about his own success with George Lewis's neg-
lected wife, the beautiful Sophia Dorothea.

Now the Count was dead. No one knew how he had died or
what had become of his body; but everyone seemed certain
that he was dead. It had been discovered that he was the lover
of Sophia Dorothea. As for this sad Princess, George Lewis was
going to divorce her and make her his prisoner, and declared
he would never see her again.

Caroline thought a good deal about Sophia Dorothea and
compared her with her own mother, for they had both found
great tragedy in marriage. It was alarming to consider that one
day—not far distant—she would be grown up and marriageable. Then she would doubtless be obliged to embark on this
perilous adventure.

\*          \*          \*

Because she was so curious she ventured to speak of the
matter to Sophia Charlotte when they walked together one day
in the gardens. She was puzzled; she would like to understand
more.

"Who is wrong," she asked. "George Lewis or Sophia
Dorothea?"

"So you have heard of this scandal?"

"They talk of it all the time. Not to me, of course. They
whisper when they see me near. And that, of course, makes me
all the more curious to know."

"Naturally, it would. Tell me what you know."

She told and Sophia Charlotte smiled.

"I see," she said, "that you are by no means ignorant of the
ways of the world. From what I have heard George Lewis is a
brutal young man, Sophia Dorothea a frivolous and foolish
woman. Who then would you say was to blame if disaster over-
takes them."

"Both of them?"

"You are wise, Caroline. I am sure both of them is the
answer. Although we must remember that even though the
blame is shared, the punishment is not."

"She will suffer more than he will."

"She is less powerful, poor creature."

"Could she have avoided this ... trouble?"

"We could by certain actions avoid all our troubles."

Caroline considered this. Yes, even her mother. She need not have married the Elector of Saxony. Perhaps if she had wept less and fought more for her rights ... In any case Sophia Charlotte thought so, and she must be right.

"I daresay you have heard a garbled story," said Sophia Charlotte. "It would be better for you to know the truth. After all, though you are only eleven years old you are much older in wisdom, I know."

Caroline glowed with happiness and taking Sophia Charlotte's hand kissed it.

"My dearest child," murmured Sophia Charlotte deeply moved. "Well," she continued briskly. "George Lewis is a man ... not unlike your late stepfather. There are many like him. It is a pattern of our times. He turned from his wife to other women. She found that intolerable and took a lover. The result—the mysterious disappearance of the lover and punishment for the poor Princess."

"It seems so unfair when he began it and she only did what he did."

"Life is unfair, my dear. More so for women than for men. He took his mistresses as a natural right. Such is the custom. But when she took a lover she dangered the succession. You see what I mean. But of course you do. That is the answer."

"So she *was* more to blame."

"It is not for us to blame. She was foolish, poor soul; and folly often pays a higher price than greater sins."

"What should she have done when he took his mistresses? Should she have accepted them. My mother ..."

"Your mother was not a proud woman like this Princess. Your mother accepted the position ... and you see here she is alive and living in peace while her husband and his mistress are dead."

"But that was by accident."

"Life is made up of accidents, luck if you like—good and bad—but often our own actions can decide the course our lives will take. If Sophia Dorothea had accepted her husband's mistresses, if she had not quarrelled with him..." Sophia Charlotte shrugged her shoulders. "Who knows what would have happened."

"So one should accept?"

"One should try to discover what is the wisest way for one's own advantage."

"I see," said Caroline.

Sophia Charlotte covered the girl's hand with her own.

"I believe you do," she said.

\*　\*　\*

Even while the Brandenburgs were visiting her Eleanor had to take to her bed. The Dresden interlude had undermined her health and it could not be expected that even though the threat to her life was removed she would easily recover.

Sophia Charlotte visited her in her bedchamber and sent away her servants.

"I have become deeply attached to Caroline," she said.

"That pleases me more than anything else could."

"I know you are anxious for her future. Your son will doubtless be secure in Ansbach but it is little Caroline who worries you."

Eleanor nodded. "I sometimes feel so weak, that I know I have not long to live."

"Nonsense, here you will recover. But..."

"But?" asked Eleanor eagerly.

"If anything should happen to you, you need not fear for Caroline. You know I love the child as my own daughter. My husband and I would be her guardians and she would have a home with us."

"Oh ... how can I thank you!"

"You shouldn't. I love your daughter. It would give me the utmost pleasure to have her with me, to educate her, to launch her in life. And ... I don't forget, Eleanor, that you met John George in Berlin ... that we persuaded you to the match."

"It is all over now...."

"It must have been ... a nightmare."

Eleanor stretched out a thin veined hand. "It is over and if you will make yourselves Caroline's guardians I shall die contented."

"Then it is done."

"And the Elector?"

"He is with me in this."

Eleanor lay back on her pillows. Now, she thought, I can die in peace.

\*　　\*　　\*

Eleanor lingered for two years in peaceful retirement at Pretsch; and on her death her eleven year old son went to Ansbach to live with his stepbrother, the Margrave, and thirteen year old Caroline to her joy was sent to Berlin to live at the Court of Sophia Charlotte and her husband.

## Suitors and Tragedy for Caroline

THERE followed the happy years. Life at Lützenberg offered even more than Caroline had daréd hope for; here were pleasures which she had not known existed. There was luxury to compare with that of the Dresden court but here it went hand in hand with good taste and the adventures were those of the mind.

Sophia Charlotte had attracted to Lützenburg some of the most interesting men of the age. Her wit and charm, her unusual intelligence, and her power over the man who was one of the most important Electors in Germany sent them flocking to her court.

Her love of everything beautiful was evident in the castle. She had collected together pictures and exquisite furniture, some of the latter inlaid with porcelain, crystal, ivory and ebony. Everything in the castle was rare and beautiful; but in spite of its grandeur ostentation was avoided.

There was no other castle in Germany where so many interesting people gathered; and the reason was due to the mistress of Lützenberg. Here came men of diverse religious

opinions—Catholics, Protestant, and Freethinkers. There was
nothing Sophia Charlotte enjoyed more than to bring these
men together, encourage them to discuss their views, and herself join in the discourse. Philosophers, historians, artists, liter-
ary men, all came to her salons, wandered in her gardens,
talked learnedly with each other; and it was Sophia Charlotte's
hope that one day because they had been able to meet at her
home they would discover some way of welding the various
versions of Christianity together and make a more tolerant
society in which men and women could discuss their ideas
freely without fear.

The coming of Caroline to Lützenberg had been a great joy
to her. She had been drawn to the girl from the first since she
had always wanted a daughter and she had been distressed
when she had heard rumours of what was happening in Saxony; she had blamed herself for having encouraged the marriage and by making herself Caroline's guardian she had
hoped to salve her conscience. But what had begun as a duty
had become a joy, and when Caroline had been with her a few
months she wondered how she could ever endure to be parted
from her. However that should not be until she had found a
suitable husband for her and secretly she hoped to avoid
separation by marrying her ward to her own son Frederick
William. Her husband, indulgent as he was, would no doubt
oppose that match, for Frederick William was one of the most
desirable matches in Germany whereas Caroline had nothing
to offer but her beauty, her charm and that alert mind which
Sophia Charlotte determined should have all the advantages
she could give it.

Neither Sophia Charlotte nor Caroline made any attempt to
hide the attraction they felt for each other. The love which
had sprung up between them was too deep to be denied. For
Sophia Charlotte, Caroline was the perfect companion, intelligent, enquiring, loving learning for its own sake and not only
because she wished to please Sophia Charlotte by her grasp of
it. And for Caroline, the goddess she had worshipped from the
distance was now a loving friend and guardian who had lost
none of her perfections through intimacy.

They were constantly together; Sophia Charlotte supervised

Caroline's education which was not only a matter of school-room lessons. They would walk together in those magnificent gardens made by Le Nôtre in the manner of Versailles; they would sit in arbours and talk with Sophia Charlotte's visitors who knew that if they would please her they must take seriously the young girl on whom she doted.

This was not difficult for the young Princess Caroline had much to contribute and in the warmth of discussion her youth was forgotten.

When Caroline had been at Lützenberg a year Saxony had become like an uneasy nightmare, something that is only remembered now and then. This was her real life, surrounded by beauty, culture and above all love—the love of the person she loved best in the world—and with it that feeling of protection and security, which, but for fears of the past she could not have known was so precious.

She was not so fond of her official guardian who was, naturally, Sophia Charlotte's husband, the Elector of Brandenburg; she found his appearance repulsive and he had no interest in those matters which seemed so vital to her and Sophia Charlotte. He was exclusively concerned with statescraft; he would rise at four o'clock in the morning and retire early which was in complete opposition to the habits of his wife, who liked to spend the morning in bed because, for her, the day did not begin until the evening.

He cared for all that seemed empty to his wife. He enjoyed colourful ceremonies and never lost an opportunity of indulging in them. Often it was necessary for Sophia Charlotte to appear with him and this she did, but it was with reluctance that she put on the robes of state, the glittering jewels which so delighted her husband, and took her place beside him; and as soon as possible she would discard them and put on some loose flowing garment, in Caroline's eyes so much more tasteful and beautiful than flamboyant purples and gold, and instead of glorifying the power of the Electorate, talk of art or literature, philosophy or music.

Caroline, while having no affection for the Elector often marvelled at his tolerance towards his wife. He would look at her wistfully and long for her to interest herself in his affairs and yet he never showed displeasure that she did not do so; only sadness. Whereas Sophia Charlotte had no desire to draw him into her life and was quite content for him to go his own way.

It was only natural that he should resent the girl who had so easily won the love of his wife in a manner which he had been unable to, in spite of everything he had done for her—particularly as, with the coming of Caroline, his wife had grown even further from him.

There were occasions when, on his way to bed, he would look in at her gatherings which were just beginning .He would stay awhile to listen to the music of a young boy named Handel whom she had discovered and was encouraging—for she was constantly discovering and encouraging someone; or exchange a word with one of her Huguenots or Catholics or perhaps Leibniz who was one of the most eminent philosophers of the day. He would not stay; he would be too weary to do anything but yawn at their learned discourse; and in any case he felt unwanted.

Caroline, very much aware of him, always relieved when he left, often felt that their happy home would have been nearer perfection if the Elector had not been there.

But growing in wisdom as she was, she knew that those moments when she and Sophia Charlotte were together could not have been quite so rapturously wonderful if there had been perpetual contentment.

For Sophia Charlotte there were the petty displays of pomp for which she had no feeling; there was the fact that she was married to a man whom she could not love; there were anxieties about the wild nature of her only son—but from all these she had her escape, and she and Caroline were together every day.

So the golden years began to pass and Caroline was growing into a handsome young woman.

*     *     *

Caroline's greatest friend in Berlin, next of course to Sophia Charlotte, was Gottfried Wilhelm Leibniz, and from him she first became deeply aware of the family at Hanover.

Leibniz had come to Lützenberg to visit Sophia Charlotte from Hanover, bringing messages from the Electress Sophia and when Caroline began her friendship with him he was in his late fifties. Recognized as one of the most learned men in Europe, he was both philosopher and mathematician, and had originally made a name for himself at two universities and later by the ideas he presented through his writing.

The Electress Sophia, Sophia Charlotte's mother, had welcomed him at Hanover; and because Leibniz was a man who had a great respect for money and position, he allowed himself to be seduced from the universities to the Courts of Princes where he hoped to make his fortune.

The Electress Sophia had given him charge of the archives at the Hanoverian Palace and one of his main duties was to write for the glorification of the house of Hanover.

Sophia, whose favourite child was Sophia Charlotte, liked her daughter to share in her pleasures and so she sent Leibniz to Lützenberg.

Sophia Charlotte had welcomed him to her band of philosophers and Leibniz was delighted to linger in such an enchanting place. He would sit in the arbours and conduct a discussion between Vota the Catholic, Beausobre, the Huguenot preacher and Toland the English freethinker, while Sophia Charlotte and Caroline listened and now and then offered an opinion. It was all very interesting and as Sophia Charlotte often said if only the same good sense could be shown all over the world as was seen in her arbours and salons, there would be no bloodshed over religion, for men would put their views forward in argument not by torture and the stake.

Although Leibniz was contented at Lützenburg he often talked affectionately of Hanover.

One day when her son Frederick William had been more difficult than usual Sophia Charlotte spoke to Liebniz of her anxieties about the boy. Caroline was present.

"He seems to grow quite unmanageable," sighed Sophia Charlotte. "His governors and tutors have no power over him."

Caroline frowned to see her adored Sophia Charlotte so worried. The boy was an anxiety. He was several years younger than she was but had begun to notice her. She was thinking of an episode which had occurred a few days before. He had pulled her hair so hard that she had cried out with the pain; then he had held her captive and attempted to kiss her, and when she had protested he had laughed at her.

"My mother will try to marry us to each other one day so I should like to try you first," he had told her.

"You are insolent," Caroline had retorted.

"And you give yourself airs, Madam Caroline. You should go down on your knees and beg me to marry you."

"That I should never do to anyone . . . least of all you."

"And why least of all me, pray? You should be very grateful for me . . . if you can get me. Do you realize that I shall be the King of Prussia one day. You do not answer, Madam Caroline."

"I was too busy feeling sorry for Prussia."

She had turned and walked away. "Don't worry, Madam Caroline," he had called after her. "My father would never agree to let me marry you. You're a nobody . . . a *nobody!* Not good enough for marriage with the King of Prussia."

Yes, he was an insufferable boy and she disliked him. She was only sorry that Sophia Charlotte cared so much for him, which was of course understandable since he was her only son . . . her *own* son which must be different from an adopted daughter.

So now she listened intently to what his mother was saying to Gottfried Leibniz.

"He has not enough discipline here," was Leibniz's verdict. "There are no other boys of his equal. The grooms and squires he spends his days with are in awe of him. He needs to be treated roughly by his equals. Why not send him to Hanover where he could be with his cousins."

"You think Hanover . . . at this time . . . is a good place for him to be?"

"The best possible place. There he can become friends with his cousin, George Augustus, and find he doesn't get all his own way."

"I often think of those poor children. Do they miss their mother much?"

"It is long ago since they saw her."

"But to know that she is kept a prisoner in Ahlden! Do they never ask for her, want to see her."

"Oh yes. George Augustus often speaks of her. I have heard that he remembers her well and talks of rescuing her."

"And my brother?"

"The Prince Elector behaves as though he never had a wife. He is happy enough as matter stands. He has his heir George Augustus and his daughter Sophia Dorothea."

"The fact that she is named after her mother must remind him."

"He gives no sign. He continues to amuse himself...."

"With Ermengarda Schulemburg?"

"She remains his favourite."

Sophia Charlotte shivered. "And you think my son would be better off at Hanover!"

"Your mother's there to take good care of him."

"Yes," answered Sophia Charlotte, "there is my mother."

And as a result Frederick William was sent to Hanover.

\* \* \*

Gottfried Leibniz liked to gossip with Caroline when they were not discussing deeper matters. He had a great admiration for the Electress Sophia, the mother of Sophia Charlotte, and he liked to chat about the court of Hanover; and since this had once been the home of her beloved Sophia Charlotte it was of great interest to Caroline.

How different a childhood Sophia Charlotte had had from Caroline's! And yet about her had whirled similar storms and passions to those with which Caroline had become acquainted at Dresden. The story of Sophia Dorothea of Hanover was far more tragic than that of Caroline's mother, for while fate had intervened to save the latter, poor Sophia Dorothea had had no such help.

Leibniz gossiped often of that tragic affair; he talked of George Lewis, Sophia Charlotte's elder brother whom as a man without learning he despised.

"If you could imagine the complete opposite of our gracious Electress Sophia Charlotte that would be her brother."

"He sounds quite loathsome," declared Caroline.

"I think that is the opinion of almost everyone except Ermengarda Schulemburg and one or two other of his favoured ladies."

"Tell me about his children."

"George Augustus is about your age ... a few months younger perhaps. He is like his father in many ways, but I think he might be an improvement on him. He is fond of music. The only sign of culture these Hanoverians have is a love of music. Literature ... art ... philosophy ... don't exist for them."

"How could the Electress have such a brother."

"She resembles her mother. The Electress Sophia is one of the cleverest women I have ever known."

"Surely not cleverer than her daughter?"

"When the Electress of Brandenburg is as old as her mother she will be as wise. I can't give her higher praise than that."

"I should like to meet the Electress Sophia."

"You will one day. She often talks of visiting her daughter. Our Electress is her favourite child."

"I can well understand that."

"I believe you and Electress Sophia would be good friends."

"Tell me more of her. Tell me about Sophia Charlotte's childhood."

"Oh ... those brothers! They were continually warring with each other. It began in the nurseries. George Lewis is such an oaf ... so uncouth, so crude. I know the Electress Sophia has always regretted that he was her eldest. She would have preferred any of the other boys as Electoral Prince."

"Did George Lewis know this?"

"If he did he didn't care. He was happy enough left to himself to pursue his two main interests."

"And what were they?"

"War and women. In the reverse order."

"And what of his father and mother. Were they happy together?"

Leibniz shrugged his shoulders. "The Electress Sophia is a wise woman. Ernest Augustus her husband was a man who would have his mistresses. Sophia looked the other way. In fact she didn't bother to do even that. She expressed a lack of interest in his extra-marital affairs."

"But why?"

"It was no concern of hers, she said. A wife should not grudge her husband his mistresses as long as he spent enough time with her to give her children."

"It seems a strange philosophy of marriage."

"The Electress Sophia is an unusual woman. Because she remained faithful to this doctrine she has been accorded every dignity, she has been a power at her husband's court and she is the mother of many children."

"And she did not care that he was unfaithful to her? I can't believe that."

"She is a great lady of higher rank than her husband; being the daughter of a Queen and the granddaughter of a King of England. She never forgets it." He smiled a little wryly. "Nor will she allow anyone else to."

"And because of this she does not care that her husband was unfaithful?"

"Her royalty is the ruling passion of her life—that and the possibility of her attaining a crown. Beside that, all else seems insignificant. She has heirs of her body. She could be Queen of England and after her, George Lewis could be King."

"England! That is far away."

"To the Electress Sophia it is home. She has never been there but she calls it so. One day she hopes to receive the call which will take her there and that it will be to mount the throne. You know what her chances are."

"Yes. But there is a King across the water. Don't you think he will come before the Electress Sophia?"

Leibniz laughed maliciously. "When the Electress engaged me to work at Hanover, one of my duties was to attempt to wield together the Catholic and Protestant faiths. But when the law of succession was passed in England, there was a clause which said that only a member of the Reformed Faith could wear the crown of England. The Electress ceased then to be interested in this wielding of the faiths. She was a Protestant and she decided to remain one."

"She is not woman of strong faith."

"Her faith is in the English crown. She believes it to be the most prized diadem in the world and England the home of all that is desirable. Religion to her is something to be of use to rulers. She maintains that only rulers unworthy of the name allow it to rule them. Every day she grows nearer to the English throne her Protestantism grows stronger."

"You find this admirable?"

"I find it ... wise."

"Isn't that a cynical view of religion?"

"It is not a matter of cynicism. You have listened to—and indeed partaken in—our discourses. We are groping in the dark. What is faith? The very word suggests that there is reason for uncertainty. Whom do you, a young woman of good sense, admire most, the man who convinces himself he believes blindly and shuts his eyes to reason, or the one who says I am not sure but eager to find out, therefore I shall listen to every argument?"

"Naturally I think it wiser to have an open mind."

"Like that of the Electress Sophia. She has an open mind. In the meantime if she has a good chance of attaining the throne of England as a Protestant and no chance at all as a Catholic, wisdom decrees that she shall be a Protestant and a Protestant she is."

"Of course it is wise but ..."

"You are too emotional, my dear young lady. That is your youth. When the tempest is blowing you must trim your sails accordingly. Always remember that. Is it wise to be wrecked for a principle? So much depends on what is involved? In life one rarely comes to a clear solution. Perhaps there is none. That is what makes our discussions here of such interest and such value."

"But you yourself, I heard declined the custodianship of the Vatican Library for a principle."

"You are wrong."

"But I heard that the Pope himself offered you this appointment and you refused because to have accepted it would have entailed becoming a Catholic."

"That is true in part. I had no intention of becoming an adherent to any one form of religion. What if I had? My freedom would have been restricted, and all avenues except one closed to me. I should have accepted this and that, because it was the law laid down by the Pope."

"But is that not declining for a principle?"

"In truth no. At the heart of my refusal was the knowledge that I could lead a fuller life at courts such as this and that of Hanover. I could become richer more famous out in the world."

"Then you are ambitious."

"I shall not know what manner of man I am until I come to the end of my life."

Sophia Charlotte joined them.

"I see as usual that you are giving Caroline something to think about," she said with a smile.

* * *

The Electress Sophia visited Lützenburg accompanied by her grandson Frederick William.

There was great preparation for their arrival for not only was Sophia Charlotte eager to have her son home again but she was delighted at the prospect of having her mother to stay with her.

Caroline was inclined to be a little jealous and this Sophia Charlotte recognized at once.

"My darling," she said, "you will love my mother and she will love you. Instead of the two of us now there will be three. We shall be a trinity."

Caroline was unsure; from all she had heard of the Electress Sophia she visualized a formidable woman.

She was agreeably surprised for although the old Electress was indeed formidable she showed nothing but pleasure in meeting Caroline.

"My daughter tells me such news of you," she said on their first meeting, "that I am impatient to meet you. Why, you have a charming face, and I am grateful to you for making my dear daughter so happy."

It was a good beginning for it was apparent to Caroline that Sophia was a woman who would say what was in her mind and it appeared that because her daughter had explained how much Caroline meant to her, the Electress was prepared to accept her too.

Her nervousness evaporated and she found herself being as natural as she was in the presence of Sophia Charlotte and with the approving eyes of the latter upon her she proceeded to find a way into the good graces of the mother.

The entertainments at Lützenburg delighted the old Electress and she was invariably to the fore in the discussions that went on. She was delighted to meet her old friend Gottfried Leibniz and even more pleased to see him so happily settled at her daughter's Court.

She liked, too, to wander in the gardens with Caroline and sound her to discover, Caroline was sure, whether she lived up to the reports her daughter had sent her. Caroline found herself playing the part of earnest young philosopher, seeking the truth, playing it in the manner she thought would best appeal to the old woman.

Am I being a little false? she asked herself. Were the Leibniz doctrines teaching her never to be herself, always to stand outside a scene, metaphorically, and look in on herself playing a part? Was it better to forget to watch oneself, to be natural, to say the first thing which came into one's mind? One would be more honest if one did. But it was so easy to do or say what was unwise, perhaps to change the whole pattern of one's life by a word or a small action.

Sometimes it seemed to her that there was no definite right or wrong way of living. Sometimes she allowed herself to believe that life would go on forever as it was now: Herself the companion, handmaiden, devoted daughter of the one she loved and always would she believed beyond all others. But common sense told her this could not be. Sophia Charlotte herself would not wish it. She would want to see her married, a mother, making a home of her own. There were only two ways in which she could ensure a life with Sophia Charlotte until death parted them. One was to remain unmarried; the other was to marry Sophia Charlotte's son.

The second prospect made her shiver.

Frederick William had returned from Hanover no better than he had gone away. He still strutted about the Court arro-

gant as ever and none of the attendants and servants dared
thwart him or he would take his revenge; he would warn them
that one day he would be their master and he would not
forget.

Thinking of marriage with him made Caroline's thoughts
turn to those far off days in Saxony.

Never! she told herself. I would rather remain unmarried.
That is the answer. I will never marry. I will stay here with
dearest Sophia Charlotte until the end of my days.

Frederick William had certainly not learned better manners
at Hanover. It was hardly to be expected that he would. He
had taken a violent dislike to his cousin George Augustus and
waylaid Caroline in the gardens to tell her about it.

"You've grown taller since I've been away, Madam Caroline," he said.

"I daresay you have too, but I don't notice."

The angry lights leaped into his eyes, and she was startled to
see how violent he could quickly become.

"Then notice now!" he demanded.

"It is of no interest to me."

"I command that you do."

"Are you in a position to command me?"

"The Electoral Prince has power to command all his de-
pendants."

Caroline laughed. He took her by the shoulder, his lower lip
projecting in an ugly fashion, and for a moment she thought
he was going to strike her.

"I've no doubt," she said. "But he should not make the mistake of trying to command those who are not."

"And you ... the penniless orphan...."

"I am here at the wish of the Elector and Electress of
Brandenburg who, let me remind you, have the power to command the Electoral Prince."

He laughed suddenly. "You have spirit for a girl who has
nothing."

"How can I have nothing if I have my spirit?"

"Now, Caroline, you're being clever. Save that for old Leibniz and the rest. Don't try it on me."

"I admit it would be wasted."

He brought his face close to hers. "Now you're afraid I'm going to kiss you. Poor Caroline, who has never been kissed. You really are getting old for such ignorance. You want knowledge. Well, why not seek it."

She pushed him aside.

"Don't get ideas," he said. "My cousin Sophia Dorothea is ten times prettier than you. I wouldn't look at you when she was around."

Disturbing! Particularly as marriages were often made without the consent of the two concerned.

A storm cloud had appeared in the skies over Lützenburg; one could not be young forever; one could not remain protected from the ugliness of the world under the cloak of an adored guardian. Change would come and Caroline was growing up.

\* \* \*

There was nothing the Electress Sophia enjoyed more than a tête-à-tête with her daughter. She admired Sophia Charlotte more than any living being and loved her more dearly than any of her children. Sophia Charlotte was not only beautiful and talented, she was wise.

The Electress Sophia could not see how she herself could better have handled her own life. She had not loved Ernest Augustus when she had married him and would have much preferred the man to whom she was first betrothed, the Duke of Celle, father of her ill-fated daughter-in-law Sophia Dorothea who was now a prisoner at Ahlden; but she had accepted Ernest Augustus and her rank and dignity had given her a certain power. All she had to do was let him go his way, let him keep his mistresses, never protest or show that she minded; and in return he accepted her position as Electress, as a Princess of royal birth, and she could have her will in all matters that did not clash with his desires. It was the kind of compact only an extremely wise woman could carry through; and she had done it.

Sophia Charlotte had one gift which her mother lacked: beauty. And this, the old Electress would be the first to admit, was a very valuable one. Because of it she had not to placate a husband who preferred other women to herself; she was able to lead her own life as determinedly as Sophia had led hers, but with greater charm and dignity.

It was a pleasure to see her here in her magnificent palace; and the Electress was most proud of her daughter.

"And what do you really think of my Caroline?" asked Sophia Charlotte.

"I find her a pleasant creature and I am ready to love her because her companionship has made you very happy."

"Few have given me greater happiness than that girl. I brought her here because I thought it my duty. Oh, I took a fancy to her from the first, but I never thought that I should find in her the daughter I have always longed to have."

"If I stayed here I should love the girl even as you do. You have made her like yourself. The other day when I heard her talking out of sight, I thought it was you I heard."

Sophia Charlotte was delighted. "I have noticed it too."

"She begins to look like you, too. She imitates you. You wear a bow on your gown one day and she does the next."

"She is the dearest creature. Sometimes I wonder what I shall do if she ever has to go away."

"Marriage, you mean?"

"I sometimes look at her with fear. She is no longer a child. Many are married at her age. I suppose the day will come..."

"Yes," agreed Sophia, "the day will come."

"You are not thinking of her for Frederick William?"

"His father would never agree."

"Wouldn't you be able to persuade him? If I know you, my dear..."

"On all but state matters. Frederick William's marriage could be that."

"A blessing for Caroline."

"You are not favourably impressed by your grandson?"

"My dearest daughter, some of us are apt to be blind where our children are concerned but you have too much sense. He is unmannerly, arrogant, ungovernable."

Sophia Charlotte looked distressed, and her mother put her hand over her daughter's.

"It happens sometimes that our children disappoint us. I can tell you I find my son George Lewis ... despicable. You and I are not the women to deceive ourselves, are we? If we are it makes a nonsense of all this fine talk we hear in these gardens of yours. No, we face the truth. There lies our strength. My eldest is a crude boor. Yours while not possessing the same deplorable characteristics has those equally bad. Face it, daughter."

"You have many children, Mother. I have only one. You were not disappointed in all."

"I had the best daughter in the world ... and so, it appears have you."

"Caroline is not my own flesh and blood."

"Now you are not being true to your theories. Caroline is all to you that any daughter could be. Are you going to love her less because you did not suffer torments to bring her into the world? Be rational. Isn't that what you say with your philosophers."

"You're right, Mother. Of what have I to complain while I have Caroline! But daughters leave their mothers when they marry—and it is that I fear, unless ..."

The Electress smiled and looked absently towards the delightful fountain playing in the midst of Le Nôtre's magnificent handiwork.

My dearest daughter will have to face a great problem, she was telling herself. To keep her dear Caroline with her through marriage with a man, who might be considered one of the biggest catches in Germany, but is almost certain to be one of the worst husbands—or to let her marry outside and go away.

Sophia could picture her daughter, torturing herself with a hundred possibilities. Keep her and guard her? Or let her go away and possibly marry as unhappily as she would at home? It was certainly a problem. But then marriage was always a gamble; and Caroline could not be protected all her life. She must go out and face the world alone, which, Sophia was certain, Caroline would be able to do adequately.

What a pity, Sophia Charlotte was thinking, that time could not stand still and charming daughters always remain young and the dearest companions of their doting mothers!

A thought had come to the old Electress. At Hanover there was another grandson who would be needing a bride: George Augustus, son of George Lewis.

Now suppose Caroline were his bride; suppose she came to Hanover. Well, that would bring Sophia Charlotte often to Hanover; the young bride could visit Berlin frequently; and the Electress Sophia would have a daughter whom she could love and respect.

A very pleasant prospect for a woman who, as she grew older, felt a longing for young companionship and affection.

Being Sophia she said nothing as yet of this idea to her daughter. So while they sat together in one of those cosy and comfortable silences which only those who are in harmony can enjoy, Sophia Charlotte was thinking of Caroline's possible marriage to her son, while her mother explored the possibility of bringing Caroline to Hanover as the bride of George Augustus.

One day, thought Sophia Charlotte, Frederick William will be King of Prussia. My Caroline would be a Queen—and she is clever enough to handle him. What other girl could?

One day, thought the Electress Sophia, George Augustus could be King of England. Caroline would be a Queen ... and Queen of England. What higher goal than that in Germany ... or in the whole world.

\* \* \*

The Electress Sophia talked to Caroline.

"My dear, do you speak English?"

"No," answered Caroline.

"Oh but that is shocking! You should, you know."

"There has never seemed any need."

"Never seemed any need! But it is the most important language in the world. What if you should ever go there? A fine ninny you would look not being able to understand what was said."

"I doubt if I should ever go there."

"Get that notion out of your head at once. Why, sometimes I think that all this talk of 'the why of the why' and 'where are we going' and 'leaps in the dark and what happens after death' leaves you a little foolish about the everyday business of living."

"But please tell me why you think I should go to England?"

"Suppose I went to England and asked you to visit me."

"Are you thinking of going?"

"Does my daughter never talk to you of her family?"

"She has done so but . . ."

"Then surely you are not unaware of our most important connection."

"Perhaps you will please explain."

"My mother was Elizabeth Queen of Bohemia and her father was James the Sixth of Scotland and the First of England."

"Yes I did know that."

"Let me refresh your memory. His son Charles the First was a King of England. You know his tragic story."

"Yes. He was beheaded by order of the Parliament, and Oliver Cromwell set up a Commonwealth."

"But it didn't last. The English have too much sense. A Commonwealth! They soon had his son back and the second Charles showed the people how much better it is to be ruled by a King than a Parliament."

"They are a pleasure-loving people who turned against the puritan ways, so I've heard."

"You heard correctly. Charles' brother James followed him but he was a fool and became a Catholic so for that reason he was turned out in favour of William and Mary. They had no children so Anne, Mary's sister came to the throne. She sits on it now and . . . she finds it hard to get a healthy son. If she fails in this, who will be the next sovereign of England?"

Caroline dared not let the old lady see her smile. This was her favourite hobby horse. Sophia Charlotte had discussed it with her. "My mother is the shrewdest calmest woman in the world, except for one thing. Over that she is fanatical. England —and her chances of becoming Queen of that country! They are remote enough, God knows, but there is a possibility. That possibility is the ruling passion of her life."

Caroline said gently: "The deposed King has a son who might be James the Third."

"They'll never tolerate him. He's a Catholic. The English turned out the father for that reason. They'll not have the son back for the same. Where would the sense be? And the English are the most sensible people in the world. Where will they turn then for a *Protestant* monarch. I'll tell you, Caroline. They'll turn to Hanover. For I am the next in the line of succession. If Anne doesn't have a son—and how can she, poor dropsical gouty lady—they must turn to me if they want the Protestant religion preserved; and they do. I should be Queen of England, Caroline. And if I were I should invite you to my Court. A fine figure you would cut—not being able to speak the language. Promise me that you will learn it."

"I promise," said Caroline.

\*     \*     \*

The Electress Sophia sadly said farewell.

"Goodbye my dearest daughter, write to me often. You know what your letters mean to me."

"And yours to me, Mother. Let me know all that happens at Hanover."

"And goodbye, Caroline, my dear. I shall miss your bright company. I think perhaps I shall send someone over from Hanover to kidnap you and bring you to me."

Caroline glowed with pleasure. She would never completely forget the horror of Saxony even though it was difficult now to compare herself with that unwanted child who had been forced to keep out of everyone's way for fear she should be noticed.

Sophia Charlotte was delighted too.

"You have made a favourable impression on Mother," she said, as they watched the cavalcade ride away. "And that is something that is rarely done." She put her arm about her. "Don't imagine though that I should ever allow her to kidnap you. No one is going to do that."

Sophia Charlotte's eyes had rested uneasily on her son who, in the party assembled to say farewell to the departing guests, was looking almost amiable. She knew it was because he was glad to see the last of his grandmother for a while.

He had come back from Hanover as unattractive as he had been before he went.

It might be that marriage would improve him, Sophia Charlotte deceived herself into thinking.

\*    \*    \*

After the departure of the Electress Sophia the old way of life was resumed at Lützenburg and Sophia Charlotte tried to forget the unpleasant subject of Caroline's marriage.

Her husband had now become King of Prussia and in this important role was able to indulge his love of ceremony more than ever. Secretly Caroline would have liked to join in the ceremonies and could have found great pleasure in putting on dazzling garments and appearing at state banquets. She did not mention this for she knew it would mark a difference between her and Sophia Charlotte and disappoint the latter.

But because the days were so pleasant they slipped quickly away and Caroline was now approaching her twentieth birthday. It was being suggested that she was never to marry for surely if she had been intended to, a bridegroom would have been found for her by now. On the other hand was she waiting for the Crown Prince of Prussia to reach marriageable age?

Caroline was aware of these whispers and made uneasy by them. Whenever she thought of marriage she was reminded of her mother's unhappy experience and certainly she had no wish to change the existing state of affairs. To leave Lützenburg! How could she ever be happy anywhere else? To stay and marry Frederick William? It was difficult to know which was the worst project—to leave Lützenburg to go to an unknown husband or to stay and marry one whom she already disliked.

The Crown Prince himself was aware of the whispers; they made him laugh and plunge into profligacy which was even more shocking than that which he had practised before.

There was a change in the air.

The King of Prussia, when he had time from state matters, was beginning to regard Caroline speculatively, pondering on the fact that she might be a useful factor in some treaty which would bring advantage to Prussia.

Caroline had a return of the nightmares which had haunted her when she had feared for her mother and which had returned now and then after her death. It was like a recurring pattern.

Oh God, save me from marriage, she prayed.

Sophia Charlotte had come to a decision. She would not lose Caroline. Anything was preferable to that.

When she went to her husband's apartments to talk to him about Caroline, he was as affectionate as usual and expressed pleasure at the visit.

"Caroline is twenty years old," she said.

"No longer a girl," he commented. "She should have had a husband years ago and a family by now."

"I have wanted to keep her with me."

"I know. But she has a life of her own to lead."

"I want to see her married but I want to see her happy too. Lützenburg has been home to her; she loves the place; I doubt whether she will ever be really happy anywhere else."

"Oh, she'll settle down with her husband."

"I want her to remain here. Frederick William will need a wife. Why not Caroline?"

"Caroline from little Ansbach! You cannot be serious. Our son is the Crown Prince of Prussia."

"He is our son and Caroline has been as our daughter."

"She has enjoyed all the advantages a daughter of ours would have had but she is not our daughter. And when it comes to marriage these things are important. The future King of Prussia could not marry an obscure girl from a place like Ansbach."

"Why not ... if we wished it?"

"But *we* don't wish it. You may, but I do not. Moreover I can never allow it."

He saw the surprise and sorrow in her face and was contrite.

"My dear," he said, "I have always allowed you to go your way. I have never interfered with your pleasures. I have tried in every way to give you what you want. This I cannot give you. This is the future of Prussia."

"I tell you he wouldn't find a better wife in the world than Caroline. The truth is he is unworthy of her."

"You are besotted about this girl. She's a pleasant enough creature, I'll admit. But she is not even outstandingly good-looking and she has nothing to commend her but her good health and serene disposition. Those are not enough, my dear, for the crown of Prussia and you must know it."

"I must talk to you. . . ."

"My dear, you will only distress yourself. This is something I cannot give you. Please put this idea out of your mind. Either find another husband for the girl or let her remain unmarried. But she shall not marry our son."

She knew that for the first time in their married life it would be useless to attempt to persuade him.

\* \* \*

It was shortly after this when Sophia Charlotte clearly a little agitated, asked Caroline to walk in the gardens with her that they might talk in privacy.

She led her to a summer house and as they sat there together took her hand and said: "Caroline, this was bound to happen sooner or later. You are not a child any more and it was inevitable that sooner or later someone would ask for your hand in marriage."

Caroline grew pale and Sophia Charlotte hurried on: "It is a great honour, of course."

"Who?" asked Caroline faintly.

"It is the Archduke Charles whom they call King of Spain. Of course he has yet to win that title but . . . you will understand it would be a very good match for you."

"The King of Spain!"

"In name only at the time. Louis is determined to put his grandson on the throne but we and our allies will not allow that, of course. Yes, it would be a very brilliant marriage."

"And he would marry me?"

"At the moment tentative enquiries are being made. You should not consider them certain but this is in the air and it would be an excellent marriage for you."

She did not say: My husband has no doubt had a hand in this because he is determined not to have you for our son. Yet if you are good enough for the King of Spain why not for the King of Prussia?

Of course Charles was only the titular King of Spain and Louis was powerful but...

Caroline had thrown herself into Sophia Charlotte's arms and they clung together.

"I never never want to leave you," she sobbed.

\* \* \*

Yet when she was alone she stood before her mirror and looked at her reflection. The traces of tears still showed on her face. She was plump and pretty; she had masses of auburn hair and blue eyes; she was talented and well-educated.

"The Queen of Spain," she said aloud.

She could never be happy away from Sophia Charlotte whom she loved so dearly; she would never never find a home such as Lützenburg had been to her; and yet she saw herself with a crown on her head, dressed in purple and ermine.

"Her Majesty, Queen of Spain," she said.

\* \* \*

Months passed without mention of the project.

Of course, said Caroline, to herself, I should never be happy away from Sophia Charlotte. No place however grand could ever be home to me the way Lützenburg is.

After a while she told herself it had been merely a rumour and she forgot that the marriage had been suggested.

Sophia Charlotte did not forget. Betrothal to the Archduke Charles might have come to nothing but there would be other suitors. There must be. Caroline was twenty years old. She could not keep her with her much longer.

The fact depressed her so much that she became unwell. She felt a pain in her throat which kept recurring—only slightly but painfully enough to be uncomfortable.

She discussed this with one of her attendants, a close friend named Marie von Pöllnitz.

"I have not felt well since this question of Caroline's marriage has been in the air." Marie looked at her sadly for she knew that it was unlikely that she would be able to keep Caroline with her for ever. Sophia Charlotte put her hand to her throat. "I have a vague sort of pain ... here. But I believe I should feel as well as ever if the King would consent to Caroline's marrying our son."

"Your Highness might be anxious then if Caroline were not happy in her marriage."

"But we should be together for the rest of our lives. I am sure that is all Caroline would ask ... as I should. Whatever happened we should be together."

Marie, looking at her friend, thought she showed signs of her anxiety. It was the first time she had noticed that the Queen showed her age.

\* \* \*

To her astonishment Caroline received an invitation from the Duke and Duchess of Weissenfels who would be delighted if she would spend a few days with them. She showed the invitation to Sophia Charlotte.

"Why should they suddenly remember me?"

"Why not? They are related to your mother. I daresay they have heard accounts of your charm and would like to see you. It is natural."

"I shall not go."

"It will seem churlish to refuse."

"You would come with me?"

Sophia Charlotte laughed. "My dearest, I am not invited."

"Oh but ..."

"You must now and then take these little trips."

"If I go I shall not stay long."

"I hope not, my dear. I shall be longing for your return."

"Then why go at all?"

"Because you have been asked."

"And why should you not come with me? I am sure if I suggested it they would be delighted to receive you."

Sophia Charlotte shook her head. Secretly she would be glad of the respite. She was often feeling very tired and she did not wish Caroline to know this. While the girl was away she would spend the time resting and on her return would feel as well as ever.

So Caroline went to Weissenfels alone.

\*     \*     \*

During her journey to Weissenfels Caroline began to feel uneasy. Had she imagined it or had Sophia Charlotte seemed as though she wanted her to go? Surely that could not have been so for she hated their parting as much as Caroline did.

But when she arrived at the castle of Weissenfels, which was a delightful spot situated among vineyards on the River Saale, she had no time for speculation; she was welcomed by the Duke and Duchess and taken to her apartments by the latter and as soon as they were alone there, the Duchess told her that a very important visitor was expected at the castle.

"Who?" asked Caroline.

The Duchess, looking a little coy, replied that it was the Archduke Charles, King of Spain.

Caroline flushed slightly but said calmly that she had heard much of him and should be interested to meet him. If she was to meet him.

"Certainly you are," was the reply. "It is to see you that he has broken his journey to call at Weissenfels."

\*     \*     \*

The Archduke Charles was clearly delighted with Caroline when with an absence of ceremony they were introduced to each other by the Duke and Duchess of Weissenfels.

Charles was nineteen and gallant; he knew that the sooner he married the better; and this young woman, a year or so older than himself with her very bright blue eyes, abundant hair and lively expression seemed delightful. He had heard of her unusual intelligence for he had met people who had stayed at the Prussian Court and been invited to Lützenburg; although she was merely the daughter of a Margrave of Ansbach she had been brought up as that of the King of Prussia.

Charles did not feel that he had made an unnecessary journey.

Although they were not allowed to be alone, the Duke and Duchess gave them opportunities for conversation; and they walked in the gardens together, with a few attendants keeping them in sight and at the same time their distance; they also sat together in the reception chamber with attendants placed too far from them to hear their conversation.

Caroline compared the Archduke Charles with Frederick William and that made her see Charles very favourably. Although there was no mention of a marriage she knew that could have been the only reason for this visit and she was vain enough to have been very disappointed if the Archduke Charles had not been favourably impressed with her.

He was so gallant that it was difficult to be sure, but she was almost certain.

King of Spain! It was a glittering title. She was discovering that she was ambitious; but how far from Lützenburg Spain was! So how could she happily contemplate marriage into that country?

She had always known that marriage would be a state into which she would enter with trepidation. Now, when she was alone in her rooms, she would stand at her window gazing over the vineyards and think of those long ago days when she had looked out at her stepfather and his mistress caressing each other for all to see, while her mother lay in her room wondering whether her punishment for marrying him would be repudiation or death.

Marriage! She had to consider it. And either way she looked she could see unhappiness. To Spain and separation from Sophia Charlotte—to Berlin, to spend the rest of her life with her beloved foster mother. And the price? Frederick William or spinsterhood.

And when she looked at the pleasant face of the young Archduke she could not make up her mind what was preferable.

He talked of his ambitions because he could not yet talk of his more romantic intentions. Before he did this his advisers must set forth their conditions, and she supposed the King of Prussia would set forth his. They would be bargained for, wrangled over, and she was glad of this because the time necessary to do the bargaining and wrangling would enable her to think; for she believed that the final decision was hers because Sophia Charlotte would never allow her to be forced into what she did not want.

"They call me a King," her suitor told her, "but I have yet to win my kingdom."

"I hope it will not be long before you do."

He shrugged his shoulders. "The Spaniards prefer the grandson of Louis XIV."

"But your claim is greater."

His smile was deprecating. "The second son of the Emperor? Perhaps. It is a pity the King of Spain died without heirs. Then there would not have to be this war for the succession."

"Well, you have great Allies."

"Yes, William of England has made the Grand Alliance, and England and Holland as well as Austria are with me. We are determined to prevent French domination of Europe which will surely ensue if Louis gets control of Spain."

"The Electress Sophia, mother of my guardian, would tell you you could not fail if you have the English on your side."

"The great Marlborough will carry us to victory I doubt not. When I leave Weissenfels I shall make my way to England, where I shall be received by Queen Anne and have conferences with the Duke of Marlborough. I should like to see a speedy end to this matter."

"And when you are victorious, you will go immediately to Spain?"

He smiled at her intently. "Yes," he said. "I shall go to Spain. It is an interesting country. Have you ever felt that you would like to see it?"

"I think it is always interesting to see new places," replied Caroline noncommitally.

The stay of the Archduke at Weissenfels was short. He had merely come to take a look at the bride he was being offered to assure himself that she was not deformed or distasteful in any way.

Then he rode on to the Hague to embark for England and Caroline went back to Lützenburg.

\*　　\*　　\*

When Caroline reached the palace she went immediately to Sophia Charlotte, embraced her and told her what had happened.

"I'll never ... never leave you!" she cried.

"But you liked him ... this Archduke Charles?" said Sophia Charlotte.

"He was pleasant enough but ..."

"He could well become the King of Spain. Have you thought of that?"

"I could only think that you would be in Prussia, I in Spain."

"And that is enough to make you want to refuse this match?"

"It is. I am certain of it."

"My dearest, I cannot be always with you."

"But why not?"

"Because I am older than you, and none of us can expect to live for ever."

"Let us swear to be together ... until death parts us."

"My darling, it is not right. It is not good. There is your future to think of. You will soon be twenty-one. In a few years they will be saying you are too old for marriage. You have no great titles or riches, remember, to attract a bridegroom. It is my duty to tell you that you might never get an offer to compare with this."

Caroline put her arms round Sophia Charlotte's neck. "I choose to stay with you," she said.

\*      \*      \*

The King of Prussia sent for his ward. When she stood before him he looked at her more intently than he ever had before. It seemed miraculous that she could have received such an honour. Of course she was a Hohenzollern and connected with the Brandenburgs, but without fortune, without honours and titles. Why had she been chosen by the Imperial family to marry one of the sons of that House? It was true Archduke Charles was a second son, but he could be Emperor one day; he could also be King of Spain. Of course the Empire was not the mighty power it had once been; and Charles was a young man with ambitious hopes rather than actual possessions; all the same this was a brilliant offer for Caroline and he hoped she realized it.

It was Sophia Charlotte who had made this possible. She had brought up the girl in such a manner as to make her a desirable wife, without dowry and titles though she might be, and all who had met her at Lützenburg had been impressed by her accomplishments for she was perhaps the most well educated and cultivated Princess in Germany. Sophia Charlotte had determined to educate her as though she were her own daughter—and this was the result.

He would be glad to see the girl married, for she was not going to have his son, and he was afraid that Sophia Charlotte would attempt to persuade him and although he was determined to remain firm, he might waver.

"Now, Caroline," he said, "I have great news for you. The Archduke Charles is asking for your hand in marriage."

Caroline sought to control her feelings which amazed herself. She was horrified because this would mean separation from Sophia Charlotte and yet at the same time she would have been hurt if the offer had not been made.

The King gave her his wintry smile. "You clearly made a good impression during your meeting at Weissenfels."

"I ... I'm pleased about that."

"Well, you don't seem to realize the honour this is. I expect at first it overwhelms you. I can tell you I did not expect anything quite so exalted. This is your great opportunity, and I am sure you are clever enough to realize that. As your guardian I am invited to meet the Elector Palatine to discuss terms, but there is one condition which will be essential. You will have to become a Catholic."

"Become a Catholic!"

"Don't look so startled. What chance do you think a Protestant would have of becoming Queen of Spain? You will have to change quickly and forget you were ever a Protestant."

"But one cannot change one's religion ... overnight."

"You are a sensible young woman and you'll understand I'm sure that in cases like this there is no time for quibbling over doctrines. You may go now and think about it, and I expect to hear before I leave for my meeting with the Elector Palatine that you are a good Catholic."

Caroline went to her own apartments to think.

If I refused to be a Catholic there would be no marriage. The thought kept hammering in her brain. It's a way out ... a way out.

\* \* \*

She sat in Sophia Charlotte's apartments and they talked of this alarming blow to their peace.

"What must I do?" asked Caroline.

"My darling," answered Sophia Charlotte, "you yourself must decide."

"If I follow my own wishes I would never never leave you," cried Caroline passionately.

"Between every mother and child of our rank this choice has to be made. I loved my own mother dearly. We were to each other almost as you and I are. But I had to leave her. The wrench was fearful ... to leave everything that is home and go to a strange land. It is the fate of all Princesses unless they don't marry and I do not think that often brings happiness."

"I would be happy to stay with you forever."

"It may be that I should not always be here."

"Don't talk like that. I can't bear it."

"My dearest, it is wrong of me. I shall always be here when you want me."

"You left Hanover for Berlin. It is not so very far. But I should leave Berlin for Spain."

"You would have children and when you hold your first baby in your arms you would regret nothing. It is nature's way of solace."

"You seek to comfort me, but I shall not leave you." She laughed suddenly. "He won't have me unless I become a Catholic. What do you say to that? Should I become a Catholic?"

"I should never presume to advise you on such a matter."

"I knew it."

"This decision shall be entirely in your hands."

\* \* \*

How rare for a Princess sought in marriage to have the

chance of making her own decision! Who else in the world, but Sophia Charlotte, would have made this possible? But to force anyone to marriage would be against all those principles which had been discussed so freely in the gardens of Lützenburg.

Caroline was torn with doubts and fears. She wanted to stay with Sophia Charlotte; she didn't want life to change. That was clear enough. And yet did she want to remain unmarried all her life? She had discovered that she was ambitious and to be the Queen of Spain would have been a glittering future for any princess.

Glittering prospects in exchange for the love and companionship of Sophia Charlotte. It was a bitter choice.

There was one fact to which she clung. She must become a Catholic. Thank God she did not have to give an immediate answer. And while she battled with her emotions she could talk of the difficulties of changing her religion.

\*     \*     \*

The King of Prussia was impatient.

"You must be mad," he said, "if you don't accept this offer. I can tell you, princes and ministers have been known to change their minds. While you prevaricate they may be looking elsewhere. The best thing you can do is say you are eager to change your religion and are ready to receive immediate instruction."

"But I am not ready and I am as yet undecided."

"Do you expect me to tell the Elector Palatine that?"

"You must tell him the truth, I suppose."

"You set a high value on yourself."

"I have been taught to be truthful and I cannot change my ideas of religion for the sake of a possible crown."

"It is all this talk you have listened to."

But he dared not force her to accept. Sophia Charlotte would never forgive him if he did.

So he met the Elector Palatine and told him that Caroline needed time to come to a decision about her religion and as a result the Elector sent Father Orban, his Jesuit confessor, to

Lützenburg to instruct Caroline and show her that the Catholic Faith was the only true one.

*      *      *

The Electress Sophia, hearing that the Archduke Charles had made Caroline an offer, came to visit Lützenburg.

When she saw Caroline she was not surprised that the Archduke was eager for the marriage.

"She reminds me more than ever of what you were at her age," she told her daughter. "So they are going to make a Catholic of her!"

"If she will become one," Sophia Charlotte reminded her mother.

"Surely anyone in their right senses would be ready to say a few masses for the sake of a crown?"

"You are cynical, Mother."

"I call it being reasonable."

"You have never been a religious woman."

"And have you?"

"I have never been able to see that one way is all good the other all bad. There are so many sides to all questions."

"And so you have talked and talked with your philosophers to try and find the answers. How have you succeeded?"

"Not with any real success. We always seem to arrive back at the point where we started. The answer is: 'It may be this, it may be that, but the truth is wrapped in doubt.' And until I die I shall not be sure what happens after death."

"And Caroline?"

"She believes as I do."

"So..."

"I am uncertain. It is a brilliant offer."

"Queen of Spain," mused the old Electress. "But he has to win his own crown before he has one to place on her head. But still she'd be a Queen of Spain if he is victorious. I can think of a crown I'd rather wear."

Sophia Charlotte smiled at her mother. "Might it be the crown of England?"

"I'd like to see George Augustus married. I'd say he has as

much likelihood of getting a crown as Master Archduke Charles."

"Do you mean you would like Caroline for George Augustus?"

"Why not? She would not have to change her religion for him."

"But the changing of religion does not shock you. I remember you had me brought up in such a manner that you could pop me either into Catholicism or Protestantism at a moment's decision, according to the offers you received for me. A Catholic Prince and then it would be 'Oh she is a Catholic'. A better offer from a Protestant and 'All her life she has been a Protestant.' Worldly wise and theologically deplorable."

"And, my darling, what happened? I have the best of daughters."

"You were determined to do the best for me as I am for Caroline. Our views differ. As I see it she shall not be forced into marriage. I despair of losing her, yet I shall make no effort to detain her. She has been brought up to respect the freedom of individuals. Now she shall have it and use it as she will."

The old Electress's shrewd eyes were speculative.

She wanted this girl for *her* daughter-in-law. She would say nothing to her as yet. George Augustus had not a good reputation and this girl had been brought up to make her own decisions. But a little persuasion would be reasonable ... and worldly wise.

\*  \*  \*

Caroline listened to the words of Father Orban.

The Catholic Faith was the true faith, the only faith, and only by adhering to it could she enter the Kingdom of Heaven. "This is the undefiled, the genuine, the pure holy truth. Break from the heretics and for the sake of your soul cling to the truth...."

Caroline was thinking: I should be Queen of Spain. And she saw herself riding through the streets of Madrid; she heard the shouts of the people. "Long live the Queen of Spain. Long live Queen Caroline!"

And the young man who would ride beside her was pleasant and courteous.

She would have children ... and when she held the first of them in her arms the pain of separation would begin to be numbed. She would love the child as she loved Sophia Charlotte and all her hopes and ambitions would be for her son.

Poor Father Orban! He was so earnest. He did not know that she had heard those arguments again and again and that they meant nothing to her. She doubted she would ever be truly religious.

When she left Father Orban she would walk in the gardens with Leibniz.

"You will never accept the Catholic Faith," he told her.

"Is it necessary to do so to call yourself a Catholic?"

"Do you think you would care for life in Spain?"

He looked at her shrewdly. How much did she know of his inner thoughts? They had made a clever girl of their Caroline ... he, Sophia Charlotte and their friends.

The Electress Sophia was against the marriage. He knew why. She wanted Caroline for Hanover. What a better prospect for Caroline ... and Leibniz ... for Sophia Charlotte ... for them all!

It was not exactly selfish to work for Hanover and against Spain. What future would there be for a free thinker in Spain, the land of the Inquisition and bigotry? Better to have accepted the custodianship of the Vatican and become a servant of the Pope than go to Spain.

"If you remember all the conversations we have had here, if they have meant anything to you, you will never go to Spain."

No, she thought in the solitude of her room, I shall never go to Spain.

\*　　\*　　\*

Sophia Charlotte showed her a letter she had received from the Elector Palatine.

He knew, he wrote, that Caroline was being instructed in the Catholic faith by Father Orban, but the Father was a little disappointed by the obstruction she put forward. She seemed to make argument rather than accept instruction. The Elector

Palatine knew that Caroline was an unusually intelligent young woman and it was partly for this reason that they were anxious for her to marry the Archduke, but they believed in Austria that she was being a little recalcitrant. If Charlotte Sophia would persuade her, for, as Caroline's guardian, she must rejoice in this brilliant offer which was being put before her, if she would point out the advantages of becoming a Catholic, the Elector Palatine was sure that Her Serene Highness the Princess of Ansbach would see good sense the quicker.

"And this is my answer," said Sophia Charlotte showing it to Caroline.

The Queen of Prussia thanked the Elector Palatine for his letter but it was her firm belief that the matter of choosing religion was a choice—like that of marriage—which should be left to the individual and she would do nothing to persuade Her Serene Highness, the Princess of Ansbach, to make her choice. It must rest entirely with her.

"It's true, my dearest," said Sophia Charlotte; "the choice must be yours."

\* \* \*

The Electress Sophia talked to Caroline. She implored her to make a *wise* decision; she herself had always felt the Catholics to be too fanatical for her taste; and she had heard such sad tales of the way Protestants were persecuted in Spain. It was, as her daughter Sophia Charlotte reiterated so often, for Caroline to make the choice, but there were matters she should consider very carefully.

"Spain is a great country. It would be an honour to be its Queen but it could not compare with the honour of being Queen of England, and England would want a Protestant Queen. I always knew it and I believe the English to be right."

The Electress Sophia felt frustrated for how could she tell Caroline that she wanted her to be the bride of her own grandson before she had discussed this matter with her son.

She thought she ought to go back to Hanover without delay and talk over the matter with George Lewis. She believed she could persuade him easily for he was not deeply interested in his son.

She wished she could say openly, instead of by hints, that Caroline should refuse the match with Spain for she might have a more brilliant possibility presented to her before long.

Sophia Charlotte said goodbye to her mother and promised to visit her soon.

"For," said the Electress Sophia, "you have allowed this matter to worry you and you are not looking as well as I should like to see you."

Get her to Hanover, thought the Electress, and there discuss the desirability of keeping Caroline in their own intimate circle.

\* \* \*

Caroline listened to Father Orban. He spoke so earnestly that he was almost convincing. Then she would walk with Gottfried Leibniz and he would be even more so.

Sophia Charlotte did not want her to go.

Of course I shall never leave her, thought Caroline.

She was not sleeping as well as she usually did. She was haunted by dreams of the past mingling with thoughts of the future. Once she dreamed she saw the Queen of Spain being crowned. She thought it was herself until she saw her mother's face under the diadem.

No, she thought, I shall never go to Spain. In any case he is not yet King; and the King of France is determined that he never shall be; and the King of France is surely one of the most powerful men in the world.

There came a letter from her brother who, on the death of their stepbrother had become Margrave of Ansbach.

"I have heard of your difficulties," he wrote. "Why not come and stay awhile in Ansbach? Here you can live quietly, away from all controversy. It would be a good place in which to make your decision."

When she showed this invitation to Sophia Charlotte, the latter thought it would be an excellent idea for her to go and stay for a short while with her brother. They had seen so little of each other and the invitation was cordial. Moreover it would be a good idea for her to get right away from Lützenburg to make her decision. There she would discover more easily what she wanted to do.

So Caroline decided she would go to Ansbach for a short stay.

\* \* \*

While Caroline had been the centre of attraction, Frederick William, piqued to find himself in the shade, had been behaving with more than his usual arrogance. Sophia Charlotte, who secretly had been feeling less well as each week passed and doing her utmost to hide this fact, agreed with the King that perhaps a tour of foreign countries might teach their son better manners.

She hated parting with him for she loved him dearly and tried to convince herself that he would outgrow his violent temper and arrogant ways, for she, who was so eager to discover the truth about life and death, could deceive herself about this son who so disappointed her.

The King was in agreement with her and while Caroline set off for Ansbach, Frederick William started his Grand Tour.

Without the two young people Sophia Charlotte found the palace unbearably lonely. Secretly she did not believe that the culture of other courts would change her son; and she was afraid of the decision Caroline might come to. If Caroline married her nephew George Augustus, their separation need not be of long duration; she could make many reasons for visiting her mother, and the Electress and Caroline could be constantly at Lützenburg.

The Electress had begged her not to delay her visit to Hanover; she knew for what reason; and because she was so lonely she decided to make plans to go at once.

The pain in her throat had grown more acute and in addition the bouts of discomfort had been more frequent. She could see the change in her appearance and wondered whether others noticed it.

The weather was particularly cold that January and Marie von Pöllnitz advised her against travelling until later.

"Shall I wait till Caroline returns?" she demanded. "Why

then I shall not want to leave Lützenburg. No, I shall go now, and by the time I return perhaps she will be with me."

So inspite of the weather she went on making her preparations.

The King protested. Why the hurry? he wanted to know. She could visit her mother in the spring. Did she guess what the roads were like?

She shrugged aside his warnings. She had promised to pay this visit. They were expecting her and nothing would induce her to postpone it.

\* \* \*

Sophia Charlotte and her retinue set out from Berlin one bitterly cold day and began the journey to Hanover. She had been feeling increasingly ill before she started and as they trundled along the frozen roads and the icy wind penetrated her carriage she became exhausted.

The pain in her throat had increased and was now almost perpetual. She was finding it difficult to swallow and consequently avoided eating; and by the time they reached Magdeburg she knew that she would have to stop and rest awhile.

Marie von Pöllnitz begged her to stay there until the spring but she merely shrugged the suggestions aside.

"There is so much to do," she said.

"But it can be done later."

"No," said Sophia Charlotte, "I have a feeling that what has to be done must be done now."

Marie looked alarmed and Sophia Charlotte turned from her; she put her hand involuntarily to her throat. She could now definitely feel the obstruction there.

A few days later, although her condition had worsened if anything, they set out for Hanover.

\* \* \*

The Electress Sophia was worried at the condition of her daughter. She put her to bed immediately and sent for her doctors. The diagnosis was terrifying. The Queen of Prussia was suffering from a tumour of the throat and there was no hope of recovery: in fact her end was imminent.

Sophia could not believe it. Her daughter was thirty-seven years old; it was too young to die, particularly as a short while ago she had seemed in perfect health.

"There is a mistake," she declared, and called in more doctors; but the answer they gave after examination was the same.

"We must save her," cried Sophia. "She can't die like this ... at her age."

But she knew that the doctors were right. The change in her beloved daughter was horrifying. In a short time she seemed to grow emaciated and her once lovely complexion had turned dull yellow.

She talked to her eldest son, George Lewis, who had been the Elector since the death of his father Ernest Augustus. "Your sister has come home to die."

"Better if she'd decided to do it in her own home," he muttered.

"This is her home. The only thing for which I am grateful is that she has come home to die."

George Lewis turned away; he was not a man to waste words. He would stick to his opinion and his mother could have hers; he still thought that a death at the Palace was an inconvenience—particularly when it should by rights have happened somewhere else.

"You're an insensitive oaf, George Lewis," she told him, for once forgetting his rank, for which she always had a great respect, and treating him as the child in the nursery whom she had never been able to love. "Don't you care for anyone but your tall malkin and your fat hen."

George Lewis received these references to his two favourite mistresses with unconcern. He muttered: "She should have stayed in Berlin."

The Electress Sophia was too distressed to quarrel with her son. She wondered then as she had so many times before how she could have borne such a son.

And he went on living and her dearest Sophia Charlotte ... but it would not bear thinking of even for an old stoic like

herself. She had lost three sons and now all that was left to her
were George Lewis with whom she could well have done without, Maximilian who was a rebel and a constant cause for
anxiety because he was continually in conflict with his brother
who had sent him into exile, and her youngest named after his
father, Ernest Augustus. Three sons and one beloved daughter.
It seemed her fate that her best loved children would be taken
from her.

That cherished project of marrying Caroline to George
Augustus must be shelved. They had death on their minds
instead of marriage.

Gone were all those pleasant plans for the future—frequent
journeyings between Hanover and Berlin, Sophia to gain a
granddaughter, her own beloved daughter's daughter.

But thus it had always been, thought Sophia. How many
times had she thought to realize a cherished dream to find it
snatched from her?

It was life; and must be borne. She, an old woman, knew
that well.

\*    \*    \*

As it became more and more apparent that there was no
hope of saving her daughter's life, Sophia was so stricken with
grief that she became ill, and had to keep to her bed.

It was as well, said her servants, for the death bed scene with
this daughter whom she loved best in the world would have
tortured her beyond endurance.

Sophia Charlotte lay back on her pillows. In spite of her
suffering there was a look of contentment on her face. A short
while before, when she knew death was close, she had talked to
her mother of Caroline, and Sophia had promised that she
would do all she could to take her daughter's place with the
girl. Sophia had talked of her plan to bring Caroline to Hanover. "There," said Sophia, "she shall be as my own daughter."

"Let her take my place with you," begged Sophia Charlotte.

"That is yours and no one can have it," answered Sophia.

"But I already love her and would always care for her."

"For my sake," murmured Sophia Charlotte.

The Electress was so distressed by this conversation that

Sophia Charlotte had been unable to continue with it; but that did not matter for she had the reassurance she needed.

And afterwards the old Electress, having to face the fact that death was imminent, broke down. Her stoicism deserted her. She could accept misfortune but not this greatest tragedy of all.

Now as Sophia Charlotte's life was slipping away she said goodbye to her brothers, George Lewis and Ernest Augustus. The latter wept; the former regarded her expressionlessly, and she remembered them so well from nursery days. George Lewis who never needed their companionship, who was content to be alone playing with his soldiers, who refused to learn to bow or converse graciously. Poor George Lewis—unloved by his family and not caring . . . only wanting soldiers, real ones now, and of course women. And Ernest Augustus the baby who was always pushed aside because he was too young to join in; she remembered his standing by wistfully pleading with his eyes to be allowed to join the game and finally out of pity being given the humblest part to play. And Max . . . dear gay mischievous Max, who was far away now because he hated his brother and could never resist the opportunity of plotting against him. There was another member of the family whom she had known for a while—poor sad Sophia Dorothea, her sister-in-law, who had had the misfortune to be chosen as the wife of George Lewis. They had not been great friends; she had found the lovely elegant Sophia Dorothea too frivolous for her, but she had been an enchanting creature. How could George Lewis condemn her to a lonely prison because she had taken a lover?

But that was the old life—a new adventure lay before her. In a short time now she would face the unknown.

"You are sorry for me," she said to those about her bed. "Why? I have always wanted to satisfy my curiosity about life after death. My friends . . . even Leibniz . . . could not explain that to me. Now I am going to find out. There is nothing to weep for."

'We have sent word to the King of Prussia," said George Lewis.

She tried to smile. "He will give me a splendid funeral," she said. "And although it will not matter to me, it will please him for he loves pomp and ceremony."

She saw her nephew and niece by her bedside—George Augustus and pretty young Sophia Dorothea named after her ill-fated mother.

"I hope you will be happy," she said and held out a hand to the girl. Sophia Dorothea, so pretty and so like her mother, came forward, took it and kissed it.

"Bless you, my dear child," said Sophia Charlotte. "I wish you a happy life. And you too, George Augustus. May you find a good wife and live as happily as is possible on this earth."

Marie von Pöllnitz had brought a chaplain into the room. And Sophia Charlotte asked him what he wanted.

He said that he had come to pray with her.

"Let me die without quarrelling with you," she said. "For years I have studied religious questions. You can tell me nothing that I don't know already. And I die in peace."

"Your Highness in the sight of God, Kings and Queens are mortally equal with all men," said the chaplain.

"I know it well," she answered.

Then she closed her eyes.

She was smiling serenely as she passed into the unknown.

*     *     *

Caroline saw the riders coming into Ansbach. She ran down to greet them for she believed they would have letters from Sophia Charlotte.

She stood impatiently in the hall of the Ansbach Palace under the Glorification of Karl the Wild as the messengers approached, and wondered why they looked so sombre.

"Your Serene Highness," said one, "there is bad news from Hanover."

"What news?" she demanded.

"The Queen of Prussia has died on a visit to her mother...."

"Dead!" She heard the word but was not sure who had said it. She was aware of a rushing in her eyes, a sudden dizziness. This was not true. This was a nightmare. There was not such misery possible in the whole of the world.

She gripped the statue of the Margrave to steady herself.

And she said again in a voice of utter desolation: "Dead!"

There was nothing more to say. Her world was shattered; there was no reason for making decisions, for caring what became of her; there was nothing more in life to live for.

## The Courtship of Caroline

WHEN the greatest catastrophe imaginable struck, one did not sit down and weep senseless tears, at least not if one were the Electress Sophia of Hanover. There was only one way of living and that was to become busily occupied in some new project.

There must be an attempt to fill the emptiness left by the irreplaceable. One must look for substitutes.

The Princess Caroline, herself emotionally crippled, could help Sophia bear a grief which they shared. That they would have in common and so much more.

Finding no comfort in prayer—either, as Sophia said, reproaching, or pleading for better treatment from, a Divine Being—she tried to set in motion a plan which, if it materialized, would at least make life tolerable.

If she could bring Caroline to Hanover, she would soothe her grief, give herself a new interest in life, and so continue living for the years which were left to her.

Poor Caroline! No one now would plan for her happiness as Sophia Charlotte had done. She was not a weak young fool, but she was without powerful friends.

The sooner I can marry her to George Augustus the better, thought the Electress Sophia; and set herself to work out a scheme for doing this.

It was exasperating to think that she had first to get George Lewis's permission. In fact it was the same in everything. He was the master now; and what a different place he had made of the court at Hanover since his father's death! He had all his father's lechery and none of his wit; although of course during the lifetime of Ernest Augustus she had had to endure the reign of the notorious Clara von Platen who had been his *maîtresse en titre* for so many years.

George Lewis at least had had the wisdom or the luck to choose stupid women for his mistresses. They would never interfere in politics as Clara von Platen had done. George Lewis was like a lumbering great ox; he had no finesses such as his father had; he was without sensitivity; but he kept his women in order, and when he beckoned to one she immediately rose and followed him; and the others dared not protest. He made it clear that women for him were of use in one place only and that was the bedchamber.

Sophia had risen from her sick bed feeling weak and exhausted, not perhaps ready to do battle with her son; and yet she felt the need for speedy action. Who could say, now that Sophia Charlotte was dead perhaps Caroline would try to forget her misery by embarking on a new life as wife to the Archduke Charles.

She went to her beloved Herrenhausen to try to recover her health and decide what should be done but even Herrenhausen which, during her husband's lifetime, she had considered hers, was not the same. For one thing George Lewis had refused to let her have the place to herself. She must be contented with one wing, he said. Herrenhausen like the Alte Palais and the Leine Schloss belonged to him and he would have her remember it.

Dear Herrenhausen with so many memories of the past, with its avenue of limes and its park which was really too grand for the rather unpretentious house which without its grounds would indeed look merely like a gentleman's house and not a Palace! One hundred and twenty acres laid out, naturally, in the manner of Versailles, with the inevitable statues and fountains; the terraces, the parterres.

Here she had walked with dear Sophia Charlotte before her marriage. How unhappy the girl had been and how it had hurt Sophia to part with her—more so she believed than it had hurt Sophia Charlotte to go. But the marriage had been a good one for she had become Queen of Prussia and the King had been indulgent to her. If their son could marry young Sophia Dorothea the family would be kept intact. Would his father agree?

In the meantime there was Caroline—the immediate problem. She must throw herself into this for the sake of Caroline, for the sake of Sophia Charlotte's memory and because when you were old there was nothing left except living through the young.

She sent a message to the Leine Schloss requesting George Lewis to come to Herrenhausen to see her since she was not well enough to go to him.

He sent an ungracious message back that he was detained that day but would, if his business permitted, visit her the next.

"He has the manners of a stable boy," she grumbled. Unfortunately it was this stable boy who ruled them all at Hanover.

\*    \*    \*

In a grudging mood, George Lewis set out for Herrenhausen which was about two miles from Hanover.

What was his mother after now? he wondered. He had been disturbed enough by the foolish action of his sister in coming to her old home to die. Since she must have known how ill she was, why hadn't she stayed at home to die decently. He hated sentimental scenes and had no intention of indulging in them.

Not that his mother was fond of them either.

No, it was more likely that she had some proposition to put to him and believed his sister's death might have put him in a mood to grant it. She was making a big mistake if she did—and his mother was not one to make mistakes.

George Lewis's plain dark face looked even more dour than

usual as he rode between the double avenue of limes. He liked
the orderliness of the Park for he could not endure untidiness.
His affairs were conducted in an efficient manner and he believed, rightly, that since he had been Elector, the prestige of
Hanover had risen in other countries. There might be more
splendid courts among the German states, but there was none
so prosperous as Hanover and this prosperity, begun by his
father, had been increased by George Lewis. He had been a
cruel husband; he was a promiscuous lover having three
favourite mistresses; he was a dour son and an indifferent
parent; but if he had no idea how to win affection, he understood very well how to rule a state. Industry had flourished
since his rule; farming prospered; he was growing richer and so
was his Electorate. Even his mother could find no fault with
his rule. And how had he done it? By keeping the women out;
by trusting no one but himself.

He was vindictive as his wife had discovered to her cost; his
manners were coarse; he had no refinements; and the only
artistic pleasure he ever received was from music. As a result
his Opera House was as fine as anything they had in Vienna.

He made his way to that wing of the house which he had
assigned to his mother, and when he threw open the door her
attendants scattered; he did not have to speak to them, only to
frown and they were gone.

He did not kiss his mother's hand; he merely nodded to her
and sprawled in the chair by her bed, his legs thrust out, his
heels resting on her carpet, while he studied the tops of his
boots as though he found them more interesting than her.

How did we manage to get this one? Sophia wondered, as
she had many times before. If I hadn't borne him myself I'd say
he had been foisted on us. How did we allow him to be
brought up without grace, without charm, without manners?
Yet he had excelled as a soldier and now was showing he could
rule.

"It was good of you to come, George Lewis," she said a trifle
acidly, "good of you to call on your mother when she asked you
to."

"I had nothing important to do today."

"Then I must be grateful for that," she retorted ironically.

He grunted. "What's your business?" he asked.

"You don't ask how I am?"

"Well, you're better, aren't you? You wouldn't have asked me to come if you were ill. So what point in asking!"

"As a matter of courtesy perhaps."

He puffed contemptuously. So they might do in the stables. And he in the presence of the granddaughter of a King of England! What would they think of him in England if he ever went there? And go there he must . . . a King. She thought of Charles, her cousin, roaming the Continent before his Restoration. He had had all the charm of the Stuarts. Who would believe that this heavy jowled awkward Hanoverian was in any way connected with the Royal Stuarts. What would the English think of him!

"No sense in asking questions when you know the answer."

"You've too much sense perhaps and not enough sensibility."

"Eh?"

My son! she thought. This is my son!

She must get down to the matter in hand before he rudely told her he had no time to waste.

"I wanted to see you about George Augustus."

The scowl deepened. George Lewis had no love for his son. His marriage had gone sour very quickly and how could it have been otherwise with such a man? Though in his way he was faithful enough to his mistresses and kept them in favour even when they lost their looks.

"What about him?"

"He's no longer a boy."

"I know his age very well."

"It is time he was married."

"Married?"

"Why not. He needs a wife. He needs to get sons."

George Lewis was silent thinking of the boy. He could not bear the sight of him. Perhaps because he reminded him of his mother. He was almost pretty and although he was fair and his mother was dark the resemblance was strong. He was small— too small for a boy, neat and willowy, as she had been; and he had a way of gesticulating which was rather French. George Lewis liked the gardens to be laid out in a French style but he did not like French manners in his son. They were clearly inherited from his mother who was half French; perhaps that was why he was constantly reminded.

It was not that he regretted what he had done to his wife. In his opinion she deserved her fate and he didn't think of her unless her name was mentioned and on those rare occasions when his son or daughter reminded him of her by their looks.

"You've someone in mind," asked George Lewis.

"Yes. Caroline of Ansbach."

"What! My sister's adopted girl?"

"Why not? We should have to act quickly for the Archduke Charles is in the field."

"You mean he's asked for her?"

"She is considering whether she will accept him."

"Then she must be a fool."

"Why?"

"She won't get another such chance."

"How do you know? Austria considered her worthy, why not Hanover?"

"The boy's not ready for marriage."

"He's nearly twenty-one."

"He seems retarded. More like a child than a man."

"How can you say that, George Lewis?"

"Posturing! Dressing himself up! Throwing his hands about."

"He is certainly more gracious than his father."

"And you think that makes a man of him?"

"I say he's old enough for marriage and I think Caroline would make him a good wife. What do you say? I tell you we should act without delay."

George Lewis grunted.

"I wish you wouldn't make those animal noises," she said sharply. "They may be intelligible to your soldiers but they're not to me."

"I've other matters to think of."

"This happens to involve the succession."

"The succession! With you it's an *ob*session."

"Surely you must admit that to be King of England would be a more inviting prospect than Elector of Hanover?"

"No! No. I don't."

"I marvel at you. Have you no ambition?"

"I'm content where I am."

"Content! To go off and fight periodically and live like a common soldier? Yes, I can see you would be well content with that. What will you do when the Spanish Succession has been settled? What will you do for fighting then? To fight ... and then come home and rule your little state and bestow your favours in turn on your three favourites! Even your choice of mistresses is laughable. Schulemburg is well past her youth— she's lost any beauty she ever had and she never did have any brains to lose. Kielmansegge-Clara von Platen's daughter! She might very likely be your own sister. When I come to think of it she's not unlike you. And the young Countess von Platen— she's the only one with any pretensions to looks. But I hear she doesn't get the opportunities the other two do to amuse Your Highness."

This was foolish. Sophia knew it as soon as she had spoken; but she was not herself and the sight of George Lewis lolling in his chair was more irritating than usual. A great bitterness was in her heart because she had lost her beloved daughter.

Why did she have to die and this one be left to her? Why had she lost the children she loved best and been left with those she cared little for.

George Lewis appeared to be unmoved by these reproaches. He yawned.

"I've work to do," he said.

"But this project of a wife for George Augustus?"

"It'll be taken care of when I'm ready."

He caught his foot in a stool and kicked it aside. The door shut behind with a bang.

She should have waited, Sophia reproached herself. She had been too upset as yet.

There was no time to be lost, and she feared her reckless handling of the situation had spoilt any hope there might have been.

\*   \*   \*

George Augustus was in his apartments in the Leine Schloss trying on a wig while his servants fluttered round him.

"This is most becoming, Your Highness. The colour is your own."

"Yes ... yes..." muttered George Augustus, looking at his neat, almost pretty face. "That is good." He fondled the tight curls of the wig. It gave him height. One of the great disappointments of his life was his lack of inches. "Another four and I'd be passable; another four on top of that and I'd be tall," he often thought. As it was, it could only be exasperating that the heir of Hanover was so much shorter than most other men about him. More so was the fact that he was not allowed to do anything that a man of his age should be doing. His father went off to the wars every year, but was George Augustus allowed to go? Certainly not. One day he would be the Elector of Hanover. But would his father allow him to take part in government and prepare himself? No! He hated his father and he was sure his father hated him.

His sister Sophia Dorothea came into the room. She was seventeen, more than three years younger than he was, and very pretty. Their mother's daintiness which they had both inherited looked well enough in her.

There was a bond between them. When they were young he had told her why they never saw their mother and they planned together how they would rescue her.

Now he dismissed his servants because he guessed she had something secret to say to him. Sophia Dorothea could never hide anything and she was clearly excited.

As soon as they were alone, she said: "Our father has gone to Herrenhausen. He is not in a good temper."

"Is he ever?"

"Yes," giggled Sophia Dorothea, "when he retires with the tall Malkin."

"No, he's in a better temper with the Platen woman."

"But he prefers the other from habit." She looked over her shoulder. "Sometimes I wonder whether he ever thinks of our mother. It was here that it happened ... in this very Schloss."

"Much he cares about her. But what have you to tell me?"

"Why has our grandmother asked him to go to see her at

Herrenhausen? His company will hardly help her to recover. It must be something important, mustn't it?"

"I daresay."

"Then what?"

"I've no idea."

"Well, I have an idea. And I think I'm right. It's about you."

"About me. He's going to let me go with the armies after all!"

"Of course not. You're a son ... the only son. You can't be allowed to go to the wars until *you've* got a son. Now I'm sure ... being just a little bit like our revered father you may have one ... two or even three by now ... but they aren't legitimate and so they can't be the heirs of Hanover. Why, if Father was to die and you were to die, what would happen to Hanover?"

"What are you driving at?"

"George Augustus, you're dense! You spend too much time admiring your pretty face. Our grandmother wants you to be married ... soon. She wants you to produce the heir which will make it possible for you or our father to be killed without calamity to the house."

"I see. But you have a pleasant way of putting it."

"It's being brought up here. Father sets us such an example in finesse and diplomatic conversation."

"I believe you hate him as much as I do."

"I have to be in the fashion. Everybody hates him ... except the tall Malkin and fat hen and of course Madam von Platen."

"What have you heard?"

"I've heard a little and deduced much. That's feminine intuition, brother. You don't believe in it—nor does father. Mind it isn't your downfall. It's time you married. It's time we both married. Father is too busy being a soldier and a lecher to remember this. But as Grandmother is neither, she does. She is talking to him now about your matrimonial prospects."

"You're romancing."

"One has to introduce romance somehow into this dreary place. Poor Mamma! I wish I could remember her. They say she was lovely. I wonder if she still is. I saw a picture of her once. She was in a simple white gown with flowers ... real flowers draped about her head. She was not wearing jewels ... and she was so beautiful. How could he! How could he!"

"I remember her at the window. She stood there with the tears falling down her face..."

Sophia Dorothea threw her arms about her brother's neck. "You tried to rescue her. My dear brave George Augustus."

"I was too young and silly. I didn't plan well enough. What was the use of escaping from a hunting party and riding to Ahlden. I thought I'd capture her and ride away with her."

"It wasn't so silly. You could have taken her to Wolfenbüttel. They would have helped there."

"It might have started a war. One doesn't think of these things."

"Well, if I'd been there I'd have helped you. And so would Grandmother Celle. Poor sad Grandmother Celle! She is the only one who ever sees our mother. She tells her all about us, George Augustus ... the things we say. I send my love to her and yours too. What right had he to take our mother from us?"

"It's all done with now...."

"Done with. When she's there ... in that prison. What must it be like to be sent to prison and kept there for years and years and years ... just because you took a lover. He had Schulemburg then."

"He thought it was different for him. And so it was."

"George Augustus, don't tell me that. If my husband is unfaithful to me I shall be unfaithful to him!"

"So you think you're going to have a husband too?"

"Of course. They wouldn't leave me unmarried. And I'll tell you something. I know who it is."

"You must have your ear to every keyhole."

"I wouldn't stoop to such indignity."

"Your intuition?"

"Partly. I shall be the future Queen of Prussia."

"What. You'd marry Frederick William?"

"And why not? What better match could I make? I shall not be far from home ... and a Queen, George Augustus. Think of that."

"I'm thinking of Frederick William. I shouldn't have

thought he would have fitted in with your romantic fancies. His manners are as bad as our father's."

"That would be quite impossible. I like Frederick William and he likes me. I know you and he fought. I know you hate him. But I like him ... and he liked me. In fact he said he would marry me."

"You're inventing that."

"I'm not. But that is for the future. First they will find a wife for you and I think I know who she will be."

"Who?"

"Caroline of Ansbach."

"Caroline of Ansbach, but ..."

"Aunt Sophia Charlotte treated her as a daughter. Grandmother liked her too. I wouldn't mind taking a bet that Aunt Sophia Charlotte travelled here to talk to Grandmother about the marriage. Why else should she have come in the bad weather and died here?"

"I don't think this Caroline would be considered suitable."

"Wouldn't she? When the King of Spain is after her?"

"The King of Spain!"

"Well, he's not King yet, I know. He's got to end this war by winning it first. But at least he's a son of the Imperial House. So if Caroline is good enough for him, don't you think she's good enough for you?"

"But if he's asked for her, she'll take him. She'd be a fool not to."

"You can never tell. Still what's good enough for the King of Spain would be good enough for you eh? And if she refused the King of Spain and accepted the Electoral Prince of Hanover well ... that would be a triumph, wouldn't it?"

George Augustus was looking in the mirror adjusting his wig, and Sophia Dorothea burst out laughing.

"I see the King of Spain is making Caroline a very acceptable bride," she said.

\*　　\*　　\*

George Lewis had paid more attention to his mother's suggestion than she had realized. It *was* time George Augustus was married, he was thinking. He was twenty-one and while he was begetting illegitimate sons he might as well produce one or two who were legitimate. He would have to be allowed to go to war sooner or later and there was always a risk of death. He himself never shielded himself—half the fun of war would be lost if he did—and although he despised this son of his, George Lewis had no reason to believe he was a coward. George Augustus had petitioned again and again to be given a command in the army.

Yes, it was time he was married.

And Caroline of Ansbach? He had heard good reports of her. His sister had brought her up and had had a very high opinion of her; she would live in harmony with his mother, and she was apparently a healthy young girl.

He himself had only two children which he admitted was a pity. If he had had a normal married life like his mother and father he would have a brood of children now—always a wise thing for a ruler. But he hadn't seen his wife for eleven years when she had been caught in adultery, divorced and sent away from Hanover to spend the rest of her life in prison. He had no intention of seeing her now, nor allowing her to have her freedom; and he felt no remorse. But he did realize that it would not be a good thing for George Augustus to make such a disastrous marriage.

His own marriage had been arranged by his parents and those of his wife—their fathers were brothers; and the marriage had been part of a grand reconciliation between them. He had not wanted marriage with the pretty silly creature; nor had she wanted marriage with him, who, she considered, was gross, crude, coarse and everything she had been brought up to dislike.

If they had been allowed to have any say in the matter that marriage would never have taken place and it might have been that a family of healthy boys would now be his.

He disliked his son but for the good of Hanover, for which he cared more than anything else, he did not want him to make a marriage similar to that of his parents. He should not be hustled into marriage as they had been. He should have a chance to see his bride, to approve of her, to be sure that he could live in reasonable harmony with her. He should not be forced into marriage ... at least not if he was prepared to make a reasonable choice.

George Lewis walked through the old Leine Schloss. He did not avoid those apartments which had belonged to his wife. Usually he passed through them without thinking; but in view of the recent interview with his mother and this talk of marriage, Sophia Dorothea was in his thoughts.

Here she had received Königsmarck on that fateful night; and after he left her he would have had to cross this large apartment which was known as the Ritter Hall where, hidden by the enormous stove which looked like a mausoleum, guards had been waiting for him.

Here, thought George Lewis, if the stories he had heard were correct, his wife's lover had been stabbed to death and his body dragged outside the castle and buried in quicklime.

Ancient history! Königsmarck was long since dead; only the captive of Ahlden lived on to repent her sins and doubtless to curse the man who had treated her with such ruthlessness.

He had no regrets. She had deceived him; she had bickered with him continually; she had shown her contempt; she had sneered at his mistresses; well now she could sneer to her heart's content within the walls of Ahlden. And he continued to enjoy those mistresses and all knew what happened to those who defied George Lewis, Elector of Hanover.

All the same, George Augustus must avoid such a disastrous marriage if possible and perhaps some immunity might be secured by letting him have a say in the choosing of his own wife.

George Lewis would call one or two of his trusted ministers together and they would discuss this matter and the best way of tackling it.

\*     \*     \*

He first sent for Count von Platen, his Prime Minister. Platen was a good minister, docile, ready to obey without question. He had climbed to his present position, it was true, through his wife who had been the notorious mistress of George Lewis's father; but having attained his position he was able to maintain it.

"I've been thinking," said George Lewis, "that it's time the Prince was married. I want him to pay a visit to Ansbach to look at the Princess Caroline at present staying with her brother the Margrave. If he likes her, we can make an offer."

"Yes, Highness. Who shall travel with him?"

"He will go incognito. This is a matter of secrecy, Platen. If she refuses him I don't want any one to know it. The Archduke Charles has offered for her and she is considering. She's got an appreciation of her own value clearly. That might not be a bad thing. If the King of Prussia knows what we're after he'll thwart us because he wants her for Charles. Therefore no one must know of this but ourselves, the Prince, and who ever accompanies him."

"And the Electress Sophia?"

"Let's keep women out of this, Platen. I don't trust their tattling tongues. Even my mother. She can't resist writing to that niece of hers, the Duchess of Orlèans ... She's the biggest scandalmonger in France and if she had an inkling of this it would soon reach the Prussian King's ears. So we'll have no women in this secret, Platen. Not even my mother."

"Very good, Your Highness."

"Who's the best man to accompany him?"

"I should say the Baron von Eltz. He was his governor and he's a good minister. He'd be discreet and see that the Prince was."

"Then that's settled. And one *valet de chambre*, no more. He'll be a nobleman travelling for his amusement. We'd better send for him and tell him."

"Yes, Your Highness."

*    *    *

Father and son regard each other with mutual dislike.

If she won't take the Archduke she'll not fancy this prancing boy! thought George Lewis, scowling.

He's quite crude, thought George Augustus. Who would believe that he was the Elector! When I'm in his shoes I shall be different.

"It's time you were married," George Lewis said. "You might fancy the Princess of Ansbach. You can go to Ansbach and take a look at her. If you like what you see we'll offer for her."

As though, thought George Augustus, she were a horse they were going to buy. What did Platen think of this crude boor? What did the elegant Baron von Eltz?

But the prospect of going to Ansbach to see Caroline pleased him, particularly as he could decide whether or not he would have her. That appealed to his conceit which ever since he had realized what a little man he was had grown out of all proportion to his accomplishments.

"You'll pose as a nobleman travelling for pleasure," said George Lewis. "You'll call at the Ansbach Court with letters from Platen. See to that, Platen."

"Yes, Your Highness."

"You will take von Eltz with you. You will be his friend, von Eltz, calling yourself Steding. But on no account let it be known who you are. If you do, you can depend upon it the King of Prussia will hear, and he'll take the Princess back to Berlin and force her to marry the Archduke Charles. No one must know. Do you hear me? Particularly women. Now go and prepare. Leave tomorrow. If you decide you want to marry her, remember delay could lose her. So could gossip. Remember that."

He dismissed them and they went off to make ready for the journey.

George Augustus was excited but he was not even tempted to tell his sister where he was going.

\*     \*     \*

Those months at Ansbach were the saddest Caroline had ever known. Each morning on waking her first thoughts were: She is dead. I shall never see her again.

She had wept until she was exhausted with weeping; she had shut herself into the bedroom which had been hers as a child and had seen no one for days. Then she had told herself that Sophia Charlotte would have chided her, would have reminded her that she must not give way to grief; that she must be brave as she had always been taught to be.

But there is no longer anything to live for, Caroline thought. How could I have believed for one moment that I could have left her and gone to Spain? This is a judgement on me because I was tempted by the glitter of a crown.

If she would only come back, I would tell her that I would never never leave her.

Her servants tried to rouse her from her melancholy. Would she not like to see the gown her seamstress was making for her? The woman wanted to know whether she would like embroidered panels or should they be of plain velvet. She had no interest in clothes. Would she care to do a little needlework? Embroidery was such a restful occupation. She had never cared for needlework. Sometimes they told her amusing stories about people of her brother's court—and of other courts, but scandal did not interest her.

She and Sophia Charlotte had talked of religion, philosophy, history, art, literature. With whom could she talk of such things now?

There is nothing ... nothing left to me, she thought.

Her brother was unusually understanding. She was grateful to him; it was fortunate that having now become Margrave he could offer her this refuge of her old home. He would talk to her of the days of their childhood before she had known Sophia Charlotte, and somehow this was soothing. Certainly here in the old Palace of the Margraves, so ornate and flamboyant as she now knew, having been educated in good taste by Sophia Charlotte, she could be less miserable than anywhere else. She liked to walk round the gallery and look sadly at the portraits of the Hohenzollerns, her ancestors, and wonder about their lives. Had they ever known grief like hers? How could any have felt such a loss? There could only have been one in the world like Sophia Charlotte.

William Frederick, her brother, seeking to bring her out of her melancholy told her that she must make a definite decision about her marriage. He was sure that once she had settled that matter she would begin to build a new life.

"I shall not marry the Archduke," she said. "I do not believe *she* wished it."

Frederick William, being piqued because he had not been consulted in the matter—after all he was the head of the family, even though younger than Caroline—was secretly pleased. The

Austrians should have consulted him. He was young and had
not long before succeeded to the title; he had been made to
feel, for so many years, that he was of little importance, so now
he felt he must continually remind people how his position
had changed.

"I think it is the right decision," he said.

"You seem very certain."

"I am sure you would never have been a Catholic."

"No. I never should. I could never be so definite in my be-
liefs. *She* was not. She always said on religious matters we must
always have an open mind."

"Then you would have been unhappy in Spain."

"I will write at once to Leibniz. He will tell me how to
handle this matter. He will draft the letter I must write. I
know he too will be with me in this."

She went at once to her apartment. Her brother was right.
Now that she had made her decision her spirits had lifted a
little.

*       *       *

Leibniz was at Hanover in attendance on the Electress
Sophia.

He read to her Caroline's letter asking him to draft the refusal.

The Electress was delighted. If only, she thought that stub-
born fool of an Elector would listen to me. If only he would
ask for Caroline for George Augustus. Sometimes I think he
refuses to do what I ask simply because I ask it!

And what could an old woman do? It had been the same
in the old days with Ernest Augustus. He had allowed Clara
von Platen to influence him, but not his wife. She remembered
how her husband and his mistress had decided to marry
George Lewis to Sophia Dorothea and had not told her anything about the plan until they needed her help to put it into
action.

And she, the granddaughter of a King, and King of England
at that, had allowed this to be. Well, at least she had kept her
place in the Electorate; she was honoured; and although
Ernest Augustus would not be influenced by her, he allowed

her supremacy in her own little Court. She had remained to bear his children—not like poor Sophia Dorothea, languishing in prison now. Had she protested as that foolish woman had, would her fate have been similar? These Germans had no idea how to treat women. How different her cousin Charles of England had been. How different was Louis XIV, the Sun King, the most admired monarch in Europe. These men were gentlemen and that fact helped them to be great rulers.

As for her son George Lewis, he was the crudest of them all. And foolish too. He was going to lose the opportunity of bringing the most accomplished of Princesses to Hanover.

Leibniz read Caroline's letter aloud.

"Heaven, jealous of our happiness, has taken away from us our adored and adorable Queen. The calamity has overwhelmed me with grief and sickness, and it is only the hope that I may soon follow her that consoles me. I pity you from the bottom of my heart for her loss to you is irreparable. I pray the good God to add to the Electress Sophia's life the years that the Queen might have lived and I beseech you to add my devotion to her."

Sophia wept quietly as she listened.

She and I alone could console each other, she thought.

Yet it was no use talking to George Lewis. What did he know of grief? What did he know of love?

\*　　\*　　\*

The clocks were striking midnight when George Augustus with the Baron von Eltz and one valet rode through the narrow streets of Hanover, past the gabled houses with their sloping roofs, past the Markt Kirche, the Rathhaus, out of the town and away towards Ansbach.

This was the most exciting adventure he had ever undertaken; the miracle was that it should be happening at his father's suggestion.

Caroline! He was half-way to falling in love with her already. He hoped she was not too clever. He didn't like clever women. He had never enjoyed studying and had avoided it when possible; a wife who knew more than he did would be intolerable. But they said she was beautiful; and if she should choose him after refusing the Archduke Charles he would be delighted with her.

The Baron was giving him some uneasy glances. He was afraid he would give himself away, afraid he would show that arrogance which was always ready to appear at an imagined slight. If he betrayed the fact that Monsieur de Busch, the name under which it had been decided he should travel, was in fact George Augustus, Electoral Prince of Hanover, the news that he was wooing Caroline of Ansbach would be all over Europe in a very short time.

"You needn't look at me like that, von Eltz," said George Augustus. "I'll play my part."

\*    \*    \*

The days were long. Caroline could settle to nothing. She could not go on in this way. She had no desire to return to Lützenburg which the King of Prussia had now renamed Charlottenburg after his wife. She had never had any love for the King of Prussia. She would stay here with her brother until her grief grew less acute—if it ever did.

She spent long hours in the Hofgarten remembering the past because the future was too painful to contemplate.

Sometimes she rode through the streets of the town, through the narrow streets, past the little houses from the windows of which people leaned out to see her go by. They called affectionate greetings. They loved her the more because she had refused marriage with the Archduke Charles. She had given up a possible empire and a crown for the sake of her faith. That was how they saw it and it seemed an admirable thing to have done.

"Long live our Princess," they called. "Good fortune to Your Serene Highness."

She smiled her sad smile and they understood her sadness and loved her for that too.

William Frederick said to her one day: "You'll be ill if you go on grieving in this way. I suggest we leave this place and take a short holiday at Triesdorf. It will be beautiful there at this time of year."

Listlessly Caroline agreed to accompany him to their

summer home and they had been there only a few weeks when
the Margrave came to his sister's room to tell her about the
new arrivals.

"Two gentlemen have come from Hanover. They bring letters from the Count von Platen, the Hanoverian Prime Minister, asking us to be kind to these two travellers."

Caroline said, "Must I see them?"

"It would seem discourteous not to as there are these letters
from Platen."

"That's true, and I might hear news of the Electress. I wonder she did not give them a message to bring to me."

"Perhaps she did not know they were coming. She wouldn't
since they are merely noblemen travelling for their own
pleasure."

"I will come down this evening," said Caroline.

So she met George Augustus, not knowing that he was
other than Monsieur de Busch.

He bowed, and murmured that he was overwhelmed by the
honour and that it was a great moment for them.

She replied that he was welcome. She was delighted to see
anyone from Hanover and she hoped he might give her news of
the Electress Sophia.

He believed he could do that.

The travellers were entertained in a homely and intimate
manner for the Margrave did not live in the same state in his
summer residence as he did at the Palace of Ansbach.

Young Monsieur de Busch talked animatedly of Hanover;
his friend, the more sober Monsieur Steding devoted himself to
the Margrave leaving his young friend to talk to Caroline.

Since she was forced to pay attention to him Caroline looked
more like her old self than she had since Sophia Charlotte's
death. Her brother noticed this and thought: We must entertain more. She must not be allowed to shut herself away.

Meanwhile Monsieur de Busch was growing very excited,
although he hid this. She was charming, this young woman.
She was the type that most appealed to him. Masses of fair hair,
blue eyes, a little quiet, always giving him the opportunity of
speaking. She seemed modest and a little sad; but he knew
why that was. She was a beauty; and she would be amenable;

and she had refused the Archduke Charles. He had made up his mind in the first half hour.

Caroline saw an animated young man—short but good-looking, with a lively expression and neat features. He was about her own age, she judged, and there was an unusual dignity about him. She liked him.

After the meal the Margrave suggested a game of cards. Monsieur de Busch asked if he might have the honour of sitting next to the Princess and this was granted.

So they played cards in a desultory manner for that was how the visitors wished it.

Caroline asked how the Electress Sophia was progressing after her illness.

"I hear she is recovering slowly," she was told.

"She is a wonderful lady."

Monsieur de Busch agreed that this was so. "Your Serene Highness should visit her. I believe nothing could speed her recovery more than that."

"I should have to wait for an invitation from the Elector. I might not be very welcome."

"I cannot imagine Your Serene Highness being unwelcome anywhere."

"You are very kind."

His almond-shaped eyes were warm—perhaps a little too warm, but strangely enough she did not mind that. By forcing her to entertain him he was making her feel more alive than she had since the tragedy.

"It would be my greatest pleasure, if it were possible for me to show you kindness."

Hardly the manner in which a casual visitor should talk to a Princess. But he was young and she liked him for he had made her feel so much better.

"It is your turn to play, Monsieur de Busch," she said.

He watched her beautiful slender fingers with the cards. She was enchanting.

I'm in love, he told himself. Caroline shall be my wife. My father will be pleased and the King of Prussia will be furious. And what will the King of Spain think when she has accepted me after refusing him!

He was in high spirits; and he was his most attractive when he was happy. His smile was sweet and he became very gay. Perhaps he was a little bold; perhaps he showed too clearly his admiration.

But Caroline even laughed now and then which made her brother look up sharply.

He was glad the travellers from Hanover had come to Triesdorf.

\* \* \*

George Augustus came unannounced to the Baron's bedchamber.

"We must leave at once for Hanover," he declared. "We must tell my father that the mission is a success. I don't propose to wait another day. I have decided."

"Your Highness has come to a very quick decision."

George Augustus threw up his hands in the gesture his father so disliked. "But I am in love with her. She is beyond my expectations. Surely you can see for yourself."

"The Princess is charming, but..."

"I have decided."

"Then in that case, in the morning I will tell the Margrave that we have been called back to Hanover on urgent business."

"Do that. I shall not have a moment's peace until she is in Hanover."

"If Your Highness is assured that you are not being too hasty..."

"I always make up my mind quickly."

The Baron forbore to mention that this was not always with the happiest results. George Augustus would not listen. He was in love.

Would he have been quite so infatuated with the Princess of Ansbach if the Archduke Charles had not sought her hand? wondered the Baron. He knew his Prince.

The Princess was a charming creature, capable of affection, as her sadness at the death of the Queen of Prussia showed. The Baron hoped she would not expect too much from his mercurial little Prince—if she decided to accept him.

In the morning he told the Margrave that they were called

back. They took outwardly regretful leave, although George
Augustus could not completely hide the fact that he was bub-
bling over with excitement.

They returned to Hanover after a very brief absence; but
the Elector was as near pleased as the Baron had ever seen
him at the result of his strategy.

*          *          *

After the visitors from Hanover had left Triesdorf Caroline
felt melancholy. They had certainly relieved the tedium and it
had been pleasant to be so obviously admired by the young
Monsieur de Busch.

Her favourite attendant Fräulein von Genninggen mentioned that his visit had been very agreeable. "I think it did
your Highness good," she added. "I am sorry he and his friend
left so soon."

"He was perhaps a little too bold," answered Caroline.

"I daresay that is the way at Hanover. But I certainly wish
they had not hurried away so quickly."

It was true, thought Caroline. Monsieur de Busch had made
her feel alive again and ... young. She was in agreement with
Fräulein von Genninggen and also regretted their departure.

But a few weeks later when Monsieur Steding returned to
Triesdorf, Caroline was disappointed that he was alone. He
told the Margrave that Monsieur de Busch had returned to
Hanover but he himself had gone to Nuremburg to meet some
friends whose arrival there had been delayed and since the
Margrave and Her Serene Highness, his sister, had been so
kind recently and had said they regretted that their stay should
not have been longer, he had taken the opportunity to throw
himself on their hospitality for a few more days.

Monsieur Steding was very welcome, but both the Margrave
and Caroline were sorry that she was not accompanied by the
charming young Monsieur de Busch.

Baron von Eltz took an early opportunity of being alone
with the Princess. He whispered to her during a card game that
he must speak to her alone so would she grant him an interview. She agreed to this but when he reached her apartment he
found Fräulein von Genninggen in attendance. He indicated

that he must be *entirely* alone with the Princess so she told the Fräulein to go into the ante-room and wait there until summoned.

As soon as they were alone the Baron told her that he came on a mission from Hanover, and that his name was not Steding but the Baron von Eltz.

The Princess looked startled and von Eltz hurried on: "Before I put this proposition to you, I must have Your Highness's promise that if you decide not to accept it you will say nothing to anyone."

"I promise," said Caroline.

"Monsieur de Busch was an assumed name. My companion was George Augustus, Electoral Prince of Hanover."

"Oh!" said Caroline faintly.

"First I must ask you whether you are free of all matrimonial engagements and are not involved in any way with the King of Spain."

"I am free."

"The Electoral Prince had heard such accounts of your beauty, your charm and wisdom that he was determined to see for himself whether rumour was true. His visit here convinced him that what he had heard was not warm enough in its praise and having seen you he has told his father that he wishes to marry you."

Caroline was too agitated to collect her thoughts. She had thought he might have had a message from the Electress Sophia, not such a proposal as this.

"I had not expected..." she began.

"Your Serene Highness, a young man in love is impatient ... and His Highness, the Electoral Prince, is both."

Sophia Charlotte's nephew! If she married him she would live under the same roof as the Electress Sophia. Surely that was getting as near to Sophia Charlotte as was possible.

"I should have to speak to my brother," she said.

"Naturally. But I pray you do not delay. And there is one other matter. If you decide that this proposition is distasteful to you, it must be entirely secret. None but yourself and your brother must know of this. The Elector would be most displeased if it were bruited abroad. There is one in particular who must be kept ignorant—that is the King of Prussia, for as your guardian he might take steps to stop your marriage. Not until the documents are signed should he be informed. Will you respect the Elector's wishes?"

"Yes, I will."

"And you will give your answer soon?"

"I must speak to my brother. There is no other House of which I would rather be a member than that of Hanover but ... I must have time to think...."

The Baron bowed and left her.

\* \* \*

Caroline walked up and down her apartment. She was thinking of the little man who had smiled at her so warmly, who had shown so clearly how he admired her.

She liked him ... as well as one could like anyone on such a short acquaintance. But she had liked Archduke Charles. If it had not been a matter of leaving Sophia Charlotte ... if it had not been necessary to become a Catholic ... Well, then she might by now be married to him.

But here was George Augustus—more ardent than Charles because he was less polished perhaps. About Charles's gallantry there had been a suavity which George Augustus lacked. Yet George Augustus was a pleasant young man; he admired her; he had helped her take one step out of the despondent morass into which the death of Sophia Charlotte had plunged her and she *had* regretted his departure.

She went to the window and looked out across the gardens now beautiful with summer roses. She could go to Sophia Charlotte's home, the Leine Schloss, Herrenhausen, the Alte Palais —of which she had talked so much that Caroline felt she knew them already. Between herself and the Electress Sophia there was already a bond—their love of Sophia Charlotte. Not only that, but they were of a kind. They were interested in discussion and ideas; and it was rare to find a companion who cared for anything but gossip, clothes and court scandal.

It was almost as though Sophia Charlotte's voice was coming to her over the immense distance which separated the dead from the living.

"I cannot be with you, my darling, but this will help you. Go to my mother; she will love you and you will love her. You have to marry sometime. It is the best way of life. You will agree when you have children. You will be there in my old home. My dearest child, it is the best thing left to you."

The best thing left! They were right when they said she could not go on mourning for ever, for one could not live with the dead.

Her brother came into her apartment. It was easy to see how delighted he was.

"Baron von Eltz has spoken to me. Why, Caroline, this is an excellent proposal. He wants your acceptance quickly. I hope you will give it. It is the best thing that could happen to you. You will accept this proposal?"

She hesitated only for a second.

"Yes, I accept."

\* \* \*

Baron von Eltz rode with all speed to Hanover and in a few days he was riding back to Ansbach with instructions from the Elector to arrange the marriage of his son with Princess Caroline.

Not until George Lewis had the documents back in his hand would he break the secrecy and it was characteristic of him that he should send Count von Platen to tell his mother what had taken place.

Sophia had risen from her bed for she was beginning to recover and when she received Platen in her audience chamber, he was smiling a little secretively as he bowed.

"Good news, Your Highness! The Electoral Prince is soon to be married."

Sophia stared at him in astonishment; anger threatened to betray itself, but long practice had disciplined her to keep it in check.

"Yes, Your Highness, your son thought it was high time, and he is sure you will agree with him. So a marriage has been arranged and we hope that it will take place very shortly as neither the Elector nor the Electoral Prince see any reason for delay."

E*

A marriage! thought Sophia furiously. But I wanted Caroline for him. Why will George Lewis never listen to me!

"The matter has been arranged in some secrecy. The Prince rode to Ansbach with von Eltz ... two gentlemen calling themselves Busch and Steding ... travelling for pleasure."

"To Ansbach!" cried Sophia. "Then ..."

"The Princess Caroline of Ansbach is to marry the Prince, Your Highness. She has accepted him and the negotiations have now been completed."

The Electress did not know which was the greater—fury at being kept out of a plan which she herself had suggested, or joy that what she so desired had come about. Being the sensible woman she was she quickly suppressed the former and indulged in the latter.

She composed her features.

"I am delighted," she said. "Pray tell my son that if I had been consulted I should have suggested that the best possible bride for my grandson would be the Princess Caroline of Ansbach."

\*    \*    \*

Hanover was in a state of excitement preparing for the wedding. It was no longer a secret. In his apartments the bridegroom was strutting before his mirror, commanding his servants to help him dress in the clothes which were being made for his wedding. He tried on his wigs and wanted them built up in the front to give him height. For the first time he was the most important person in the Court, the focus of all attention; and he was delighted with himself. Even his father treated him with a new respect. George Augustus was a happy bridegroom.

In the kitchens there was great activity; banquets to surpass all banquets must be prepared to celebrate the wedding; comedians and actors were commanded to concoct plays and entertainments to enliven the celebrations. Even the Elector, usually inclined to be parsimonious, had implied that a little extravagance was warranted on such a happy occasion. It was a unique occasion. For the first time most people remembered the Elector was pleased with his son.

Sophia Dorothea was as excited as her brother.

"Marriage is in the air," she declared. "I shall be next. And I'll tell you something, George Augustus, the Crown Prince of Prussia is asking for me."

"You think his father will allow that. He's furious about my marriage. He wanted Caroline for himself, some say." George Augustus stood on tiptoe and studied himself in the mirror. "The King of Spain wanted her; the King of Prussia wanted her; but she wanted me."

"Well, you're the last one to be surprised at that!" retorted Sophia Dorothea. "And it's no use anyone's saying I'm not to have Frederick William because I've decided that I am ... and so has he."

"He told you this?"

"He said he would make life unbearable for everyone until consent was given to our marriage."

"There's a bold lover for you!"

"The only sort of lover I would have." Sophia Dorothea was serious suddenly. "George Augustus, I wonder what our mother *feels* about this."

"Feels? What should she feel?"

"Can't you put yourself in her place. Her son, her first born, is about to be married and she is shut away and not allowed to join in and be happy with the rest of us."

George Augustus was silent; his mouth turned down angrily. "I hate our father for what he did to our mother."

"You hate him for a lot of other things besides," Sophia Dorothea reminded him. "Grandfather Celle is on his way, did you know? He is coming to congratulate you and say how happy he is. But I don't think he's very happy. I don't think he was happy from the day he allowed our father to marry our mother. We're lucky to *choose* our partners ... or more or less choose them. Fancy being presented with our father and told you had to marry him! No wonder our mother was unhappy; no wonder it made Grandmother Celle turn away from Grandfather Celle and never love him again in quite the same way."

George Augustus was thinking of his childhood. He remembered his mother more clearly than Sophia Dorothea. He could still recall the fear when she had disappeared; and how he had once tried to rescue her.

"I shall always hate our father," he said. "Even though he didn't try to force me into marriage I'll always hate him."

Sophia Dorothea nodded. "Marriage!" she said. "They all dance and make merry and congratulate. But is it a matter of congratulation?"

"Mine will be."

"Of course. George Augustus and Caroline are going to live in harmony for ever after."

"Why shouldn't they?"

"Because no one ever does. All you can hope for is a compromise like Grandmother Hanover had. She was Queen of the household because she never interfered with Grandfather Hanover's mistresses."

"Caroline will never interfere with mine."

"Oh, won't she? I shall not allow my husband to have any."

"You think any husband would allow that?"

"Mine will."

"You have strange ideas of marriage."

"Perhaps Caroline shares them."

"Caroline!" George Augustus smiled dreamily into the future. "She is very beautiful, sister. And she is docile. She is quiet when I wish to speak; she is a little sad; and she will be grateful to me for ever because I married her."

"Yours is certain to be a happy marriage," said Sophia Dorothea scornfully. "Grandmother Celle has gone to Ahlden. She will not come here because she hates our Father. She has never forgiven him for what he did to our mother. I saw Fraülein von Knesebeck once. She loved our mother and suffered with her and she told me. She said that she never saw a pair of lovers like Grandmother Celle and Grandfather Celle. He lived for her until our mother married our father and then they quarrelled, because Grandmother was against the match and he for it, and when the tragedy happened she blamed him and never loved him again. All her love was for our mother. Isn't that sad, George Augustus? Doesn't it make you hesitate when you think about marriage?"

"My marriage will be different. We shall not quarrel. Caroline will understand me."

"Frederick William does not understand me ... but it will

be fun learning about him . . . and for him to learn about me. I don't think I ask as much from marriage as you do. You want a wife who is a sort of exalted slave, to give way to all your whims, to look up to you as a god. Oh, George Augustus, you have to grow up."

"Listen to who's talking! I believe you're comparing me with our father."

"I wouldn't compare anyone with him. Do you know our mother wanted to write to you. She wanted to say how happy she is that you are going to be married and she wanted to wish you joy. But Father wouldn't let her."

"He is a monster. I shall always hate him. I shall always be kind to Caroline."

"So *good* of you." Sophia Dorothea laughed lightly. "Let us hope that she will be as good to you as you are to her."

George Augustus narrowed his eyes. "What do you mean?"

"Wait and see. Wait till five years . . . ten years. . . . Just wait and see."

With that she decided she had had enough talk of marriage. She was tired of looking at George Augustus strutting in his new clothes. She would go and see about her own.

*         *         *

About eight weeks after Baron von Eltz had made the Electoral Prince's proposal, Caroline, with her brother, set out for Hanover.

Caroline was a little nervous. She had made a complete break with the old life and was now ready for the new. She had determined that her marriage would be a success and that she would find a tolerable life at Hanover—though not to be compared with that which she had known at Lützenburg, for what could compare with the companionship of Sophia Charlotte?

As they left the hills of Ansbach behind them and their coach carried them towards the northern plains Caroline was thinking of the letters George Augustus had written her when he knew that she had consented to become his wife.

"I owe you every imaginable obligation for permitting me

the greatest happiness that I desire in my life ... I hope to show you my inviolable respect and eternal affection...."

"The time of your departure seems infinitely distant and I count every day and hour until its arrival..."

"I desire nothing so much as to throw myself at my Princess's feet and promise her eternal devotion. You alone can make me happy. But I shall not be entirely convinced of my happiness until I have the satisfaction of testifying to the excess of my fondness and love for you."

The words of a lover, but a man whom she had seen only during one short visit. Still, happiness ... or at least satisfaction ... was apparent in everything he wrote to her. She was not a romantic girl. Life with Sophia Charlotte and her own mother's tragic story had taught her realism. Marriage with this ardent dapper little man would no doubt be a compromise and she was ready for it.

As she listened to the sound of the coach on the road she believed she had been wise to come.

She needed a new life.

Now she was on the threshold of it.

\* \* \*

At a village outside Hanover Caroline made the acquaintance of her father-in-law.

It was not a very reassuring encounter and had she not been warned of the man she must expect she would have been depressed. Certainly she would have been surprised had she known that George Lewis was being unusually gracious.

He actually muttered that he was pleased to see her and was glad she was marrying his son.

Dour, having no love for ceremonies, he cut short the interview as quickly as possible, but left her with the impression that he was looking her over to assess what sort of a breeder she would be. She then began to have qualms as to the difficulties of settling into a household of which this man was the head.

Her brother consoled her. George Lewis was a just man; he ruled Hanover well; and it was clear that in spite of his curt manners he was delighted with the match.

Caroline was glad when he returned to Hanover and left her for the last evening alone with her brother.

\* \* \*

Just before Caroline made her entry into Hanover the Duke of Celle caught a chill when hunting and died. This cast a gloom over everything—not so much because a member of the family had died, but because it brought an inevitable reminder of the Elector's wife. It was scarcely a pretty rumour to be in circulation at the time of a wedding.

However George Lewis decreed that the period of mourning should be very short in the circumstances.

\* \* \*

The coach containing Caroline and her brother entered the main courtyard of the Leine Schloss. The trumpets immediately sounded their welcome and the soldiers formed to make a guard of honour. Standing waiting to receive the bride, was the entire Electoral family headed by the Elector and on one side of him his son and on the other his mother.

George Augustus's eyes were shining with pleasure and happiness; George Lewis's were grimly content. And the Electress Sophia was saying to herself: This is the happiest moment since my dearest daughter died.

"Welcome ... welcome to Hanover." That was the theme of the day.

But it was the Electress Sophia who, with an unusual show of emotion, embraced Caroline and held her in her arms, and whispered: "Welcome home, my dear."

\* \* \*

That evening a large company assembled in the palace church to celebrate the marriage of George Augustus, Electoral Prince of Hanover and Caroline, Princess of Ansbach.

## The Court at Hanover

DURING the first weeks of the marriage Caroline was happier than she had believed possible. George Augustus was an attentive husband and being in love was a delightful adventure which appealed to him. Caroline was beautiful; she had grace and charm; she was much admired. George Augustus never tired of reminding people that she had refused the Archduke of Spain to marry him.

"They were made for each other," said the Empress Sophia. "And she will be the making of George Augustus."

George Augustus strutted about the Court; all he needed was a son—with other children to follow, of course—and a brilliant record in the army. As yet he had only taken the first step.

Caroline basked in his affection; they were constantly together; he delighted in showing her the pleasures of Hanover; she found the court a little vulgar but she gave no hint of this; instead she planned to change it when she became Electress; then she would endeavour to make Hanover another Charlottenburg. Leibniz was already here; she would invite other philosophers.

It was a pleasure to ride through the streets of Hanover to the cheers of the people. They were particularly friendly towards her and the Electoral Prince—doubtless, she thought, because for all his qualities as a ruler, George Lewis would never inspire any affection in his people.

She thought Herrenhausen delightful—mainly for its gardens; she liked the little Alte Palais; but the Leine Schloss was a little gloomy—haunted, she thought, by the shadow of a tragedy.

George Augustus, when showing it to her pointed out the Ritter Hall, the place where it was believed Königsmarck had been murdered.

"There is one member of the family whom you will not meet," he told her. "My mother."

"Isn't it possible?"

George Augustus narrowed his eyes and his face grew red with emotion. "He will not allow it. I am not allowed to see her. She can't even write to me. I tell you this, Caroline. I shall not always allow him to have his way."

"Perhaps if you explained your point of view."

"Explain to my father! You don't know him yet, Caroline. Wait until you do."

"I believe you hate him."

"Of course I hate him. Everybody hates him except his women and I expect they only tolerate him for what they get. You'll hate him too."

"I hope not."

George Augustus turned his red face to her. "You'll hate him, Caroline, because I do."

She smiled. "But we don't have to hate the same people do we?"

"Those who love me hate my father."

It was almost a command.

As she looked at his flushed face and saw the purpose in his eyes she felt the first twinges of uneasiness.

\*      \*      \*

George Lewis decided that she should receive an income of nine hundred and fifty pounds a year, and summoned her and George Augustus to his presence to explain this to them.

It did not seem a very princely sum to Caroline and she looked dismayed.

"It will be adequate," said George Lewis. "I shall pay your servants and they will be answerable to me."

"To you?" Caroline had spoken without thinking. George Lewis scowled and she hurried on: "That would put an unnecessary burden on Your Highness."

"They will be answerable to me," repeated George Lewis. He turned to his son. "You'll provide your wife with a carriage and horses and you must set aside two thousand pounds a year to be hers should she be left a widow."

Caroline gasped in dismay but George Lewis threw her a contemptuous look. Women were fools about money, he thought. She thought it was bad taste to refer to her husband's death. She'd thank his foresight if George Augustus died and left her poor.

Having settled these facts, he dismissed them.

In their own apartments, George Augustus's anger against his father broke out.

"Nine hundred and fifty a year!" he sneered. "Generous, isn't he? Now you begin to know him."

"He is paying for my servants," said Caroline.

"You're making excuses for him!"

"It's true. But they're answerable to him."

"Ah, there you see! If you say a word about him in their hearing they'll report it."

"Then I must be careful not to."

"You'd never please him whatever you did."

"I wish that you and he were friendly towards each other."

"As if that's possible!"

"Why not?"

George Augustus laughed. "You wait until you know him, Caroline."

She began to realize that this was a divided household. She had hoped to make a good impression on the Elector. There was one characteristic she had regretted in Sophia Charlotte and that was that she had not been interested in the politics of her husband's court. Caroline could imagine nothing more exciting than helping to govern. She had quickly learned that George Augustus did not possess an intellect to be compared with her own. That at first had not displeased her. It was well, she believed, for the woman to be the dominant partner, even if—and perhaps it was better so—the husband was unaware of this.

She had hoped that the Elector, who for all his boorishness was a shrewd man, would have recognized this and she could, while having a say in Hanoverian politics, put an end to the strife between father and son.

It suddenly occurred to her that that would not be possible if she were to retain her husband's affection.

This discord had been going on too long—ever since George Augustus had known that his mother had been sent into exile.

It would be necessary for her to make a choice. She must support her husband or lose his affection because it was not possible to be on friendly terms with both of them. Thus Caroline quickly learned that she had no choice. She must take sides and join in the conflict.

*　　*　　*

She made another unwelcome discovery.

Leibniz was delighted that she was at the court of Hanover. As she walked with him in the gardens of Herrenhausen he told her how the presence of a cultivated person was needed here.

"This is very different from our dear Lützenburg," he said. "They are not very interested in ideas here. Perhaps now that Your Highness is come that will be changed."

"But the Electress Sophia is here."

"Yes, that's so. I should not be here otherwise. I could not exist in this slough of ignorance. But the Electress is ageing. She has not been well lately and I have been very anxious about her. Besides, it is for the young to lead opinion. You will set a new fashion in Hanover—a fashion for learning and culture."

"That would be very pleasant."

The Electress Sophia who liked to spend a certain time of

the day out of doors joined them and they sat on one of the terraces talking together.

They were speaking of Sophia Charlotte and her theories about death when they were joined by George Augustus and one of his friends.

"I think she preferred always the open mind," said Caroline. "She used to say that to have faith one must first take a leap in the dark."

"What's this?" asked George Augustus.

"We were talking of the blessings of faith, Your Highness," explained Leibniz.

"Why?" asked George Augustus rudely.

"It's an interesting subject," said Caroline. "The Queen of Prussia loved to discuss these matters. We did it constantly at Lützenburg."

"Well, you're not at Lützenburg now."

"But we can have equally intelligent conversations here at Hanover."

"I don't care for these intelligent conversations."

"You would soon learn to. If you would read some of the philosophers..."

She stopped for he was looking at her oddly and the Electress Sophia said quickly: "Oh the philosophers were never much to my grandson's taste, were they, George Augustus?"

"They would be if I wanted them to. I just don't, that's all. Caroline, are you ready?"

She was on the point of saying that she wished to stay with Leibniz and the Electress, when she caught the old woman's eye.

She rose at once and went with George Augustus into the palace.

As soon as they were alone he turned on her.

"So you would flaunt your cleverness?" he said unpleasantly.

"My ... cleverness?"

"Oh yes ... I am to read the books you give me. I am to learn to be as clever as you."

"But I did not say that."

"In front of that old fool Leibniz!"

"He is not a fool. He is one of the cleverest men living."

"Clever! Clever! Books, books, books. I tell you I won't have you trying to make me look a fool."

"But .... I had no intention ..."

"No intention!" he screamed in his rage. It was the first time she had seen these rages. He took off his wig and stamped on it. "Listen. I married you. You had nothing much to offer ... no dowry to speak of ... nothing ... but I married you."

She was about to say: Because the King of Spain had asked for me. But she stopped herself in time, and remained silent.

It was the right thing to have done for it stemmed his rage.

"I'll not have it," he said. "No wife should be cleverer than her husband, should she? Should she?"

If she is, she thought, there is no help for it.

"Should she?" he cried again, kicking his wig to the other side of the room.

In the silence that followed it was as though the sad ghost of the young Sophia Dorothea was warning her: Be careful. Don't go my way.

No, her way was not the right one. Caroline thought fleetingly of her own mother's miserable marriage.

Clever women took the reins in marriage, but they often did it by seeming docile.

"No," she said slowly, "she shouldn't."

A slow smile spread over his flushed face.

He walked to his wig, picked it up and crammed it down on his head.

He came to her then, his smile loving and very affectionate.

He kissed her with fervour—her lips first, and then he slid her bodice from her shoulders.

"You are the best wife in the world," he said thickly; and he reminded her of his father.

She wanted to cry out: No. Go away.

But she had learned her first lesson. She could not love this boy with his pitiful arrogance. But she could win nothing by letting him know that she was beginning to despise him.

\*     \*     \*

When George Lewis retired to his bedchamber he found the

Countess von Platen waiting for him. He had not intimated that he would need her services that night but he was not surprised because she was the only one of his three established mistresses who now and then took the initiative.

George Lewis was not displeased. Although he liked variety it was among a selected circle; he was a faithful lover and once a mistress had a firm position she usually kept it. George Lewis was a man who had always dispensed with romantic wooing which he considered a waste of time; therefore a mistress who knew exactly what was expected of her—be she old and ugly as his two favourites Schulemburg and Kielmansegge undoubtedly had become—was more to his taste than any coy and shrinking virgin.

The Countess von Platen differed from the other two in the fact that she was both beautiful and fairly young, but he would never have selected her in the first place if she had not brought herself to his notice. When she had come to the Court as the wife of his first minister's son he had been unaware of her; until one night he had discovered her in his bedchamber where she threw herself on her knees and demanded to know why she had offended him.

He had replied in his blunt way that he could not see how she had since he was unaware of her existence. Whereupon she implored him not to be so cruel. Did he object to her looks?

Studying her closely he replied that he could not do that for he could see that she was very beautiful. In fact he thought she must be one of the most beautiful women at his court.

"If you think so," she replied, "why do you spend all your time with Madam Schulemburg and my sister-in-law Madam Kielmansegge?"

George Lewis gave this question consideration. Pre-occupation with state matters had offered little opportunity for looking round, he said, but since she had been so kind as to bring herself to his notice, he saw no reason why he should not extend his patronage. At which the young Countess dried her tears, fell on her knees, told him he was the most beneficent ruler in the world, and from thence forward George Lewis had three established mistresses instead of two.

Schulemburg and Kielmansegge were too lethargic and too

well established to care. Schulemburg had only one passion in life, apart from her genuine devotion to George Lewis, and that was adding to her wealth. Kielmansegge's great delight was in the adventures of the bedchamber, but unlike her royal patron she liked a constant change of scene. As neither of these ladies had to fear youth and beauty, the young Countess von Platen was a welcome member of the trinity as it meant a little relief from duty.

Now the Countess von Platen did not immediately state the reason for her visit. She would let George Lewis believe what, in any case it did not enter his mind to doubt—that she had come to enjoy his company.

It was not until the morning that she said: "Her Serene Highness the Electoral Princess has not invited me to her soirée yet. I fancy she considers that I should not be a suitable guest."

George Lewis grunted: "Why not?"

"Since Mesdames Schulemburg and Kielmansegge have not been invited either and we seem to be the only three ladies who have been treated in this way, the reason seems obvious. It is because of our relationship with you. I know you won't allow the silly creature to be so foolish."

"Go without invitations," he said.

The Countess von Platen pretended to shiver. "And incur the wrath of her Serene Highness the Electoral Princess."

"You go ... and tell the others."

"It is your command?"

He grunted.

"And you will be there?"

He nodded.

The Countess von Platen was well pleased. The Princess Caroline had better learn without delay the etiquette of the Court of Hanover.

\* \* \*

Sophia Dorothea had taken a liking to her sister-in-law. She pitied her for one thing. Fancy being doomed to spend her life at Hanover! It was Sophia Dorothea's home, of course. But with such a father, it had never been a happy one. He had shown no affection for his children, although she fancied he did not hate her as bitterly as he did George Augustus. In fact, if he had been a man who knew how to express affection, he might have shown some for her. She was beautiful; she was gay; so perhaps she was too much like her mother.

Her mother! There was the shadow which hung over their lives. Which ever way one looked it was there. She, Sophia Dorothea would be glad to get away and she would soon, for marriage negotiations were being conducted. Frederick William had kept his word; she knew that his father, the king of Prussia had not wanted an alliance with Hanover. In fact he was angry with Hanover for carrying off Caroline right under his nose, which was understandable when he was her guardian. He had wanted her either for the King of Spain or for himself. Poor Caroline, she was in demand, and she had been awarded George Augustus!

Sophia Dorothea grimaced. He was her brother and she had some affection for him, but he was very conceited and he would be like his father in some ways in his attitude towards a wife. I am the master; you are the slave.

That would not please me, she thought. And Caroline? How would she react?

It was not easy to know with Caroline. That was what made her so interesting. So far she had been docile and the more docile she became the more devoted was George Augustus. But once let her show defiance and that would be the end of George Augustus's affection. He might even be as callous towards a wife as his father had been.

Life with Frederick William would be different. She was certain of that. They had learned a good deal about each other on the few occasions when they had met because they had been drawn together irresistibly. He was wild and ungovernable; and she was not the one to accept the role of patient Griselda. No, there would be quarrels and reconciliations. But life would never be dull.

In a rush of pity for her poor sister-in-law Sophia Dorothea went along to Caroline's apartment where Caroline was being dressed for her soirée.

Sophia Dorothea watched her women at work.

"You have lovely hair, sister," said Sophia Dorothea.

Caroline smiled, pleased at the compliment.

"And the blue gown is becoming."

"You are kind to say so."

How could she be so serene, so grave, so outwardly contented when she was far too intelligent not to know that she had been sent into a den of ... Sophia Dorothea paused for the word. Lions? George Augustus was not strong enough nor dignified enough. Foxes? Not cunning enough. Wolves? Yes, wolves wasn't bad.

"You are thoughtful," said Caroline.

"Have you finished?" Sophia Dorothea asked the woman. "I want to talk to Her Highness."

"Yes, in a moment, Your Highness."

Sophia Dorothea sat in a high backed chair watching the finishing touches to Caroline's toilet. I think George Augustus would be every bit as cruel as our father, she thought, if his vanity were wounded. That's it. His vanity! Ever since he knew he would not be very tall he has felt the need to remind everyone that he is as good, as strong, as important as people who are. How cruel life is! To deny George Augustus those inches as well as a mother. And poor Caroline will have to suffer for it too.

The woman had gone and Caroline said: "It is kind of you to come and see me."

"You're my sister now and I shan't have many more opportunities of calling on you like this."

"Are you uneasy about your coming marriage?"

"No. Only waiting to leave Hanover for Prussia."

"Then I'm glad."

"I'm fortunate. If I had loved my home I shouldn't want to leave it. But because I can't wait to get out of it, I'm happy. There's life for you. Taking away with one hand and giving with the other. I hope you will be happy here, Caroline."

"I think so."

"*I* think you have a great gift for being happy. How do you do it? I may need to know when I'm quarrelling with my wild Frederick William."

"Then you are a little uneasy about going to Berlin?"

She shook her head. "I'll deal with Frederick William. You and I should have a good deal to say to each other for while you have come into my old home, I am going into yours."

"Berlin will be quite different from when I was there. Nothing could ever be the same now that Sophia Charlotte is dead."

"No, I suppose not. You loved my aunt very dearly, didn't you?"

Caroline nodded, her eyes clouding. "But I've stopped grieving for those happy days. I'm trying to look ahead. That is the advice she would have given. It is always rather difficult adjusting oneself to a new life ... a new home. Women of our rank invariably have to face it. I am fortunate in having the Electress Sophia who is already my friend as well as my grandmother-in-law."

"George Augustus does not like to be crossed," said Sophia Dorothea.

"Who does?" answered Caroline with a sinking heart, for she recognized the warning in her sister-in-law's voice.

"He more than most. He so very much wants to be ... appreciated."

"I understand." Caroline changed the subject abruptly; she did not want George Augustus to discover that she discussed him with anyone. Whatever her opinion of her husband, she knew she must keep it to herself. "Tell me about Madam Schulemburg and Madam Kielmansegge. It has been suggested that I should invite them to my soirée. I have no intention of doing so."

"Oh, they are my father's mistresses."

"What sort of women are they?"

"The Schulemburg is very tall. She is quite ugly now but was a beauty in her youth. Since she had the smallpox she lost most of her hair, her skin is pockmarked, and she's a real scarecrow. Particularly now that she's so thin—and looks thinner because she is so tall. She is as pale as a ghost under all her rouge which looks dreadful over the pock marks; and the red wig she wears makes her look worse than ever. But she has been there for so long that no one notices her. She has been my father's mistress for years and she's still the favourite. He doesn't seem to notice how ugly she is ... or perhaps he doesn't think so. He has no sense of beauty."

"I meant rather what sort of woman is she."

"Oh ... stupid. Quite stupid. But that's in her favour. She never argues. That to my father means more than silken locks and peach-like complexion. Lips are fascinating to him not because they are luscious but because they keep silent."

"You think that she has kept her hold on your father because she never disagrees with him?"

Sophia Dorothea nodded. "Her stupidity is one of her main attractions."

"Do you really mean that?"

"Of course. Some men like to feel superior. My father doesn't consciously feel superior. He's merely convinced he is. If anyone disagreed with him he would think they were stupid. Some are different. They have to be continually reminded of their superiority because they doubt it. They perhaps are the more dangerous ones."

"I see what you mean," said Caroline slowly; and then more briskly: "Tell me more about Schulemburg."

She came to the court when she was a young girl and was introduced to my father by the Countess von Platen—not the present one ... the wife of the elder Count von Platen. She was my grandfather's mistress and she ruled the Court."

"Then your grandfather did not share this love for stupid women."

"No. He was different. But even he liked them to be clever enough to know when to keep quiet and was as determined to have his own way as my father is. Only he was gallant and witty whereas my father..." Sophia Dorothea shrugged her shoulders. "To get back to Schulemburg: Countess von Platen was in love with Königsmarck who was my mother's lover so she hated my mother. She advised Schulemburg how to keep my father's favour and my mother quarrelled with him over the creature. He wouldn't have interference from his wife any more than he would tolerate her having a lover. You see how unfair it is for us women?"

Caroline nodded.

"Well Schulemburg suited my father. She's really fond of

him and he of her—as much as he could be of anyone. When
my mother was sent away Schulemburg was treated like his
wife. But she never argued; she never quarrelled; she never
criticized him even when he took another mistress, but was
always waiting gratefully when he came back to her. That is
what the Hanoverians expect of women."

Caroline's eyes narrowed. "So she kept her place all those
years. It must be nearly twenty. And although she is no longer
beautiful she still keeps her place. It is quite an achievement."

"To succeed through stupidity!"

"But not so stupid."

"Oh it's not by design. That would be clever. No Schulemburg is as she is because nature made her that way."

"And the other ... Kielmansegge?"

"Ah, she is a different kind altogether."

"Yet she keeps her hold too."

"Yes. It must be because my father is too lazy to change. But
you could scarcely call him lazy. No. It is habit, perhaps; and
the conviction that all women are more or less the same and
the only ones who are disagreeable to him are those who voice
opinions. Kielmansegge is as ugly in her way as Schulemburg is
in hers. She's the daughter of the Count von Platen. You see
how useful that family is. Schulemburg introduced by Platen;
Kielmansegge the daughter of Platen; and the Countess von
Platen, the latest addition to the seraglio, the daughter-in-law
of the Platens. Kielmansegge could well be my father's sister. In
fact it is more than likely. My grandfather was Clara von
Platen's lover over many years, and as her husband was the
complaisant kind—he did very well through it as you know—it
is more than possible that the children he accepted as his were
other people's."

"And she is not in such favour as Schulemburg."

"There is very little in it. She is not so docile ... at least
when my father is not about. Schulemburg is completely faithful to my father and always has been. No breath of scandal
attaches to our tall malkin; it's a very different matter with
Kielmansegge. She is like her mother. The sight of any person-
able man makes her eyes glisten. She doesn't see why she
should reserve herself for my father, particularly when she has

to share his favours with others. I doubt whether he could satisfy her if she was the only one. She is as ugly as Schulemburg—only her wig is black instead of red but it's as unbecoming. She's as fat as Schulemburg is thin; and her complexion is so ruddy that she has to tone it down with white powder which is every bit as unbecoming as Schulemburg's rouge."

"I see that your father likes variety. These two are exact opposites."

"Perhaps you are right. Then there is the young Countess von Platen, a most conventional mistress, being young and beautiful. And while she is not entirely faithful like Schulemburg and not as promiscuous as Kielmansegge she is not averse to take a lover now and then."

"I begin to understand," said Caroline. "The Elector has tried to have all women represented in those three. It is what I would have expected of such an orderly mind."

"I think you admire him a little."

"He is a good ruler and I am sorry there is such enmity between him and George Augustus. I should like to change that and make them friends."

Sophia Dorothea shook her head.

"You're beginning to understand them. No one has ever been able to teach them anything. My grandmother gave up long ago and she is a wise woman."

"I shall not receive those three women at my soirée. I believe that that will please George Augustus. In fact I know it will. I think perhaps the Elector would realize then how much happier everyone would be if he showed a little kindness to your mother. I don't suggest that she should come back to Hanover. That would be too painful for everyone. But I do think that if he would allow George Augustus and you to see your mother, everyone would be happier and the dreadful enmity in the family might come to an end."

"You are a reformer, Caroline."

"That amuses you."

"In a way because I don't think you know us here very well. But you will learn." Sophia Dorothea stood up. "I keep you from your duties. But I have enjoyed our talk. We must make the most of our opportunities before I leave for Prussia. There

I shall have to concern myself with my own problems. Ugh! Settling ourselves into new homes, is a delicate business. I suppose all wise princesses should remember my mother. Perhaps if she had her chance over again she would behave differently. Who wouldn't? I daresay like me you would accept a great deal rather than be a prisoner in a lonely castle for years and years?"

There was no doubt about it. Sophia Dorothea was warning her sister-in-law.

\*   \*   \*

Caroline looked startled. Coming towards her was the Elector; his expression was cold, his mouth grim. Behind him walked two of the ugliest women Caroline had ever seen. They were like grotesque creatures from some fantastic play, one being so tall and thin, the other short and fat. And with them was the young and beautiful Countess von Platen.

The Elector stood before her.

"I present to you Madam von Schulemburg, Madam Kielmansegge and the Countess von Platen...."

Caroline hesitated. She could say that she had not invited them. And if she did?

She looked into the cold cruel face of the Elector, and saw the determination there.

The Electress Sophia who was beside her spoke suddenly: "Now is your opportunity to meet these ladies. I know it has for some time been your desire to do so."

Warnings all about her. From the Electress, from her sister-in-law, from the sad prisoner of Ahlden, this band of women who knew what could happen to one of them if they did not accept the right of men to use them, to insult them, to humiliate them.

But there are other ways, thought Caroline as graciously she extended her hand to the tall woman with the raddled skin who came forward.

"It gives me pleasure to see you here," she said coldly.

But the Elector was satisfied. The first hint of rebellion had been quashed.

\*   \*   \*

The English were beginning to arrive at Hanover in large numbers. The passing of the act of Succession naming the Electress Sophia as the heir to the throne should Queen Anne fail to produce a child had sent many, whose popularity at home was not great, scurrying to Hanover to ingratiate themselves with the Queen's possible successor.

The Electress Sophia seemed to have become younger. She was an old woman, older than Queen Anne, but the latter had been sickly for years and Sophia did not believe she could out-live her now. If this were so she would have the infinite pleasure of visiting a country which she considered the greatest in the world, and going as its Queen.

Such a prospect was rejuvenating in the extreme. She received the visitors from England with great honour and she entertained them as lavishly as she could and did her utmost to make George Lewis do the same.

Her son however was not so enamoured of the English project as she was. There was no place on earth to compare with Hanover as far as he was concerned and he preferred Germans to English.

What would they think of him? Sophia asked herself. They would take home reports of this crude boor, and the English would ask themselves whether they were wise to pass over the Catholic Stuart for the sake of such a man, Protestant though he was—for Sophia had to face the fact that she was an old woman and there could not be many more years left to her and when she died who was left to be King of England other than George Lewis?

Among those who came to Hanover was the famous Duke of Marlborough. George Lewis received him with pleasure, for although the Duke was a charming handsome man with impeccable manners and some gallantry, the greatest interest to them both was soldiering; and they could discuss the war and future campaigns together to their mutual benefit and pleasure. Each year a Hanoverian army left for Flanders; and often George Lewis was with it. Marlborough had had a great respect for him ever since when quite a young man George Lewis had distinguished himself in the field.

George Augustus longed for military glory. He had repeatedly begged his father to allow him to go to the wars but always he had been met with a refusal.

But the sight of Marlborough there in all his military glory and everyone talking about his successes and repeating the legend that he was unbeatable in the field, that the enemy knew it and lost heart before the battle had begun, George Augustus's desire for equal fame was more than he could endure.

He went to his father and cried out: "Why ... why can't I be a soldier?"

George Lewis turned away in disgust. "Get a son," he said. "Then you shall go."

Get a son. He had been married for some months and there was no sign.

He went to Caroline and told her that they must get a son because he wanted to go to war and his father would never allow him to until their son was born.

"I hope," he said crossly, "that you are not going to be one of those women who can't get children."

She was serene outwardly but inwardly the anxious qualms were troubling her.

It was an unfair world where an intelligent woman must accept the supremacy and domination of her intellectual inferior simply because he was a man and she a woman.

\* \* \*

There was always the Empress Sophia to offer her comfort. They walked in the gardens of Herrenhausen together among the statues, clumsy German replicas of French artistry, beside the water works which were faithful copies of those at Marley and Versailles.

"You were wise to receive my son's women," she told Caroline.

"I confess I almost refused."

"It would have been a great mistake to have done so. My son would never have forgiven you and he is a vindictive man."

"Yes, I know that."

Sophia shook her head. "When I go to England, you and George Augustus will come with me. George Lewis will have to also. We shall have a better life there, a more cultured life. I can assure you the Court of St. James's will be a little different from this of Hanover."

"But if the Elector is the Prince of Wales he will doubtless introduce something of Hanover into England."

Sophia shivered. "I shall prevent that for I shall be the Queen."

Caroline had never before seen her so enraptured. She was a different person from the sober serene woman she had known, and it was clear that she could think of little else but the prospect of going to England.

"George Augustus is eager to be a soldier."

"He will in time."

"Not until we have a son."

Sophia turned her gaze on Caroline. "You are anxious about that? You must not be. It is early days yet."

"George Augustus seems to think I am a little tardy in giving him his heart's desire."

"Poor George Augustus!" sighed Sophia. "I am sorry my grandson is such a fool. But you my dear have intelligence enough for both. You must make good use of it. You did right about my son's women. Don't try to fight what can't be fought. And don't worry about not becoming pregnant; it's the worst thing in the world. You are far less likely to conceive if you worry about it. I am sure you will soon be telling me you are pregnant and the joy bells will be ringing in Hanover. I shall be delighted to hear them ... unless I should be in England by then."

Oh yes, her thoughts were far away in England.

"I want to see Sophia Dorothea settled before I leave. I do hope there will be no delay. It will be pleasant to think of her with my dearest Sophia Charlotte's son. I'm sure she would have been delighted. It was a dream of hers that you should come here, Caroline."

But, thought Caroline, not that I should have to subject myself to the whims of a mentally retarded boy.

"Now I want you to come with me and talk to Mr. Howe, the English Envoy. He will tell us about England. It's a pity your English is not better my dear. You have such a German accent and you are far from fluent. We shall have to speak in German, and Mr. Howe would far rather speak in English."

Caroline felt alone. The Electress Sophia, whom she had regarded as a bulwark was now inclining away from her—so wrapped up was she in her own glorious future as Queen of England.

\*   \*   \*

The Electress had to take her mind from England to celebrate the marriage of Sophia Dorothea to the Crown Prince of Prussia. As both bride and groom were her grandchildren she was quite delighted with the match; and she was certain that the pretty, not exactly clever, but spirited Sophia Dorothea would be a match for the rather violent Frederick William. In any case they were both eager for marriage and there had been no reluctant tears from the bride, no protests from the groom. In fact their eagerness was the reason why they were being married at such an early age.

Frederick William was nearly five years younger than George Augustus but he seemed more mature in many ways. They disliked each other intensely so it was fortunate that the newly married couple would not live at Hanover to add to family strife.

In spite of her friendship with Sophia Dorothea Caroline was glad when the celebrations were at an end and the young couple left Hanover. George Augustus's jealousy of his cousin was painful to watch.

She fancied she had grown a little closer to her husband through her friendship with his maternal grandmother the Duchess of Celle, the Frenchwoman who still showed signs of great beauty and who at the end of her life was so sad. The Duchess mourned her husband deeply, even though the last years of the marriage had been soured by the Duke's siding with Hanover for state reasons while the Duchess had one motive in her life which was the care of her daughter. The Duchess would never forgive her son-in-law for what he had done to her daughter. She it was who visited Ahlden regularly, who took accounts of her children's lives to their mother. She would tell of the marriage of the young Sophia Dorothea, of Caroline the wife of her son.

Caroline was attracted by the Duchess, a woman of great culture and charm, as clever as the Electress and far more beautiful. And Caroline knew her friendship towards Sophia was weakening because of that she immediately felt towards the Duchess. The Duke of Celle had refused to marry Sophia, had given up lands and titles rather than do so; and that was something, even so many years later, that Sophia found hard to forgive. Particularly when he fell so deeply in love with the woman he married and with whom he remained deeply in love, until the marriage of their daughter brought such bitterness into their lives. Sophia had hated the Duchess of Celle with a vindictiveness which appalled Caroline; and after that she did not feel so friendly towards the old woman. Moreover Sophia's preoccupation with the English had already driven a rift between them and a coldness had sprung up, which a few months before would not have seemed possible.

George Augustus was delighted with Caroline's friendship towards his mother's mother. At the same time he was doing his best to please the English visitors. It was a natural instinct to go against everything that his father stood for.

It was a great relief when Caroline realized that George Lewis was indifferent to her friendship with the Duchess of Celle. She supposed it was because he thought the Duchess too insignificant to be of importance. If she attempted to see the prisoner she would be sternly reprimanded, but of course she would do no such thing. She was learning how to be a Hanoverian wife, outwardly docile. But there was something they did not understand: inwardly she was in revolt.

Domestic storms could blow up quickly in Hanover. Violently and suddenly they arose out of the most insignificant incidents.

George Augustus marched into his wife's apartments, his face red and puffed, his eyes watering with emotion.

"Have you heard the news?" he demanded.

Alarmed she asked what catastrophe had happened.

"That puppy Frederick William is going to the Netherlands."

"Oh?" said Caroline surprised.

"Don't stand there saying Oh. Can't you see what this means! He's going with the armies. He's going to fight. *His* father has not stopped him. He doesn't have to get a son before he goes. He's five years younger than I and yet I'm kept out and he's allowed to go!"

"Your time will come . . ." began Caroline soothingly.

"Yes, when you have given me a son. When will that be? What signs are there? Do you think you're barren? God knows you ought to have shown signs by now. And my father is laughing at me with those scarecrows of his. George Augustus . . . married to a barren wife . . . we'll keep him at Hanover till he's too old to make a soldier."

"George Augustus, this is absurd."

"Absurd, is it? I tell you he's gone. Gone to win honours on the battlefield. And they're laughing at me because I'm not allowed to be a soldier . . . because I can't get a son. They're jeering at me . . . me . . . the Prince. And all because you are barren. If I'd known it . . ."

He stopped and looked at her. He hadn't meant to say that. He was proud of her. She was beautiful. She had never really crossed him . . . she never showed off as he called it, after that one attempt when he had made her understand that he didn't like it.

But he was angry. He was too unsure of himself to accept the fact that he could occasionally be wrong. He always had to be in the right, always the injured party. If his father would not let him go to war that was because his father was jealous of the honours he might win. If he was not yet a father that was Caroline's fault.

He picked up his wig and throwing it on the floor stamped on it; then kicked it round the room. It was a favourite outlet for outraged feelings; and after that display of physical violence he felt a little better.

He took up his wig, slammed it on his head and walked out.

He would show them whose fault it was that he had no son.

Caroline did not see him that night. The next day she

learned that her husband had a mistress. Such news travelled fast in Hanover.

\* \* \*

If only Sophia Charlotte were here, she would have advised her what to do. Life was so disappointing, so unfulfilled. How she longed for Lützenburg, and intelligent conversation beneath the trees!

What was life at Hanover? There was no culture. Leibniz was still with them but he despaired of bringing distinguished scholars to the court, and even the Electress was no longer interested in philosophical discussion now she had one aim in life—to gain the crown of England before she died.

And here was Caroline—young, beautiful, vital and above all clever, doomed to be the typical German wife, to remain silent when her husband spoke, to accept his word as law—even though he had the mind of a boy of fourteen and the manners and control of one younger—to be humble, docile, suppressing all desires but to be a good wife and bear many children.

No! said Caroline.

But what was the use of rebelling when one was in a Hanoverian prison? There was at least a pretence of freedom here which was more than there was at Ahlden.

There were times when she felt she could give way to despair but in her heart she knew that because she had a more alert mind, a deeper power of concentration, because she had considerable more knowledge than her husband, there must be a way of eluding his domination. She was certain that in time she would find it. And until she did she must allow him to believe that she was the wife he wanted her to be. That was the way she would always have to live. She would always have to let him believe that he was the master. There was no harm in playing a game of pretence so long as in reality she was in command of her own destiny.

And she would be.

\* \* \*

It was with great joy that Caroline was able to announce that she was pregnant.

George Augustus came to her in a mood of contrition. He had been angry, he explained. Not with her, of course, but with his father. It was always his father.

"He frustrates me, Caroline. He does everything he knows to annoy me. I shall never be happy until he's dead."

Caroline told him he must not say such things; as for that other matter, since it was over they would say no more about it.

He fell upon her embracing her. She was the best wife in the world. It should never happen again. And now they would have their son. His clever beautiful Caroline had at last become pregnant. He would have a son and she should have a husband whose military exploits were the wonder of the world.

Once I have a child, thought Caroline, that child's interests will be the centre of my life. Then I shall not care that I have an adolescent boy for a husband.

\* \* \*

"The Crown Prince and his wife are reconciled," said the Court. "There was never a more devoted husband. Why he is with her every minute of the day. She will grow weary of his company."

If she found his company a little tiring she was pleased to have it. It was a triumph for that policy which the Electress Sophia had used to her advantage.

The Electress complimented her on her tact.

"It is the first which is often a little difficult to accept. I remember my own case. I was young then and a little unworldly, I suppose. I was quite grieved. I quickly learned though, as you will, my dear. Never interfere with a husband's mistresses and you may find that you can have charge of almost everything else. It was a rule I followed with my husband; and Ernest Augustus was a clever man; your husband is a fool."

Caroline did not deny it.

But relations between her and the Electress were still lukewarm because her friendship with the Duchess of Celle continued to make a rift between them, although Sophia did not mention it. But that difference was almost obliterated by Caroline's attitude towards the English.

Caroline had decided that it was impossible to pursue a solitary course at Hanover. She had to take sides either with the Elector or his son; it would be folly, she knew to alienate her husband, so she had ranged herself beside him. That meant that she must delight in the English as George Augustus was doing—not because he liked them, but because his father didn't care for them.

Therefore the rift between the Electress and herself was slowly being bridged.

Sophia was also delighted by Caroline's pregnancy.

She hoped with her that the child would be a boy.

\* \* \*

Everyone was waiting for the birth of the heir of Hanover. The child should be due by November, it was said, and the Court was preparing to celebrate; even the Elector realized that the birth of a grandson should be heralded by a little extravagance.

But November passed and although the Electoral Princess continued to look as though she were in the last stages of pregnancy still the birth did not take place.

The Electress Sophia was worried. At last here was something to turn her attention from the English throne.

She talked to Caroline as they walked in the gardens together.

"You are feeling well?" she asked.

"Yes, as well as can be expected in the circumstances."

"But ... shouldn't your time be at hand?"

"Doubtless I miscalculated."

A week or two, yes, thought Sophia. But December was upon them, and the child was very much overdue.

She talked to some of the doctors.

It sometimes happened, she was told, that when a woman ardently wished for a child she had all the outwards symptoms of pregnancy, but there was no child. This seemed hardly likely in the case of the Princess Caroline. She was not a nervous type; she seemed so serene, so certain. But it was strange that the child did not arrive. It might be that she was not pregnant after all.

George Augustus was having his uniform made. He was certain that he would soon be going into battle. One thing in the favour of his father was that he kept his word.

All through the December they waited and still there was no birth.

*          *          *

Christmas passed and the New Year Carnival was celebrated throughout Hanover in accordance with the old custom. There were fancy dress balls in the Palace and the Town Hall; for the New Year was brought in with revelry among the high and the low.

In the Opera House of which George Lewis was justly proud operas were performed—the one divertisement that George Lewis could tolerate.

Caroline appeared at the revels, obviously pregnant; but everyone was saying now that there would be no child. Only Caroline was certain that she would soon bear a child; and George Agustus, dressed as a General at the fancy dress ball, was certain he would soon be at the wars.

On a cold January night Caroline went to bed and during the night her pains started.

The next day the long awaited child was born.

It was a boy.

*          *          *

Exhausted and triumphant, Caroline lay back on her pillows. She had succeeded when all the court had thought she would never give birth to a child at all but was the victim of some strange disease.

But there he was, a strong healthy child, bawling with a good pair of lungs to let the world know that he had at last arrived.

George Augustus came to show her his uniform and to admire the baby at the same time. He looked with fond admiration at his wife. Clever Caroline! She had produced a son and given him his heart's desire; he was overcome with love for her; he knelt by the bed and covered her hands with kisses.

The Electress came to see the baby.

"It's to be hoped," she said, "that he will have more sense than his father."

The child was christened Frederick Louis and was known as Fritz; Caroline called him Fritzchen.

*       *       *

So he had his son; now he could go to war.

He must first fit himself for the task, said George Lewis; but he could now study military tactics and be ready perhaps to leave Hanover with the next expedition which would not be for some months.

To argue with George Lewis might mean some fresh embargo so George Augustus curbed his impatience and set about learning how to become a soldier. He enjoyed the life; he was certain it was the one for him; meanwhile he was attentive to his wife and liked to watch the progress of little Fritzchen.

When the baby was six months old Caroline thought she had caught what was said to be a chill and kept to her bed for a day but as she grew worse the doctors were sent for.

Her blood had become overheated, she was told. It happened sometimes after childbirth.

She said she would rest in her apartments for a few days and asked that Fritzchen be brought to her.

Fritzchen was sleeping, she was told.

"Then as soon as he is awake," she said, "bring him to me."

But the child was not brought and it suddenly dawned on Caroline that the doctors had not told her the truth.

She sent for them and demanded to know it.

The doctors exchanged glances; she would have to know sooner or later.

"Your Highness, we fear the smallpox."

The smallpox! That dreaded scourge which either killed or ravaged. And it had come to her!

*       *       *

Someone was at her bedside.

"Who is there?" she whispered.

"It is your husband."

"George Augustus. What are you doing here? Don't you understand . . . ?"

"I understand," he replied dramatically.

"But you are running a risk."

"Who but I should nurse you at such a time?"

She was incredulous. He nurse her! He could not do it. He would be of no use whatever in a sick room. Yet he was determined to share her danger. What a fool . . . but a brave fool! If he could not show his valour on the battle fields of Flanders he would in his wife's sick room.

"George Augustus," she said weakly. "You must not stay here. It is folly."

He leaned over her, unnecessarily close. "Did you think I should desert you at such a time?"

"You have convinced me of your devotion. I am touched by it. But please . . . please don't stay here."

"Rest assured that I shall never leave you."

"For my sake go, George Augustus. I am so anxious for you."

He leaned over the bed and kissed her.

For her sake. No, for his own, she thought in weary exasperation. He wanted the whole court to be talking about the brave devotion of its little Prince.

\*       \*       \*

Through her illness—and she was very ill—she was aware of him. She heard his voice through her delirium; she heard the sound of breaking china; she was aware of the shape of him close to the bed, the touch of his hands.

Go away, George Augustus, she thought.

She heard his voice. "She is in the critical stage, I know. Tell me . . . tell me the worst. It will break my heart but I can bear it."

She was too ill to care whether he went or stayed. And throughout Hanover they were saying: "The Electoral Princess is dying."

\*       \*       \*

There came a day when the crisis passed and she found herself still alive.

George Augustus was sitting by her bed, holding her hand. You ... fool, she thought.

She heard his voice, high pitched with self-satisfaction. "You're better, Caroline. I've been with you the whole of the time. I never stirred from your bed except in the evening. Then I took a horse and rode for miles. I had to take some exercise, and I thought that would keep me well after staying the whole day at your bedside. I nursed you, Caroline. They are saying in the palace that no Princess ever had a more devoted husband."

"Thank you, George Augustus."

"That shows you, doesn't it? That shows you!"

Contrition for infidelity, she thought; although all the time he was with his mistress he was telling himself it was his right.

She murmured faintly: "You are very good, George Augustus."

"Oh yes, they told me I was running a terrible risk. They told me I should catch the pox. You've been very ill, Caroline. We didn't think you'd live. And I was there all the time ... even at the most contagious time. They begged me not to stay but I wouldn't go. I said: Caroline is my wife. No one can nurse her as I can."

Nurse her? How had he nursed her? She pictured him, fussing round the bed, getting in the way of doctors and nurses, talking too much not about her needs, but his own courage.

Oh go away, go away, she thought wearily. Leave me in peace.

But she said: "Thank you."

And his voice went on telling her a little of how ill she had been and a great deal about how brave he had been.

\*     \*     \*

Caroline sent for a mirror. It was brought with some reluctance. This was the moment which all sufferers from the smallpox had to face. It could be terrifying.

Caroline held it up and caught her breath. There was change, and although she was not disfigured, the pox had not left her unscathed. When did it ever do that? But she was not badly marked although her delicately coloured complexion had gone.

She sighed. It was sad for a woman, who needed all her weapons to fight for and hold her place in the world, to find one of her valued assets though not entirely lost, blunted.

\* \* \*

It was inevitable, said everyone, that George Augustus should have caught the smallpox after his attendance in his wife's sick room. Very soon the news was brought to Caroline that he could not visit her because he was sick.

She was relieved because she could not visit him, but as she lay thinking of him she felt a new tenderness for him. She knew him well enough to understand his need always to call attention to himself; she knew that his devotion to her—in fact every action in his life—was directed by this motive; and yet he *had* braved this dreaded disease; he *had* shown his devotion to her.

Lying there, thinking of George Augustus, she came to new terms with her life. She would try to understand him, to help him conquer that feeling of inferiority which being smaller than most men had given him and which manifested itself in arrogance and apparent conceit.

Their destiny lay together. There should be no discord between them.

She must remember that in future. She must curb her impatience; she must try to give him the confidence he needed and perhaps she could do this by letting him know she valued him.

She would try to make him understand this when ... if he recovered.

If he recovered? She shivered at the possibility of his not doing so. And it was not only because of the uncertainty his death would place on her, for after all she was now the mother of little Fritzchen who was one of the heirs to Hanover and possibly the crown of England. No. It was not that. Could it be that she really had some affection for the little man?

*    *    *

The Prince's attack was a slight one and he soon came to Caroline's apartment in good spirits.

The need to go to war was temporarily forgotten; he had won his laurels for bravery in the sick room.

Caroline was still very weak having suffered a more severe attack and George Augustus was delighted to prove his great resistance to the disease, having taken it after and recovered sooner than his wife.

The Electress Sophia came to see them as soon as there was no danger in doing so.

She embraced them both and was delighted she said to see them well again.

"It has been a very anxious time," she told them. "The whole Court was plunged in melancholy, so fearful were they. The English were very disturbed. They think very highly of you both."

She looked at them proudly as though it were more commendable to please the English than to recover from an attack of the smallpox.

She was thinking that poor Caroline looked very wan. She will never again have that bright young beauty, that freshness, she thought. Although she has come through better than I expected; but the change is there.

As though reading her thoughts Caroline said: "You are thinking I have changed."

"Very little," answered the Electress. "And you have to get really well yet. You have had a very bad attack, remember."

"And do you think *I* have changed?" demanded George Augustus.

"You don't look as if you've had the pox at all," replied his grandmother. "The people might wonder whether some fleas had bitten your face."

George Augustus was examining his face at a mirror.

People would look at him and say: Have some fleas bitten his face? And the answer would be: No, he caught the smallpox, you know. He could have avoided it, but he *would* nurse his wife. He saved her life. Brave. I should say so! How many men or women would risk their lives like that!

His grandmother and wife watched him, understanding his thoughts.

They smiled.

Sophia said: "I am pleased to see you two so happy together."

George Augustus came and taking his wife's hand kissed it. "I'd do the same again," he said.

It was a happy convalescence.

\*     \*     \*

George Augustus was more contented than he had ever been.

He had a son; he had nursed his wife through the smallpox, had caught it himself, had recovered, and was training to go into the army.

He was a very loving husband.

Caroline became pregnant again and to George Augustus's great joy he was allowed to join Marlborough's army in Belgium.

George Lewis spoke to him before he left telling him that he was fortunate to be with the greatest captain in the world; and for the first time in their lives father and son seemed almost fond of each other.

With George Augustus away Caroline was able to spend a great deal of her time with the Electress Sophia and in the gardens of Herrenhausen they talked with Leibniz and other visitors to Hanover. It was almost like being in Lützenburg again, for the little coldness which had sprung up between the old Electress and Caroline was over. There were so many English in Hanover now that it was known as Little England, and Sophia secretly called herself the Princess of Wales and longed for news from England that Queen Anne was no more.

They were happy days, for Caroline believed that his war experiences would give George Augustus maturity and that she might eventually learn to make a good life with him.

Fritzchen caused a little anxiety by not being able to walk; he was a pretty child but small for his age and backward.

When it was discovered however that he had rickets special care was taken of him and he began to show improvement.

As with Fritzchen, Caroline had miscalculated and when the time came for her child to be born nothing happened, but she remained calmly waiting. So pleasant it was to wander in the gardens of Herrenhausen; to stroll through the orangery while music was played for them and Leibniz talked to them; with George Augustus away and no one to reprimand her for talking like a scholar rather than a Princess, she was happier than she had been since the death of Sophia Charlotte.

Together they discussed the religious controversy which was taking place in France at the time between the Jesuits and the Jansenites and Caroline was in her element in the centre of discussion, surprising them all with her knowledge for she had always possessed an extraordinarily retentive memory and remembered everything she read.

Those were happy days.

There came news from the battle front. Oudenarde had been won under Marlborough's command and George Augustus had distinguished himself by his bravery. At the head of the Hanoverian Dragoons he had led them to victory and although his horse had been shot under him, he had plunged into the thick of the fighting and to the admiration of all had proved himself as fine a soldier as his father.

The English at Hanover were talking about his bravery and Marlborough had written to the Elector congratulating him on the Prince's action. He had played his part in the great victory, said Marlborough.

Even George Lewis was pleased with his son ... for a time; then he realized that his success on the battlefield had made him a hero in the eyes of the English and as those at Hanover had already reported back to London that the Electoral Prince was more favourable to the English than the Elector, the old antagonism was as fierce as ever. Was his son trying to ingratiate himself with the English? wondered George Lewis. Was he hoping that they would want to pass over the father and take the son?

George Lewis had no great desire to accept the crown of England; but on the death of Anne and Sophia it would be his

... not his son's. George Augustus could only have it on his death.

George Augustus returned to Hanover flushed with triumph, ready to receive a hero's welcome. There were many ready to give it and he was content. For his father's grim disapproval he cared nothing; in fact he was glad of it. He had no wish for the hatred between them to be diminished. He revelled in his new popularity. The people of Hanover, he liked to believe, as well as the English, loved him better than his father.

There was his devoted wife, large with child. There was little Fritzchen shouting with glee at the sight of his brave Papa.

George Augustus had never been so happy in his life.

And on a dark November day Caroline's second child was born—a healthy girl.

"We will christen her Anne," said the Electress, "in compliment to the Queen of England."

Caroline agreed that this was an excellent idea and Anne of England graciously consented to be godmother to baby Anne of Hanover.

George Augustus who had to leave before the birth wrote of his joy in the event and in his wife who had given him so much happiness.

"This token of your love attaches me to you more deeply than ever. The peace of my life depends on knowing you are in good health and upon the conviction of your continued affection towards me. I shall endeavour to attract it by all imaginable love and passion and I shall never omit any way of showing you that no one could be more wholly yours, dear Caroline, than your George Augustus."

When she read that letter, holding her newly born child in her arms with little Fritzchen beside her, she told herself that she had passed through the dangerous years of marriage. She would know how to find happiness in the life that lay ahead.

## The Prince Improves his English

THE wagon trundled into the main square of Hanover and came to a stop before the inn. Among the passengers who alighted were a man and woman who were obviously foreigners, but in the last years there had been so many foreigners in Hanover—and particularly English—that little notice was paid to these two.

They were travel-stained and weary and seemed to have one thought: to provide themselves with food and a room for the night.

They followed other travellers into the inn where they were assigned a room and told that supper would be ready within an hour. The woman wrinkled her nose at the smell of sauerkraut, sausages and onions which came from the kitchens, as she and the man were conducted to a room.

As soon as the door shut on them, she threw back the hood of her cloak and taking the pins from her hair shook it out. It fell like a golden brown shawl about her shoulder and immediately transformed her into a beauty.

"My head aches," she said in a quiet voice.

The man nodded and took a bottle from his pocket. He drank deeply while she looked at him with contempt.

"Not too much, Henry," she said. "We cannot afford any drunkenness now."

He scowled at her. "Nag! nag! nag!" he said. "What a life you lead me."

"If you'd listened to me," she began.

"I know. I know. We shouldn't be in the state we are today. We should be at the Court of Good Queen Anne not trying out our fortunes here in Hanover."

"Don't forget we need all our wits."

"You won't let me."

"Henry, we can't afford to fail. We've got to consider very seriously where we go from here. If we're clever, if we can win the favour of these people, we'll go back home with them and it'll be our turn to hold high places at Court."

"Yes, and there are a hundred other people here with the same idea."

"We're in good time. If only we can bring ourselves to their notice. If only we can please them. But if you're going to drink yourself silly . . . if you're going to drink away all the money we have . . ."

"Have we any money?"

"Scarcely any. I've got to think . . . think seriously what we're going to do. We've got to get an introduction to the old Electress. If only I can get that we'll go forward from there. You only have to be English to please her, they say. And if we haven't money we have background . . . both of us."

"Well, you're the clever one."

"I'll have to think. But I want your help, Henry. You've got to give me your help."

He sat down on the bed and regarded her gloomily. He was wondering why he had married her; she was wondering why she had married him.

Furiously she went to the mirror which was tarnished and mottled and threw ageing shadows on her face which momentarily alarmed her. That was how she would look in reality in a few years time if they continued to live this hole and corner life. She put up a hand to stroke her hair. It was magnificent, her greatest beauty and she was more than averagely good looking even without it. Her features were neat, her eyes very good, her smile most agreeable and her figure slender without being thin.

She was an attractive woman; and appearances were so useful.

At home in Norfolk they had expected her to make a good match, and so, they thought, she had; for it had seemed that the eldest daughter of Sir Henry Hobart had done very well in securing a son of the Earl of Suffolk. Of course Henry was only a third son and he had disgraced himself in his family before the marriage, which was why he was allowed to throw himself away on the daughter of a Norfolk baronet—only of course the Hobarts had not known that until after. He was a drunkard; he was immoral; he had an alarming temper which could at times be violent; and he had long before his marriage run through his own patrimony; therefore Henrietta Hobart with her dowry of six thousand pounds seemed an attractive proposition.

Henrietta soon realized the mistake. Often she wished she were back in her father's house in Norfolk, sitting under the apple tree or in the rose garden with her sisters talking of the men they would marry. The peace of a country mansion had often during the last few years seemed the most desirable thing in the world.

But Henrietta was not a foolish girl to sigh for the impossible. In marriage she had found disappointment but it need not be disastrous. Fortunately, besides being blessed with beauty she had a placid temperament; and although not brilliantly clever she was resourceful.

It was her suggestion that they had come to Hanover and she was going to get to Court somehow. Once there she would seek to find a niche for herself, if not for Henry, and when she found it, would do her best to remain in it, comfortably secure, ready to leave for England with the new Queen when the time came.

It could not be long now. Anne was constantly about to die and miraculously recovering. Abigail Hill, Lady Masham, had long since driven the Duchess of Marlborough from favour

and she guarded Anne like the dragon she was for all her insipid looks. Henrietta had often thought that if she had had
an opportunity of bringing herself to the Queen's notice she
might have had an opportunity of winning her favour.

But it was an impossible task, moreover one did not seek to
travel on a sinking ship. Wise forward-looking people were
now turning to Hanover and were bringing themselves to the
notice of the Electress Sophia.

And that was what the Howards must do.

"We must find a way," she said quietly, and began binding
up her hair in readiness for their descent to the dining room.
Sausages and sauerkraut. Not very delectable. But they would
not for long be taking their meals like common travellers in an
inn parlour.

*       *       *

The next day Henrietta secured a small apartment in
Hanover. It was grander than she could afford but even so
it was too humble. But that, she decided, was a necessary
expense.

There were so many English in Hanover that it was not
difficult to introduce herself into society. After all she was well
born—herself the daughter of a baronet, her husband the son
of an Earl. She had been most excellently educated and was
every bit a court lady; and in Hanover, where manners were
considered coarse compared with those of England, she seemed
a very grand lady.

What she needed was an audience with the Electress but this
was not easy to come by. In spite of the crudities of court life
there was a rigid protocol. The number of people employed in
the service of the royal household must rival that of Queen
Anne's Court. Henrietta learned that there were chamberlains,
ushers, pages, physicians, barbers, waiters, lacqueys, a dozen
cooks the chief of whom was French, pastry makers, pie makers,
scullions, officers in charge of the wine, officers in charge of
beer; and all these people had their assistants. There were the
court musicians: organist, numerous trumpeters and fiddlers,
singers and writers of songs and music; for the one field of
culture the Elector cared to explore was that of music. To see

the Electoral coach leave Hanover for the short trip to Herren-hausen, with its accompanying guardsmen, outriders and glittering escort was enough to warn Henrietta of the diffi-culties which lay before her.

Easy enough to remain on the fringe; but of what use was that?

She must choose carefully. She must select those who could help her obtain an audience with the Electress and somehow wheedle them into making the introduction. These Germans were great eaters and drinkers; and it was under the influence of food and drink that they would be most expansive.

She must give a dinner party, select her guests carefully, and choose the right moment to get the promise she so urgently required.

She talked it over with Henry. Not that he was much use, a hindrance rather. He had easy charming manners—it was those which had first delighted her and made her visualize a very different life from that to which he had brought her—but he was feckless and his chief preoccupation was how to get money to spend on drink. Still, he could be relied upon to play his part for an evening and he was, after all, the son of an Earl and a member of the great Howard family. She couldn't really do without him at this stage and if he did drink too much, it was very probable that their guests would too. Indeed, that was what she wanted, in order to extract that promise.

"It's a good idea," said Henry. "But how are you going to pay for the dinner party?"

She had counted her small store over and over again. It was inadequate. If she spent all she had she could provide the banquet ... and what then?

Yet it was necessary, she knew; and this was the moment. She knew that if she delayed and lost this opportunity it would mean waiting for another; and by the time that came it might be possible that they would become known as the poor Howards, deeply in debt ... hangers-on like so many more.

No, now was the time. Everything depended on the next few days.

And ... how to find the money?

Henry shrugged and yawned; he could see no way.

He's quite useless, she thought, putting on her cloak and going out into the streets.

\* \* \*

It was a crazy idea. As soon as it occurred to her she refused to consider it. Rather anything than that.

Nevertheless she paused before the window of a shop in one of the little streets; it was an expensive little shop and on a stand in the window was a solitary wig—a profusion of chestnut coloured curls.

She stared at those curls and at the inscription over the shop window. "Wig makers to the Electors of Hanover."

She turned away and walked a few paces but she came back again to look at the wig.

Then determinedly she opened the door and stepped down two steps into the shop.

A man came forward clasping his hands together, recognizing a lady of quality.

"Madam, I can be of assistance?"

"You are the wig maker?"

"Yes, Madam, at your service. Whatever you need we can provide."

She took off her hood and shook out her hair which she had left unpinned.

He stared at it almost reverently.

"It is good hair," she said. "Fine, yet abundant. Feel the texture."

He put out a hand gingerly.

"I suppose," she said, "that people come to you and offer to sell their hair. I am not the first one."

He was silent. Girls came to him—serving girls, working girls, sometimes a mother who had a baby to provide for ... but not ladies of quality.

"I want to know," said Henrietta clearly in her English-German, "whether you would consider buying my hair and whether it would be worth my while to sell it."

"I would consider buying it ... yes."

"Ah," she sighed. "You admit it is good hair and plenty of it."

He nodded and named a sum. Her heart leaped. It was considerable but she needed a considerable sum to entertain those who were going to open up the way for her.

"Not enough," she said, and started to pull up her hood. But he was fascinated by that hair; he was terrified that she would go straight to the rival wig maker in the town who would make it into such a wig that everyone would be transferring their custom to him. He had never seen hair of such a rich colour, such a texture which although fine was not too fine; he had rarely seen such rippling waves.

He could afford a little gamble. Moreover she was a lady and it was always well to be on the right side of the quality.

He put up his price but she seemed to hesitate.

He said: "I would take it from the level of the chin and I don't think we should argue about a thaler this way or that."

Henrietta hesitated once more; it was a great effort not to run from the shop; she felt that her entire future was being decided in this moment.

"Very well," she said, and seated herself in the chair he offered.

In a few moments, her shining hair lay on a table and she herself looked like a handsome boy—her hair clustering thickly about her neck like that of a page boy. It was not unbecoming, she comforted herself as the wig maker was counting out the thalers.

She hurried back to her lodging; there to begin preparations for the dinner party which was going to change her life.

\* \* \*

The Electress Sophia was delighted to meet Henry and Henrietta Howard. Certain friends of hers had dined with the couple in their lodgings in the town and had found them charming. They had just arrived from England and knowing how interesting the Electress found such people it was wondered whether she would graciously grant them an interview.

"I am always delighted to meet anyone from England," was the expected reply.

Sophia made Henrietta sit beside her and talk about England. Had Henrietta met the Queen? Yes, said Henrietta, for she had seen Anne from a distance and how would Sophia ever know that they had never exchanged a word.

"Tell me about her."

"I fear, Your Highness, that she is not long for this world. There are occasions when she has to be carried in her chair throughout the palace. The gout and dropsy will surely kill her soon for Her Majesty is a martyr to them."

"It grieves me to hear it," lied Sophia.

Henrietta had chosen the right subject when she enlarged on the infirmities of the Queen; as she listened Sophia saw herself arriving in state, being crowned Queen of England.

I should die happy, she thought, if I could die Queen of England.

How ironical that this great hope of a lifetime should come to her when she was so old she must surely herself be only a step or two from the grave. But not until I have been crowned Queen of England, she told herself firmly.

And what entertaining tales Henrietta had to tell of Court life in England. Sophia had heard most of it before but she never tired of hearing it again. Sarah Churchill, that virago, had been dismissed. Imagine it. The great Duke's wife. And he was in disgrace too. Mousy little Abigail Hill queened it over the queen. She was a wise one; she did not stamp and storm like Sarah. She had won the day with soothing hands that knew how to poultice aching limbs; she had never demanded that this man be given office, that man be put down. But she had had her way all the same. It was said that Robert Harley, Lord Oxford, who was her cousin and the Queen's chief adviser, owed his position to her, and that she was responsible for the downfall of the Marlboroughs.

"Fascinating! Fascinating!" murmured Sophia. "Now tell me about the people of England."

"They like to be amused. They like sport and laughter and hate to be serious. Your Highness would be interested in some of the lampoons that are written about events. The coffee houses are full of scribblers like Swift and Steele, and men such as Harley use them to write their lampoons and hold up to ridicule that which they wish to destroy."

"How I should love to be there!"

"Your Highness will soon be there. The poor Queen suffers so with her gout and dropsy. Her life is despaired of at least once a month."

"And tell me how much support is there for the King across the water?"

"Only that of the Catholics, Your Highness. Most of the people of England swear they will never have a Catholic on the throne; it was for that reason that James II was sent into exile."

"Then they are happily looking to us in Hanover?"

"Most happily, Your Highness."

Sophia was enjoying the company of this young woman from England who seemed to have such a grasp of affairs.

"You must come and see me again," she said. "Soon."

Henrietta replied promptly that she would present herself next day and every day until the Electress had time to see her.

She went away well pleased. She had achieved her purpose. It was easier than she had hoped. As for her hair, it would grow again, and the approving eyes of several men and the envying ones of women had assured her that short as it was, it was still admired; and in its unusual fashion attracted as much attention as when it had been coiled heavily about her head.

\*　　\*　　\*

The Electress came into the nursery to see her grandchildren. Fritzchen her favourite scrambled up on her knee and asked if she had brought him any cake or sweetmeat.

"You're a greedy boy, Fritzchen," she told him indulgently. "And where are your sisters?"

There were two of them now for two years after the birth of Anne little Amelia had appeared.

Anne, independent and self-important, had been known to exchange blows with Fritzchen; Amelia, a sturdy two-year-old, adored him. Fritzchen liked being adored and was very kind to his younger sister thus winning more adoration.

I hope, thought Sophia, he is not going to take after his father.

Hearing that her mother-in-law was in the nursery, Caroline came to see her and talk about the children.

"My dear Caroline," said Sophia affectionately. "You are looking very well."

She studied Caroline's figure; she certainly looked pregnant and by ordinary standards would soon be giving birth; but Caroline's pregnancies always seemed to last so long. It had certainly been so with the two elder children. What a satisfactory daughter-in-law she was, and how bored she must be with George Augustus; yet she never showed it. Clever Caroline. At least, thought Sophia, I had a clever man, even though he preferred his mistresses to me all through our married life. It wasn't quite so with George Augustus. Somehow he appeared to be in love with his wife even while he was unfaithful to her; and he had never set up a mistress to equal Clara von Platen who had had such influence with Ernest Augustus.

Yes, Caroline was a clever woman and she was glad George Augustus had had the good fortune to have her for his wife.

"I hope for a boy this time," said Caroline.

"Well, you've a whole lifetime before you. We're good breeders. Not like poor Queen Anne ... fortunately." Sophia could be frank with Caroline who was so sensible and was already sharing Sophia's ambitions, for after all if Sophia was Queen of England it was certain that Caroline would be also one day.

Sophia was off on her favourite topic. "Imagine all those pregnancies ... all those miscarriages! Seventeen, so I've heard. Poor soul! And then when she did rear one boy, to lose him just when she thought at last she had given the nation its heir."

Sophia could not hide the satisfied smile.

"It means everything in the world to you," said Caroline.

"I've said it once and I'll say it again. I shall only die content if I die Queen of Great Britain and Ireland."

"It seems certain that you will."

"I've heard disturbing rumours. Anne is unpredictable. She's so sentimental and suffers from her conscience, I was told. She

thinks that if she puts her half-brother on the throne her sins
will be forgiven."

"He's a Catholic. The English will never have him."

"There will be some who are ready to call him James III."

"Only the Catholics. And the English have already clearly
shown that they'll have none of them. What would have been
the point in turning James II from the throne if they were
going to put his son there?"

"Perhaps it wasn't so much the people who made him into
an exile as William of Orange. I remember him. He was half
Stuart but you would never have known it. He had none of the
grace nor the charm. I wish you could have known my mother.
She was Stuart . . . all Stuart. Orange was a man who knew
what he wanted and wouldn't rest until he'd got it. He wanted
the three crowns—England, Scotland and Ireland."

"And he won them. But the English would not have
accepted him if they hadn't wanted him. They'll never have a
Catholic. I think you will be Queen of England soon."

Young Fritzchen was listening intently, but Caroline knew
he did not understand what they were saying. He liked to
watch their lips moving. The little girls took their cue from
Fritzchen and were silent too.

"Have you been telling Great Grandmamma how you enjoyed the sugar cake she sent you, Fritzchen?" asked his mother.

Fritzchen nodded happily and hopefully.

"If you are good and learn your lessons you may have some
more," Sophia promised him. Then she turned to Caroline.
"There is an interesting woman from England whom I want
you to meet. Henrietta Howard. You'll know that the Norfolk
Howards are one of England's premier families. She's married
a third son and is a charming creature—pretty and intelligent.
Come to my apartments and meet her. I thought you might
have a place for her in your household."

Caroline promised; and that was how Henrietta achieved her
goal; she had not expected to get so far in such a short time. It
was a great honour to become one of the *dames du palais* in
the household of the Princess Caroline.

\* \* \*

Caroline liked Henrietta Howard and as a result Henrietta
was often in attendance. An excellent conversationalist she
was able to hide a certain lack of knowledge and could talk
with apparent ease on many subjects. She was even at ease
in the company of Leibniz who was writing a history of the
Princes of Brunswick which had been commissioned by the
Elector.

Henrietta had good reason to believe that she had shown
great foresight in selling her hair.

To the Princess Caroline's apartments came George Augustus, the devoted husband, always interested in his wife's affairs.
Henrietta noticed immediately how the Princess made certain
that proper deference was paid to him and she realized that if
she were to retain her place with the Princess, she must not
displease the Prince. With that skill at which she was an
expert, she conveyed her awe of the little man in such a way
that he was immediately aware of it. He was delighted that this
charming English woman should notice him.

At this time the biggest court scandal was that created by the
Countess von Platen and a young Englishman named James
Craggs, and because of the antagonism between the courts of
the Elector and his son it was discussed with gleeful malice in
the presence of George Augustus.

Since the Countess, the youngest and most beautiful of his
father's three mistresses, was deceiving him, this was considered
highly amusing; and as the young man concerned was newly
arrived from England, Henrietta was able to tell a story about
him which had not been heard before.

Thus she entertained the company.

"He's a Whig," she explained, "and he's ambitious like his
father. He has come to Hanover because he knows the Queen
cannot last forever and he wants to find favour here."

"So he thinks to find favour with my father by seducing his
mistress!" cried George Augustus.

"Why, Your Highness, I do not believe he seduced her; it
was she who seduced him."

This was the sort of remark which seemed witty and highly
entertaining to George Augustus. He looked afresh at the
handsome young woman. She was so different from the Han-

over beauties who all somehow contrived to look the same. It was the fashion at the moment to die the hair black; so everywhere one looked one saw black hair; scarlet cheeks were considered fashionable with the new black hair, so everyone had scarlet cheeks. But Henrietta was different. Her thick lustrous hair fell to her shoulders in a fashion all her own. If others tried to copy it they could not do so for they lacked Henrietta's shining locks, which were the colour of honey and glistened so delightfully in the sunlight. George Augustus was charmed by her appearance.

"Well," said George Augustus, "this Craggs looks like a man of experience."

"To be sure he is. He has come far ... through experience."

George Augustus laughed. "Perhaps, Madam, you knew him in England?"

"I have no acquaintance with him, Your Highness, but I knew of him. A connection of mine, the Duchess of Norfolk, employed his father. He was very good in the capacity in which she engaged him."

"And what capacity was that?" asked George Augustus, prepared to be amused.

"The Duchess was on terms of great friendship with the King. That was James II, Your Highnesses."

"I believe," said Caroline, "that many ladies were on terms of friendship with that King."

"He and his brother, King Charles ... were very friendly people."

Oh, she was amusing, thought George Augustus. She was witty. He looked at Caroline who seemed entertained too.

"This young Craggs' father was butler to the Duchess. He was very discreet in helping her in her negotiations with the King. Such servants are very necessary, as Your Highness knows, where such delicate operations are concerned."

"I know it well," replied George Augustus, fearful that she might have heard of his devotion to his wife and despise him for it. He was secretly more interested in Caroline than any other woman, but he had been wondering whether to be a faithful husband might not be a slur on his manhood. He was years younger than his father who had three mistresses. George Augustus would not like it to be thought that he was not exceedingly virile.

"He proved himself to be such a good intriguer that when the Duchess no longer required his services in that direction she recommended him to the Duke of Marlborough who found him very useful for a different kind of intrigue. He amassed a fortune and entered Parliament, being a very ambitious man. I should say his son is also ambitious!"

"He's a good looking man," commented George Augustus.

"Your Highness means he is good looking in his way. Tall, strong ... oh yes he is that, but he has the looks of a porter to me." She smiled admiringly at George Augustus. "One sees that there is no breeding there."

"Of course ... of course," said George Augustus. "Well, I wish the Countess well of him."

"She is bringing him to the notice of the Elector," Caroline pointed out. "I hear that he has been promised a good post if the Elector goes to England."

Henrietta lifted her hands prettily as though to say that, versed as she was in the ways of St. James's, the manners of Hanover were a mystery to her.

George Augustus watched her thoughtfully.

\*　　\*　　\*

When he left his wife's apartments he did not stop thinking of Caroline's new *dame du palais*.

She was amusing and witty; but at the same time modest. A very unusual combination; and she was beautiful.

He had been moderately content with life lately. He had a good wife of whom he was becoming fonder every year; they had a growing family—a boy, two girls and another child on the way; and they had years before them. He had distinguished himself on the battlefield. People could no longer laugh at him behind his back because he was below average height. He had proved himself to be a man.

He thought of his father; he thought often of his father and was always soured in doing so. George Lewis's great strength was that he would never care what people thought of him; George Augustus cared deeply. So George Lewis could have three mistresses as well as casual affairs and not care if one or all of the women were unfaithful to him; he wouldn't have cared if he gave up all his mistresses, which he would if he wanted to. George Lewis kept mistresses purely for the physical pleasure he received from them. What impression he was making had no effect at all. For instance he did not care that Platen was deceiving him with this Craggs fellow; he didn't care that Kielmansegge had been in and out of every bed in the court; the promiscuity of Platen and Kielmansegge meant no more to him than Schulemburg's fidelity.

But George Augustus never did anything without wondering what effect it was having on the spectators.

And now it occurred to him that they might be laughing at him because at the moment he had no mistress. He was not eager to have one. He liked Caroline; he liked family life; he was fond of the children, and Caroline was, and he assured himself always would be, the best woman in the world. But a man should have a mistress. If he did not his virility would be doubted.

"Why is he such a devoted husband?" people would ask. "Poor George Augustus, one woman is enough for him."

"One is not enough!" he said vehemently.

He had made up his mind. The pretty Englishwoman was amusing and she would not be domineering. His father was anxious that he should not become too popular with the English; it was for that reason that he had shown his geniality with every English visitor at the Court.

An English mistress. That would irritate his father and prove his own manhood.

He began to court Henrietta Howard; and as she had come to Hanover for advancement, what better opportunity could she have than friendship with one who could in time be a King of England. The courtship progressed with the utmost speed and satisfaction; and in a short time Henrietta Howard became the mistress of George Augustus.

\* \* \*

When Caroline heard of her husband's infidelity she was angry. She had befriended this English woman, had given her a place in her household, had done everything she could to help her and this was her reward.

She restrained herself from speaking to George Augustus but when she was alone with Sophia expressed her annoyance when Sophia gave her the opportunity by remarking that she looked out of humour.

"I have every reason to be," retorted Caroline. "That English woman Howard has become George Augustus's mistress."

Sophia nodded, but she did not look disgusted.

"You seem to think this is a matter for rejoicing."

"It should improve his English," Sophia reminded her.

Caroline looked at her mother-in-law in astonishment. "Is that all you have to say?"

"It is enough. If he is to be a King of England he must speak English. That is where his father is such a fool. He refuses to make an effort. I should be delighted to hear that he had added an Englishwoman to *his* seraglio. Still, George Augustus who speaks adequately already—although with the most atrocious accent—should very shortly improve."

Caroline did not speak and Sophia went on: "There is nothing like being in close contact with foreigners for learning their language. You my dear, should engage an Englishwoman to converse with you, for your accent is as bad as that of George Augustus."

"I really believe you are pleased that he has taken up with this Howard woman."

"My dear, do you still let these unimportant matters distress you? George Augustus admires you; I'll swear he loves you—as far as he is able to love anyone other than himself—more than anyone else. Do not irritate him. Accept this woman, show no rancour, and you will still continue to have all that you need. Why, I believe you will rule your husband more than I was ever able to rule mine, providing of course you do not allow your annoyance over these little irritations to show. You know George Augustus. You are ten times more clever. Don't forget it. Now what you must do is find someone to teach *you* English, so that he does not outstrip you."

Caroline was silent. Her mother-in-law was right, of course. So the Princess's response to her husband's infidelity was to engage a young woman who had been to England and spoke the language to converse with her daily.

And while George Augustus dallied with his new mistress learning English in the pleasantest way, Caroline struggled with conversations between Fraulein Brandshagen and herself, and learned to speak the language but alas, with a deplorable accent which was exactly like Fräulein Brandshagen's, for in spite of that long stay in England, the Fräulein had not been able to lose her German accent.

In due course her child was born—another daughter. They called her Caroline and George Augustus showed in a hundred ways that he was very satisfied with his wife.

As she lay in bed, her newly born child in her cradle nearby, Fritzchen, Anne and Amelia at her bedside, come to look with interest at the new addition to the family and with awe at their mother who had provided it, she knew that she should be reasonably content.

The future looked bright. She had caught Sophia's enthusiasm for the crown of England; for it could be hers, if she was wise.

She must never antagonize George Augustus. She must always remember the terrible example of Sophia Dorothea, the prisoner of Ahlden. George Augustus might, in certain circumstances, be as vindictive as his father. And one thing which could make him so would be if his manhood or self importance was doubted.

How right she had been to listen to Sophia. Let him have his Englishwoman; while she, Caroline, threw him a mistress as one threw a dog a bone, she would remain the woman he most admired in the world, the one he really loved. Love? There was of course only one person whom George Augustus could love and that was George Augustus. As long as she remembered that and never did anything to disturb his image of himself, she had a good chance of ruling him, and in due course, England. The first she must do in secret, of course, and he must be the last to suspect it; but there would be little secret about the second; and when she thought of being crowned Queen of

England she knew that she differed in this one way from Sophia Charlotte. The pomps and ceremonies of royalty would mean a great deal to her.

Therefore what was a little discretion now to win such glory?

So she appeared to be contented with her nursery, to look up to her husband, and take it as a wifely duty to accept his infidelities.

# The End of a Life and the Beginning of a Reign

SOPHIA was growing anxious. She had noticed lately that the arrivals from England had decreased in the last months and this was a bad sign. Fewer people were leaving the sinking ship—and there was no doubt that Anne was sinking ... fast. She could not live much longer; and she was growing more and more sentimental about her half-brother, talking of him continually, remembering the wrong she had helped her sister Mary and her brother-in-law William do to her father. Her great love was the Church—the English reformed Church—and this was the hope of Hanover. Yet news was brought that James had declared he would maintain the church of England. What if the dying woman, to expiate her conscience, believed this? Would the people prefer to keep the Stuarts than to bring in the Guelphs of Hanover?

Sophia could not rest. She pondered the matter night and day, talked of nothing else, and Caroline was her chief confidant. The more Caroline learned of England, the more she

longed to be there. She had grown to accept Sophia's valuation
and was as certain as she was that Hanover was like a little
country town compared with a great kingdom. She and Sophia
had fought to bring a little culture to Hanover but what up-
hill work it was! She had an idea from the visitors from that
country, how different it would be in England. Marlborough
had been dismissed from all his offices and he and his Duchess
were in exile now. They were waiting, it was said, for the
Queen to die; but there had been unpleasant rumours about
Marlborough, always a clever man where his own interests
were concerned, except when he married Sarah—the one occasion when he was prompted by his heart and not his head. And
look where that had led him! If Sarah had not quarrelled with
the Queen—and how easy it should have been not to—he
would have been in his old place now. But Marlborough, it
was said, was in secret correspondence with James, ready to
jump with whichever side was going to be victorious. One
should be wary of such men.

The Treaty of Utrecht had been signed and received with
joy in England by the people who were heartily sick of war;
but the fact that there was peace meant that the ties between
Hanover and England were slackened.

There were rumours that Bolingbroke and Ormonde were
rising in favour—and both these men were suspected of supporting the Jacobites—while Oxford was falling into dis-
favour; he had offended Lady Masham; he had appeared
drunk before the Queen; and it was said that he would soon be
obliged to relinquish his office. Anne was ready to be advised
and the nearer to death she came, the more ready was she to
sway towards the return of her brother.

It was intolerable. Sophia saw the dream of a lifetime re-
maining a dream. For once James was proclaimed James III of
England, she would never be the Queen. George Lewis was not
sufficiently attracted by the crown of England to fight for it.
Oaf that he was, he had no desire for a better way of life. He
was satisfied with Hanover.

She was becoming ill with anxiety; she slept little; she could
concentrate on nothing but the English succession. She would
walk in the gardens of Herrenhausen with Caroline and Leib-

niz—the two in whom more than any others she could confide her true feelings—and discuss the possibility of Anne's secretly sending for her half-brother and leaving the crown to him. All he would have to do was promise to maintain the Church of England—and how easy it was to give such promises!

"You'll be ill if you go on in this way," said Caroline.

"My dear, you do not seem to understand what this means. If James becomes King of England, we shall never be anything but Electors of Hanover. You will never be Queen of England. Don't you understand?"

"I do understand, of course."

"And that it could so easily happen?"

"That's true. But you can do no good by making yourself ill."

"George Lewis will do nothing. He has not even bothered to learn English—though he speaks French well enough. How could a man be so perverse! And this is my son. What help is he? If his father were alive how different it would be! But he isn't. And I have to think for us all ... while I have no power to act."

"So in the circumstances Your Highness should not disturb yourself so."

"My dear Caroline, you astonish me. The English throne is about to be lost. What can we do? I cannot remain here ... just waiting."

"There are evidently intrigues at the Court of England," said Caroline. "If you were there ..."

"If I were there!" echoed Sophia. "Of course. My dear, I knew you would have a wise suggestion to make. Of course I must be there."

"Your health ... ?"

"Nonsense. What I need to make me well and strong is the crown of England. I have told you often that I should die happy only if the words Queen of England Scotland and Ireland were engraved on my tomb."

"I pray you do not talk of dying," said Caroline with a shiver.

Sophia laughed. "Die. Why should I? You are right. I must go to England."

"The Queen has been against a visit from Hanover for so long," Leibniz pointed out.

"That's true, but everything is different now. She must understand that I should be there."

"She has a superstitious fear that to see any member of the house of Hanover in England would be an indication that she could not live long. It is hardly likely that she will feel differently now when even she must know that death is close."

"I must go to England," said Sophia.

And watching her Caroline was surprised that the old woman, who had always behaved with shrewd and calculating calmness, could over this one thing for which she cared more than anything else on earth, so betray her eagerness and become vulnerable.

She hoped that, however urgently she desired something, she would never betray it as Sophia was doing now.

\* \* \*

Caroline was summoned to the Electress's apartments, where she found the old woman in bed.

"A slight indisposition," said Sophia.

"The tension and excitement have caused it," added Caroline. "You could not think of making a journey to England in your condition."

"Perhaps you are right. I have left it too long. I should have been there by now. Sometimes I think that I should not go to England except as its Queen."

Caroline nodded.

"But that does not mean that Hanover should not be represented there. I should like to speak to you about that. You know whom I have in mind. George Augustus speaks English ... tolerably. He is popular with them, and he has always shown his approval of all things English. I have been thinking that he should go to England."

"Yes," said Caroline slowly. "I am sure you are right."

"George Lewis could not go ... nor does he want to. It would be the end of our hopes once they set eyes on his sullen face. Besides he doesn't speak a word of their language. Can you imagine that a man could be such a fool! He may be King of a country and doesn't bother to learn the language! No, George Augustus should go. Do you agree with me?"

"I do," said Caroline, her eyes shining. Let George Augustus go to England. Let him ingratiate himself with the English. Then when Queen Anne died . . . if Sophia became Queen and eventually George Lewis was King, it would be the Prince of Wales who would enjoy the popularity of his new country— not the King. Caroline was uncertain that they would ever get to England, but if they did, there would without a doubt be a feud between George Lewis and his son.

She must not forget that and must in fact begin working for the good of her husband—and therefore her own.

Yes, it was an excellent idea that George Augustus should go to England, to represent the House of Hanover at this important time.

*       *       *

George Lewis set his jaw firmly and faced his chief minister Bernstorff who had worked for him ever since, as chief minister to the Duke of Celle, he had conspired against his master for the sake of Hanover—at considerable profit, it was true. But he was too shrewd a minister to lose sight of, and on the death of the Duke of Celle, when Bernstorff could no longer work for Hanover at Celle, George Lewis had welcomed him to work for him openly.

"My son wants to go to England," he said. "And the English appear to be eager to have him there."

"Only the Whig faction, Your Highness. The Queen would not welcome him."

"He's not going, in any case."

"No, Your Highness?"

"Come, Bernstorff. You know my son. What will he be at do you think? Poisoning them against me before I get there . . . if I ever do. Certainly George Augustus shall not go."

"You are right as usual, Highness. He could do us a great deal of harm."

"Picture him, making himself pleasant. They might not see through him until it was too late. Go and tell him he can stop thinking about such a journey. We do not want *him* to represent Hanover."

"Your Highness would consider making the journey?"

"I do not consider it. I wish to stay in Hanover. My mother has a picture of England which she has had as long as I knew her. Some Valhalla, I fancy. I don't share her view. I've no wish to go to their island. They can keep it."

"Three Crowns, Your Highness. William of Orange thought they were worth making a bid for."

"He had a small kingdom."

Bernstorff spread his hands.

George Lewis grunted. His minister was right, of course, if the crowns of England, Scotland and Ireland came to Hanover, the power of the Guelphs would be greatly increased from a little German state to a great country.

George Lewis was not a deeply ambitious man. He did not want to be disturbed; he was happy enough in Hanover which he, following his father's rule, had strengthened and made rich; he governed judicially; here he lived with his own people; he did not like what he had seen of the English who came to Hanover, nor did they—and they made this quite clear—like him.

For some strange reason they accepted George Augustus, the little popinjay, the arrogant, quick-tempered, self-opinionated little man—which in case showed they hadn't much sense.

Was he going to allow George Augustus to go to England to ingratiate himself further? And to take with him that wife of his. She was a clever one, a sly one. George Lewis was not at all sure of her. She had ten times the brain of George Augustus and shrewdly she was with him in all he did.

No, George Augustus was not going to England.

\* \* \*

George Augustus kicked a stool across the room.

"I am not to go to England. He forbids it. I am a grown man, am I not? I have proved myself on the battlefield. And I think I have given proof of my manhood. But . . . I am not to go to England. Papa forbids it."

"He is jealous of your popularity," said Caroline quietly.

George Augustus stood still smiling. What a pleasant construction to put on this irritating matter! His father refused him not because he feared he might be incompetent but because he was jealous of him!

"That," continued Caroline, "is the reason why he will not allow you to go to England."

"He is such a crude boor. He will never be liked in England."

George Augustus was studying his reflection in the mirror seeing himself arriving in England, the crowds cheering. What a handsome man! Have you heard how he distinguished himself on the battle field? A favourite of the ladies ... but at the same time a good husband. His wife adores him, but of course, he being such a man, there are his mistresses. His wife forgives him? With such a man, such natural frailties are forgiven.

He could hear their cheers ringing in his ears. They had always liked him; and he had liked them. But his father wouldn't let him go.

George Lewis, the Elector, was jealous of his son. It was almost worth not going to England to know that. And Caroline had seen it.

He smiled at her. She was a good wife.

He went to her and taking her arm made her sit down beside him. He always felt happier sitting, when his lack of inches did not show.

"Well," he said, "I shall not go to England then. And that pleases you?"

"It pleases me to have you here in Hanover, yet I am sure it would have been good for you to go to England. When we get there ... if we ever do ... the strife between you and your father will continue. I want us to make sure that the English are on your side ... not on your father's."

He kissed her. She was a clever woman, as women went. He was fortunate to have such a wife ... and such a pleasant mistress as Henrietta Howard. Two women who adored him so much that they never made trouble. Henrietta was demure in the presence of Caroline, never betraying by a hint that she enjoyed the special favours of her husband; as for Caroline she continued to treat Henrietta as a friend; she knew of course of the intimacy between him and Henrietta; but she accepted a mistress as necessary to a man of his virility.

He was certain in that moment that he loved Caroline very much.

* * *

There was acute conflict between the Elector and his son; Sophia held conferences with George Augustus and Caroline in her apartments; the Elector was angry, chiefly with Caroline. He had always respected his mother and despised his son; but Caroline's turning against him angered him. He respected her mentality; he would have welcomed her as an ally; that she supported her husband he did not regard as a natural action but a foolish one.

The tension was rising. News came from England that Queen Anne was on the point of dying.

"It cannot be long now," said Sophia to Caroline.

They had settled in at Herrenhausen for the summer and Sophia was always happier there than anywhere else. She walked every day in the gardens, but she liked to have a companion with her and this was almost always Caroline.

The conversation was mainly about England; in fact Sophia showed her impatience if any other subject was mentioned. Caroline often attempted to turn the conversation because she was afraid that the excitement this matter of the throne of England roused in Sophia was not good for her. There were times when the old lady looked her age—she was eighty-four— and that was something she had never done before. She would grow breathless in her indignation and often Caroline had to urge her to sit down.

This irritated Sophia who on one occasion demanded to know whether Caroline thought she, not Anne, was on the point of death.

Anne, growing more and more feeble each day, grew also more and more aggravating. News came that she was continually praying for her half-brother, that she was favouring the Jacobites, even that she had written a document, which was to be produced after her death, to the effect that James was to inherit.

"George Augustus must go to England," said Sophia. "Oh, Caroline, he must. He must let them see that he will be a good Protestant. He should leave without delay. George Lewis is mad to prevent him. He is letting his jealousy overrule his common sense."

Caroline agreed that George Augustus must go and as they were discussing how they could bring George Lewis to his senses the courier arrived with letters from England.

The two ladies went into the palace where George Lewis was receiving the courier, and waited for a while in Sophia's apartment, but as George Lewis sent no message, they went along to George Lewis's apartment.

He looked surprised to see them and barely greeted them, but Sophia was far too anxious about the news from England to care.

"What news is there?" she demanded.

"There is a letter from Queen Anne," muttered George Lewis.

"From the Queen. What does she say?"

"She is annoyed because of these suggestions to send George Augustus to England. She doesn't want him."

"She doesn't want to see George Augustus!"

"Strange as you think it, she doesn't. In fact she hints that if any of our family set foot in England while she is alive she will alter the succession."

Sophia gasped. "I don't believe it."

George Lewis went to his table and picking up a document handed it to his mother.

She read it and grew pale. It was exactly as he had said. She was feeling faint and gripped the table to support herself. Nothing seemed safe and secure.

The throne which had seemed so near had begun to recede. So much depended on the whim of a woman who should have been dead long ago but who obstinately clung to life.

She could in a moment destroy all their hopes; and surely if they were to inherit the throne they should be in England now.

George Lewis said to her with more tenderness than he usually displayed: "Sit down. You look a little shaken."

She sat down, still holding the letter. She tried to read it through again, but the writing danced before her eyes.

George Lewis was watching her intently. She handed the letter to him.

"I felt a little unwell for a moment or two," she said. "I am all right now."

\*    \*    \*

Sophia sat in her apartments at Herrenhausen writing a letter to her niece, the Duchess of Orléans, the most notorious scandal-monger at the French Court. It was a habit of Sophia's to write to this niece whenever she was particularly disturbed and even though she realized that Elizabeth Charlotte was completely mischievous and what she wrote would be discussed freely at the French Court, she could never resist writing to her. The letters were a safety valve for one who had so often been forced to curb her true feelings.

She was smiling as she wrote, telling her niece how badly the Queen of England was behaving, first by being so long in dying, secondly by flirting with the idea of placating her conscience and naming her half-brother as her successor. And here she was, at Herrenhausen, when she should be at the Court of St. James. George Lewis was worse than usual—a crude German boor who had never tried to learn English and had no love for England, the country she hoped he would one day rule; followed by George Augustus, who really had *some* sense since he had managed to make friends with a number of English people and had married a very sensible wife whom Sophia was sure would guide him through any difficulties which lay ahead.

Something must happen soon. Queen Anne could not live for ever.

Caroline came to her apartments accompanied by one of Sophia's women, the Countess von Pickenbourg.

"I thought you might care to take a walk," said Caroline.

"Excellent idea," replied Sophia. "As you know full well I'm always ready for that. If people walked more then we would enjoy better health." She rose smiling. She would finish the letter later. "I have lived so long because I have walked every day in the fresh air ... never as a task, mind you, but always as a pleasure. Give me your arm, Caroline, my dear."

Caroline obeyed and the Countess stood on the other side of the Electress.

"Let us walk in the orangery," said Sophia. "I always enjoyed the orangery, and I think it is particularly beautiful on a summer's evening."

As they came into the orangery, Sophia began to talk, as usual of England.

"I should like to know what the people of England think of Anne's refusal to invite us. Surely they would wish to see us there."

"The Queen's health is even worse than usual, so I believe," replied Caroline. "But she has been on the point of death so many times."

"Poor soul!" sighed Sophia. "I am sorry for her. Hers has scarcely been a happy life. As a girl she was so delicate. Why, when her sister Mary was being married to Orange, she was on the point of death through the smallpox. She has faced death so many times that she must be prepared. How grateful *I* am for my good health. I hope death, when it comes for me, will snuff me out like a candle. That's the best way."

"I believe it to be the best way," agreed Caroline. "What a pity we cannot all choose our way of going. But the subject is a morbid one. If Marlborough were here he might be able to give us some news, although I confess I don't altogether trust Marlborough."

"There are very few one can trust, alas," said Sophia. "I am fortunate to have you here with me, my dear. I can talk openly to you of these matters which are of such importance to us all. I only wish I could feel so confident of everyone. These are difficult times ... and full of significance for our house. Once I am in England everything will be so different. How I long to be there!"

"It can't be long now," said Caroline.

"Perhaps Your Highness would care to sit a while," suggested the Countess.

"No, I prefer to walk. As I have often told you there is nothing so good for the health as walking. What a beautiful day it has been."

Sophia was silent suddenly for through the greenery she had caught a glimpse of George Lewis walking in the gardens with Schulemburg on one side and Kielmansegge on the other.

She sighed. "What a spectacle! Are there two more unattractive women at this Court. But I suppose when they first became his mistresses they were more attractive."

"The Elector is faithful, according to some standards," replied Caroline.

"I prefer the tall malken to the fat hen. The first is at least faithful to him. I don't understand my son. I never did since he was three years old. Sometimes I think he is a clever man, at others a fool."

"There are so many different sides to all of us," said Caroline; and she was thinking of Sophia—so discreet at Hanover, so reckless in her correspondence with Elizabeth Charlotte; so restrained in the matters concerning the Court of Hanover; so transparent in those concerning the Court of St. James's. A woman with a single purpose—to be Queen of England. Perhaps that was the explanation of every action.

"Take care," said Caroline, suddenly realizing that Sophia was growing very breathless. "You are going too fast."

"I daresay I am," replied Sophia.

"Your Highness," began the Countess and stopped for Sophia had swayed towards her. Between them the Countess and Caroline caught her.

"Help me to get her to a chair," said Caroline quickly; but even as she spoke she felt the Electress's body limp in her arms.

Tenderly they lowered her to the ground; she lay back, an odd pallor in her cheeks, her eyes turning glassy.

"Call for help ... quickly," cried Caroline; and the Countess ran out of the orangery into the grounds.

As Caroline knelt beside Sophia a terrible desolation came to her. "Can you ... speak to me ... " she whispered.

Sophia's glassy eyes were on her face ... fixed ... lifeless.

You must get well, thought Caroline. I can't lose you as well. ...

George Lewis had come into the orangery. Caroline was

aware of the startled faces of his two mistresses, but all that was admirable in George Lewis was uppermost on an occasion such as this.

Without showing the least sign of agitation he knelt beside his mother and felt her pulse. Then he sent one of the guards to bring him some *poudre d'or*. "Quickly," he said. "There may be time."

Caroline brought a cushion and placed it under Sophia's head.

"When did it happen?" asked George Lewis.

"Quite suddenly. We were walking and talking . . . and suddenly she fell."

George Lewis nodded and said no more and a few minutes later the guard returned with the *poudre d'or* which George Lewis forced into her mouth.

"It may revive her," said Caroline.

"If it is not too late," replied George Lewis, in a flat unemotional voice.

What was he thinking? wondered Caroline. How much did he feel for his mother? Did he recognize her virtues or had she been to him nothing but an interfering old woman? Whatever he felt George Lewis would not betray it.

The physician had arrived. Kneeling beside the Electress and looking from George Lewis to Caroline he said: "There is nothing we can do."

"So she's dead," said George Lewis, final, matter of fact.

"I fear so, Your Highness."

"It can't be so," began Caroline; but George Lewis ignored her.

"She should be carried into the palace," he said.

So the body of Sophia was carried into the palace which she had loved beyond all others. Queen Anne lived on, but Sophia, whose great ambition had been to succeed her, had been as she herself would have said 'snuffed out like a candle'.

\*   \*   \*

No one mourned Sophia as sincerely as Caroline. Not since the death of Sophia Charlotte had she felt so desolate. It was true that now she was married and had her own children; but the Electress had been like a mother to her and she had loved her dearly.

Now there was no one to share her liberal ideas, no one to whom she could turn for advice.

She was very melancholy but after a while she became philosophical. Nothing ever stood still. The Electress Sophia, like her daughter Sophia Charlotte, had taught Caroline invaluable lessons, and she would best preserve their memory by profiting from them.

Yet the gap left by Sophia's death was immeasurable. The children were too young to be of much help to her. George Augustus? She had long since learned that she could expect little from him. She must however be grateful to the Electress who had taught her how to govern without seeming to, how to win through secret diplomacy.

"I shall never forget," said Caroline. "Never."

\* \* \*

July was an uneasy month. Rumours came thick and fast from England. Queen Anne could not live much longer.

George Lewis shrugged his shoulders. He was not deeply concerned. He had no wish to go to England; Hanover was good enough for him.

"If the English showed any sign of not wanting mè," he said, "I would show them very clearly that I did not want them."

He had thought of being King of England at some future date; but Sophia's death had placed him in the direct line.

To go to England would be a great upheaval, and at fifty, if one were not an ambitious man, such disturbances were to be avoided.

"The English!" he said. "Bah! It is not long since they lopped the head off one King, and that King's son was sent into exile. What sort of people are they?"

If it had been her burning desire to be Queen of England, George Lewis's might be said to be to stay in Hanover.

During the first days of August James Craggs came riding breathlessly to Hanover; before even seeing his mistress, the

Countess von Platen, he presented himself to her protector, George Lewis.

"This really is the end, Your Highness," he assured him. "The Queen is dying. Indeed I am ready to stake my life she is already dead."

George Lewis looked at the young man—one whom he regarded as his own kind—bucolic and shrewd without any fancy manners; the fact that he was the lover of George Lewis's mistress was a further bond between them.

George Lewis thanked James Craggs and told him that he appreciated his loyalty and James went to his mistress and told her that soon they would all be in England.

George Lewis retired early and alone. It had come; he was sure of it. It would be an entirely new life. He would have to go to England—but he could postpone that; he would become ruler of a country of some standing in the world. Different, as his mother had often pointed out, from a little German state.

But, George Lewis promised himself, even though I may have to reside in England, I shall frequently visit Hanover. Hanover is my own country. I shall never forget that—nor shall the English.

He settled himself to sleep.

\*     \*     \*

George Lewis was aroused out of his sleep.

"What hour is it?" he demanded.

"Two o'clock, Your Highness."

"Then what is the meaning of this."

Before his servant could reply he was aware of a man at his bedside whom he recognized as Lord Clarendon Envoy Extraordinary from England.

He did not like Clarendon whom the Queen had sent to Hanover, because as first cousin to Anne he had worked entirely for the Queen, and George Lewis had always regarded him as a kind of spy. Moreover he knew that Clarendon had not been in favour of the Hanoverian succession and was at heart a Jacobite; so, having been awakened at two o'clock in the morning by a man whom he disliked, who had come to tell him something which he knew already, this disturbance did not give him great pleasure.

"Clarendon," he said, raising himself on his elbow. "What's this, Clarendon?"

"The Queen is dead, Sire. Long live George the First of England Scotland and Ireland."

George Lewis grunted.

"Your Majesty, I await your commands," said Clarendon.

"You'd better stay in Hanover till I leave," said George.

"Yes, Your Majesty. And for the moment?"

"Leave me," said George Lewis and settling down into his bed, promptly fell asleep.

Thus George Lewis, Elector of Hanover, had become George the First of England.

## Royal Arrival

IF the new King was not excited by the prospect of leaving
Hanover for England, everyone else at the Court was. Who
should accompany him? Who should stay behind? These were
the important questions of the hour.

In their apartments Caroline discussed the change of fortune
with George Augustus. They both now had a new and glorious
title: Prince and Princess of Wales. George Augustus was carried away by excitement. One day he would be the King of
England.

"George the Second," he murmured to himself.

All he had to do was wait for his father to die and the old
man was already past fifty.

He could scarcely wait to get to England. He discussed the
matter continually with Caroline, to whom he had grown
closer since the death of his grandmother and that, to him,
much more significant event, the death of Anne.

Caroline was a good wife and he had no regrets at having
married her. She had proved herself to be reliable in the past
and was doing the same now. Always she talked of *his* interests,

as a wife should; and since these were in direct opposition to those of his father, this made an intriguing subject.

"We should get to England as quickly as possible," she reminded him. "Your father's delay is nothing short of foolish. What will the English think of a King who holds their country in so little regard that he delays going immediately to accept the crown they are offering him? But I'm glad he is so stupid. It gives us an opportunity to show we are different."

George Augustus nodded. "We will show them how much more agreeable we are."

"Speaking English is a great advantage and yours has improved greatly in the last months."

A reference to Henrietta Howard but it was given genially and sensibly and accepted in the same manner.

"And yours is good. Just imagine! My father cannot speak a word. What a fool that man is."

"Yes, but let us be glad of his folly. When do you think we shall go to England? It will be wonderful. I picture us riding through the streets with little Fritzchen beside us and all the girls. The people will see that we can give them heirs. How much more we can give them than your father. They'll know about your mother...."

George Augustus's face darkened as it always did at the mention of his mother. "It's his own fault," he said. "He treated her badly and the people of England won't like him for it."

"They won't. And we shall be there with the children ... speaking in English, showing them how much we, at least, appreciate being in the country. There are glorious days ahead of us. And George Augustus, we shall always work together. We shall always be loyal to each other. Your father will regret the day he left himself without a wife."

George Augustus was content. He had been the wise one. His father had been the fool.

He would go off now to see his mistress, which he did regularly to the actual hour; he would tell her that he had the best wife in the world, and she would agree with him.

He was indeed a lucky man.

\*　　\*　　\*

George Augustus would have been dismayed if he could have heard the conversation between his father and chief minister Bernstorff.

"It'll be necessary to watch the Prince," Bernstorff was saying "His knowledge of English will be a great advantage to him, and you may be sure he will seize it."

"Perhaps it would be better to leave him in Hanover."

Bernstorff was thoughtful for a moment, then he said: "Who knows what harm he would do at home! Better perhaps to keep our eyes on him. In that case he should come with us. The English will want to see the Prince of Wales."

The King grunted. "Would I could send him to England and stay here."

"Fatal, Your Majesty. Fatal. The Jacobites would have James on the throne in no time. In any case we don't know what opposition we have to face when we get there."

"I know it. We've had them here swearing allegiance, but I wouldn't trust any one of them. They're all like Marlborough ready to turn their coats with a change of the wind."

"We must remember it, Sir, here in Hanover and more especially when we set foot in England. That is why I think that while we must take the Prince of Wales with us, we might leave the Princess to follow later."

George looked surprised and Bernstorff hurried on: "The Prince relies on her more than he realizes. She will have to follow. It will be expected. But let her come later. Don't have the Prince and his family there when you make your entry into the capital. All attention will be for them; they are young; they have children. It will detract from Your Majesty to have your son and his family there."

George never minded plain speaking if it seemed good sense to him. He did not want to go to England. He would delay as much as possible; but since he had to go he must do his best to make a success.

"She shall follow later," he said, dismissing the matter.

Bernstorff hesitated. "Was Your Majesty thinking of taking Madam Schulemburg with you?"

"I doubt she would agree to stay in Hanover if I went to England," said George unemotionally. Of all his mistresses he was most fond of Ermengarda Schulemburg; she had been with him so long; she was truly fond of him as, he was shrewd enough to know, none of the others were. She was like a wife and he could not imagine life without her.

"And Madam Kielmansegge?"

George shrugged his shoulders. It was hardly likely that if Schulemburg went with him Kielmansegge would agree to stay behind. He said so; and knowing the habit forming ways of his master, Bernstorff agreed that it might be necessary to take these two women to England.

Bernstorff's mouth hardened imperceptibly. The Countess von Platen was not going. He was going to have his revenge on her. She would be taught a lesson. She was a dabbler, therefore could menace his power. It was enough for Schulemburg to be as a wife to the King; Kielmansegge was content as long as she could have her lovers; but von Platen was an ambitious woman; she had secured the place of cofferer for her lover Craggs and when Bernstorff had heard about it second-hand, his fury was great. In the past those who sought favours had come to him. He would not tolerate a woman who sought to deprive him of his privileges.

"I think the Countess von Platen should remain in Hanover, Your Majesty," he said. "Two ladies ... and both of an age to have earned respectability ... that is well enough. But the Countess von Platen should remain in Hanover for I think if she accompanied you, the English might feel three was too much."

George considered this, fleetingly thinking of the beautiful countess hiding in his apartment, a robe over her naked body, coming to beg him to show her a little honour and not bestow all on those two ageing ladies. It had been a moment of rare amusement and he admired her shrewdness. She was a beautiful woman; but there would be many beautiful women in England—slightly different, as foreigners always were, but he liked a little variety now and then. Schulemburg and Kielmansegge to satisfy habit and a few new ladies to make a change.

All women were very much alike; and the Platen was inclined to meddle. He had never really liked meddlers.

So he nodded. It should be as Bernstorff suggested.

\* \* \*

When he went to Ermengarda's apartment he found her in tears. He was surprised for she rarely showed any emotion except a pleasant complacency in his company.

"What's wrong?" he asked.

She tried to smile but it was no use. "I'm afraid of what will happen to you," she told him.

"What should?"

"You are going to England as the King. Not very long ago they beheaded one of their Kings; they drove another away. If he had stayed he might have lost his head."

He looked at her with affection. She had even tried to learn a little history for his sake.

"They wouldn't dare kill me."

"They might try. Let us stay here in Hanover. What does it matter if you are a King or an Elector?"

She had always been concerned for him; it suddenly occurred to him that she was one of the few persons in his life who had a genuine affection for him.

"The king-killers are on my side," he said with a guffaw. "So you see there's nothing to fear."

"I shall come with you," she said.

"You're coming," he told her. He made a sign for her to disrobe; he never wasted time in words. She knew why he had come at this hour as he had been doing for years. He did not like habits to be broken.

Meekly she rose; her attraction had always been her meakness; she had been such a contrast to the haughty Sophia Dorothea. If Schulemburg had been his wife, he reflected briefly, they would have lived in harmony and would doubtless have a brood of children to show for their long relationship. She would ride with him in the state coach through the streets of London and the people would cheer him.

Now they would think of the wife who would have been with him if she were not a prisoner—his prisoner—in the castle of Ahlden.

Yes, Bernstorff was right. They couldn't have George

Augustus riding through the streets with Caroline and their
children. But that matter was settled and Ermengarda was
ready.

\*    \*    \*

Caroline was eagerly awaiting departure. This was the best
thing that could happen to make her forget the loss of Sophia.

She must think ahead to the future and never look back on
the past. That was the advice Sophia Charlotte would have
given her and how wise it was.

England! Land of promise! The Princess of Wales. It was a
fine sounding title; and in time, if all went well, she would be
Queen of England.

Her position would be a difficult one, for the very fact that
the King's wife would not be in England meant that she would
immediately be the first lady in the land. The people would
know she was their future Queen; they would seek her favour.
Her task would be to control George Augustus—oh, so discreetly—and on the day when he became King of England she
could be the real ruler of that country; a glorious, dazzling
prospect. She could scarcely wait to leave for England.

She sent for Leibniz to come to her apartments. He was one
of the few to whom she could talk frankly of her hopes. He had
taken the measure of George Augustus; he was well aware of
the absurd vanities of the little man; he knew that it would be
clever Caroline who would in time rule; and she needed the
help of clever men such as he was.

When he came to her, she said: "You should make ready to
leave for England, for you must certainly come with us. I shall
need your help in so many ways."

Leibniz looked sad. "Your Highness has not heard then?"

"Heard what?"

"That I am to remain in Hanover."

"But who gave such an order?"

"His Majesty . . . through Bernstorff."

"But you are my friend. It is not for them. . . ."

"To give orders, Highness? His Majesty has always given
orders in Hanover. It is only when he was not interested that
others were allowed to do so."

"But for what reason should you remain in Hanover?"

"To finish my task," he says. "I am here to write a history of the Princes of Brunswick and that is what I am to do."

"I shall speak to His Majesty myself," said Caroline.

Leibniz shook his head but Caroline was insistent.

She went straight to the King's apartments.

*     *     *

The King was surprised to see her. He glanced at her sullenly and noticed her handsome looks. The pox had dimmed them a little but she was still a beautiful woman; and with the colour in her face the slight ravages were scarcely discernible. Proud too. She would have to be watched. Bernstorff was right. She would be a meddler ... given the chance. She must therefore not be given the chance.

"I have come to speak to Your Majesty about Gottfried Leibniz."

"What?"

"He is too brilliant a man to leave behind in Hanover. We shall need him in England."

"I do not need him."

"But I ..." She stopped realizing that for the moment she had forgotten her own rule of conduct.

"He is completing his history, so he remains."

"He could do more useful work."

"So you do not think his work here is useful?"

"I do. But I think he should accompany me to England."

"No. He remains."

"Your Majesty, I ask you as a favour to me ..."

The King shook his head. "He remains," he said.

"But we shall be leaving very soon and I had arranged ..."

"You will not be leaving very soon."

"I don't understand."

"You are not leaving with the Prince and me. You will follow later."

This was a shattering blow, even worse than the knowledge that Leibniz would not be accompanying her.

"But I had thought ..."

"No. You will come later. You will be given instructions."

Indignation burned in her eyes. She hated him and all the will power she had built up during the years was necessary at that moment to hold back her hatred.

"You will follow us a month later. You and the little girls."

"But my son . . ."

"He is to stay in Hanover."

"Oh no!"

The King looked surprised. She was a woman indeed who would have to be watched.

He said quietly: "It would not be wise for the two heirs to the throne—your husband and your son—to be in England together . . . not until we have discovered what our reception will be. Frederick will stay behind to represent us."

"Little Fritzchen is only seven. Did Your Majesty remember?"

"I remember Frederick's age. He will stay here, and you will follow a month or so after we have arrived in England."

It was useless to argue, useless to plead. Leibniz would not be allowed to go to England; Fritzchen would stay behind in Hanover; and she would not go to England with the King and her husband; she would wait until she was sent for.

This was indeed a frustrating discovery.

*        *        *

Ermengarda Schulemburg was preparing to leave for England. The King had managed to soothe her fears and since he said it was safe she accepted that it was; her great charm was that she believed he was always right.

Madam Kielmansegge was in difficulties because, learning that she was preparing to depart, her creditors—and she owed vast sums—swooped on her from all directions and demanded that she settled their bills before she went. Frantically she begged the King to settle them but he told her he could do no such thing and she must deal with the matter herself. She was desperate, for there was no one who would help her if the King wouldn't. Ermengarda was smugly secure; she had incurred no debts; her greatest characteristic, next to her placidity, was her avariciousness and during the years she had managed to amass a considerable fortune. She was not inclined to dip into this to help a rival. No, Kielmansegge must fend for herself. The Countess von Platen, too, was an angry woman; but any who had known the King for any length of time must be aware that once he had declined to give assistance it was useless to beg for it.

He himself was not in a happy mood for as the time grew nearer for his departure the more he realized how deeply he loved Hanover and how loath he was to leave it for a country of which he knew little except that he disliked it.

He had been there once before as a young man—about thirty years ago—when it had been decided he should make a bid for the hand of the Princess Anne. That had been a most unsuccessful journey; the English had hated his German speech and German manners; the Princess had shown her dislike for him and he his for her. His stay had necessarily been brief; and afterwards he had come back to Hanover to be hustled into marriage with Sophia Dorothea.

He would have liked to delay—and he had to a certain extent—but he knew that it would be unwise to wait longer.

It was a month after the first news of Queen Anne's death had been brought to Hanover when George the First set out for England.

* * *

The King's yacht lay off Gravesend in a thick fog. It had been a rough crossing and everyone aboard was regretting it had ever been necessary to leave Hanover—most of all the King.

He felt irritable. Hanover had never looked so beautiful to him as it did on the day he had left it. He knew he would have been a fool to decline the crown of England for himself and his heirs, but how he wished it had never been necessary to claim it.

The sight of George Augustus added to his discontent. There he was, enjoying himself, rehearsing how he would show himself off to the English; he had already uttered the most flowery eulogies on his new country and the English, although sensible enough in some respects, were not shrewd enough to recognize the gross flattery. Before they had set foot in England

George Augustus was trying to rival his father, trying to turn any devotion they might feel towards him to his son.

It was a bitter thing when there was strife between families. His own father had taught him that and by God it was true.

The *Peregrine* had been a fine sight when it had set out from The Hague with its escort of twenty ships. It was a little less splendid certainly after the rough storm they had encountered—and now here at Gravesend was this accursed fog.

When shall I return to Hanover? wondered the King.

The mist was already lifting and they could go ashore. The sun broke through and it promised to be a glorious day.

The bells were chiming; the guns had begun to boom a welcome. The people of England wanted to show him that although they might not be glad he had come, they preferred him to Catholic James.

It was the eighteenth day of September in the year 1714. Hanover had come to England and this was the end of the House of Stuart. At least it was to be hoped this was so, for who could say what the man whom many called James III was preparing to do even now. George wondered how many of these men who were bowing before him, welcoming him to their island, swearing allegiance to him, would if the Stuart were victorious, turn to *him* with the same loyal greetings.

George had few illusions.

There was Marlborough, all smiles and friendliness: a great soldier but a dangerous politician. George was well aware that Marlborough like the majority of these men was not to be trusted.

He received them noncommittally—Marlborough, Ormonde, Oxford, Harcourt. They would discover that he was not a man to be led by the nose. He might not speak their language but they should soon become acquainted with his desires for all that.

The King noticed the gracious smiles of his son as the people called a welcome. It was George Augustus who secured most of the limelight.

He must be watched, thought George. He must be kept in his place.

Greenwich Palace was very grand but the King was home-sick for the Leine Schloss and Herrenhausen.

"Your Majesty," he was told. "If you would stand at the window with the Prince the people would be pleased."

He stood there—with George Augustus beside him. George Augustus was bowing, smiling, waving—most gracious, most affable. And the King saw that the people liked it, and that it was the Prince of Wales they cheered rather than the King.

\* \* \*

On the river craft of all kinds were assembled; crowds jostled each other in the streets; every window was occupied; people shouted to each other; and it was clear that London was in a festive mood. Sellers of pies and ballads called to the crowds to buy what they had to sell. The coffee and chocolate houses were full to overflowing; so were the taverns and even the very select mug houses. Under the brilliant painted signs—Mother Red Cap, The Merry Maidens, The Blue Cockade—knots of people gathered to talk excitedly of what the coming of a new King would mean.

There were the Jacobites who muttered darkly and whispered that this was an evil day for England; but these were few compared with the Protestants who were relieved that a new King had been chosen who would be true to the Reformed Church of England.

But even they talked of Germans. A pity, they thought, that the Stuarts had turned to Catholicism. How much more comfortable if King James's son across the water had never become a Papist; then they would never have been obliged to bring in the Germans.

But today King George was making his entry into London and whatever had happened to bring him here, whatever would be the result was not to be thought of today. For this was a holiday, a day of pleasure; and every apprentice in the capital, every milkmaid, every merchant and his wife were going to see that a good time was enjoyed.

The Jacobites were the only ones who had been hoping for a

dismal day. They would have preferred to see the rain teeming down in torrents or a cold wind to drive the people off the streets. But fate was on the side of the Guelphs that day; and the sun shone brilliantly. It was a glorious, golden September day.

Coaches emblazoned with arms led the procession from Greenwich and the spectators had an opportunity of seeing representatives of all the noble families of England.

There were exclamations and shouts as the coaches trundled by; and breathless with excitement the spectators waited for that which they had come to see—the royal coach.

And there it was—its glass glittering in the sun and on the front seat the Duke of Northumberland and Lord Dorset; and inside—the new King and his son the Prince of Wales.

"So that's the King!" There was a titter of dismay. He was not exactly what they had expected. A man past fifty on whom the royal robes did not hang very becomingly; he had a rather sour expression and it was quickly noticed that although he bowed his head in acknowledgement of their cheers and put his hand on his heart as he did so as a token of his determination to be their very good King, he did not smile.

Beside him was a much more pleasant personality: The Prince of Wales. There was a young man, not exactly handsome, but with a pleasant expression and manner. He seemed to enjoy wearing his magnificent robes, and his gracious smiles showed that he liked the people too. Now there was a man who seemed glad to be in England.

"God bless the Prince of Wales!" cried a voice in the crowd and others took it up.

The young man placed his hand on his heart and bowed.

"Don't do that," said the King sharply.

"But..."

"I said don't. It is for me to bow. You sit still and do nothing."

George Augustus's affable expression turned to one of hatred, but he quickly changed it knowing that he was watched.

"The Prince of Wales!" cried the crowd. He was delighted.

They liked him—not his father. This was triumph. They were accepting him as they never would his father. He wished Caroline were here to see him.

So he must not bow. Very well. He could do as much with a smile. They seemed to think so for they continued to shout for him.

The King noticed and his expression grew more grim.

I'm glad we came to England, thought George Augustus. England is the place for me.

He was already planning the Court he would have to rival that of his father; and the thought gave him much pleasure.

The royal coach passed on and in the cavalcade following it were the coaches in which rode the Hanoverian friends and servants whom the King had brought with him.

In one of these were two women—one very tall and thin, the other short and fat. They made a grotesque sight, the raddled cheeks of one painted scarlet, the purple ones of the other covered in white powder; the wig of one flaming red, the other jet black.

"Who are they?" was the cry; and the answer came promptly: "They are his mistresses."

This was the occasion for which they had been waiting. George had pleased them at last; he had given them something to laugh at and there was nothing they liked better.

"So that's how he likes them. What kind of man is this they have brought us from Germany?"

"Look at her. The Maypole, I mean ... not the Elephant! Though look at her too! Did you ever see the like?"

"Why did he bring those with him. Did he think we could not offer him better than that?"

The King's mistresses had their nicknames—the Maypole and the Elephant and because one was so tall and thin, the other so short and fat, they gave rise to ribaldry which went echoing through the crowds.

In the coffee houses the Jacobites reminded each other, and any who cared to listen, of the King's cruelty to his wife and how even at this time she was languishing in a prison to which he had confined her many years ago.

"This is the man you have brought here!" cried the Jacobite

speakers. "This man who hasn't learned how to speak our language or even to smile."

And even those who didn't care whether a Guelph or a a Stuart sat in the throne thought the new king was a sour looking fellow.

The guns of the Tower boomed out and the Lord Mayor and City Father greeted the King while the Recorder read his speech of welcome. Then—over London Bridge to St. Pauls where children had been assembled to chant "God Save the King", and flags were waved as the glass coach passed through the triumphal arches; the guns were booming and the bells from every church in London ringing.

Several people were already drunk on the wine which flowed from the fountains, and among the shouts of "God Save the King" could be heard a growl or two.

If the King heard them he gave no sign; he was merely thinking that he would be glad when the procession had passed through his capital city and had reached the comfort of St. James's Palace for then the nonsense would be over. His new subjects were a frivolous lot; he had gathered that much. They were shouting for him now, but they would be shouting for James if he were offered to them; anything for free wine and a day's holiday!

St. James's at last. He was glad it was over. Now for the banquet and more expressions of loyalty and then the comfort of bed.

George Augustus was flushed and triumphant; no doubts there as to his feelings for his new country! Bernstorff was right. He would have to be watched; and when his clever wife appeared even more so.

He listened to the loyal addresses; he presided over a meeting of his Council; and after that to bed.

In the streets the feasting continued. The lights of a hundred bonfires sent a glow into the sky; there was dancing and singing; there were brawls and lovemaking. A typical holiday for the people of the new King's capital who had always chosen any opportunity for making merry except in the days of the Puritans, since when they had been doubly merry to make up for those lost years.

"Long live King George!" sang the Protestants.

"Damn King George," sang the Jacobites.

And, in his new palace, alas many miles from Hanover which he knew now how much he loved, the new King of England serenely slept.

## God Save King George

FROM the deck of the ship which was carrying her to England Caroline had her first glimpse of the land which would be her home and of which, if all went as she hoped, she would be Queen.

She had few regrets for what she had left behind, having caught the Electress Sophia's enthusiasm for this land, compared with which, she fully believed, Hanover was a backward little state. True she had been unable to bring Leibniz but this was the land of Newton, Swift, Addison and Steele—and she would have an opportunity of meeting these men. Here they wrote their satires and their lampoons and through these they moulded public opinion and so had as great an influence on the conduct of the Kingdom as any ruler.

Of this land she would one day be Queen, unless the Jacobites arose and drove them away. The future seemed full of stimulating possibilities.

It was true that she had left two of her children behind. How sad and angry she had been to part from Fritzchen; the parting was so unnecessary. Why should a little boy of seven be separated from his parents because he must act as the representative of his grandfather and father! How typical of the new King of England to care nothing for the tender feelings between a mother and her son. She would not rest until she had brought Fritzchen to England. And then baby Caroline had become ill just as they were about to depart and it had been thought wise to leave her behind. She would follow soon, but still it was sad to part.

The little girls Anne and Amelia, five and three years old, now stood beside her, excitedly chattering as the land grew nearer and nearer. Anne pointed out the land to her little sister and told her what fun they were going to have in England; Amelia burst into tears now and then when she remembered Fritzchen, but Anne did not care. She was secretly pleased that he was left behind and there would be no one to strut and bully, and call attention to himself. She had explored the yacht *Mary* on which they were travelling; she had asked questions which had delighted the sailors; and she had shown great interest in the squadron of English men-of-war which had provided their escort.

And now land was in sight. The town of Margate was waiting to welcome them; and after the ten days journey from Hanover it was a pleasure to know that they were nearing the end of their destination.

As the *Mary* came into the town, crowds had gathered to catch a glimpse of the new Princess of Wales. The people of Margate, who were both fishermen and farmers, rarely enjoyed such excitement and were determined to make the most of it; and the appearance of the newcomers pleased them. The Princess was a stately, comely woman, inclined to be plump but they liked her none the less for that. She was gracious to them and seemed genuinely pleased with their welcome; as for the little girls, they were quite enchanting in their excitement. Here was a lady who would have many children and give the country frequent reasons to celebrate. Poor Queen Anne—good Queen though she was—had been disappointed again and again in her hopes and there had been little cause for rejoicing on her account.

The two little girls squealed their delight in a foreign

tongue, but that would soon be remedied, for England would be their home in future.

They did not stay in Margate for at Rochester the Prince of Wales was waiting to greet his family and it was desirable that the Prince and Princess meet as soon as possible.

So out of the town of Margate rode the Princess and her escort, bowing and smiling to the people with the little Princesses beside her in the carriage, unable to restrain their pleasure.

It was October and the Kent countryside, though not at its best, showed signs of its fertility. Caroline scarcely saw it; she was more interested in the people who had come to give a loyal greeting—a more exuberant people than those of Hanover. They sang and danced to welcome her and some threw flowers at her carriage.

There was no sign on that journey to Rochester that the English were not delighted to have the Guelphs in England although there was one whom some might call the King across the water.

And at Rochester George Augustus was waiting for her.

There in the sight of the crowds he embraced her; he lifted up the little girls and held them to his heart while the crowd cheered. How different was the dapper little Prince of Wales from his sour-faced father who had come riding into England accompanied by two grotesque mistresses, already known throughout the land as Elephant and Maypole; but here was the Prince with his affable smile, greeting his wife and children. And even those who had cried "Damn King George!" had a greeting for the Prince and Princess of Wales.

"It was too long to be parted from you," said George Augustus; and Caroline smiled her pleasure. "My one regret is that Fritzchen and Caroline are not with you."

"Caroline will soon follow."

His face darkened. "But Fritzchen will remain. By God, I'll never forgive him for this."

"Let us talk of it later." It was a gentle reminder that they were being watched, and she added hastily: "I see you have made a good impression."

He was smiling. "You will too." Then he presented the Dukes of Somerset and Argyle to her.

The next morning they began their progress to London and when they reached the capital the crowds lined the streets to see them. The Prince and Princess of Wales sitting side by side, hand in hand, smiling happily, and the little girls jumping up and down laughing with delight was a sight to please everyone.

The journey to St. James's was a triumph.

\* \* \*

Caroline was a success. Her majestic appearance combined with affability, her friendliness which went side by side with a royal manner, the fact that there was no Queen and she was the first lady in the land, the knowledge that the King had separated her from her son, all this made the English warm towards her. She spoke English—which the King could not, nor did he make any attempt to, a fact which displeased the English—and although she had a German accent which in itself was not pleasing, she peppered her speech with French and German words and had a quaint manner of expression which amused and therefore charmed.

Whenever she was present she was the centre of attraction. The King's friends noticed it. Madam Kielmansegge pointed it out to him. George wished he could have left the she-devil in Hanover with her son, but that would have been too much; the people would never have sanctioned his separating a husband and wife. He was sickened to see that young popinjay of a son of his strutting about, making himself popular, ogling the women; if he wanted a woman why not get on with it. That was not the way of George Augustus; he must always call attention to the fact that he was a sensual man—which, it was clear to his father, he was not, at least no more than any normal man. He loathed his son because he despised him; but he was beginning to realize that however much he deplored the presence of Caroline he could never despise her.

That woman has to be watched, King George repeatedly told himself.

\* \* \*

A week after Caroline arrived in England the Coronation took place. There had been scarcely time to prepare herself for this important event. She was a little piqued that she was not to play a major part in it and would not walk in the procession. Had there been a Queen of England she would have been there; here was yet another reminder of the fate of women who fell foul of their husbands. What, she wondered, was the captive of Ahlden thinking on this day? Would she know that her husband was being crowned King of England? Would she be thinking of how she might have walked by his side and as Queen of England shared in his coronation? On such an occasion what would be the thoughts of a Queen who was not a queen, a queen without a crown?

There was too much with which to occupy herself to spend time in hypothetical brooding on another woman's tragedy. She was too clever to make the mistakes of Sophia Dorothea; and George Augustus was not as ruthless as his father. Yet could he be if his vanity were hurt? She shrugged aside such thoughts. I shall take care ... the utmost care that I keep my place and when the day comes for me to walk beside *my* husband and receive the crown, I shall be there.

She sat before her mirror while her attendants bustled round her. She had had to select them rather hastily but as she had been importuned during the years at Hanover when so many seemed impatiently to be awaiting the death of Anne, the selections had not been quite so speedily completed as might appear.

Henrietta Howard had accompanied her and remained in attendance in spite of her relationship with George Augustus. She had little to complain of about that woman who always behaved with the utmost discretion and treated her with deference. As she had learned from the old Electress, it was wiser not to interfere with a husband's mistresses and if at the same time one could keep them under observation, so much the better.

Henrietta was at the moment trying to conceal her suspicions of Charlotte Clayton who had joined her as lady-in-waiting to Caroline. There was something about Charlotte which had immediately attracted Caroline and at the same time antagonized Henrietta. Caroline had taken Charlotte into her household because the Duchess of Marlborough had suggested she should, and Caroline, having met Charlotte, saw no reason why she should not be as useful as the forceful Duchess declared she would be.

Charlotte had come determined to please the Princess and place herself at the head of her women; and while she was wise enough to know she must never mention in her mistress's presence that she deplored being obliged to employ the Prince's mistress, when Caroline was not present she made her disapproval of Henrietta clear.

Caroline looking into her mirror, smiled from one to the other.

"That will be all," she said in her own quaint version of the English tongue. "After all I shall the ceremony only be watching." She lightly touched a curl which hung over her shoulder. It was a simple hairstyle but very becoming, and as the low cut of her dress showed the beginning of her magnificent bust, the effect was pleasing.

"All eyes will be on Your Highness," said Henrietta.

"And Your Highness need have no fear that you will not please," replied Charlotte. "The crowd in the Mall when you walked there with His Highness the Prince yesterday was remarkable."

"They vant most to see the King's son."

"But it was his Highness's wife who attracted all the attention," said Charlotte.

"You should not to His Highness tell this." Caroline spoke lightly, but it was a warning to Henrietta.

"The women are always eager to see a Princess's gowns and headdress," replied Henrietta with her usual tact.

Yes, thought Caroline, it's to be hoped she retains her hold on him, for no one could be less of a menace than she is. Her husband, who was a useless sort of fellow had become a gentleman usher to the King, a post George Augustus had been able to secure for him as a sop for his complaisant attitude towards his wife's relationship with the Prince of Wales. It was a matter which had been discreetly settled and was conducted with the utmost decorum.

Not many women would have behaved so modestly as Henrietta Howard. She, Caroline, must protect her, if need be, from Charlotte, who was so eager to serve her mistress that she might be over zealous.

"I look forward that I shall make the many pleasant promenades," said Caroline. "That vill be very goot."

"I heard it said that Your Highness will set the fashion for sauntering which King Charles II made so popular."

"It is goot, this promenade," said Caroline.

She turned her head for in another part of the room putting away the jewellery she had decided not to wear two of her young maids-of-honour were whispering together in the belief that she could not hear them.

They stopped immediately at her gesture and she smiled faintly. They were charming, Mary Bellenden and Molly Lepel, two of the prettiest creatures she had ever seen. In fact, if she had been asked to decide which was the more beautiful she could not have said.

Charlotte made a mental note to warn the girls that they must show more decorum if they wished to remain in the service of the Princess. The chief culprit she was sure would be Mary Bellenden for that girl had the most irrespressible spirits she had ever encountered. She was delighted no doubt to discover that she was one of the beauties of the court—and the attention she received was enough to turn anyone's head. As for Molly Lepel, she was lovely too, and it must be a matter of taste which of the two were preferred.

Charlotte went to the girls and told them that as soon as they had finished putting the jewellery away they had leave to retire. Henrietta watched Charlotte, restraining her slight annoyance. Did Charlotte think she might give orders in the Princess's apartment?

This little scene was interrupted by the entrance of the Prince of Wales who liked to come into his wife's apartments unceremoniously.

"Vy, my dear," he said. "You are ready." Like Caroline he insisted on talking in English since he had come to England and his accent was as German as Caroline's. "You are in good time. I haf not yet put on my robes."

"You should then," smiled Caroline. "*You* must not be late."

He sat down on a chair which Henrietta hastily put for him near his wife's dressing table. He was placed so that he could face her and the rest of the apartment as well.

His expansive smile took in the women. The wife with whom he was well content; the mistress who pleased him also. He felt life was good. He was about to see his father crowned King of England and his father was turned fifty. The day would not be far distant when he would be crowned King of England and Caroline his Queen. She was clever, but not too clever. It would never do for a Queen to be cleverer than her husband. He must watch that. His Caroline was inclined to be a bit of a scholar. And Henrietta, his mistress, was discreet, always ready, meekly flattering. It was a very good existence. If there was no such person as George I life would be very good indeed.

All the women were suitably impressed by his presence. The two girls who were closing the doors of the cupboard were glancing his way and about to curtsey before slipping discreetly away. What pretty creatures! thought George Augustus. I like these English.

"You haf not present to me these young ladies, my tear."

Caroline signed to the girls, who came forward, not shyly because they had been well versed in court manners, but with exactly the right amount of deference.

"Mrs. Molly Lepel, daughter of Brigadier General Nicholas Lepel," Caroline explained.

George Augustus nodded. Pretty creature. And a bold one too. He could see that in her eyes.

"And Mrs. Mary Bellenden, daughter of Lord Bellenden."

The girl curtseyed and raised her magnificent eyes to his face. She was a lively creature, that one; and until he had closely scrutinized her he had thought Molly Lepel must be the loveliest girl at court—now he was not so sure. No, the Bellenden girl was his fancy.

"It please me that you haf to the Princess's household *kommen*," he said. "I can see you both vill it decorate ... in a pretty vay."

"Your Highness is gracious," murmured Molly Lepel; and Mary Bellenden merely lowered her eyes and smiled.

"Vell," went on George Augustus, "you must serve the Princess vell. You vill find she is the best mistress in the vorld."

He turned his eyes to his wife; they were misty with emotion. Oh dear, thought Caroline, he is beginning to make plans for one of these girls—or perhaps both of them. Henrietta was alert too. Poor Henrietta, if she lost her position, her fortunes—and those of her complaisant husband—could change drastically.

"I am sure they vill me serve vell," said Caroline. She nodded dismissal to the girls and they retired. George Augustus's eyes were on them until they disappeared and then he continued to gaze at the door in a bemused fashion.

"They are pretty *filles*," said Caroline. "Not very *serieuse*, I am afraid. I must see they are told of the dangers that could come."

George Augustus looked at her a little sharply and she was immediately uneasy. Had she betrayed a criticism of his behaviour? That would be the quickest way to drive him to some indiscretion. Caroline had an uneasy vision of some pert young woman attempting to show insolence to the Princess of Wales because the Prince of Wales had made love to her.

Yes, she had betrayed that she had noticed his interest in the girls. They were both a little wary.

George Augustus looked at his wife, sitting there dressed for his father's coronation, a long curl hanging over her shoulders, at her dazzlingly white neck and the beginning of her magnificent bust.

His eyes rested there.

"You haf the finest bosom in the vorld, my love," he said.

At least, thought Caroline, he wishes to placate me.

She smiled. "I you vatch throughout the ceremony."

He bent forward and kissed the finest bosom in the world.

\*      \*      \*

Those who supported the House of Hanover had decided that the coronation must be the most splendid of its kind. The people must be reminded that this was not only the crowning of a King, it was the heralding of a new dynasty. On street corners, in coffee and chocolate houses, in riverside taverns, the Jacobites gathered. Who could say what might not happen on Coronation day. They hoped the wind would howl and the rain pour down, because sunshine could have such an effect on the spirits that the people would be ready to believe life was good while it shone. It was October the 20th, so surely unsettled weather was not impossible.

But the sun shone brilliantly; and the crowd was more eager for a day's pleasure than for the uncertain excitement of rioting. When the fountains flowed with wine, when there was an opportunity to dance and cheer at the procession as it passed, to see the fireworks, to get drunk and make love after dark, who wanted to gamble with death? What did it matter what King was on the throne as long as there were feast days and holidays for the people?

As soon as the Jacobites saw the sun steady in the sky, they knew that the coronation of George I was going to be a day of rejoicing.

In the streets the flower and orange girls, the pie men and the ballad sellers were already gathering, while pickpockets and confidence tricksters made their plans for a day which should provide a record harvest. On the pavements seedy men and women sat with their dice boxes inviting passers by to throw the dice with them and indulge in a little gamble. Already there was evidence of drunkenness. In the October Club the Jacobites had gathered to make gloomy comments on the prospects for the future and drink a secret toast to the King over the Water. On the river there were crafts of all description and from many of these came the sound of music.

Ladies and gentlemen of fashion made their appearance in the streets—the ladies in brilliant gowns, their hair piled high under their enormous hats, their skirts flounced, their waists incredibly small, their bosoms liberally exposed. Patches to show off a fine pair of eyes a luscious mouth or a straight little nose were much in evidence. And the men were every bit as colourful as the women, with their splendidly embroidered waistcoats, their three cornered hats and buckled shoes, their quizzing glasses and their snuff boxes.

The sun, the mood of the people, the gaiety of music and the laughter all had a depressing effect on the Jacobites.

Still, they consoled themselves, it won't last. These people who are cheering the German today will be calling for his blood in a few weeks' time.

Driving to Westminster in his state coach the King was wishing the day over. He had no taste for this sort of thing! He looked grimly out at his cheering subjects and found it hard to raise a smile. He could not much like these English and he, who had never believed himself to be a sentimental man, often thought longingly of Hanover.

To Westminster Hall in accordance with English tradition, where under the canopy of state he received the peers and court officials. A dreary ceremony and he was weary of the whole affair already. He accepted the sword and spurs while the regalia with the crown, chalice, paten and Bible were given to the lords and bishops, to be transported by them in the procession to the Abbey.

I'm a plain man, thought George, though I am a King. They want to crown me. Why can't they put the crown on my head and have done with it?

But no, there must be this ceremony. And there was George Augustus, very much enjoying himself in the rôle of Prince of Wales. George felt a twinge of annoyance to see that his son looked almost handsome in his crimson velvet state robes, edged with ermine. There he was, not forgetting to smile at the people, trying to win their support. Support! For what reason? So that he could have them on his side in any quarrel with his father. A fine son I've got, thought George bitterly. And only one. There could have been more, if his wife ... But that was a subject he refused to think of. He had one son who was a constant irritation to him and that was his misfortune. He was glad in any case that the wife of his had no place in the procession. Put them there, side by side, playing the ideally happy married couple, with the children beside them and all sympathy would have been for the Prince of Wales.

If they turned me out, he ruminated, I should go back to Hanover and that would be no bad thing.

It might well be. The cheers died on their lips when they looked at their king. There he was in the ceremonial robes worn by his predecessors—crimson velvet, with ermine lining, bordered with gold lace, a cap of the same crimson velvet trimmed with ermine encircled by gold and glittering with diamonds. He was dressed like a King, but he had no smiles for his subjects and he looked as if he was not so very pleased to be crowned their King.

There were whispers in the crowd. If German George did not want England, England did not want him.

Caroline watching from her canopied chair in the Abbey placed near the sacrarium was amazed at the almost sullen demeanour of the King. Could it really be true that he had no wish to be King of England? How different was George Augustus, who was sycophantish in his attitude towards his new country and could not show the people often enough how he admired them. King George was a fool, thought Caroline, unless of course he really did want to return to Hanover. How could he want to leave this great and exciting country for a little German principality? He had no ambition. She felt an excitement grip her. She had enough ambition for them all.

The Archbishop of Canterbury was saying in a voice which reverberated throughout the Abbey: "Sirs, I here present to you King George, the undoubted King of these realms. Wherefore all of you who are come this day to do your homage, are you willing to do the same?"

Caroline held her breath. The silence seemed to go on a long time, but was that only her imagination? How could they want this dour unattractive man who could not even speak their language?

But the cry rang out: "God Save King George."

The trumpeters were filling the abbey with the sounds of triumph.

## At the Court of St. James's

THE people had accepted their new royal family. They were amused by the love of walking which the Prince and Princess of Wales displayed; Caroline with her husband and sometimes the little girls could often be seen promenading in the Mall; now and then they even strolled all the way from St. James's to Kensington, surrounded by friends, courtiers and ladies of the Princess's household and followed by a crowd of spectators. This habit endeared them to the people who wanted to see their rulers; and the affable Prince and Princess were very much to their taste. Germans, yes, but at least they spoke some sort of English and the Prince had already made his admiration of his new country obvious.

"I haf not a drop of bloot in my veins vich is not English," declared the Prince. "This I am proud of. The English is the best, handsomest, the best shaped, the best natured and lovingest people in the world. And if anybody vish to make his court to me, he must tell me I am like an Englishman."

Such blatant flattery was irresistible.

Caroline was not far behind her husband. "As for me," she

contributed to this praise, "I vould as lief live on a dunghill as return to Hanover."

Such remarks were repeated in the crowd who cried: "Long live the Prince and Princess of Wales!" and were very intrigued to learn that the King and the Prince were not on good terms. Their royal family was going to provide some amusement with their family quarrels and it was a royal family's duty to amuse its subjects.

So they were pleased with the Prince of Wales if they did feel resentful towards the King.

On the Prince's birthday there was a ball and at this both Prince and Princess increased their popularity. The Princess with her magnificent bust decorously veiled but not enough to disguise its charms, a fair curl over her shoulder, danced very charmingly with the Prince in her low heeled shoes to make him look less short than he actually was. Her gown sparkled with gems and she was a gay and glittering figure.

The King was present, dour as usual, but even he brightened a little when in the company of women. He was making it clear that although he had brought Mesdames Schulemburg and Kielmansegge to England with him and they were secure in his affection and his habits—which he did not care to change—he could appreciate the charms of other ladies and he implied that although he was not exactly enamoured of the country of which he had found himself king, he certainly was of the women of that country.

He had already shown interest in Lady Cowper even though that lady had made it clear that she had no intention of sullying her virtuous reputation and he was roused from his lethargy by the sparkling conversation of the Duchess of Shrewsbury who had no such reputation to protect, having been Shrewsbury's mistress before he married her. Being Italian she could speak French much better than most of the English women and as the King used that language, which he spoke fluently and which was understood in England better than German, she had an advantage and she did not let this slip. The King was constantly at her house where he went, he said, to play sixpenny ombre; but both Schulemburg and Kielmansegge were a little uneasy.

After one of these visits the King asked the Princess of Wales to come to his apartments and when Caroline arrived, he said: "I want you to offer the Duchess of Shrewsbury a place in your household."

Caroline taken aback replied that there was no vacant place in her household.

"That is not true," replied the King. "You have not yet filled all posts, have you?"

"They are not in fact filled but I have so many applicants for them that I cannot consider any more."

"This is one you will now consider and appoint."

Anger was in Caroline's heart. She wanted to cry out: It is my household. I shall decide.

But she knew the folly of that. The dislike they felt for each other was turning to hatred and she must not forget that he held the power.

She bowed her head.

"You will send for the Duchess," said the King.

\*     \*     \*

In his longing for Hanover the King grew critical of everything English—except the women. The language he dismissed as gibberish; the food he could not stomach. These islanders turned up their noses at sausages and sauerkraut, while relishing oysters. He declared they were stale when they were served to him, although he had never tasted them in his life before. The climate was terrible, he said. "The climate is the most beautiful in the vorld!" said the Prince of Wales. In truth the climate was very little different from that of Hanover. "The people are noisy and undisciplined," said the King. "The people are full of a natural charm and gaiety," retorted the Prince of Wales.

It was small wonder that the people took the Prince and Princess to their hearts and disliked the King.

George was in no mood to admit he liked anything in his new country, but he could not disguise his love of music. This love was deep in his family and his fellow Hanoverians, and the musicians of his household were treated with greater respect than any other of his servants. Opera he had always delighted in and he often spoke lovingly of the opera house at Hanover, yet he would not admit that the entertainment London had to offer excelled that of his native town.

The play began to fascinate him. In London it had been an important feature of town life since the days of Charles II, who had loved the playhouse and most of all its actresses. There were excellent players and playwrights to please the enormous public who thronged each night to Drury Lane and Lincoln's Inn Fields and the King would have liked to be among them. He was not however going to show these people that the playhouses of London were a novelty to him and admit that they had nothing like them in Hanover. All the same he could not resist attending and the only way he could do this was to go incognito.

Even so, his heavy features might be sufficiently known for him to be recognized, so he would take a private box, remain hidden at the back of it and watch the players on the stage. He could not understand the words they spoke, but he enjoyed watching their antics and some of the women were very attractive.

But after a while this habit became known and the King could no longer hide his interest in the play. From thence he was often seen in the royal box and because of this he found some favour with actors, actresses and all those connected with the theatre, for many people would come to the theatre to see German George, as much as the play.

The King's lack of English was a drawback, so managers began to look for plays with the minimum of dialogue.

Caroline pointed out to her husband that the King had become less unpopular with the people by this playgoing habit.

"Perhaps," she said, "we should go more to the theatre."

George Augustus saw the point at once and the whole royal family took to visiting the theatre frequently.

There were more cheers, Caroline noticed with satisfaction, for the Prince of Wales than for the King.

He and Caroline would be bowing and smiling from their box and the King would be scowling from his and they could laugh at the jokes of the players while the King could not begin to understand them.

This rivalry was becoming a matter of great delight to the Prince and more and more irritating to the King.

It was noticed that at Betterton's *The Wanton Wife* the King ignored the Prince and Princess, never once looking their way while the Prince threw many a scornful look at the King's box. The audience was delighted. A feud in the royal family aroused interest, enabled them to take sides; and sentimental feeling was, of course, with the Prince and Princess who smiled on them so affectionately and loved all things English, rather than on sour-faced George who clearly would have preferred to go back to Hanover.

James Stuart could not have provided more entertainment; he would have had French mistresses instead of German ones and they may have been more attractive—in fact how could they have been less?—but there was a lot of fun to be had from the Elephant and the Maypole.

"Long live King George!" cried the theatre crowds. "Long live the Prince and Princess of Wales."

The King was thoughtful; he was fully aware of what was going on in the coffee houses. The Jacobite writers were sending out their lampoons and the supporters of the Stuart were drinking to the King across the water.

At a ball given in the Haymarket at which the royal family were present and to which, since it was a masked ball, all sorts of people could find a way in, the King in his mask, was approached by a woman. She was young and seemed attractive and George was never one to forego an adventure. He had to admit, of course, that he could not speak English and found to his pleasure that she could speak tolerable French.

She said: "It is sad for England since we have had Germans among us."

"You do not like them?" asked the King.

"Who could? They are so crude. They are not like us. I should be glad to see them turned away."

"You think they will be?"

"Without a doubt. We don't want German George here and many say he doesn't want to be here. Let him go back to Hanover and no harm done."

"It mightn't be a bad idea."

"Let us drink a health," said the woman; and taking his hand she led him to a buffet where she filled two glasses.

She lifted hers. "To King James III now across the water. May he soon be in his rightful place."

George looked into his glass and she went on: "Come! Why don't you drink? Drink to King James!"

"I drink with all my heart to the health of any unfortunate prince," said the King.

After that he was in no mood for possible seduction and he left early.

He was not liked by his new subjects. It was possible that he would be sent back to Hanover.

It would, he reflected, be rather pleasant to end his days there.

\* \* \*

George Augustus was watching his wife's maid of honour and Caroline was watching George Augustus. They were in church, for the King's advisers had pointed out that it was essential to show the people that the new dynasty was determined to support the Church of England.

The King knew, even in his most nostalgic moments, that he would be a fool to lose this kingdom. Even though he himself longed to go back to Hanover he must make the three crowns of England, Scotland and Ireland secure for his descendants. As far as George Augustus was concerned, he could go to hell for all he cared, but there was young Frederick now in Hanover who would in his turn be Prince of Wales and King.

Therefore to church went the King but the long sermons in a tongue he could not understand were a trial to him and he could not pretend they were otherwise. He slept through most of them, or if he couldn't sleep he would discuss state matters with whoever was next to him. The preacher had to accept that. Now he was asleep, a fact made obvious by his intermittent snores. The Prince however was alert, his eyes speculatively on lovely Mary Bellenden.

Caroline was wondering whether she had been wise to accumulate such a band of beauties and bring them into her household. Yes, she decided, better to have them under her surveillance, and Mrs. Clayton and Mrs. Howard would be excellent watchdogs—particularly Henrietta who had her own position to think of.

Margaret Meadows, the oldest of the girls was sitting up primly in her pew and giving side glances at the girls who, taking their cue from the King, showed no attention to the preacher—on this occasion the renowned Bishop Burnet. Mary Bellenden and Molly Lepel were whispering together. Fair and pretty Bridget Carteret, who was a niece of Lord Carteret, was doing her best to suppress her giggles which was more than Sophia Howe could manage. Every now and then the girl's choking laughter could be heard. Sophie was very frivolous. I should dismiss her, thought Caroline. But she was the grand-daughter of Prince Rupert—although on the wrong side of the blanket—who was a brother of the Electress Sophia, and such a close connection could not be ignored; but the girl would have to be spoken to.

Bishop Burnet had turned his scornful gaze from the snoring King to the giggling maids of honour and made it very clear that he was displeased with the House of Hanover. Queen Anne had been most devout in her attitude to the church; Queen Mary had been the same; it was true King James had been a Catholic and been dismissed for it; and King Charles had made comments during sermons, but at least they were witty. Bishop Burnet had implied that these were newcomers to England and if they wished to retain their popularity they must show due respect to the church.

He was right, of course, thought Caroline; but in fact her thoughts were more occupied with George Augustus's interest in Mary Bellenden than Bishop Burnet's criticism of her maids.

How far would Mary Bellenden seek to impose her will, she wondered. She was very very pretty and could no doubt have a great influence on George Augustus if she wished. She re-minded herself that she had been lucky so far.

The King gave a louder snore than usual which woke him up; he looked about him startled for a moment and then saw that the service was almost over, so yawning inelegantly he prepared to leave. The maids of honour—Sophia Howe still giggling—trooped out of their pews, and the royal party left the church for the palace.

\*   \*   \*

Bishop Burnet bowed to Caroline.

"I am grieved, Your Highness," he said, "to make this complaint to you, but it is no use taking it to His Majesty whose snoring through my sermons—and those of others—shows clearly that he has little respect for the conduct of his servants in church."

"For me too there is the grief," replied Caroline. "I too have these naughty girls seen."

"Your Highness will agree, I am sure that such behaviour cannot continue."

"I agree," replied Caroline.

"The Church is becoming nothing but a meeting place for the purpose of flirtation. It is full now of young men who come simply to gaze at the maids of honour and attempt to make their acquaintance. Your Highness will agree that that is not the purpose of the service."

"You are right, Bishop."

"It cannot go on."

"Do you vish that they stay away?"

"Stay away and imperil their souls, Your Highness? Those girls are half-way to perdition already. No, their pew should be boarded in and the board should be high enough to prevent their being seen by the young men."

"You mean ... put them in a *petit* ... box?"

"Your Highness might call it that. They must listen to the service but not be seen."

"Oh, it is ... *traurig*. They are so pretty."

"Your Highness we must not concern ourselves with their physical perfections but the welfare of their souls."

"Ah, yes, yes. There shall be this ... box, if you so say."

Dr. Burnet left the Princess satisfied with his interview. She was a good woman, a sensible woman; and he would not be displeased when the time came for her to mount the throne as Queen.

\*   \*   \*

The Prince had waylaid Mary Bellenden.

"You are von pretty *mädchen*," he told her.

She made a pert curtsey.

"I you like very much."

She took a few paces backwards and head on one side regarded him, slightly insolently, but she was so pretty that even so she was delightful.

"And you like me? That is vell, eh?"

"It is the duty of a good subject to honour the Prince of Wales," replied Mary demurely.

"So, you vill this duty do?"

"It depends how far this duty extends."

"Vat is dis?"

"Your Highness I am a virtuous young lady."

"Ah ... yes ... you are very pretty."

"So I am told, Your Highness. But I am constantly having to tell others how virtuous I am. They won't believe me. But I have to convince them. And it will be the same with your Highness, I fear."

"Vat is dis?"

But she had already made a sweeping curtsey and moved to the door; she smiled at him provocatively for one second before she disappeared.

"Got damn it," said the Prince.

* * *

There were wails of protests from the gay gallants of the court when they saw the boarded-up pew but this was something they could not blame on the Hanoverians. This was their own Bishop Burnet who had decided to hide the pretty creatures from sight. The whole object of going to church was spoilt; for it was small consolation to hear the giggles of Sophia Howe, always louder than the rest, behind the high wooden wall.

They didn't go to church to be bored by Bishop Burnet or any preacher; and the amusement the King had at first caused with his snores and loud conversation during sermon time had worn thin.

Soon the lampooners were busy.

*"Bishop Burnet perceived that the beautiful dames*
*Who flocked to the chapel of hilly St. James*
*On their lovers alone their kind looks did bestow,*
*And smiled not on him while he bellowed below."*

There followed more verses to explain what had happened
and these ended with:

*"The Princess by rude importunity pressed,*
*Though she laughed at his reasons, allowed his request;*
*And now Britain's nymphs in a Protestant reign*
*Are boxed up at prayers like virgins of Spain."*

The King read copies of the lampoon and saw for the first
time that these English could mock their own kind, if they
thought they deserved it, as readily as any stranger. He saw too
that they were no respecters of persons.

He felt a little warmer towards them and was more than
usually disturbed when reports of new Jacobite riots were
brought to him.

\*   \*   \*

His unpopularity increased with the passing of the months.
His two German mistresses were loathed by the people and
jeered at whenever their coaches were seen in the streets.
Schulemburg, who remained his first favourite, had proved
herself to be of a very avaricious disposition and was continually seeking to enlarge her fortunes. George knew this and
made no effort to stop her. The English, he said, were the most
grasping people he had ever met. He was constantly being
pestered by those about him for posts for this and that relation
or friend. Therefore he was sardonically amused that Ermengarda should get what she wanted from them.

She came to him one day in a state of some agitation. She
had been riding through the streets of London when the crowd
had stopped her carriage and shouted insults at her.

"They call me Maypole," she said.

"There's nothing new in that," replied George. "It's the
name they gave you when they first saw you."

For once Ermengarda could not be placated; her face under her red wig was sweating with indignation.

"I look from the window and I spoke to them in English," she explained. "I said this: 'Good pipple, why you abuse us? We come for all your goots.' And what do you think they shouted at me? 'Yes, damn you,' they cried, 'And for all our chattels too.' "

When George understood the meaning of this he laughed sardonically. They were a garrulous lot, his new subjects. They seemed in love with words; no wonder the lampooners were so effective.

He told Ermengarda that she must not take the matter to heart.

"For," he said gloomily, "we are here, and here we must try to stay."

"And you think they will not send us back to Hanover?" she asked, little lights of fear shooting up in her eyes. If they returned to Hanover what would happen to her plans for amassing future wealth. England was a great milch cow and her dear George Lewis, whom she had truly loved for so long that she was as a wife to him, would help her to the milking.

"I think some may try," said George, "but they won't succeed."

"No, we must stop them. It could never be that they should turn you out. Silly people. Do they not know you come for their good."

"And their chattels?" added George with a rare touch of humour.

\* \* \*

The King was thoughtful while being dressed by the only two servants whom he allowed into his bedchamber. This in itself was a complete disregard of royal etiquette for the ceremony of dressing the King had been one of the most important in the household and those courtiers who took part in it consequently of high standing. And that these two servants should be Turks was yet another insult to English custom.

Mustapha and Mahomet might be a pair of rogues, but they were no more avaricious than the fine ladies and gentlemen who surrounded him. He doubted they had ever learned the art of peculation as thoroughly as the great Duke of Marlborough a man whom George would never trust. Oh, he was friendly enough now and he had his uses, but there was a man who could turn his coat with more rapidity than most. George had heard that even while he accepted office with him he was in secret communication with James Stuart, just in case the Jacobites should succeed in bringing him back.

Life was very different here from in Hanover. There it had been far less complicated. There, although he had been Elector of a small community he had received more respect than he did as King of this great country. The Germans were by nature more disciplined than the English. He wished he were back.

These people had no respect for anyone. Only recently on the occasion of his birthday he had, because he had been told it was the custom, provided his Guards with new clothing. He was not a man who cared to waste money and naturally he had given the commission to the company which had given the cheapest estimate. It seemed that the shirts were much coarser than those previously supplied and as a result the Guards had marched through the City throwing off their jackets to show the quality of what the lampooners were soon calling "Hanoverian shirts".

That brought Marlborough to the King. One could not, said the Duke, afford to upset the soldiery. It was possible that a small affair like the cheap shirts could be the very spark to set off a mutiny.

Marlborough, George reflected cynically, must be of the opinion that the House of Hanover was in a stronger position than that of Stuart for he immediately ordered a double supply of shirts and jackets of the very best quality and added to it an extra donation of beer.

Such incidents made the King aware of the insecurity of his position.

Then again he enjoyed walking but he had no desire to be followed by a crowd who watched him and laughed and talked about him in a language he could not understand.

St. James's Park was beautiful but, in his opinion, spoilt by the people who crowded there and used it as their own. It belonged to the King. Why, he wanted to know, should not the King reserve it for his own special use?

He had talked of this to his Secretary of State, Lord Townsend, who had taken over that office on the dismissal of Bolingbroke, because the latter being a Jacobite naturally could not retain his position when George came to England.

"I want to know," George had said, "how much it would cost to shut up St. James's Park and keep it for my private use."

Townsend had hesitated only for a second and then replied; "It would cost you three crowns, Sire."

A witty remark such as these English loved—but very much to the point this one. And it brought home to him yet once more how very precariously he sat on the throne of England.

Mahomet was placing his wig on his head, and George looked at the reflection of the dark face close to that with the heavy sullen jaw which was his own.

Bolingbroke! he thought. There was a man who could make trouble. And it was not long ago that he had fled to France.

He was an ambitious man, that Bolingbroke; in the last reign he had aspired to lead the government. He had quarrelled with Harley and helped by that woman of devious character, Lady Masham, might have succeeded very well indeed if Anne had not died, or if he had been able to bring James Stuart to England. He was too confirmed a Jacobite to change coats with sufficient alacrity and naturally he was dismissed—but dismissal was not all he had to fear. Walpole had wanted to impeach him and impeached he would have been had he not taken action. He had known this so he had artfully assumed an indifference he was far from feeling.

"I shall devote myself to literature," he had declared; and had gone to the opera, where he had greeted all his friends and generally called attention to himself by making appointments to see them in the following weeks. But when he left the opera he had gone to his house, put on a large black wig, dressed himself as a valet and made for Dover; and once there he crossed to France.

It was obvious to whom he was now offering his services.

The throne was very shaky.

Well, thought George, if I lose it, I shall go back to Hanover.

Herrenhausen would be very beautiful now; it would be good to smell the sausages and sauerkraut cooking in the old kitchens of the Leine Schloss.

And yet...

Was he beginning to have a little affection for this adopted country? Scarcely affection. But he must think of the generation to come—the future Kings and Queens of England.

\* \* \*

Shortly afterwards on a bright September day Lord Townsend and the Duke of Marlborough called on the King.

Prince James Francis Edward Stuart had landed in Scotland and had been welcomed there as King James III of England Scotland and Ireland.

## *Rebellion*

ALARM spread through the capital. Civil war seemed imminent. There was no longer secret drinking in the cafés. The Jacobites were singing their songs in the open; in every tavern they were drinking their toasts to the King who would soon no longer be the King over the water but in his rightful place; in the streets fighting constantly broke out between Catholics and Protestants.

"Down with the Pretender!" cried the Protestants.

"Damn George!" responded the Jacobites. "Send the German back to Hanover."

News from Scotland filtered through, but none could be sure how much was rumour, how much was truth. James had already been crowned at Scone. James had not yet crossed the sea. James came with arms and men supplied by the French. James came with nothing but a few miserable followers.

Ormonde and Bolingbroke who had both fled from England on the accession of George were fighting to restore the fortunes of James—and their own. Toasts were drunk to "Job"—the combined initials of James and these two men. There was tension and rising excitement everywhere.

None was calmer than the King. Ermengarda wanted to go back to Hanover, but George just waved her aside. It was only in moments of panic that she would have dared to advise.

The Prince of Wales was in despair. He came to his wife and she had never seen him so perturbed.

"My father is von fool," he lamented. "These pipple do not him vant."

"It is not important for the pipple to him vant so much as it is for him to stay."

"The English pipple will have vat they vant and they vant this Stuart. There are riots in the Park this day. I vas nearby. I heard them shout: 'Damn George!' They cheer for James."

"It is von mob," replied Caroline scornfully.

"And two mob . . . and three mob. All over London there are these mob."

"Ve vill stand strong."

"And be sent back to Hanover?"

"God forbid."

"Ah, ve are of von mind, my Caroline. I fear . . . I fear very much."

"Let us take a valk. Let us valk in the Mall. Let us show this pipple that ve love them."

"And you think that vill make them love us?"

"I am sure of this," replied Caroline.

So he walked with her in the Park which his father had wanted to make private; and they chatted together and with their attendants; they showed no fear; they only expressed their affection towards the English people.

"I vould rather on a dunghill live," declared Caroline, "than go back to Hanover."

Even as she spoke the shouts of a Jacobite mob could be heard in the distance; but Caroline, smiling at her husband made no sign that she heard.

"At least," said the spectators, "these Germans have courage."

Caroline knew she was right to have suggested the walk in public.

As they returned to their rooms George Augustus was flushed and happy.

"It vas good this idea of mine ... to show ourselves, eh?"

Caroline was about to protest that the idea had been hers. She stopped herself in time and nodded.

"An excellent idea," she agreed.

\*    \*    \*

From her maids of honour Caroline learned what was going on in the streets outside the Palace. They were uneasy many of them, wondering, she knew, whether the end of the Hanoverian reign was in sight. Girls like Molly Lepel and Mary Bellenden chatted freely and in the highest of spirits. Caroline made no attempt to restrain them for she realized the importance of learning all she could.

"The Chevalier de St. George is very handsome!" sighed Mary Bellenden. "At least so I've heard."

"A trifle melancholy, I believe," whispered her companion.

"But women love him."

"They love all Stuarts. . . ."

"Different from . . ."

Suppressed laughter. Yes, different from the Guelphs, thought Caroline, who though none the less fond of women managed to be graceless in their manners towards them.

She called to the girls. "You speak of the Pretender," she said.

They admitted it, just a little defiantly, she thought. How many of those who now called themselves her friends, wondered Caroline, would support the Stuart if he were successful.

"I think of the battle of Oudenarde," she said.

"Oudenarde, Your Highness?"

'Yes. At this battle the Prince my husband is on the side of the English. The Pretender he fights for the French."

The girls did not answer.

"It is forgotten, you think?" asked Caroline. "I do not think so. The English are the most grateful pipples in the vorld. They do not forget their friends, I think."

"No, Your Highness," murmured Molly. "They don't forget these things."

Caroline nodded: and the girls noticed later how often she introduced Oudenarde into the conversation and the honours the Prince had won there. Others began remembering Oudenarde; and it was talked of at Court. And as what was discussed at Court spread to the streets it was soon remembered throughout the City how bravely the Prince had fought for the English at Oudenarde and that the man who now desired to be their King had fought against them.

\* \* \*

During the vital months that followed luck proved to be on the side of the Hanoverians.

Bolingbroke, exiled from England, and therefore joining with the Stuart cause, was appalled by the character of the man who would set out to capture a kingdom. There was no fire in him; he was a pessimist through and through; and although he had made elaborate plans, first for the capture of Scotland and then that of England, his natural melancholy always overcame his belief in his success.

"The time is not yet," Bolingbroke urged him. "A rebellion now would have little hope of success."

But James, at heart feeling certain of failure, yet wanted to make the attempt. Ever since the accession to the throne of England of the Hanoverian branch of the family, messengers had been going back and forth to Scotland. The Earl of Mar assured him that the whole of the Highlands were with him; there were riots in England—and in London the Jacobites were secretly drinking his health and awaiting the signal to rise against George and acclaim James III King.

Bolingbroke continued to advise. He had recently left England; he knew the temper of the people; they were Protestant at heart; a few riots in riverside taverns did not alter that. They liked the thrill of secretly plotting against the reigning monarch but did they want a civil war? Did they want to plunge themselves into bloodshed for the sake of replacing a German by a Frenchman—for his upbringing in France had made James that in their eyes? In the place of the Maypole and the Elephant there would be James's mistresses—French, elegant and beautiful. More pleasant to look at certainly than those German ladies, but were the English prepared to go to war for that?

James turned from Bolingbroke; he was not the man to listen to advice he did not want to take.

When Louis XIV had died they had lost their best friend, Bolingbroke pointed out.

James retorted that the French would always support him against the German, for one thing he was a Catholic and the German a Protestant. But Bolingbroke, who was unsure of the Duc d'Orléans, was acting as Regent for the little Louis XV, and continued in his belief that this was not the moment to make the attempt.

Meanwhile John Erskine, Earl of Mar, a man who at the accession of George had been prepared to throw in his fortunes with that King but had not been favourably received by him, was eager to set up the standard for James in Scotland and rally the clans to his help.

Even in this fate was against the Stuart, for when Mar, with a small company of sixty men, set up the flag pole an ornament fell from the top, and the suspicious Highlanders, looking at each other gravely, declared it was an ill omen. The Stuarts were notoriously unfortunate. This poor James's father had lost a crown; even his brother, the gay and charming Charles, had had to wander in penury on the Continent of Europe for years before he attained his; and one only had to mention the name of their ill-fated father to recall how he had lost his head.

No, the Stuarts' luck had not changed; and the incident with the flagstaff was certainly an omen.

Those who had watched the moving ceremony, even as they saluted the flag when it fluttered nobly in the breeze, crossed their fingers, and wives implored their husbands to wait a wee while and not become too embroiled in the Stuart cause until the German was sent back to where he belonged.

Even so Mar marched South, and nobles and their followers joined them; and the band of sixty who had watched the planting of the flagstaff had grown to five thousand when they came marching into Perth.

*      *      *

Now there was alarm at the Court. Mar and his followers were preparing to march south. In London some bold men and women were actually wearing the white cockade.

Ermengarda was in despair.

"You must leave at once," she told the King. "It is unsafe for you to stay here."

But George only told her to be quiet.

"These people chop off the heads of Kings they do not want."

"Only when they can't get rid of them in any other way. They know they only have to tell me I'm to go back to Hanover and I'll go."

"Let us not wait to be sent."

"You know nothing of these matters."

"I know I fear for your safety."

George regarded her with mild affection. Dear Ermengarda! They had been together for so many years and while she loved adding to her fortunes, at the same time she had a genuine affection for him. It must be so for she could gain more by staying in England than leaving it—and she was ready to leave this country and all those new treasures which she had accumulated, for the sake of his safety.

He would never discard her; in fact he did not see her as she was now—raddled and rouged, scraggy as an old hen, her enormous red wig with its luxuriant curls slightly askew on a head that was almost bald. He saw her as the beautiful young woman she had been when he had turned to her and found her character such that he wanted in a woman.

He allowed himself a rare moment of tenderness.

"We'll see it through," he said. "The worst that can happen will be that we're sent back to Hanover, and that does not seem such a bad idea to me."

Ermengarda replied that anything that put him in danger was the worst possible idea to her; but he knew best, she was well aware; and she was comforted.

And when she rode out and was recognized and jeered at, when she saw men and women wearing the white cockade, she said: "The King knows what is best. He will stay if he wants and go back if he wants."

But she hoped she would stay. She could not be homesick for Hanover when England offered unlimited opportunities for increasing her fortune—for although the King had first place in her heart, money ran him very close.

*       *       *

The Duke of Marlborough was with the King and George eyed the great soldier suspiciously. Here was a man who could have been a great bulwark ... if he could have been trusted. He was no longer in his prime and the years of exile from the Court of Queen Anne had taken more toll of him than all the exigencies of war.

But now he was offering his help and George, himself a soldier, could judge that it was good.

The situation was grave. Already five thousand men were in arms against them. Let them cross the Border, let them set up their standard in England and the Crown would be in very grave danger indeed. This must not become a civil war; it was to be nothing more than a rebellious rising; but it must not be forgotten how easily the first could become the second.

"And what will you do?" asked George.

"Muster all the men we can and send them north. We have eight thousand men only; if we send all these north and are troubled with risings in the south, we shall be defeated. We must immediately raise new regiments; we must send for Dutch troops; and we must set up a camp in the Park, complete with cannon to show the people of London what they can expect if these riots become really menacing. The Prince can be useful. He and the Princess have some popularity with the people which ... er ..."

The King looked at the Duke and scowled. "Which I have not?" he said gruffly.

"Your Majesty's lack of English is a great barrier, naturally."

"The Prince's is far from good, I gather."

"It exists, Your Majesty, and the accent is quaint. This amuses and you know how your subjects enjoy being amused."

"They'll never find me amusing them by aping their gibberish."

"No, Your Majesty, but the fact that the Prince has done so gives him a certain popularity. He will be with the troops in the Park; he will review them with Your Majesty and the Princess. And I think I should be with you. We will show that in adversity the royal family can stand together and that any little differences of opinion which may have existed are forgotten in the present danger."

The King grunted. He could see the wisdom of Marlborough's suggestion and being a soldier himself he knew that, however devious the Duke was, however unreliable, he must admire him as the greatest soldier living—perhaps the greatest who had ever lived.

Marlborough was in command of the situation. The camp was set up in the Park; the Habeas Corpus Act was suspended and the Riot Act was read on the smallest provocation.

The people began to realize that although there might be excitement in the streets there was also danger.

The Prince reviewed the troops in the Park. That he enjoyed very much. Beaming with pleasure he would strut among the soldiers, complimenting them always on their good appearance, their obvious bravery and above all for being English.

The King was often with him and always managed to curb any outward sign of his dislike; and when Dutch troops arrived in England, when certain Jacobites were arrested and sent to the Tower, when the Duke of Argyll, Commander of the King's Forces, marched to the Border, tension relaxed. It seemed that Hanoverian George was more firmly on the throne than many had believed possible.

\* \* \*

James arrived at Peterhead on a bleak December day which matched his mood.

He could not forget Bolingbroke's warnings and he was wishing that Bolingbroke had never come to France. For so often he had planned this invasion; he had talked of nothing else during the last years of Anne's reign; but in his heart there was a fatalism which made him believe that the throne of England would never be his. He had inherited many of his father's characteristics and had no power to win men to his side. Handsome as he was, possessed of the notorious Stuart charm, he had only to spend a little time in any company for it to doubt his success. He was melancholy by nature; he believed in failure rather than success.

In the circumstances it seemed strange that he should have embarked for Scotland; but he knew that once the Queen was dead an occasion would arise which would force him to take this action. His friend Louis XIV who fervently hoped, for the sake of Catholicism, that he would become King of England, had expected him to make a bid for his throne; and he had always implied that when the opportunity arose he would do so. It had come; Mar had set up his standard in Scotland and loyal friends were waiting for him.

In his small craft with only eight guns and six friends, in the uniform of French naval officers, his spirits did lift a little when he saw the land. Scotland should be particularly dear to all Stuarts; it was natural that he should land here and find loyal friends. It was anathema to good Scotsmen to see a German rule them when they had a good Stuart King living.

At Peterhead he was welcomed by a very small company but the welcome was warm; and keeping his identity secret he crossed Aberdeenshire to be met by the Earl of Mar, who welcomed him in the name of Scotland and for his services was awarded a dukedom.

"Your Majesty," said Mar, "if it pleases you we shall crown you James VIII of Scotland and III of England at Scone in January."

"That will give me pleasure if it comes to pass," murmured James.

"It shall be so, Your Majesty," Mar assured him.

\*     \*     \*

And so to the palace of Scone there to make a court for James III! This must be set up with all the pomp and ceremony of the Court at St. James's that there might be no doubt that this was indeed the palace of the King.

This was pleasant. James allowed himself to be treated as a King; he was gracious and charming. So different, it was said, from the crude George of Hanover.

There must be a ball and a banquet to celebrate the return of the King.

There was little money but that must be found somehow; all those who possessed jewels must give them to make a crown for the King and provide the money for the necessary celebrations.

And so while Mar and James celebrated his arrival in Scotland, while they busied themselves with plans for the coronation at Scone, Argyll was marching north with the Dutch troops who had now arrived in England.

\* \* \*

When James heard the news he shook his head sadly.

"We are lost," he said. "What hope against Argyll?"

"Argyll is a Scot, Your Majesty," pointed out Mar. "I have heard it said that he is delaying his advance in your cause, not that of the German."

"Nay," murmured James, "too many come against us. I shall at least not be surprised if I am unfortunate, for so have I been from the day of my birth. It was doubted then that I was the King's son; and shortly after my birth my father was driven from his throne. What luck can I expect now?"

"All fortunes have to change, Your Majesty."

"Not mine," he mourned. "Not mine."

The Highlanders were restive. They demanded of each other why they had been brought south. Why should there be this dismay because the enemy were approaching when they had gathered together to meet the enemy. And what of King James? Why did he not show himself? Why did he never mingle with his soldiers? And why when he was seen did he have the look of a man whose cause is hopeless?

There was only one answer to those questions: these things were so because the cause was hopeless.

James and his Council decided they must retreat in the face of the advancing army; and while this marched north, Mar and James made their arrangements for James to return to France.

So the great rebellion known as the 1715 was quashed almost before it started.

What could the Highlanders do when they heard that their

leader had left? There was no point in fighting without a cause.

They returned to the Highlands, there to hide until the '15 was forgotten.

Good luck, not skill, had given the victory to George I.

In London the streets returned to normal; the Jacobites drank their toasts in secret; the camp disappeared from Hyde Park; and the soldiers returned from the north.

Ermengarda settled down happily to discover more opportunities for amassing a fortune; George grunted and was not sure whether he was pleased or sorry. He still thought with deep nostalgia of Hanover. The Prince and Princess of Wales took their walks in the Mall with their band of attendants and friends, talking their German-French-English which never failed to amuse, telling everyone how much they admired England and the English.

They were secure. James would make no more attempts. They felt safer than even before. The attempt had been made and failed; it was as though the people had given their verdict.

But the scribblers were still busy and the rhyme which won the most acclaim at that time and which was repeated in every coffee house, tavern, or wherever men and women congregated, was John Byrom's:

> "God bless the King, God bless our Faith's Defender!
> God bless—no harm in blessing—the Pretender!
> But who Pretender is and who is King?
> God bless us all! That's quite another thing."

## The King's Departure

MARY BELLENDEN was leaning out of the window trying to see the last of a handsome man who had crossed the courtyard and was about to disappear through a door which led to the Prince's apartments.

As he waved and was gone, she sighed and turning sharply was aware of two of the maids of honour who had been watching her.

There could not have been two girls less alike than Margaret Meadows and Sophie Howe. Margaret had now folded her arms and was looking extremely disapproving while Sophie was giggling sympathetically.

"Such unbecoming conduct!" muttered Margaret.

"I see nothing unbecoming," retorted Mary.

"Of course you do not. You are accustomed to such manners that you believe them to be acceptable. It's more than I do."

"Really Margaret," protested Sophie. "Tell me what harm can they do by waving to each other from a window?"

"They've made an assignation no doubt."

"There's nothing wrong in *making* an assignation," pointed

out Sophie. "Of course it depends on what happens when they keep it." She began to laugh so hilariously that, thought Margaret, she could only be remembering her own indiscretions.

"Be silent both of you," commanded Mary, "I won't have you say such things about John."

"So it's John?" cried Sophie.

"Yes, it's John and he is an honourable gentleman and I don't want either of you to start a gossip about him. Do you understand?"

"Oh, we understand, we understand?" cried Sophie. "We understand our Mary is at last in love."

"Don't shout so," reprimanded Margaret. "I never saw such behaviour. And you, Sophie Howe, are the worst of the lot. As for you, Mary Bellenden, you should be careful. These men will talk of love until they get what they want and then . . ."

"'Tis true, Mary," agreed Sophie. "Oh, how they talk of love! And afterwards they laugh and tell their friends all about the submissive lady while they advise them to try *their* luck."

"You don't understand . . . either of you. You're too much of a prude, Margaret, and Sophie's too much of a flirt."

"And our dear Mary is . . . just as she should be?" laughed Sophie.

"I'm . . . serious."

"But is he?" laughed Sophie. "I could tell you a few things. In fact if you want to know anything about the most fascinating subject in the world come to Sophie."

"And what would that be?" demanded Margaret.

"Men!" laughed Sophie.

"If you know anything about them, Sophie Howe, it's all you do know," retorted Margaret.

"There's no need to know anything else, I do assure you, Margaret."

Mary listened to them dreamily. Colonel John Campbell was the handsomest man in the Prince's bedchamber; one day they would marry but for the present they must be content to wait for each other. Poor John had little money; and she, as one of the greatest beauties of the court, was expected to make a brilliant match. In fact everyone knew that the Prince had his eye on her. Not, thought Mary scornfully, that that will do him much good. She was not going to take the easy road to honours by becoming a Prince's—and later perhaps a King's—mistress.

In fact, thought Mary, she would be a fool to take any notice of the Prince's insinuations. He was not really very interested in any woman as a woman; his great desire was to prove his manhood and this he thought he could best do by implying that he was the insatiable lover.

How trivial, how foolish these vanities seemed when compared with the love she and John Campbell had for each other.

One day, John, she was thinking, we'll be married. Perhaps secretly at first ... but shall we care about that? John had told her about the great love of his hero the Duke of Marlborough for his Duchess; they had been married secretly in the days before he had become famous; and whatever might be said of the great Duke or his termagant of a Duchess, none doubted their affection for each other. Their love had endured through all their fame and their misfortunes.

"It shall be so with us," John had said.

He would be as great a soldier as Marlborough, she had replied, but she trusted she would never be such a quarrelsome woman as the Duchess.

She would never be anything but the most charming, the most beautiful woman in the world, he told her.

"You're one who has made up his mind," she had retorted, for the rival charms of herself and Molly Lepel were continuously sung in the court and there were continual arguments as to which of the two was the more beautiful.

"Be careful of the Prince," John had fearfully said; and she had laughingly assured him he had no need to warn her.

Sophie Howe was saying: "I told the man I could not pay him yet. I told him it should be payment enough for him to serve a maid of honour."

"If he complains to the Princess you will be reprimanded I can tell you."

"Oh Margaret, how tiresome *good* people can be! I tell you I owe such a lot that I dare not try to calculate how much. In fact when a bill is sent to me I hide it ... quickly."

"Which is just what I should expect of you. Don't forget you

ɪ*

were one of the chief offenders in church and it's due to you
that the maids have to be boarded up. You will be getting a
bad reputation, Sophie Howe. I'm surprised that Her Highness
keeps you in her service."

"She can hardly dismiss the granddaughter of Grandpapa
Prince Rupert ... even though there is a slight blot on the
family escutcheon."

"You are a frivolous creature and you'll come to a bad end
one day."

"Well I shall have lots of fun on the way there, you can be
sure. Oh how I wish I were rich! How I wish I had a nice kind
friend who would pay all my bills so that I need not be bothered to hide them."

"That's what we should all like," said Mary, coming out of
her day dream. "When I think of all I owe, I shudder."

"Goot day to you, ladies!" The door had been opened and
the Prince of Wales, accompanied by the Duke of Argyll, with
his brother Lord Islay, and a few of his gentlemen came into
the room.

The three girls immediately curtsied and the Prince smiled
benignly on them all, but his eyes rested on Mary Bellenden.

"And very pretty you look," he commented.

"Your Royal Highness is gracious," answered Margaret
Meadows.

"Always ready to be gracious to pretty young ladies."

His eyes were almost pleading but Mary refused to look at
him.

He rocked on his heels and put his hands into his pockets.
He brought out some coins which he jingled in his hands.

"Alvays ready to be gracious," he went on; and this time
Mary could not avoid his eye. "Very ready," he added.

She bowed her head.

"Your Highness would wish us to acquaint the Princess of
your presence?" she asked boldly.

"The Princess, yes. Ve are come to accompany her to the
theatre. You like the theatre?"

"Very much, Your Highness."

"It is goot."

Little eyes, alight with desire, implied that, like John Campbell, he thought Mary Bellenden the prettiest girl at Court; and it was fitting, surely, that the Prince should choose the prettiest to be his mistress.

"We must not detain Your Highnesses," said Mary.

And she hurried from the ante chamber to the Princess's apartment.

\*      \*      \*

Caroline enjoyed riding through the streets to Drury Lane. Since the rebellion she had become so popular—more so, she believed, than her husband; and she was secretly pleased that this should be so.

When the Prince became the King she would be Queen and she had no intention of being a background figure, she meant to choose the ministers who would serve them; and she was determined that everyone should realize the importance of the Queen, for, she often wondered, when George Augustus betrayed some foolish vanity, what would become of royalty if she did not take the lead. George Augustus was a fool; he must be to grow angry when he remembered how short he was, and keep a mistress like Henrietta Howard for whom he had no great fancy, merely because he wanted it to be known that he had a mistress. George Augustus was a fool; but his wife was a wise woman.

Therefore it was a pleasure to know that she was becoming known to these people and that they liked what they heard.

She was not only wiser than the Prince but than the King also, for George I cared nothing for his unpopularity which showed he was a fool. He clearly betrayed his preference for Hanover—and that was almost as great an offence in the eyes of the English as his refusal to speak their language. The Prince, though not unpopular like the King, missed opportunities—and the scribblers saw through him and did not hesitate to make their vitriolic pen portraits of him.

Caroline learned that the English enjoyed treating their rulers with derision, and decided she would give them no opportunity to treat her so if she could help it.

"Long live the Princess! Long live the Prince!"

She gazed at him uneasily. Did he notice that the cheers for the Princess were a little more prolonged than those for the Prince? She hoped not, or he would be angry with her. How well she was beginning to know this little husband of hers! That was all to the good. The more she understood, the easier it would be to handle him.

"They like us vell," he murmured; and he bowed graciously, his hand on his heart, to a young woman in the crowd.

"It gives me pleasure," said Caroline, "to see how you they like more than your father."

"Ah, they hate that old devil. And I love them for it."

George Augustus laughed happily and those watching said that the Prince and Princess were on the best possible terms, and they gave an extra cheer for the Princess, reminding each other how good she had been during the winter, which had been a hard one.

There was a special cheer from the boatmen who earned their living by ferrying along the river. They had much to be grateful for to the Princess of Wales who had helped them when they were starving.

They would remember the season just passed as that terrible winter when the Thames had been frozen over, when it had been possible to drive a horse and cart from bank to bank and roast an ox on the ice.

That would in future be known as The Winter of the Great Freeze and the Great Hardship, when it had not been possible to ply a waterman's trade. The Princess had concerned herself with their sufferings, had raised money for them. So there was many a poor waterman who would give a cheer for the good Princess every time her carriage rolled by.

There were others who remembered how she had pleaded for leniency towards those poor devils who had been caught up in the '15 rebellion. Not that her pleading had had much effect on sour old George. He didn't seem to want his English crown but he was pitiless enough with those who had tried to deprive him of it. They had seen the executions of Lord Derwentwater and Lord Kenmure. They had heard how the Countess of Nithsdale had implored the King for leniency towards her husband and of George's brutal rejection of that distracted lady.

They were still talking of Lord Nithsdale's miraculous escape from the Tower which was romantic and exciting enough to win the sympathy of even the staunchest Hanoverian. Nithsdale had been in the Tower, doomed to die, and his wife was unable to move the King with her entreaties. She was not only a brave woman but a determined one; she had taken a companion with her to the Tower, and while she had worn two cloaks her companion had worn two gowns; and in the condemned prisoner's cell they had hastily dressed Lord Nithsdale in the extra gown and cloak, had painted his face, drawn the hood over his head, and Lady Nithsdale and her husband had left the prison while the companion had remained behind.

Such a romantic story caught the imagination of all. The Nithsdales escaped to the Continent; even George realized that he could not punish the lady who had helped in the deception, for the mood of the people was not strong enough in his favour; and even though James had retreated to France that did not mean that the people loved George.

But while the Prince and Princess rode through the streets on their way to Drury Lane it was remembered that the Princess had pleaded with the King for leniency towards the prisoners of the '15, among them Lord Nithsdale; so the Princess's name was linked with the nobleman's escape, and the people liked her for it.

As for the Prince, he was not unpleasant. And his father hated him, which was in his favour.

So, decided the crowd, a special cheer for the Prince and Princess of Wales.

To Caroline the streets of London were always an exhilarating spectacle. The noise and colour were so different from anything she had known before coming to London. The shouting of the street vendors who pushed their way between the carriages of the great and the occasional Sedan chair, never failed to fascinate her. She could only be amused when some grinning pieman would catch her eye and shout: "Good hot pies. They warm the cockles of your heart." Her smile would be gracious, appreciating the joke; and the pieman would add his cheers to the rest. She had learned the art of being affable and dignified at the same time; something which neither the Prince nor King could achieve.

They had arrived at the theatre—Caroline in her tight-waisted dress, the bodice of which was cut low enough to give a liberal view of the "finest bosom in the world", her skirt a mass of flounces, jewels at her throat, on her arms and fingers; hair dressed in her favourite style with a curl over her shoulder—not high because that would have added inches and called attention to the fact that she was taller than the Prince. Her heels were low for the same reason.

Drury Lane! And the crowds closing in to have a closer look at the Prince and Princess.

"Who's King and who's Pretender?" cried a voice in the crowd.

"Silence! Three cheers for our Princess."

Still smiling Caroline threw a quick and uneasy glance at George Augustus. He had not noticed the omission, as smilingly he battled his way through the crowd which closed about him.

"Good pipple, I am happy to be here. You are the best pipple in the vorld."

Such blatant flattery, thought Caroline, yet spoken with a beaming sincerity which made it acceptable.

"Long live James III."

"Long live King George."

"Damn King George. Go back to Hanover."

There was loud and ribald laughter. One did not take too much notice of the shouts of an excited crowd.

The Prince and Princess were conducted to their box. They seated themselves in full view and Caroline bowed and smiled as she was greeted from the pit. The Prince beside her beamed.

"They love us, I think," he whispered.

The two guards had placed themselves in the shadows at the back of the box; and now that the Prince and Princess were in their places the curtain could go up.

Caroline's eyes were on the stage. The play was interesting; it was called *The Wonder, A Woman Who Keeps a Secret;* and it had been dedicated to the Prince, therefore there was a special reason for their presence. She was listening for some allusion to the Prince, perhaps some ridicule, for there was nothing that pleased them so much. The Prince was contented, laughing with the audience, letting them know how much he liked to be among them.

If we had had to go back to Hanover we should have been regretful for the rest of our lives, thought Caroline. Thank God that's over. They've accepted us. James will never make another attempt. He has had his chance and failed. We're safe.

Echoes from the crowd came back to her mind. "Who's the King and who's the Pretender?" That was nothing—merely a quotation from verses which had caught the people's fancy. "Long Live James III!" Oh, these people lived for excitement. One only had to ride through a London crowd to know that. They wanted to laugh and be amused; and one of the duties of royalty was to provide that amusement. They liked to think there was a king across the water; they liked the thought of conflict. But they did not want war; and because they were essentially lazy, they did not greatly care which king was on the throne . . . as long as they had their chance to make merry.

We are safe, safe! thought Caroline. This is our home for the rest of our lives. Soon Fritzchen must join us. She had been delighted when little Caroline had arrived in England but she longed for Fritzchen. After all he was her only son; he was their heir—after his father he would be King of England, yet because his sour old grandfather decreed that he should stay in Hanover, there he remained.

Why? she wanted to know. What use to keep him there? How could a boy of nine rule over even a place like Hanover? A figure-head? What nonsense! George I of England was still the Elector of Hanover; ruling over the Electorate was his business; and only the most insensitive of men would separate a boy of nine from his mother.

But then George I was insensitive. I could hate that man, thought Caroline.

But she must not show it, of course. She must still play the gentle game; she must still play the meek woman.

It would not always be so. One day . . .

One should not wish for another human being's death, of course. But she was ready now to be Queen of England.

George I was no longer young and when he died ... She smiled at the man beside her. He would be the next King of England and when he was she would be Queen. Queen Caroline, the real power in the land!

She was awaiting her time.

It happened without warning. First the loud report; then it was as though in the second or so of silence which followed that the whole of the theatre had become petrified. Silence ... not a sound. George Augustus beside her, his face ashen beneath his towering wig. The actors and actresses on the stage stood as though grouped in a tableau. Then the silence was broken when someone in the pit started to scream.

"Get him!" shouted a voice. "He's shot the Prince."

The cry was taken up all over the theatre.

Then Caroline was aware of the dead man in their box, and she knew that the bullet which had been intended for George Augustus had, by a miracle, missed him and buried itself in the body of one of the guards who were standing at the back of the box.

George Augustus was about to rise, but Caroline put out a hand and gripped his.

What was the mood of those people down there? Riots could be ignited by such an action as had just taken place. She and the Prince were trapped here in a theatre, easy prey for their enemies. One false mood and that could be the end of all hope, perhaps the end of life.

The manager had come into the box.

"Your Highnesses...." He stopped and stared in horror at the man on the floor.

"The Prince is safe," said Caroline.

"Your Highnesses...."

"Let the man be taken away.... Get him to a doctor...."

"He is dead, Your Highness."

"Then take him away."

"And Your Highnesses?"

"We will remain here. Let the play go on."

The manager was astounded. The Prince was looking at his wife. Even at such a time he resented her taking charge.

"Perhaps if you speak to the people they would listen,"

she said. "You could tell them that a man has been killed."

She looked down at the scene below. There was great confusion. The tableau on the stage had sprung to animation; the actors were climbing down into the pit; there were shouts and screams as people began rushing for the doors.

"There'll be a riot," said the manager.

The Prince stood up in his box.

"Good pipple," he shouted, "the trouble is over. A madman tried to shoot me. He has not done so . . . you see. We haf come here to see the play."

He was at his best, for no one had ever been able to call him a coward, and the thought that he had narrowly escaped death even stimulated him. This was what he always wanted to be: the centre of the scene, the hero of the occasion.

He stood there, waiting for silence. It came and all eyes were now on the royal box.

"The murderer is caught," he said. "And now there is the play. . . ."

A man was being hustled out of the theatre and attention was divided between the scuffle and the Prince in the box.

"It is a goot play, eh, my frients?"

There was a short silence during which Caroline felt anything might have happened.

Then the people below began to take their seats. The actors climbed back on to the stage and the play continued.

\* \* \*

The King walked in the gardens of Hampton Court discussing an exciting project. His ministers, Townsend, Walpole and Stanhope had never seen him so animated and Walpole was thinking that if the people of England could see him now and know the cause of his pleasure he would be less popular than ever.

"Now that all is orderly there is no need for me to be here. I can take a little respite. After all I have Hanover to consider. I must pay my brother a visit and see how he is faring."

Walpole and Townsend exchanged glances. If he went the affairs of the nation would be left in their hands, and what could please them better than that? In any case George had never meddled extensively. He was not sufficiently interested in his realm to want to govern it.

"I can see no reason why Your Majesty should not pay a visit to Hanover," said Walpole.

"And does Your Majesty intend that the Prince and Princess shall accompany you?"

George was thoughtful.

"The Prince should surely remain in England as Regent," suggested Stanhope.

"Regent!" cried the King. "Never shall this be. You know the Prince. He will be wearing the crown by the time I return."

The ministers were thoughtful. "It is the usual procedure, Your Majesty. The Prince is of age...."

"I care not. He shall not be Regent. The Prince is a fool."

"Then what does Your Majesty suggest?"

"I suggest that he is not Regent. That he has no power to govern."

"The people would think it strange."

"The people!" cried the King. "Why one of them tried to shoot him the other night."

"Proved to be a madman, Your Majesty. And the Prince's action in the theatre has made him very popular."

"What action?" growled the King.

"He was very calm; and they are saying that his behaviour—and that of the Princess—prevented a riot. He is very popular at the moment. And the Princess has been ever since she came."

"She is cleverer than he is. He is a fool; she is a she-devil."

The ministers looked uncomfortable; and the King for once was roused from his usual indifference.

"Oh yes, she must be watched. She is the clever one."

Walpole was inclined to agree. He would either have to be the friend or the enemy of the Princess of Wales if she became powerful. She would not, of course, while the King lived; but wise politicians planned ahead.

Already she had shown a desire to meddle in politics, and had hinted that she would like the post of Secretary of the Treasury for the husband of Mrs. Clayton, one of the women of her household for whom she had a great regard. Walpole had no intention of allowing her to have the post for her friend; in the first instance she must not be allowed to acquire the power which friends in high places would give her; for the second he wanted the post for his brother Horatio.

"The Princess is perhaps ambitious," suggested Walpole, "and too ambitious to be content with merely social activities. It may be that she will attempt..."

He stopped; Stanhope was giving him a warning look but he knew very well what he wanted to imply.

"Attempt what?" asked the King.

"Attempt to make a circle ... a little court ... apart from Your Majesty's. It is not the first time it has been done."

Angry lights shot up in the King's eyes. "She would not dare."

"Not openly perhaps, Your Majesty. But it would not be good to have a rival Court. The friendship with Argyll, for instance...."

"Dismiss Argyll."

There was silence. The King could scarcely order the Prince to part with a member of his own household. After all the Prince was adult, and heir to the throne; he had some say in the management of his own affairs.

"Dismiss Argyll," repeated the King. "I will send an order to the Prince at once. Well, why are you silent?"

Walpole said: "Your Majesty, I doubt the Prince will agree."

"He will agree or face my displeasure."

A quarrel in the royal family—an open one this time. What effect would that have? The King's ministers considered the effect on themselves. Townsend was telling himself that the King would not live for ever; and when the new King came to the throne he would be more inclined to favour those who had been with him before he took the crown rather than those who hurried to stand in line when he did. If this was going to be a quarrel between King and Prince, perhaps the far-seeing man would take his stand beside the Prince.

Stanhope and Townsend were silent and Walpole said: "Your Majesty will know how to deal with the Prince, and when Your Majesty is in Hanover..."

"I'll not make him Regent. The care of the realm will be left in the hands of my ministers."

Not an unsatisfactory arrangement, thought Walpole. It was in the hands of his ministers now, for George's heart was in Hanover and he did not seem to care much how this country was governed—as long as the Prince had no hand in it.

Family quarrels were bad for a royal family, but very often offered advantages to ministers.

\*    \*    \*

When Caroline heard that the King was going to Hanover she forgot her usual discretion. He would see little Fritzchen; and surely he would be made to understand how a mother felt about her only son.

She asked for an audience with the King which was grudgingly granted. George thought she should have kept away particularly in view of all the bother about Argyll.

When she came to him he dismissed his attendants and looked at her suspiciously. Oh yes, he thought, George Augustus may be a fool but this one isn't.

He waited in sullen silence for her to speak.

"Your Majesty is going to Hanover and will see your grandson. Will you please tell him how I miss him here, how I long to see him and hope that you will soon allow him to join his father, mother and the girls."

"Unsettling," said the King shaking his head.

"But he will come to England . . . in time."

"In time. Not yet."

"But he will be the heir to the throne. . . ."

George scowled. He did not like any reference to his death; one of the reasons for his great dislike of his son was because he was continually referred to as the next King, a title he could only take on his father's death.

"He has his duties in Hanover."

The mother took possession of the diplomatist, and Caroline cried out: "What duties can a little boy of nine have? It is cruel to keep him from his mother."

"You're hysterical."

"I am not." It was something of which she had never been accused; and it was undeserved. She was a natural mother crying out against an unnatural separation. "Like any mother I want my son."

"You are a Princess and know that Frederick has his duties."

"And how do you think he is growing up there ... without his family?"

"He has his guardians ... and his duties."

"You are hard."

George looked bored.

"You must listen to me."

He stared over her head. "There's nothing more to be said."

The colour in her cheeks hid the slight imperfections made by the smallpox; her auburn hair was simply dressed with a curl hanging on her shoulder. She was an attractive woman, with her magnificent bust accentuated by her small waist and her ample hips. She had a figure which George admired. In fact, had she not been his daughter-in-law ... But she was and there was no sense in involving himself. Not that she would allow herself to be involved.

All women are the same in the dark, thought George with a yawn.

"There is a great deal to be said," she replied. "I want my son to join his family. After all, he is my son."

"He's my grandson. He has his duties."

"I beg of you . . ."

"You waste your time."

"Have you no heart ... no feelings?"

"No."

"Can't you understand how a parent feels towards a child. . . ."

He yawned again, this time significantly. He understood very well how he felt towards his son. He despised the fellow; in fact there were times when if he were a more violent man he might have hated him.

"Frederick remains in Hanover," he said.

"I see it is no use appealing to you," she retorted; and for once her calm deserted her. She could not help it. She thought of the birth of Fritzchen and how happy she had been; what plans she had made for his future; and how, even when this monster had given the order that he was to remain in Hanover, she had not really believed he would stay there for more than a few months.

"He must learn to rule," said George.

"As you do?" she cried. "You do not rule! Your German friends rule ... Bernstorff, Bothmer and Robethon, helped by Townsend, Walpole and Stanhope. These are the men who rule England ... and you are content to let them do so. Yet Fritzchen with such an example before him must stay in Hanover to learn to rule. What do you think he is doing in Hanover ... learning to rule like his grandfather does?"

The King was astonished; so was Caroline.

In moments of stress, all one's restraint fell away.

"You get too excited," said the King.

"Your Majesty's pardon."

The King nodded his head and Caroline was dismissed.

She went slowly to her own apartments. What a fool I was! she thought. He'll hate me now. I've shown my true feelings.

There was no point in pretending to be a docile wife and daughter-in-law now she had shown her true feelings. She would come out in the open and if she could not have her son, at least she would have her separate court; she and George Augustus would have their own friends, men of influence; so there would be the court of the Prince of Wales as well as the King's. And the Prince of Wales's Court would be that to which all men of intellect would want to belong.

She would send for Leibniz. But the King would not allow him to come. Still, she would attempt to get him over. Perhaps if the King refused to let her have Fritzchen he would give her her old friend as a consolation. As if George would care about consolation!

Still, it was open warfare from now on.

George was thinking of her, which would have surprised her: "Damn fine woman. A pity she's that fool's wife. He can't appreciate her. If she wasn't ... Oh, well, all women are alike in the dark. She's a she-devil too. We'll have to watch her. George Augustus is nothing but a fool—but not that one."

\* \* \*

The whole Court was interested in the battle for Argyll.

"He shall be dismissed from the Prince's household," said the King.

"I only shall decide whom I keep in my household," said the Prince.

Caroline was beside her husband in this. "We will stand firm," she told him. "He must be shown that we demand some consideration."

Her petition that Leibniz be allowed to come to England was met by a blank refusal from the King.

"We don't want these intellectual men here. There are enough of them in England already. Besides he has work to do there."

Caroline was now firmly ranged against the King and this brought her closer to her husband. To quarrel with his father had always been a favourite pleasure of the Prince's and in the past it had been Caroline who restrained him. It was different now. She could not forgive George for separating her from Fritzchen in the first place and refusing Leibniz permission to come to England in the second.

"He cannot force you to dismiss Argyll," said Caroline. "All you have to do is stand firm. You have friends."

"Do you think they'll stand with us against the King?"

Caroline nodded.

"Who?"

"Mr. Prime Minister."

"Townsend!"

"He is playing for safety. He thinks of the time George II is on the throne."

Contemplating such a time always gave George Augustus the greatest pleasure.

"Ah, he is von clever man, this Townsend."

"And ve vill be clever too."

"I think I am, my tear."

She smiled at him. It would always be so. She must learn to

accept the fact that she was the one who made the decisions
and he was the one who thought they were his.

"Yes, of course you are. I think the King is very foolish. He
does not govern. He dreams of Hanover ven he has this great
country. He is *fou*."

"Let him be, Caroline. Let him be. All the better for me the
more *fou* he is, eh?"

"All the better," she agreed. "So we'll keep Argyll, just to
show him that if he keeps our son from us at least we can
choose our own servants."

"I vill this show him," cried the Prince.

\*        \*        \*

George felt more at ease discussing this family disagreement
with his German ministers than his English ones. He would
never be sure of the English; and he fancied his Prime Minister while not exactly supporting the Prince was trying hard
not to offend him. There were three whom he could trust:
Bernstorff, Bothmer and Robethon. His own countrymen on
whose loyalty he could rely.

Bernstorff had worked for his father when he was in the
employ of the Duke of Celle and it was largely due to him that
George's marriage with Sophia Dorothea had come about.
True, that marriage had been disastrous and George now
wished it had never taken place, but at the time it had been
the wish of George's father that it should, and it had been a
most advantageous match ... financially. That Sophia Dorothea was a harlot whom he had been forced to put away was no
fault of Bernstorff's. And when the Duke of Celle had died,
after keeping an eye on his affairs for the benefit of Hanover,
of course, it had seemed natural that Bernstorff should openly
serve the House of Hanover which had been his real master for
so many years. Bernstorff's fortunes were bound up in those of
George I; therefore he could be trusted.

Then there was Count Hans Caspar von Bothmer; he had
been very useful as George's ambassador at St. James's before
his accession and it was due to his efficiency and diplomacy
that George's arrival in England had come about so peacefully.
Now he was able to advise his master on foreign affairs.

Jean de Robethon was a quiet man. A Huguenot who had found refuge in the German court, he was ready to serve efficiently behind the scenes. He never sought the limelight, but he was aware of what an important part he played—and so was George.

To these three the King now turned in this quarrel with his son, for as he said he did not trust the English. They were out for gain. By God, he thought, I never knew such men for looking after their own pockets. He didn't trust them; while they bowed to him and swore allegiance they were weighing up how much longer he was likely to live and wondering how they could curry favour with the man who would be George II.

So now the King called his three German friends and advisers to his private chamber and there they were closeted to discuss the imminent journey to Hanover and the recalcitrance of the Prince of Wales.

"If he thinks he is going to play King while I'm away he's mistaken," said George.

"Depend upon it," replied Bernsorff, "he will make full use of his opportunities."

"He is a fool," said the King.

"The Princess is no fool," added Robethon.

"That's true enough. But they shall have no power."

"It will be necessary to take this before the Parliament," Bothmer suggested.

"Oh these English and their parliaments!" cried George.

"Of which Your Majesty is head," Bernstorff reminded him.

"We must act carefully," cautioned Robethon. "And one of us should remain behind to watch what is happening in Your Majesty's absence."

The King looked at his three friends; he saw the apprehension in their eyes for they were as homesick as he was and the longing to see Hanover again was great.

"It's true," he said.

Bernstorff he must have with him; Robethon was too useful a man to leave behind. As for Bothmer, he had been the ambassador at St. James's and was the diplomat who understood the ways of the English far better than the others. There could be no doubt who should be the one to remain and act as spy on the Prince of Wales.

They all knew it.

Bothmer said: "I should be the one to remain."

George nodded. That was all; but it was a recognition of a good servant. He was not a man to forget a friend any more than he would forgive an enemy—he could be as loyal as he was vindictive.

It was agreed then that Bothmer would remain.

"Your Majesty must insist on the dismissal of Argyll," said Bernstorff, for his ministers always respected the King's custom of not wasting time on a matter which had already been settled.

"It seems it is not so easy," replied George.

"There is a way," put in Robethon.

They were all looking at the clever one who worked in the shadows.

"Make a condition," said Robethon. "If the Prince does not please you in this matter of Argyll you recall your brother, the Duke of Osnabrück, to act as Regent."

George, taken aback, stared at his secretary and the other two caught their breath. They turned to the King to see his reception of the news.

"You think these English would allow that?"

"They will not have to. The Prince will give way to your wishes over Argyll."

"But to bring my brother here!" George was thinking of his youth when he, the eldest of a family of brothers was hated by them all because they were jealous of his inheritance. Bring Ernest Augustus to England! Let him act as Regent! He saw trouble there.

"You would never have to bring your brother here, Your Majesty. The very mention of his coming would so alarm the Prince that he would agree to do whatever you asked of him to prevent it. No, it is a threat merely. Let me see that it reaches his ears as a rumour—that is all. If it does not have the desired effect well then, we shall have to allow him to keep Argyll. But it is not good for Your Majesty to be flouted. We have

beaten off the Jacobites; we cannot allow the Prince to triumph over the King."

George grunted; then he slapped his thigh.

"All right," he said, "we'll try it. But I'd rather keep Argyll
in the Prince's service than have Ernest Augustus here."

"If Your Majesty will leave this little matter to me, I will see
that it reaches the Prince's ear ... unofficially."

\*      \*      \*

The Prince stalked up and down his apartment, his eyes
bulging with rage while Caroline did her best to calm him.

"And you think ve can be calm! This is an outrage. Bring
my uncle to England! Vat vill the people think? That I ... the
Prince ... am not capable enough to have the charge of this
country?"

"He vill not bring your uncle here."

"But this is vat I hear. I hear they are vorking out their
plans. He ... and his Germans! The English vill not haf it.
They vill vant their Prince."

"Of course. This is a threat ... it is no more."

"But I tell you this: they are planning it. Bernstorff that
man ... I do not trust. I tell you the English vill not have."

"Of course they vill not have. They vill say 'Ve vill haf the
Prince. Ve love the Prince. He is von brave man.' They vill
remember how you acted in the theatre."

George Augustus's face lightened at the memory. "No." he
said, "the people vill not haf."

"But," went on Caroline, "the King may bring his brother
here. Ve cannot say vat the King vill do."

George Augustus stamped. "I vill not haf it."

"In time," said Caroline, "ve haf our own court ... our own
friends. It is not yet. So far ve cannot be sure. So it is better
to ..."

George Augustus was staring at her.

"I do not think Argyll is vorth ve should make such trouble
for ourselves."

"You mean ... ve give vay!"

"It is sometimes better to ... at the beginning, as you tell
me."

He had not told her but he was ready to believe he had and it was the way to make him accept the idea. Caroline saw clearly that they could bring great trouble on themselves by clinging to a principle. What mattered now was that the Prince should have power when his father was away. That would give them the opportunity they needed to build up a court, to seek friends and supporters. It would be George Augustus's rehearsal for that day when he was in fact King of England.

He was hesitating.

She went to him and slipped her arm through his. He liked these little displays of affection between them.

"You vill be von great ruler," she said, "People do not understand this until you have had this chance to show them. This vill give you the chance. Many are already on your side. They do not like the King. He does not like them and makes no pains to hide this. They do not like. But you will be their hero. You will show them how much better ruler you are. Then if the King tries to rule you ... he vill not be able to because the people vill be vith you ... and it is at the last the people who decide who shall be their Kings."

He looked at his wife, but he was not seeing her. He saw himself riding through the streets of London, acclaimed by the people. It was true he was more charming than his father. Who could be less? The people cheered him in the streets. He was almost English already and his father would never be.

"Your father must not bring your uncle here," said Caroline. "Ven the King goes to Hanover you must be Regent."

"It's true," he said, "Nothing must stop that."

"Nothing," she agreed. "Not even Argyll."

"Then ..." he began.

"You must go to your father. You must say you vish to please him. This you must say."

"I hate to do it."

"This I know. But as you say it must be done. If you say to the King: 'I vill give up everything to please you and live in amity with you. I vill as you vish part with the Duke of Argyll, then he can haf no excuse. The Regency vill be yours. It is a small price to pay for the Regency'"

He stood still scowling, his heavy jaw thrust out giving him the sullen look which made him resemble his father.

"It vill be goot," she said. "You vill be as King. Who knows he may be away ... months ... a year or more. Then you vill show this pipples how much better king you vill be. Your court vill you have. Nothing vill be the same after that ... even ven he comes back. If he ever does. He is a fool. He loves Hanover better than he love England. Let him have Hanover. Let us make England for us."

The Prince nodded slowly.

"Go to him I vill," he said. "I vill tell him that I vill dismiss Argyll because it is his vish."

"Go now," she said. "Vaste no time. If he sends for your uncle it vill be too late."

The Prince went at once to the King, and Robethon was delighted with the success of his plan.

* * *

In spite of the fact that George Augustus had given way and the Duke of Argyll and his brother Lord Islay had been dismissed from their public posts, the King was still determined not to give his son the Regency.

He argued with his Council that the Prince was too irresponsible.

His German advisers were firm in their views that harm could come of giving the Prince too much power; the English ministers declared that the Prince being of age must necessarily take the Regency.

If George had not been so eager to see Hanover he would have abandoned the whole project; but he was so heartily sick of his new country and so fervently longing for his old, that he was determined to make the trip whatever the consequences. Moreover war was imminent—war which would involve Hanover and he wanted to make sure that if Hanover should need the support of England, Hanover should have it.

Marlborough, backed by his forceful wife, always ready to seek a way back to power, suggested that six men should be chosen who would support the Prince in his Regency and have equal power with him. This idea enchanted Marlborough, for he saw himself as one, with four of his friends—possibly members of his family—who would sit in Council with the Prince and in fact govern the realm with the Prince as their mouthpiece. A project after his own heart.

But the days of Marlborough's glory were long behind him. Walpole and Townsend laughed at the Duke's temerity behind his back. The old man must be getting senile to think he could get away with that one! They smiled to think of him hatching it with Sarah—and being so unaware of the decline in their fortunes as to think such a suggestion could be anything but laughable.

Townsend, as Prime Minister, had made his decision. The King did not like him so he already had one foot in the Prince's camp and he had made up his mind that his support was going to the Prince.

He addressed the Council, telling them that there was no precedence for what was suggested. Never before when a Prince of Wales had been of an age to become Regent in the absence of the King had he been asked to agree that others should join with him. The Prince would be working in collaboration with the Parliament and that was according to the laws and customs of England.

"I will not have him Regent," cried George. "This would give him too much power. He would have a position similar to that now held by the Duke of Orléans. This is a different matter. Louis XV is a minor, and the Duke is in all but name King of France. To be Regent at this time in France is to be King. It must not be so here. Regent he shall not be called. My son must not have the power of a Regent. His talents do not justify this."

The members of the Council were silent for a while; and then Townsend said: "There is another title which was once used in England. It is Guardian and Lieutenant of the Realm. It implies a guardianship without the power of a Regent. Does your Majesty think this could be bestowed on the Prince of Wales? It would give him a title without great power. It would thus preserve his dignity while giving Your Majesty less cause for anxiety."

"I will look into this," said George. "I think it may well be what we need."

* * *

"Guardian and Lieutenant of the Realm!" cried George Augustus taking off his wig—a familiar habit when incensed—and first stamping on it and then proceeding to kick it round the apartment. "I am Regent. I vill be Regent."

"This is not bad," soothed Caroline. "Vait till he is gone ... just vait. That is all. Vat we must do is make this pipple love us. This ve can do. Ve vill have our court. It vill be as though ve are the King and Queen. And if anything goes wrong ... it is not your fault. You are only the Guardian of the Realm ... not the Regent. As soon as he has gone ve shall show the pipple how much more pleasant it is ven you are King."

"Guardian of the Realm!" growled George Augustus.

"Vat do the pipple know of that? Vat do they care? It is the pipple's love ve vant, George Augustus. It is friends ... Ve vill have our court. To it vill ve invite those who vill help us most ... and those who are not pleased vith the King. Never mind if they call you Regent or Guardian. This is your chance to show this pipple vat a King you vill be."

His scowl lightened; he picked up his wig and put it on his head. He stood on tiptoe; he looked in the mirror. He was already seeing himself as King.

"This is my chance, Caroline," he said. "That is how I see it. Guardian of the Realm! It is an insult. But vat does the name matter? They vill see, these dear good pipple, vat a King I shall be. They vill long for the day ... just as I do. And it vill come."

She smiled at him; she was growing more fond of him as time passed.

* * *

There was excited activity at St. James's, but no one was more excited at the project of leaving England than the King; he was almost jovial—a mood in which many of his subjects had never seen him before.

Mustapha and Mahomet were, of course, going with the

King; but they were not very pleased. Life in England had offered them far more than it had in Hanover. They had been able to give out many of the smaller posts in the King's household and they had quickly discovered how they could make a profitable business of this.

They had laughed together at the grumbles of the King's courtiers who asked: Who ever heard of a King who would have only two Turkish servants to assist him at his toilet? This had been a longstanding ceremony in the life of English Kings and this German had substituted two Turks for all the gentlemen who could have had lucrative posts in his household.

Just another crude habit of a coarse-minded King, said the disappointed gentlemen; but Mahomet and Mustapha had developed a talent for greed; so they were not pleased to be taken from the happy hunting ground.

Stanhope was uneasy. He was to accompany George to Hanover leaving Townsend and Walpole behind. He would, of course, have the ear of the King which was important, but how could he know what was going on in the mind of Townsend and the even more wily one of Walpole? What would they be doing while he was away?

The King's two mistresses naturally accompanied him—the Maypole and the Elephant. Kielmansegge was not eager to go; she had found lovers among the English and she was growing to like them better than the Germans. Moreover, in Hanover was their old rival the Countess von Platen, who would of course welcome George very affectionately—and even a man of habit as he undoubtedly was could not help being glad of a change.

And Ermengarda? A little while ago she would have been delighted to go to Hanover. That was when she was afraid for the King's safety. But why go now when the horrible Pretender had shown he could do nothing against the King and had scuttled back to France? Why not stay in England where life was really more comfortable and there were so many perquisites for those in favoured places? Oh, yes, Ermengarda would rather have stayed in England.

At the same time she was fond enough of George to be

pleased to see him happy. So with her usual placidity she prepared to accompany her lord to Hanover.

There was one other at St. James's who rejoiced as wholeheartedly as George—and that was Caroline, for she saw clearly that the pattern of life had changed. She was no longer going to pretend she was trying to please the King. She had had to come out into the open.

Very well, they were rivals. And while he was away she was going to lay the foundations of that Court of which she would one day be Queen.

\*     \*     \*

They understood each other, and George could not help admire Caroline.

He found himself saying now and then: If she were not my own son's wife...

She was a damned fine woman. Large enough to please him physically; and it occurred to him that he might even enjoy pitting his wits against hers. It was the first time he had ever thought of a woman having wits—except his mother, of course; and there was his sister Sophia Charlotte who had been a clever woman.

Then he would yawn and think of Ermengarda on whom he had come to depend. She would never have been the comfort she had been if she'd had wits.

Uncomfortable things wits in women. It was a good thing Caroline was his son's wife. A good thing, too, that he was never a man to put himself out to pursue a woman. He'd always thought that a waste of good time. There were women enough about for his needs.

To Caroline's astonishment the King announced that he would spend his last evening in her apartments.

She expressed her pleasure and arranged that a brilliant gathering should be there that he might honour them with his company.

He came—almost excited. No one had ever known him so pleasant.

It was not a very good impression to make, thought Caroline gleefully. He is happier than he has ever been since his coming to England—and the reason? Tomorrow he is leaving it. Oh, his English subjects will love him for this!

All to the good. They could turn their affection to his son.

George Augustus was there. She could hear him talking.

"How happy I am that I do not leave with His Majesty. That is a thing I could not endure. It is because I find the English the best pipple in the vorld...."

The King is a fool, thought Caroline, to go away and leave the field to us.

And what had brought the King to their apartments that night? Was it a woman?

Caroline looked about the apartment with interest. Who? There were the black and red wigs of Kielmansegge and Schulemburg—nothing extraordinary about that. They accompanied the King everywhere and whatever woman he wanted, he would always keep those two.

Now I wonder, thought Caroline, and shrugged the matter aside.

The King had come to talk to her. A matter of policy, she thought; he wants to show the company that we are not enemies and there are no quarrels within the family.

"I envy your seeing Frederick," she said. "I want you to tell him that I think of him often. Will you tell him that his sisters are growing big now. They are always talking of him and even baby Caroline who never knew him speaks of him as though he is familiar to her."

"I shall have much work to do in Hanover."

She flushed angrily. "And no time to give a few messages to your grandson?"

How ugly he was, with his heavy jaw and his protuberant eyes. She was thankful she had a husband like George Augustus. How tragic to be married to a man like this! He was coarse, crude and without feeling.

She had raised her voice a little and he was anxious to show that there was no real discord in the family.

"I will tell him what you say."

"And you will tell Gottfried Leibniz that I hope he will soon visit me in England."

The King was silent. He was not going to be pressed too far.

Sullen old boor! thought Caroline; still he did look happy tonight and he was more genial than he had ever been before; he was even smiling at her.

And soon he would be gone and she would have her opportunity.

Momentary irritations could not spoil her pleasure in this night—nor the King's.

\* \* \*

The next morning the King was in good spirits while Mahomet and Mustapha dressed him. He had awakened at dawn, which came early for it was July and, eager to waste no time, arose.

By ten o'clock he was at the Tower where he would take boat for Gravesend. The Prince of Wales accompanied him and George even addressed a few pleasant remarks to his son during the trip from the Tower to Gravesend where his yacht was awaiting him.

"We want everyone to know that we are good friends," he told his son.

George Augustus put on his most affable manner, never forgetting to return a greeting from the few on the bank who stood watching the King pass along the river. Very few of them, the Prince noted with pleasure. They were not interested in seeing their Sovereign start on his journey. Let him go back to his sausages and sauerkraut, would be the comment of most of them.

This was indeed a great opportunity.

To Gravesend and aboard the yacht.

Father and son embraced—something they never remembered doing before. But each made the other aware that there was no affection in the gesture; it was merely to show the spectators that there was no family quarrel.

The Prince came ashore.

Back to St. James's to start his reign as Guardian of the Realm while the King sailed away to his beloved Hanover.

## The Days of Glory

OH, the joy of being rid of the King!

On her bed in the Wren wing of Hampton Court Caroline lay dreamily looking up at the ceiling. It was a magnificent apartment with the windows looking out on the Great Fountain garden and the park beyond.

She was pregnant and pregnancies were uncomfortable but it was a good state for a Princess to be in and she was hoping this time for a boy—a boy whom she would keep with her. She loved the children; and they were always happy to be with her. One of the pleasantest hours of the day was when they were brought to her—Anne in charge. She was seven and thought herself the head of the family, keeping five year old Amelia and three year old Caroline in order. Oh, it was cruel of the King to keep Fritzchen from his parents and his sisters! But what could one expect from a man who allowed his own wife to remain a prisoner for twenty years.

But she must not think of Fritzchen. Nothing must spoil the perfection of these days. She had never really been so happy; in fact if she could have her son in England and her father-in-law in Hanover she would ask nothing more of life.

She loved England; and the most beautiful place in England in her eyes was Hampton. The lovely peaceful river; the palace; the grounds. Never would she want to be in any other place. She continued to gaze at the high ceiling. The apartment was a lofty thirty feet in height and on the ceiling only a year ago Sir James Thornhill had painted Aurora in her golden chariot rising from the sea; her attendant fat little cupids reminded her of baby Caroline. She would not look at the portraits on the wall; to contemplate either of the subjects made her unhappy for one was the King, morose and forbidding, to remind her that this was only a temporary release; the other was Fritzchen to remind her of their separation.

No, she would luxuriate in her bed, for it was the custom which they had brought from Hanover to eat a heavy meal and then retire to rest in the afternoon—one of the few pleasant customs they had brought; but the English said it made them fat.

There were many sly comments made behind their backs, she was certain. The English did not like the Germans. Well, we must try to be as English as possible, she thought; for we are English now.

She was wishing that she had learned to speak the language without this atrocious German accent of hers which must remind people whence she came as soon as she spoke. She remembered the old Electress Sophia who had been so anxious for her to learn English and how she had been pleased when George Augustus had become Henrietta Howard's lover because he would improve his English.

How did George Augustus feel nowadays towards Henrietta? She had become a habit; he was like his father in many ways. Still, she would not complain for she had nothing to fear from Henrietta, who had no wish to come into conflict with her, nor to show her power. A wise woman, Henrietta.

Such luxury to lie here in the quietness of the Palace. May the King stay long in Hanover, prayed Caroline. We can do so much while he is away. Make our position strong. Lay the foundation for the future.

Down in the gardens her maids of honour would be walking

with their admirers, frolicking and flirting, taking advantage of the after dinner drowsiness of the Prince and Princess. It was as though since the departure of the King a pall had been lifted and everywhere there was gaiety. Even the weather was exceptionally good.

In his apartments George Augustus would be sleeping deeply, perhaps snoring gently, a smile on his face, for he had become a very happy man since the departure of his father.

Yes, this was indeed a foretaste of glories to come.

Even in a few weeks they had begun to create a new way of life—gracious and luxurious, splendid and *royal*. That was something the King could never do.

Caroline thought of those few trips she and the Prince had taken down the river in their barge which was decorated with crimson velvet, a royal barge; the Prince in his wig, his blue velvet coat ornamented with silver, his tall wig, his beaming smile; herself magnificently dressed, glittering with jewels—looking as a Prince and Princess should look. How different from dour George—and the people showed by their interest, their comments and their cheers that they preferred their royalty this way.

That was important. Never must they lose sight of the need to placate the people. But that was not all. To Hampton Court came men and women who were dissatisfied with their present positions. They had seen that it might be possible to build another court in which they would be appreciated.

These were not the people Caroline wished to gather about her. She did not want the malcontents; but they would do for a start. She had her eyes on men like Walpole and Townsend. But it was necessary to show that she and the Prince were interested in state matters; and all the time every man and woman at court must be aware that the King was an ageing man.

First, she had thought, let us make a court. Let it be gay, a miniature Versailles; for under the cover of gaiety, intrigue could begin—an intrigue to make the court of the Prince and Princess not only more amusing and entertaining but more rewarding.

In surrounding herself with beautiful girls like Mary Bellenden and Molly Lepel she had drawn men of all ages to Hampton; and once there they realized that there was something more to be had than flirtation. The King would be surprised if he came back now and saw the traffic on the river; barges, gaily decorated, containing exquisitely dressed men and women came sailing from London to Hampton; the sounds of music constantly broke the quiet of the afternoon.

George had only been a few weeks away and life was changing, becoming gay, colourful and amusing.

If she had a son and if she could have Fritzchen with her, she would be completely happy. At least she had insisted that he have an English tutor; she wanted him to speak the language fluently when he did come. Fritzchen must not have an accent like herself or George Augustus. The girls were speaking English beautifully, and she loved to listen to them.

Of course she thought, if our court becomes powerful, which it may well do, we can demand the return of Fritzchen.

There was a discreet scratching at the door and Henrietta Howard came in.

She moved gracefully to the Princess's bed. She was a charming looking woman—although not exactly beautiful. Her hair was lovely, abundant and fine and she wore it simply dressed with a curl over her shoulder—a fashion which Caroline favoured a good deal herself. What was it about Henrietta? A serenity, Caroline decided. Like herself, Henrietta made her way by gentleness, never making demands on the Prince, always ready to bow to his wishes. Clever Henrietta!

"Is it time to rise then, Henrietta?"

"Yes, Highness. The children are waiting outside."

"Then bring them in."

They came in and Caroline held out her hand bidding them come to her bedside.

Anne, as the eldest came ahead of the others, almost pushing them aside in her eagerness to be there first. Not, thought Caroline, because she wishes to be with me; but because she must be first. She is too proud, too conscious of her dignity, this one, too much aware of being a Princess.

"Vell and vat have you been doing this day?" asked Caroline.

"What have we been doing today, Mamma?" A gentle correction, this. Caroline was glad she could make it but wondered whether the slight arrogance should be reproved or ignored. "We have been walking in the park and playing in the pond garden. Caroline fell into the pond. It was rather stupid of her. But she is stupid."

Little Caroline's lips began to tremble and her mother held out her hand. The child took it and Henrietta lifted her on to the bed.

"There," said the Princess, "is that better? I remember when I was von little girl I fell into a pond."

The child was happy nestling close. She is too thin, thought her mother. I must tell them to take special care of her. Does Anne bully her?

Amelia would not, of course. Contemplating her second daughter Caroline was proud of her charming looks. Amelia already showed signs of being the beauty of the family and, although two years younger, was as tall as Anne. Although, like Anne, she was fully aware of the dignity due to a Princess she was not spiteful and would stand by her little sister.

I wish I could see more of them, thought the Princess.

"Now you must me tell how you fall into the pond."

"She slipped," said Anne. "And Lord Hervey pulled her out.

"Mrs. Lepel was there and she said she must change her clothes; and Lord Hervey carried her into the palace."

Caroline was trying to remember Lord Hervey ... a young man new to the court, she supposed. She must ask Molly Lepel sometime.

"And Mrs. Bellenden helped, and they made such a fuss. They made her change her clothes."

Little Caroline was smiling, so evidently she had enjoyed the adventure.

"Let Caroline tell me herself," said her mother.

She loved to listen to the prattle of their voice—English voices. A pity that however much she tried she could not rid herself of her German accent. Oh dear, what was happening to Fritzchen? Would he arrive speaking English like his father and mother?

There were voices outside; Caroline recognized the booming tones of her husband. So he had had his sleep and was already dressed. She had not noticed how the time was flying.

"Ha, my dear! So this is how I find you. In bed, eh? It is goot ... for your condition."

He was beaming. The part of first gentleman suited him. His great desire, like hers, would be that his father remained in Hanover and never returned.

"So ... our little ones are here too."

Anne and Amelia looked at him with awe; young Caroline drew a little closer to her mother.

He was smiling jovially enough, but somehow he had not the knack of winning their confidences. Perhaps it was because, with the intuition of children they sensed beneath his *bonhomie* a boredom with them.

Caroline was disappointed because he had disturbed her interview with her children—and she always looked forward to these meetings with the utmost pleasure—but this was something he must never know.

"So you grow up," he said. "Ha, you are von big girl now."

"Yes, Papa, I am a big girl."

"I am as tall, Papa, although I'm two years younger," Amelia pointed out.

"She is too tall," said Anne.

The animosity between the two sisters was visible, and that it should be over a matter of height was disturbing on account of the Prince's preoccupation with his own lack of inches.

"My tear," said the Prince, "it is time I should take you for your valk. I vill vant to speak vis you of the celebrations for the anniversary of our coming. It is just two years and it is expected."

"That shall be very interesting."

The Prince sat down on a stool and looked tenderly at his wife. A fine woman—and these their children. Fine children; and Caroline soon to have another. He had done well.

Henrietta came to the bed and lifted off young Caroline. She took the little girl by the hand and with the others went to the door.

The Prince followed them with his eyes. His wife, his chil-

K*

dren, his mistress ... here together ... happy together. His father far away; men and women everywhere seeking his favour.

He had never been so contented in his life.

\* \* \*

Those were enchanting days at Hampton—not only for the Prince and Princess and those who flocked to their court but for simple country folk. George I had wanted to close St. James's Park and had been told that his three crowns would be in jeopardy if he did; in direct contrast George Augustus appeared to delight in the presence of his father's subjects, however lowly, in the grounds of Hampton Court. He and Caroline, taking their walk there often stopped to say a word or two to some countryman and his wife and left them gaping after them, loyal supporters for ever after.

Hampton Court was the gayest, merriest Court that had existed since the days of Charles II. Old men and women, such as the Duchess of Monmouth, recalled the court of that monarch and the excitement of long ago. They told tales of the witty King and his merry Court. Like the Prince and Princess of Wales he had spent a great deal of time in what he called sauntering. It was an excellent custom for it enabled his subjects to see him often and even talk with him now and then. But whereas Charles had strolled with a bevy of mistresses and his spaniels, the Prince of Wales strolled with his wife—and wonderfully tender he was to her on account of her condition; it was true his mistress was in attendance too; but a man might be allowed one mistress, and since his wife appeared to have no objection, why should anyone else?

The Prince and Princess of Wales were very quickly forming their own special entourage and at the same time winning the approval of the King's subjects.

No wonder they were satisfied!

There was one who was not.

Count Hans Caspar von Bothmer, never far from the Prince of Wales, watched in consternation. The King was enjoying his visit to Hanover. He had heard rumours that there was rejoicing there at the return of the Elector, that his German subjects were delighted that he was back with them and appreciated him more than ever now that he brought English money and English support for Hanover.

He was at Herrenhausen reunited with the Countess von Platen though Schulemburg and Kielmansegge were in attendance. "The King gives every sign that he has forgotten the misfortune which happened to him and his family in August 1714," said one report.

"The King so clearly loves Hanover that he will never willingly leave it," said another.

And meanwhile in England his son was playing King.

In his apartments Bothmer wrote down everything he noticed at Hampton Court and sent it to the King. It was a warning, but the King had never wanted the crown of England; his heart was in Hanover and he could not bring himself to leave his old home.

\*   \*   \*

Fanning herself, for the sun was warm, Caroline sat in one of the pavilions with her little girls, her ladies and some of the gentlemen of the court, while the Prince presented prizes to the winners of the races which he had organized.

Caroline loved the pavilions which had been built at each corner of the Green and had been luxuriously furnished. Like the Prince, she was fond of being out of doors and spent a great deal of time here, so that although her condition prevented her walking as much as she would like she could enjoy the fresh air. In the late afternoons she and her friends would drink a dish of tea and the country folk would see them chatting or playing cards. This was what the people wanted from their royalty. The less privacy the better.

Caroline, sensing this, readily accepted it; George Augustus was so anxious to be the centre of attraction that the sacrifice of his privacy was no hardship. They had grown accustomed to being watched at dinner and if at times they were a little weary of it, they reminded themselves that one of the main causes of the King's unpopularity was his refusal to show himself and be gracious to his subjects.

Mary Bellenden was talking quietly to Colonel John Campbell and Caroline reflected that Mary had become more serious
lately; Sophie Howe was flirting with several young men,
throwing them provocative glances, whispering, and now and
then suppressing her giggles; Sophie would never be serious;
and Molly Lepel was talking to one of the young men
from the Prince's household, Lord Hervey, a very amusing
young man, she suspected, if she could judge from Molly's
smiles.

Henrietta was close to her, solicitous as ever of her needs,
and Lady Cowper and Mrs. Clayton were at hand ready to
criticize everything Henrietta did because they did not
approve of her relationship with the Prince.

One could not explain to them that it was better that he
should have a mistress on whom she could keep an eye, and
certainly one like Henrietta who never flaunted her position
and performed her duties in the Princess's bedchamber as
efficiently as she did those in the Prince's.

There was a burst of applause as one of the winners curtsied
to the Prince. Caroline clapped her hands and bade the little
girls do the same. George Augustus presented a quilted petti-
coat to the girl.

"It vill you most become," he told her to the delight of the
crowd.

And for another a smock and another a sarcenet hood.

"You vill not forget this day . . . not never, eh?"

Even the Prince's German accent sounded charming on that
day.

"And I am sorry for all those who haf not von. Everyone
cannot vin. Is it not? For all there shall be vine and cakes.
Then ve are all happy."

The Prince came to the pavilion.

"And you are not in a vind, my tearest? Ve must of you take
care."

Mrs. Howard sprang forward to place a scarf about the Princess's shoulders.

"No, it is not necessary. It hide the Princess's neck . . . and
that is von shame. The Princess haf the most beautiful neck in
the vorld. The people should see."

"I am not cold," said Caroline.

The Prince sat beside her, beaming, contented.

"It is goot," he said, "to see our peoples so happy."

His eyes were misty as they rested on lovely Mary Bellenden. What a charming creature! Should not a Prince have more than one mistress? Would the people, who so often talked of Charles II with affection, particularly now that he George Augustus had shown them what a gay court he would let them share in, say "Ah, but he will never be as Charles. Charles had many mistresses; he would stroll in the Mall with three or four at a time."

He called to Henrietta to stand beside him.

"You haf enjoyed this day, my tear?" he asked.

She assured him that it had been amusing to watch the races and it gave her great pleasure to see everyone having such a pleasant day.

He pressed her hand.

"I shall visit you this evening," he said.

"Your Highness is gracious," replied Henrietta.

\*　　\*　　\*

Henrietta was giving a little party. She was popular and these occasions were always well attended, for she was so good hearted that she could never take sides between Whigs or Tories but longed for a peaceful existence and this she seemed to achieve.

To her party came the Prince of Wales. The Princess had retired early on account of her condition; and there was cards and music. The Prince treated Henrietta with almost luxurious tenderness; she had become such a habit with him. Although when Mary Bellenden was present he would turn a definitely lascivious gaze on her. As for Mary she was quite content to be in the Prince's company as long as there were others present. Perhaps, she thought, I could get him to do something for John, for John was so poor that difficulties would be made if they tried to marry just yet. But I'll have no other, Mary thought fiercely, and reminded herself she was foolish to think the Prince would grant honours to his successful rival. He was not that sort of man.

She noticed that Lord Townsend was present tonight which was a compliment to Henrietta Howard; and he was beside her showing her great attention, and it seemed as though he respected her.

Mary wanted to laugh. Did Townsend think that he could find favour with the Prince through Henrietta Howard! He was not very discerning if he did—and he a Prime Minister —for Henrietta had no influence at all with the Prince; in fact the only reason why she held her position was because she made no attempt to meddle. The Prince of Wales resembled the King in as much as he liked his women docile. Mary knew that any woman's favour with the Prince would depend upon her ability in getting her way without letting him know it.

Henrietta would be no good at that; so she was wise enough not to try.

Now the Princess . . . that was another matter. It was obvious to Mary that the Princess had her way far more often than the Prince realized.

Sophie Howe had come up to her.

"Look who's here," said Mary.

"My lord Townsend, the Prime Minister?"

"It's the first time he's been here."

"I don't find him attractive," said Sophie. "He doesn't interest me."

Mary laughed. "You seem to be obsessed by one idea."

"It's a very nice idea," retorted Sophie.

\*       \*       \*

Mary was not the only one who had noticed the presence of the Prime Minister. Lady Cowper was watching him, and knew very well why he had come.

She did not approve of Henrietta Howard; in fact she liked to imply that had she been a woman of a less rigid moral character she might have borne the same relationship towards the King as Henrietta Howard did to the Prince of Wales.

She was fond of saying that she had quickly made the King aware that if he wanted an English mistress he should look elsewhere, and had gladly taken up her post in the Princess's household.

She and Mrs. Clayton, both having serious natures, deplored the frivolous behaviour of some of the maids of honour, and in particular Sophie Howe. If Lady Cowper could have had her way that girl would have been dismissed long ago.

So now, she noticed Townsend and was very certain that there was a purpose behind his visit to Henrietta Howard's rooms. She was faintly disturbed too for she believed that if important politicians began paying attention to Henrietta Howard, very soon the woman could become important. That was something Lady Cowper would prevent if it were possible.

She made her way to Townsend's side.

"A pleasant party, my lord," she said.

"Very pleasant." He looked at her without interest. The man is not subtle enough, thought Lady Cowper. Knowing my position with the Princess he should be careful. But of course he did not realize the importance of the Princess.

She decided to speak to him frankly.

"If you seek the Prince's favour you have come to the wrong place."

Townsend looked startled.

"Mrs. Howard has no influence with him whatsoever."

Townsend hesitated. Then he said: "I should like to hear the Prince's views."

"Knowing you are his father's Prime Minister he is scarcely likely to trust you."

"This is unfortunate ... this feud between the King and Prince."

"Oh, doubtless it will enable some men to make their fortunes."

"It is not good for the country."

"And you ... as the King's man would like to hear the Prince's case."

"Naturally."

"And therefore you seek the friendship of his nearest confidante?"

Townsend was silent.

"You are in the wrong apartment, my lord. I did not think

your manner particularly gracious to the Princess in the pavilion today. The Princess may have noticed it. She is not a figurehead, you know."

"It was the Prince's views in which I was interested."

"My lord, you are not aware of the truth. The woman who guides the Prince in all he does is the Princess. If you wish for the Prince's favour first seek that of the Princess."

Townsend was looking at Henrietta who, being a little deaf, was straining to hear what the Prince was saying to her.

"She is his mistress, yes," said Lady Cowper. "She is a habit with him, or it might be that he would have discarded her. She dare not attempt to advise him."

"And the Princess dares?"

"The Princess is the cleverest woman at this court, my lord. Until you have discovered that you will not get far with the Prince. She will be at cards in the pavilion tomorrow. If you wish it I will present you to her. She will be gracious and forgive you for past neglect. She will know of course how you blundered."

Townsend looked alarmed.

"I'm right you will find," laughed Lady Cowper. "In time you will realize that."

\*     \*     \*

To his surprise Townsend discovered that Lady Cowper was right. The Princess of Wales while bearing the heirs to the realm had time to spare for dabbling in politics. In fact, once Townsend had gained her confidence she was ready to show that the subject was to her the most fascinating in the world and that when the time came for her to be Queen of England she would do everything in her power to play a big part in its government.

She was clever because she was controlled. Her gift of deceiving the Prince into thinking that she followed him in his ideas when the facts were the complete reverse, was masterly.

Here, thought Townsend, is a true statesman. And he wondered at his folly in not realizing this before.

Walpole was aware of it also, but he was more cautious; he was not going to be on with the new before the old was out. He had warned Townsend that that old spy Bothmer was watching them and reporting everything to Hanover.

Those were days of excitement to Townsend and even more so to Caroline. Sitting in the pavilion sipping tea or coffee, listening to music, watching the card players, sometimes joining in herself, but preferring to sit apart with the Prince or such men as Townsend talking cautiously; it was almost as though she were already the Queen.

It was what she longed for—to be the Queen. Her first command would be that Fritzchen be brought to England. She would also send for Leibniz. What pleasure to have him here! How he would enjoy talking to the brilliant men with whom she was filling her court!

That was what she needed for complete happiness. In the meantime it was pleasant here at Hampton, sitting in the pleasant warmth of late summer. Late summer alas! She would always remember this summer as the happiest she had known since the death of Sophia Charlotte—and it was passing for the warm days were already growing sadly short; soon they would leave Hampton for St. James's ... and the King could not stay away for ever.

Townsend was saying: "I greatly fear that England will be drawn into war. The people of this country do not want war. They hate war. It means to them death and taxation ... and no gain. What gain would there be for us in war? Of course there might be some gain to Hanover. But the people of this country can hardly be expected to make sacrifices for Hanover."

"They should not be asked to," replied Caroline quickly.

Townsend drew a deep breath. Were those the Prince's views? he wondered.

Caroline seemed to sense his thoughts for she added: "The Prince and I vould be strongly against this country making the sacrifice for Hanover. Hanover cannot expect it."

"Hanover does expect. The King and his German ministers are of the opinion that England and Hanover should stand as one."

"That," said Caroline with a laugh, "is a Hanoverian view and not, I believe an English one."

"Your Highness is right. But..."

"A strong opposition in England vould mean that this could not be."

"It is the wish of the King and many of his Hanoverian ministers. But ... what of the Prince?"

"I believe the Prince, nay I am sure the Prince vould not agree to his father. My lord, you vill know that there is hardly von matter on vich they agree. And certainly it vould not be this von."

Townsend was alert. If he could get the Prince of Wales to support him, if here with the Prince and Princess he could build up a strong opposition to those who could put Hanover before England, he might get his way *and* remain in office.

"If I could speak to the Prince..."

"He vill be delighted to giv you von audience."

"And Your Highness will be present?"

Caroline smiled. This was what she had always wanted. She would prepare the Prince who would be only too eager to intrigue against his father. Nothing would delight him more; and it would not be difficult for her to guide him along the way she wanted him to go.

She noticed that the Count von Bothmer was talking to Lord Hervey. The German made a point of attending any gathering at which she or the Prince were present. The King should have chosen a less obvious spy. But they must be careful. If the King knew that the Prime Minister was conferring with her and the Prince, surely he would realize the need for returning to England at once.

She said: "I vould like to hear some singing. Mrs. Bellenden has the voice *très charmante*. Mrs. Howard, I pray you tell Mrs. Bellenden I vould hear her sing. And perhaps aftervards Lord Hervey would recite to us some of his verses."

Townsend bowed and said he would acquaint Lord Hervey with Her Highness's wishes.

He understood perfectly why she had interrupted their conversation. Bothmer would undoubtedly report what he had seen to his master.

The Prime Minister was uneasy. The Prince of Wales could have little power while his father lived. But of course the King was not a young man—and in the political field it was often necessary to take risks.

*    *    *

The Prince watching Mary Bellenden sing, thought: This is the most beautiful girl at court!

She had spirit ... too much spirit. He would have preferred her docile, eager, very honoured to be noticed by the Prince of Wales.

Alas, she was not so. Sometimes her eyes flashed scornfully and he wondered why he pursued her. She was tall and slender —not plump and rounded. She was very English.

It is the English I love best in the world, thought George Augustus, as though repeating a lesson.

In the streets people sang verses about her. The beautiful Mary Bellenden and the fair Molly Lepel were rivals for beauty. But give him Mary; and it would be right and proper that either one of the reigning beauties should be his mistress. Could she not see that?

He hummed under his breath a song he had heard one of his gentlemen singing:

> *"What pranks are played behind the scenes,*
> *And who at Court the belle?*
> *Some swear it is the Bellenden.*
> *And others say Lepel."*

I say the Bellenden! he thought.

He had betrayed his feelings for her and she was not the only one who was aware of them. It was undignified that the Prince of Wales's desires should go unsatisfied.

He had always believed though that in time she would be his mistress. She was no prude, so why delay? He could only think that like most of the people at Court she wanted something. And what could she want but money?

He knew she had her financial difficulties like most extravagant young ladies, for he had heard her complain of bills. He must therefore take an opportunity of letting her see that if she would become his mistress she would have so much money that she need never be bothered by bills ... while she continued to please him.

Mary had finished signing and had gone to sit in an alcove in the pavilion with Margaret Meadows and Mrs. Clayton.

The Prince made his way by degrees to her corner, stopping to chat on the way, believing that by so doing he disguised his intention of singling out Mary.

When he reached the table at which she sat he beamed at the three of them.

"It vos von beautiful song," he said.

He sat down and took a purse from his pocket which he put on the table. The three stared at it in surprise. He emptied it of its guineas and began to count them.

"It seems I much money haf," he said with a smile, and gathering up the money put it back in the purse, jingling it while he smiled at Mary.

Mary however was looking beyond him as though she was quite unaware of what he was doing.

Molly Lepel had begun to sing at the Princess's request; there was silence at the table while the Prince continued to look expectantly at Mary; and Mary stared stonily ahead.

*       *       *

The Prince came to the Princess's apartments where she was resting on her bed. He waved away her women and going to the bed kissed her.

"It is goot that you rest," he said. "And how are you, my tear?"

"Vell, but shall be glad when the child comes. It is long waiting."

"You always have the difficult time. You are certain you have the right time? You were wrong before, remember."

"I'm sure of it. Cowper and Clayton have been bothering me. And Mrs. Howard too."

The Prince looked shocked at the mention of Henrietta.

"Oh, they serve me vell. They think I should have the doctor instead of the midvife."

"Instead of the midvife! A man! You could not, Caroline."

"No, I could not. They say that in France royal ladies have

*accoucheurs* instead of midvives. They say they have the skill ... and it is safer. But I shall have the midvife. I vould not vish for Sir David Hamilton to attend me."

"I should not vish either."

"I must scold these ladies."

"They do it for your good, but scold."

"I feel vell .. .very vell. And I vish to speak to you about the Prime Minister."

"Tell me."

"He vishes an audience. I believe he vould rather serve you than the King."

The Prince's eyes gleamed with pleasure.

"Of course you vill say ve must be careful," she said warningly.

"Oh, ve must be careful."

"If the King hears that the Prime Minister talks business vith you he vill angry be. He vill come back from Hanover ... *toute de suite.*"

The Prince nodded; but there was triumph in his eyes.

"The weeks at Hampton have been so *wunderbar.*"

The Prince nodded.

"It has done me so much goot to see you. You have shown them what a King you vill be."

"And you a Queen."

She put her hands on her stomach. "Oh, I must bear the children.... That is for the vomen."

"But I vould always talk to you, Caroline. There is no von else I vould talk to as I do to you."

"You are so goot to me. Ve shall be careful with Townsend. Should ve send for him now? I vill dress and we can receive him in the Queen's gallery. Vould you give your consent to this?"

The Prince nodded eagerly.

"I believe the King is trying to make England declare war. Do you think that will be goot for England? Goot for Hanover yes, but vill it be goot for England? The people do not vant it. Do you think it would be goot for England to declare var vhile you are the guardian of the realm?"

"It would be bad. I vould not allow it."

"I thought you vould not. I vill summon my women and join you in the Queen's gallery. I vill have vord sent to Townsend that he is to come there."

* * *

Caroline, in a long robe which did its best to disguise her advanced state of pregnancy, walked up and down the gallery between the Prince and the Prime Minister.

Townsend was saying: "The English will never willingly go to war for the sake of Hanover."

"They must never do so," replied the Prince.

"I am glad of Your Highness's support," replied Townsend, "for the Cabinet are of your opinion. It was against my advice that we sent a squadron to the Baltic. This was said to protect our trade but our trade was in no real need of protection. It was meant to protect Bremen and Verden ... for the sake of Hanover."

"Hanover must fight her own battles," said the Prince.

"The King does not think so."

"The King is von fool," reorted the Prince.

Both Caroline and the Prime Minister lowered their eyes.

"I repeat ... von fool," went on George Augustus. "He must be to prefer Hanover to England. But then he is not English ... as I am ..."

"As ve both are," added the Princess.

The Prince smiled across at her. "Yes, all things English ve love."

"There are new propositions from Hanover," said Townsend. "I do not agree with them and I should like to know that I have Your Highness's support in refusing them."

"You have my support if it is for England's goot. I vould never put Hanover before England."

"Vell spoken," murmured Caroline; and again he smiled at her.

"Denmark offers Bremen and Verden to Hanover on the condition that England declares war on Sweden and pays to Denmark £150,000."

"And vat goot vill this bring to Englandt?" asked the Prince excitedly.

"No good to England, but Hanover will get Bremen and Verden, of course."

"And Englandt would be at var with Sveden and Russia," added Caroline quietly.

"It shall not be!" cried the Prince clenching his fist, while the veins at his temples became swollen.

"I am delighted to have Your Highness's support in this as I intend to place Stanhope's proposals before the Cabinet. I can assure you they will be rejected ... particularly in view of the fact that we have Your Highness's support."

The Prince was delighted. When the Prime Minister consulted him he was truly playing the King.

\* \* \*

The golden September days were passing. Each day Caroline wondered whether there would be news of the King's return. But he stayed on in Hanover and left them free to enjoy the blessing of his absence.

To the Prince's great joy, Townsend, with whom he was now on excellent terms, suggested that he make a tour of the countryside. He had seen little of England, except during his journey from the coast to London on his arrival and the English liked to see their sovereigns.

Townsend was already talking to him as though he were the King and he was thinking of himself as such.

The Prince immediately began making his preparations.

"There is but von thing that grieves me," he said. "You, my tear, vill not come vith me."

"You vill manage very vell on your own," Caroline told him.

"It vould have been happier for me if I could have had my tear vife beside me."

"I shall be thinking of you ... all the time. And you see I am in no condition to come vith you."

"Take care of yourself. I vill give Mrs. Howard very special instructions."

"You need not. She is the best of vomen."

The Prince smiled at her gratefully. It seemed there was nothing to spoil his pleasure.

And what joy it was to travel through the countryside of Hampshire, Sussex and Kent where the people lined the roads to cheer him as he rode by and he told himself and his attendants that he would never tire of smiling for the English people.

To signal his approach bonfires were lighted all along his route and girls with flowers and leaves came out to dance in his path. At Portsmouth he was entertained at military as well as naval reviews. He went aboard the finest of the ships and guns were fired in his honour.

His eyes shining with sentiment, he told those who welcomed him that he had never been so happy in his life. He loved England; he loved the English people; he was English; he would not have it otherwise. Every drop of blood in his veins was English; he had inherited it through his grandmother.

He would never willingly leave England; the best and lovingest people in the world were the English.

He loved the English and the English loved him.

He was different from his dour old father, said the people; let that old fellow stay in Germany with his Maypole and Elephant, let him stuff himself with sausages and sauerkraut. His son was quite different. He was English, although he spoke with an atrocious German accent. He was one of them because he was determined to be.

So the bonfires were lighted; and the people sang and danced; and the theme of the day was "God Bless the Prince of Wales".

October was well advanced by the time he returned in triumph to Hampton. He found Caroline delighted to see him, eager to hear of his triumphs; but although she was more heavily pregnant than ever, there was no sign that her confinement was imminent.

\*    \*    \*

Bothmer sat in his apartments writing to the King, to Bernstorff and to Robethon.

"The Prince," he wrote, "has become the King. The Prime Minister confers with him. Townsend has in fact become his man. His Highness has just returned to Hampton from a royal progress through Hampshire, Kent and Sussex. He is treated as the ruler of the realm."

\* \* \*

Caroline was delighted and yet apprehensive. The more popular the Prince became the more determined the King would be to suppress him. Their only hope to go on living this delightful existence was for the King to discover that he loved Hanover so much he would stay there.

She believed there might be a faint possibility that he would. She prayed that it might come true. But while his father lived George Augustus could not be King. Still, to live as pleasantly as they had been living for this wonderful summer would be very delightful while they waited.

Yet as the days grew shorter her apprehension grew. There were no longer charming afternoons in the pavilion. The wind was too chilly. Walks had to be taken early in the afternoon if she was to be back in her apartments by dusk. It was not so exciting playing cards by candle-light as in the fresh air.

It cannot go on, of course, she thought sighing.

News came from Hanover which saddened her.

Leibniz had approached the King and begged leave to come to England and this had been curtly refused. Poor Leibniz! He had been unpopular enough in the past but he was more so now. Then he had merely been disliked as a man of intellect and a friend of the Princess's, when the King had considered her to be an unimportant woman whose only function was to bear children. Now he would know that she was not so stupid. Bothmer would have reported how Townsend had first approached her; and she would have her full share of the King's animosity.

Leibniz had not been wise to approach the King at such a time.

"The King has been so incensed by what was happening at home," she read, "that he could not endure to look on Leibniz who has always been a supporter of the Princess of Wales. He turned his back on him and in consequence of this action Leibniz had no alternative but to leave court."

Poor lonely old Leibniz, whose only fault was that he was loyal to his old pupil and that he was a man of wit and understanding! So he had gone to his home in Hanover and lived there. He had left Court for ever and he despaired of ever coming to England.

Caroline pictured him, thinking of all those talks he had had with the Electress Sophia when she had embued him with her love of a country neither of them had ever seen.

He was heartbroken—deprived of his work, deprived of his friends, despised because he had a good brain and liked to use it.

Could a man die of a broken heart? Perhaps, thought Caroline, for Leibniz had died in Leibnizhaus, his house in Hanver, and had been buried quietly, for the King had had no wish that he should be remembered.

"He was buried," ran the letter, "more like a robber than an ornament to his country."

Dear Leibniz who had tutored her, who had reproved her, and who had loved her!

It was another link with the old life broken; and at the same time it was an evil augury for the future.

George was harsh to those he believed did not serve him well. So poor Leibniz had suffered.

How much more harsh he would be to those who had deliberately flouted him—his own son and daughter-in-law! What would happen when he returned? That was what Caroline wondered as she sat awaiting the first signs of her child's arrival on those rapidly shortening days.

*  *  *

The crimson-decked barge made its way slowly up the river. On the banks the people cheered while the Prince, his hand on his heart, bowed and smiled, and the Princess, who looked as though she might give birth at any moment, sat back, with smiles as gracious as those of the Prince. The young Princesses, Anne, Amelia and Caroline, were with their mother and there was a special cheer for them; and on the elaborately decorated barge it was possible to catch a glimpse of those rival beauties,

Molly Lepel and Mary Bellenden, and of Sophie Howes of whom many verses had been written, of Henrietta Howard, the Prince's mistress, who was on the best of terms with the Princess, and of other personalities of the Court.

If the last month had been a foretaste of what the future reign would be like the people certainly would not mourn the passing of George I.

Caroline was a little sad. She had wanted to lie in at Hampton but Townsend had warned her that the child she was going to bear could be an heir to the throne, and heirs to the throne were not born at Hampton. The last thing Caroline wanted to do was ignore English custom, so regretfully she gave up the idea of staying at Hampton, and she could not throw off this feeling of sadness because she knew that when she left the Thames-side mansion, with its scarlet-bricked walls and its magnificent state apartments, and most delightful of all its gardens with its fountains and flowers, its greens and pavilions, its wilderness and maze, she was leaving more than a country house. This was the end of a phase—the most delightful phase of her life.

Moreover she felt ill, for a few weeks before she had almost miscarried. She wanted children—many more—but the months of discomfort while she awaited their arrival were very trying.

So to London and St. James's, and soon she hoped her child would be born.

I shall feel better then, she promised herself. More ready to face the storm which will inevitably come when the King returns.

*        *        *

A week after the royal party had returned to St. James's Palace, on a dark November Sunday Caroline's pains started.

All through the day officials were arriving at the Palace and the Prince summoned certain members of the Cabinet that they might be present when the child was born.

The German midwife, who could speak no English, but whom the Prince had commanded to attend to his wife, was growing anxious. As the labour was going on and on and there was no sign of the child, Mrs. Clayton and Lady Cowper were apprehensive.

"This is no ordinary confinement," said Mrs. Clayton.

"The Princess's are always difficult," Lady Cowper reminded her, "and for that reason it is folly to leave her in the hands of this old German woman."

"An old country midwife!" agreed Mrs. Clayton. "We should call Sir David Hamilton."

"I will speak to the Princess," said the forthright Lady Cowper.

She went into the apartment where Caroline was walking up and down clearly in great pain. With her was the old German woman who was obviously very worried.

"Your Highness, would you allow me to send for Sir David Hamilton?" asked Lady Cowper.

Caroline stopped in her perambulations and stared at Lady Cowper.

"For vat reason?"

"Your Highness may have need of him. He is a trained *accoucheur*."

"I do not vish a man to be here at this time," said the Princess.

"Your Highness . . ."

But Caroline had turned away, but as Lady Cowper went to the door she gripped the bedpost in a spasm of fresh agony. The midwife was shaking her head and letting out a stream of German.

"This is folly," said Lady Cowper; and went back to consult with Mrs. Clayton.

"But if the Princess will not have a man to attend her confinement, what can we do?"

\* \* \*

All through Monday and Tuesday the Princess continued in labour. She lay on her bed exhausted and still the child could not be brought forth.

"This is madness!" said Lady Cowper. "She cannot go on like this. Her life is in danger."

The Princess's ladies waited in their apartment for news

terrified and tearful. Lady Cowper raged that she had never heard such folly. The Princess's life was in danger and the only one she would have to attend her was that old fool of a midwife.

Selecting one of the Princess's German attendants, the Countess of Bückeburg, Lady Cowper commanded that she go to the Prince and tell him that the Princess needed the expert attention of Sir David Hamilton and that he must be sent for without delay.

The Countess went to the Prince where he was waiting with his Council.

As he listened to her his face grew red with anger—and with fear.

How dared they suggest that all was not well. Life had become so good. He was treated as a King; he was popular; he had shown himself to be a virile man. His wife was fruitful; he had a mistress. Very soon he would have another for Mary Bellenden would not hold out much longer. Everything was well.

"Nonsense," he said. "The Princess's confinements are alvays like this. Ve alvays think the child vill come earlier . . . it is alvays so. She is vell . . . vell . . . I tell you."

The Countess retreated in haste and when she reported back to Lady Cowper, the latter with Mrs. Clayton to support her, decided that something would have to be done.

They were certain that the Princess's life was in danger.

Lady Cowper went into the lying-in chamber and called to the midwife.

"What is happening?" she demanded in German.

The old woman raised her eyes to the ceiling. "It is a difficult confinement . . . very difficult."

"And you are not competent enough to deal with it . . . you know it."

"I do my best."

"Admit you're afraid."

"It's a difficult confinement."

'Go to the Prince and tell him you can't manage . . . tell him you need help. Ask that a trained *accoucheur* be sent."

"It is a difficult confinement. The Princess's confinements are always difficult."

"And you are incompetent. I tell you this ... if the Princess miscarries you will be hanged by the neck until you're dead."

The midwife screamed and ran into the ante-room which was thronged with many people who stared at the screaming woman, not understanding a word of what she was saying.

The Prince and Townsend came hurrying into the room followed by several of the ministers who had assembled for the birth.

"What is wrong?" demanded the Prince.

The midwife burst out that she wanted to go away. She could not proceed when the ladies had threatened to hang her.

"Vat is this!" cried the Prince, his face purple with rage.

The midwife cried that she would not go near the lying-in chamber, for if the Princess miscarried they were going to hang her. She had done no harm. Was it her fault that the Princess's labours were difficult?

"Who says they will hang you?" yelled the Prince.

"The ladies ... all the ladies of the Princess. They say they will blame me because I am here and it should be Sir David Hamilton. They say they will kill me..."

In the lying-in chamber the Princess was moaning in her agony.

"You must go to her," said the Prince.

"No ... no ... I dare not. They are going to hang me. I will not stay to be hanged."

"The Princess needs you," said the Prince. "Oh, we know her labours are always difficult. Go in now and attend her."

The midwife went on screaming that she dared not for they were going to hang her. They had said she should have Sir David ... and they were going to hang the poor midwife.

The Prince shouted at the top of his voice. "Of this meddling I am sick. If anyvon meddles more I throw him out of this vindow."

There was silence in the room; the Prince's wig was awry his face a choleric purple, his eyes blazing with hot anger.

Both he and the Princess had decided she should not have a

man to attend her—trained *accoucheur* that he was. She should have the midwife, as Germans always had.

But the midwife was terrified. "They will hang me," she said.

Townsend took her by the arm. He could not speak German but he smiled at her reassuringly and tried to draw her towards the Princess's chamber. But she kept screaming that they were going to hang her.

Everyone gathered round her and began talking at once. German and English mingled; an effort was made to push the woman forward but she would only whimper that they were going to hang her.

A woman's voice was heard shouting above the noise.

"Will you come at once. The Princess is lying very still." There was a deep silence. Then the midwife forgot her fears. She ran into the lying-in chamber followed by the Prince and Townsend.

After five days of labour the Princess had at last given birth.

Her child—a boy—was born dead and she herself was critically ill.

*       *       *

Considering how near death she had been Caroline recovered quickly. Deeply she regretted that she had lost her child but she consoled herself that there would be others.

There was news from Hanover. The king was pleased with his grandson Frederick and had created him Duke of Gloucester.

All very well, thought Caroline, but when is he coming to England? Perhaps the boy would return with his grandfather. If that were so she might almost look forward to the King's return.

But whenever she thought of that—which could not now be far distant—she shivered with apprehension. What had been happening during his absence was almost an open declaration of war between them.

While she lay recovering from her ordeal Townsend came to see her.

The Prince was with her and as soon as the minister entered the apartment George Augustus dismissed their attendants, for both he and Caroline saw at once that something was wrong, Townsend lost no time in telling them.

"I am dismissed from office," he said. "On the King's orders. Stanhope is now Prime Minister."

"Dismissed!" cried the Prince.

"Townsend nodded. "Bothmer has been reporting to Hanover. The King does not approve of our friendship. It was the last straw when I asked that you might have special powers to open Parliament since he was so long away."

The Prince was speechless.

Caroline lay back on her pillows and thought: The battle has begun.

\*  \*  \*

The King was coming back to England, and the Christmas celebrations had been soured by this knowledge. It could not be long now. The days of glory were coming to an end.

The Prince, clinging to power as long as possible, strutted in the Park reviewing the troops. He made more public appearances than ever, bowing, smiling, showing the people how he loved them; and his popularity was at its height. One early morning when a fire broke out near the Palace he rose from his bed and helped to put it out. Not content with that he sent money to people who had lost their homes. Everyone was talking of his bravery and consideration for his father's subjects; when the news that the mad man who had tried to shoot him at Drury Lane had made an attack on his warders in Newgate, the story of his courage was recalled.

"This is truly the Guardian of the Realm," said one newspaper.

The Prince was pleased and more able to live in the present than Caroline, who now fully recovered in health awaited the return of the King with growing apprehension.

And one day at the end of January George I returned to England.

The Prince met him at Blackheath. When his coach came to a halt the Prince alighted and went to that of the King.

As a crowd had gathered to see the meeting the King could do nothing but alight.

They faced each other and embraced while the people cheered.

Then they got into the King's coach together as though they were the best of friends. But the Prince had caught the cold dislike in the eyes of his father.

They continued the journey to St. James's in stony silence.

## The Fateful Christening

It was once more summer at Hampton Court. But how different was this summer from the last! There was common talk now of the Prince's Party and the King's Party and it was well known, not only at Court, but throughout the country that the King and his son were enemies.

The only way in which peace was maintained was by seeing that the Prince and the King were kept out of each other's way, and as they had no wish to see each other this was not difficult. The King declared himself most dissatisfied with his son; the Prince made no secret of the fact that he hated his father.

Caroline alone kept up a pretence that all was well; and however vehemently she expressed her dislike of her father-in-law in private, she always behaved with the utmost respect in public.

They had moved to Hampton Court for the summer; the King was not as displeased to be back in England now as he had been in the winter, for he had promised himself another trip to Hanover in the not too distant future while he resigned himself to the fact that as King of England he must spend some of his time in that country.

And at Hampton Court the King made an attempt to gain a little popularity, since his son had acquired a great deal during his absence. It was not easy for George, but he did try; he allowed conversation at the dinner table in which he sometimes joined, speaking French for he still made no effort whatsoever to speak English. He would sometimes sit in the pavilion and watch the bowl players, or take a turn at the cards; he often listened to music; he liked to take supper alone with Ermengarda, who was now the Duchess of Kendal, making sure that they retired early to what he called "a seasonable bedtime".

Caroline was pleased that they were at Hampton. She was once more pregnant and this time was determined to take more care of herself. She longed for a son; and the very root of her resentment against the King was the fact that he would not allow Fritzchen to come to England.

The Whig Ministry had been reformed with Stanhope and Sunderland at its head. Sunderland however, had become a great favourite of the King's for two reasons. One was his intense dislike of the Prince of Wales; and the other that he had become fast friends with the Duchess of Kendal, whose long association with the King had made her as a wife to him, and also with Bernstorff who was the King's chief adviser. Even Stanhope, brilliant master of foreign affairs that he was—and the King appreciated his worth—could not compete with that. As for Townsend, although he had lost his office, he was, with Walpole, still of some importance; yet, to the chagrin of Caroline and the Prince, since the return of the King, the friendship towards them and these two men had waned considerably. They seemed as though instead of being the support they had promised to be, they merely wanted to remain on good terms, ready for the day when the Prince would be in power.

Still, there were Whigs who were very dissatisfied with the reigning ministry and these formed the nucleus of the Prince's party.

There was one man whom the Prince and Caroline disliked and distrusted more than any other and that was the Duke of

Newcastle. The Duke had shown his contempt for the Prince and stood firmly against him. That was something George Augustus and Caroline found hard to forgive.

But there was fortunately no obligation to see much of the man. In fact, because of her pregnancy, and moreover because of the last confinement which had ended so disastrously, Caroline made every excuse to live quietly in her own apartments.

This she did, and it was pleasant to have her little girls with her. They had become devoted to her now that they could be so much together, but she was rather alarmed to notice that Anne was aware of certain follies in her father. She had seen the child watching him when he betrayed his vanity, or quick temper, or some lack of perception. If Anne became critical of her father she would have to correct that. She shuddered to think of having her children in conflict with *their* parents. Anne was old enough to know of course, of the strife between her father and grandfather. On no account must that be repeated.

So with the family together and the excitement of intrigues with those politicians who, even though the King had returned, remained faithful to the Prince, life was far from tedious. Although at times when Caroline was made aware of the choleric temper of her husband and the soured vindictiveness of his father she did feel as though she were sitting on gunpowder.

There was storm in the sultry air all that summer when everyone was comparing it with that of the previous year.

And in October Caroline and the Prince returned to St. James's to be ready for Caroline's lying-in.

*       *       *

Exactly a year after the disaster when she had lost her child and almost her own life through her prudery in not allowing Sir David Hamilton to attend her, Caroline gave birth to a son.

She was delighted, but not more so than the Prince. He came to her, his face pink with emotion as he knelt by her bed and kissed her hands.

"My tear, my tear, this the happiest day ... Now you vill not miss little Fritzchen so much, eh?"

"*Wunderbar ... wunderbar!*" whispered Caroline.

"And vere is this little fellow?"

He was brought and placed in the Prince's arms.

Caroline watched her husband awkwardly nursing the child.

"He is goot ... he seems goot. Vere are my daughters. Send my daughters here. They must their *bruder* meet."

Caroline lay back on her pillows watching them; the three little girls; her husband and the new child.

"There! Is he not von fine little fellow?" The Prince was strutting round the apartment. "See how happy he is to be in his father's arms."

Anne was watching a trifle scornfully.

Amelia said: "Is it not Mamma's baby too?"

"Ha!" laughed the Prince. "It is Mamma's baby too."

"Perhaps," said Anne coolly, "she would like to hold it now."

"Ha! ha!" laughed her father. Caroline held her breath. He did not see the criticism. He would not have thought it possible that his daughters could be critical of him.

It must not grow, thought Caroline.

"Your father is very happy now," she said. "He was anxious for me and now it is goot that all is vell."

Little Caroline was standing by the bed, clinging to her mother's hand, fearful that the coming of the new child might lose her her mother's attention, wondering what it would be like now that she was no longer the baby.

The Prince had laid the child in her arms and the little girls came round her to look closely at him.

"Do you think he is like his Papa, eh?" demanded the Prince.

"No," replied Anne. "I think he is more like Mamma. I like him."

The Prince rocked on his heels, well pleased with his happy family.

When the little girls had gone he said: "I'll swear my father is envious of us."

"This quarrel does little good," replied Caroline. "Ve should try to mend it ... if only outwardly."

"Oh, he is von old scoundrel."

"I know, but he is the King; and he can make things very unpleasant for you."

"Let him try."

Caroline sighed. Then she said: "I should like to call the child Lewis."

"Lewis..." repeated the Prince. "Oh but it's his name."

"Perhaps you vould agree that he might be pleased to have the child named after him."

"Vy should ve please him?"

"Because after all he is the King. Ve lose by this quarrel."

The Prince was thoughtful. "And you vish, my love, that this should be the boy's name?"

"Yes. I vish it."

"Then it shall be Lewis."

"And I should like your sister to be sponsor."

"My sister! You think she would come from Prussia?"

Caroline thought of Sophia Dorothea from whom she heard now and then, living her stormy life with Frederick William who was now King of Prussia. They quarrelled violently and incessantly but there was a bond between them which, in spite of this, held them together. It would be a great joy to see her sister-in-law again and recall those days at Hanover.

"But perhaps she vould send a proxy."

The Prince nodded. It seemed fitting that his sister should be sponsor to his child; he had always been fond of her since those days when they had lost their mother and gradually became aware of the tragic circumstances of her disappearance.

"Ve should ask her," he said.

"And beside her perhaps your uncle the Duke of Osnabrück and York."

"Vat! He whom my father threatened to make Regent ven he vent avay!"

"It vould please your father."

"I do not vish to please that old scoundrel."

"Outwardly..." she said with a smile.

The Prince began to smile and his eyes lit up with mischief.

"Yes," he said, "this is not a bad idea. Ve vill please him in this..."

"Show the people that ve do our best to end the family quarrels."

"A goot idea," replied the Prince, every moment becoming certain that he had thought of it.

\* \* \*

The King came to St. James's to see his grandson. Caroline received him in bed and he was gracious to her.

A fine woman, he thought, looking at her lying back on her pillows, her hair simply dressed, a curl over either shoulder. Too clever for a woman though. Bernstorff had discovered it; so had Bothmer and Robethon. They must watch this one.

"It is good of Your Majesty to come," she said meekly enough but he didn't trust her meekness. She was the guiding hand in this partnership against him. George Augustus was a fool who allowed his wife to lead him by the nose; and a bigger fool because he didn't know it.

"I come to see my grandson," he retorted with characteristic tactlessness.

The Prince came into the apartment. Uneasily Caroline watched the two regard each other. The Prince bowed; the King nodded and quickly turned back to the bed.

"Your Majesty will wish to see the boy," said Caroline, and signed to one of the attendants to have the child brought to the King.

The nurse came and stood before George, holding the child in her arms. The King looked down into the little face and grunted.

"The Prince and I have decided to call him Lewis," said Caroline, and waited for the sign of pleasure in the grim old face.

Instead the lips tightened; and there was no show of pleasure.

Thinking it was because he was trying to hide his pleasure she hurried on: "And as sponsors we have chosen the Queen of Prussia and the Duke of Osnabrück and York."

The King was silent for a moment. Then he said: "His name shall be George William and I shall let you know who his sponsors will be."

With that he gave her a curt nod and without another look at his son strode out of the apartment.

\*   \*   \*

The Prince was furious. There before his attendants, the nurse and some of the bedchamber women he took off his wig and kicked it over the bed.

"He is von old scoundrel. Whose son is this? Is it mine or is it his? I tell you his name is Lewis. I vill not have his sponsors. . . ."

With a nod Caroline signed to Henrietta Howard to pick up the wig and present it to the Prince.

This she did; he took it ungraciously and slammed it on his head. It was awry, and his face purple with rage looked almost comic beneath it. Caroline believed that Molly Lepel and Sophie Howe were having great difficulties in suppressing their giggles.

"You may leave us," said Caroline to all present.

And when they were alone she set herself the difficult task of persuading the Prince that they would have to fall in with the King's wishes because he had the power to make them. They must be patient, remembering that it would not always be so.

\*   \*   \*

Caroline was in bed for the christening. She was both angry and apprehensive. The King had shown his animosity not only by forcing them to have the name of his choice but by selecting for one of the sponsors the Duke of Newcastle whom he knew —and the whole court knew—was a particular enemy of the Prince and Princess of Wales.

She was terrified that George Augustus would be unable to control his rage. If he insulted the King in public the consequences could be disastrous. She dared not warn him of this for it might put the idea into his mind; and his very fearlessness could make him reckless.

When Newcastle came into the apartment she saw the Prince turn his back on him. Newcastle was an extremely ugly man and it was obvious from his demeanour that he knew the Prince deplored his presence, and was amused by this.

The Duchess of St. Albans was co-sponsor with the King and Newcastle. Caroline had no great feeling for or against her, except for the fact that she had not chosen her and she thought that a Prince of the royal house should have had royal sponsors.

How relieved she would be when the ceremony was over! She must try to forget her chagrin, and persuade George Augustus to do the same, for this matter, while extremely irritating and humiliating would not damage their reputation with the people, which was more important than anything. In fact, the people would be indignant on their behalf which might mean it was a good thing after all.

The ceremony was over quickly and the King left immediately. The Prince however was glaring at Newcastle on whose unprepossessing face there was a faint sneer. The Prince had grown scarlet; the veins stood out at his temples and rushing to Newcastle he shook his fist at him shouting in English which was always more imperfect than usual when he was disturbed: "You are von scoundrel. I vill find you."

What the Prince meant to imply was that he would discover what intrigues the Duke was engaged in; but the Duke thought he was trying to say he would fight him; and he gathered that this was a challenge to a duel.

He bowed and hastily left the apartment.

\* \* \*

He went at once to his friends Sunderland and Stanhope who listened intently to what he had to say.

They said they would consult the King's minister, Bernstorff, who would know better than anyone else what the King's reaction would be to such blatant indiscretion on the part of the Prince.

The four men talked the matter over.

There would be no duel. The Prince would not be allowed to fight.

Secretly all but Newcastle, when they heard what the Prince had said, realized that it was his imperfect English which had given the wrong impression; but as they were eager to increase

L*

the animosity between the King and the Prince they thought it wise to keep to the original construction.

The Prince was a fool, but a fool with a clever wife. Therefore he was a danger. He was their enemy, so if it were possible to incense the King more deeply against him all the better.

"The Prince is clearly a danger to the King's ministers," said Bernstorff. "I will put this matter before him."

\*     \*     \*

To the Prince's apartments came the Dukes of Kent, Roxburgh and Kingston.

"Vat you vant?" demanded the Prince.

"We come on His Majesty's instructions."

"Vell, vell, vat is it?"

"We have to question Your Highness on the challenge you have made to the Duke of Newcastle."

"Challenge? Vat is this challenge?"

"You have challenged him to a duel."

"You are mad."

"The Duke of Newcastle complains that Your Highness has challenged him to a duel. He cannot accept your challenge. In the name of the King...."

"In the name of the King vill you get out of here."

"We come to question Your Highness on the King's order."

"I answer not questions ... to the King, that old scoundrel, nor to you. I made no challenge. Newcastle is von liar. Get out or I vill you out throw."

The Dukes retired and went to the King who after listening intently gave the order that the Prince should be placed under arrest.

\*     \*     \*

Throughout the Court and all over London the news of the Prince's arrest was being discussed.

He was shut in his apartments with the Princess and neither of them was allowed to venture out. Even those attendants who had not been in the apartments at the time of the arrest were not permitted to go to their master and mistress.

In the coffee houses there was excited speculation. Sympathy was with the Prince who, when he was Guardian of the Realm, had shown them how much more gay and colourful life would be if he were King. The Princess was popular too, so the people were on their side.

The King was a sour old man; his mistresses were ugly; he rarely smiled; he made no concessions to popularity; he preferred Hanover to England. Let him go back and live on sausages and sauerkraut. He had a wife whom he had kept shut up in a prison for more than twenty years. He was a wicked old ogre. Did he now think to imprison his son as he had his wife!

The people would not allow it.

They wanted to see their Prince and Princess riding through the streets, walking in the parks.

A royal quarrel was exciting only for a while. They would allow no locking up of their Prince and Princess.

Besides the poor lady had just given birth to a boy. What a shock this must be for her, and her still recovering from a difficult confinement!

The people were for the Prince and Princess.

\*       \*       \*

Aghast at what had happened, Caroline tried to plan what they should do for the best.

She knew they had a vindictive man against them. She had lived long enough in the shadow of the Leine Schloss where the ill-fated Sophia Dorothea, the Prince's mother, had learned what could happen to those who offended George Lewis.

Why should he be any more lenient towards a son than a wife?

They must not be foolishly proud. They must act quickly.

She tried to convey her fears to George Augustus, who after his first storms of rage had subsided was prepared to listen to her.

He too remembered the fate of his mother.

Between them they composed a letter to the King which the Prince wrote.

"If I have had the misfortune to offend Your Majesty, contrary to my intention, I crave his pardon and pray him to be persuaded of the respect which I have for him. I will show no more resentment to the Duke of Newcastle...."

Caroline read the letter slowly.

"Must I send this to that old scoundrel?" asked the Prince almost tearfully.

"I fear so," she said. "He has great power. Ve must not forget your mother."

\*　　\*　　\*

They had humbled themselves and the King was glad of that. Not that he intended it to do them any good. He despised and hated his son. He would never forget the day when as a boy he had broken away from a hunting party and tried to rescue his mother. It had been an attempt doomed to failure from the start but the boy had been reckless enough to make it, and it had earned him the admiration and affection of too many people. It had called attention to the vindictive cruelty of his father; and more than that, it had been the beginning of the enmity between them.

The boy had been on the side of his mother, which meant that he was against his father.

George Lewis never forgave, never forgot an insult, or an injury. Sophia Dorothea, still in prison, was a confirmation of that.

He wanted to forget that woman; and her son—who was unfortunately his also—would not let him forget. For instance, there were times when he even looked like her; and he knew she was often in his mind. His son had never forgiven him for what he had done to his mother. Very well, he would have to learn what it meant to have his father for an enemy.

When he read the letter his son had written he laughed scornfully. He knew who was responsible for that. That she-devil. George Augustus would never have had the sense to try to placate him.

Well, Madam, you have failed, said the King; and he put the letter into a candle flame and let it burn.

Stanhope, with several of his ministers, was asking for audience to discuss this unfortunate matter of the Prince. He received them with no change in his usual dour expression.

"Your Majesty we cannot keep the Prince in confinement indefinitely," Stanhope explained. "It is a breach of the Habeas Corpus Act. The Opposition will create a great disturbance if we keep him confined much longer. It could lead to great trouble."

"If I were in Hanover I should know what to do," said the King. "Here in England ... there are different laws. You must explain to me. But one thing I will not have—and I know there is no law to stop this. I will not live under the same roof with the Prince."

Stanhope replied: "Your Majesty is right. There is no law to prevent the Prince having a separate establishment."

"Then I will banish him and the Princess from St. James's Palace."

"The Cabinet would have to approve Your Majesty's decision."

"Then let them approve ... quickly. I will not tolerate him here much longer."

"I will call a meeting of the Cabinet without delay," said Stanhope.

\*     \*     \*

Caroline had risen from her bed, although still weak. The quarrel with the King had not helped in her recovery and she was very anxious as to the outcome. The Prince was more subdued than usual. The days of confinement to his apartments had sobered him considerably. He considered the power of his father and was alarmed as to what the next move would be.

Caroline thought of her daughters in another part of the palace and wondered what stories they were hearing of the differences between their parents and their grandfather. She asked that they might be sent to her, that if they were under arrest the whole family might be together, but was told that the King's orders were that the girls were not to visit their parents.

She was more alarmed than ever when she heard this.

He is capable of any cruelty, she thought. And again she thought of his wife who had been separated from her two young children.

What next? she wondered.

She felt faint and feverish, and this was an additional anxiety for she knew that in this crisis she needed all her wits.

Their sentence came to them, explained in a document which the King had prepared. They were free to go, but they were banished from St. James's.

George Augustus read the document aloud to her.

"Banished!" he said. "Good riddance to him and his miserable court. Ve'll have our own. A fine goot court. He von't like that. Oh no, my old rascal."

"And is that all?" she asked.

"No, there is some more."

She was out of bed and taking the document from his hands. She felt dizzy as she read:

"It is my pleasure that my grandson and granddaughters remain at St. James's where they are. The Princess will be permitted to see them when she has a mind, and the children will be permitted from time to time to go and see her and my son."

Caroline dropped the document and stared at the Prince.

"Do you see vat he is doing?"

"He is sending us avay." The Prince snapped his fingers. "Let him. Ve vill have von fine big court ... better than his. To ours vill come his enemies. He is von big fool."

"He is going to keep the children from us."

"He says you can see them ... from time to time."

"From time to time! My own children. They are going to be taken from us. And the baby. . . . He is so young. He needs his mother."

"You are distressed, my tear. That old scoundrel ... his is von vicked old devil ... but ve vill outvit him yet."

"My children," murmured Caroline. "My little baby. Don't you see. This is his punishment to us! He is going to rob us of our children?"

He could not share her grief. He was planning ahead. He would have his court and the Prince's Court would be a rival to the King's. It would be no different from before, except that the people would be sorry for him; they would be on his side. The old devil had not been so clever after all.

But Caroline was heartbroken. This was the cruellest blow he could have inflicted. Perhaps he knew it and that was why he had planned it. He was going to separate her from her children.

* * *

There was no time for grief. They were expected to leave on receipt of the King's order.

"Where to?" asked Caroline in bewilderment.

No one knew. All that mattered was that they left St. James's without delay. It was the King's wish that they did not spend another night under the same roof as himself.

Caroline called for Henrietta.

"Tell all the women to make ready. We are going at once."

"Where, Your Highness?"

"That I cannot say. All I can tell you is that we are leaving St. James's."

"And the children?" asked Henrietta.

"They are to remain," replied Caroline, bitterly, "on the King's orders."

"But . . ."

"I can tell you no more," replied Caroline. "We are to leave at once."

Mary Bellenden asked leave to give a note to the Prince or Princess. It was Caroline who took it and saw that it was from the Earl of Grantham. He had heard what had happened and wished to place his house in Albermarle Street at their disposal.

"So," said Caroline blankly, "we have somewhere to go."

At the same time the King's messenger had arrived with a note to her from the King.

She read it eagerly hoping that he had had some change of heart with regard to her children.

The King wrote that he understood she had not recovered from her confinement and was not well enough to move at present. He would therefore grant her permission to stay at St. James's with her children providing she made no attempt to communicate with her husband who must leave the palace without delay. Unless she kept this promise she would be banished with her husband while her children remained at St. James's.

Caroline re-read the letter. He was offering her her children or her husband.

Never in her life before had she had such a decision to make.

The Prince came to her. "Vat now?" he asked; and when she showed him the letter, his face grew scarlet with rage.

"He vould try to separate us ... he vould try to tempt a vife from her husband!"

"There are the children."

"You vill them see," he told her. "He does not say you vill not see them. From time to time, he says. But it vill not be for long. Ve vill think of something, my tearest."

And she looked at him and knew that she must choose to be with him. She was necessary to him. What would become of him without her? What would become of them both? He was as one of her children and she dared not desert him now.

She wrote to the King: "Where my husband goes there must I go too."

\* \* \*

The maids of honour were packing hastily.

"This is disastrous," said Margaret Meadows. "It is the beginning of real trouble between the King and the Prince."

"We'll have a better time in the Prince's Court than in the King's," commented Sophie Howe. "Of all the dreary places in the world ... St. James's is the most dreary!"

"I wish it were like that summer at Hampton," said Molly Lepel. "That was a glorious time."

Mary Bellenden joined them; she was in high spirits, for where she went John Campbell as gentleman of the Prince's bedchamber would go.

"Are you ready?" she cried. "Then come—over the hills and far away!"

\* \* \*

The coach jolted along to Albemarle Street. Already there were little knots of people in the streets to watch the party.

The Prince of Wales turned out of the Palace! Who ever

heard of such a thing! These Germans had no family feeling. They didn't want Germans here. King Charles had always been jovial and kind to members of his family. It had been a pleasure to see him with his little nieces. And his brother James had doted on Anne and Mary; Anne's love for her only child who lived past his infancy was quite touching. But German George had been really cruel to the poor Princess. Not only had he taken her daughters from her but he had separated her from her newly born baby.

Family bickering was one thing, but to drive a woman from her children, soon after she's risen from childbed was real cruelty.

"Damn George," said the people. "Damn the German. And God bless the Prince and Princess of Wales."

\*　　\*　　\*

In Grantham House the Princess was in a state of collapse. Her women got her quickly to bed and feared that she would not recover.

The Prince sat beside her bed covering his face with his hands and crying quietly.

Rumours that the Prince and Princess were ill circulated in the streets and little knots of people stood outside Grantham's house waiting for news of them while in St. James's the King gave orders that any foreign ambassadors who visited the Prince would not be received at his Court.

And now, he said, that the troublesome Prince is no longer with us let us enjoy some peace.

\*　　\*　　\*

A new drama soon arose. The newly born child, deprived of its mother, became ill. The nurses whom the King had commanded to care for the little boy at first assured themselves that this was nothing but a normal childish ailment, but as the child grew more wan and fretful they could no longer deceive themselves and sent for the physicians, who, when they saw the child, decided that the King should be informed, without delay, of its condition.

"Well," said George gruffly, "what do you recommend?"

"That Your Majesty should send at once for the child's mother."

"That's impossible," snapped the King.

"We fear, sir, that if you do not the child will die."

"Nonsense. What can she do that you can't? Are you doctors or not?"

"In our opinion, Your Majesty, the child is pining for his mother."

George looked at them suspiciously. He was inclined to suspect them of working for the Prince.

"She is forbidden to come to the palace, so she must stay away."

And with that he dismissed the doctors.

\*     \*     \*

But the people were too interested in the family quarrel not to have discovered what was happening in the Palace, and when it became known that the newly born child was ill and not allowed to see its mother, the crowds grew angry.

"Keep a babe from its mother!" they cried. "What sort of a monster is this we've got as a King."

Stanhope came to see George.

"If the child dies, Your Majesty, and his mother is not allowed to see him, there might be riots. These people are sentimental about children."

George was thoughtful.

"The Princess may come, but not the Prince."

"I will send a message to her immediately," replied Stanhope.

\*     \*     \*

When Caroline received the message she immediately prepared to leave Albermarle Street for St. James's. The people crowded the streets to see her pass and shout their good wishes.

She smiled wanly; and when they saw how ill she looked and how sad they shouted: "God bless you. And down with the unnatural German monster."

Caroline felt comforted and wondered whether she would be

allowed to stay at St. James's and nurse her baby; and whether she would have a chance of seeing her daughters.

On reaching the Palace she was hurriedly taken to an apartment which had been prepared for her and when she saw her child she was overcome with grief for she realized how ill he was. He was suffering from fever and his cough was so incessant that she was afraid she had come too late.

She took him from his nurses and said she would have charge of him now, and all through the night she sat with him and although he continued to cough and his fever was as high as ever, she fancied he knew her and was comforted.

\* \* \*

The child was sleeping in his cradle. He looked very ill, but at least he slept. Caroline kept her place at his cradle, rocking it gently to and fro and turning over in her mind whether she might not plead with the King at least to allow her to have care of this child.

Henrietta, whom she had brought with her, came silently into the room and said that the little girls were outside and longing to see their mother.

"Oh Henrietta, bring them in to me!"

The door was flung open and the girls ran in to throw themselves into their mother's arms.

"Anne ... my dear ... and Amelia ... and where's my baby Caroline?"

"Here, Mamma! Here!"

"Oh, my darlings!"

She was weeping; and they had never seen her weep before. They would not have thought their stately, wise Mamma capable of tears. And because she was crying for them that made them sad and happy at the same time; and very soon they were all crying with her.

"But ve are *fou*," said Caroline. "Here ve are together ... and ve veep ven ve should be laughing. Oh, it makes me happy to see you. Are you goot girls? Do you miss Mamma ... and Papa?"

"We miss you, Mamma," said Amelia, the truthful one.

Caroline pretended not to notice the omission. She thought:

What do they hear of their father? There must be whisperings about him in the King's court.

"We are like charity children," said Anne.

"Charity children?" cried Caroline.

"Yes ... although we have a good mother and we have a father ... we are not with them and that makes us like charity children."

"Ve shall be together soon ... you children and Papa and myself."

"When Mamma, when?" demanded little Caroline.

"Ven it ... is permitted."

"I do not like grandfather much," said Amelia.

"He is the King," put in Anne in a shocked voice looking over her shoulder.

Were they being furtive? wondered Caroline. Did they talk together about the King, about the family quarrel? Did their servants whisper gossip to them? 'You must not mention this ... or that...'

It is so bad for them, she thought. Oh, why cannot I bring up my own children in the way I want. It is so cruel. He knows what hurts me most.

"That doesn't make me like him," said Amelia.

"I like Mamma," said young Caroline.

Caroline held her more tightly. "Tell me please ... what do you do all day?"

"Lady Portland is our governess," said Amelia.

"She is kind to you?"

They nodded.

"We walk and we read and we say prayers. And Mr. Handel is going to teach us music."

"You must be goot ... goot ... and learn. And soon ve shall be together."

"Why can't we be now?" Caroline wanted to know.

"Because of Grandpapa and Papa," said Amelia. "They have had a quarrel and it is to punish Mamma."

Oh, what do they hear? wondered Caroline again.

"Mamma is punished because she loves us," said Caroline.

And the Princess was weeping again, straining them to her breast. It was wrong, but for once she could not control her emotions. These were her beloved children and how did she know when she should see them again?

*     *     *

"The Princess has been with my granddaughters!" cried the King. "This is forbidden. Of what use for me to give orders if they are not obeyed? Who took my granddaughters to their mother's apartment?"

Bernstorff pointed out that it was deplorable that His Majesty's wishes had been disregarded but if the people knew that he prevented their mother seeing the children there might be demonstrations against him in the streets. The people were a little placated because the Princess had been allowed to see her sick son; but if they knew someone had been reprimanded for taking her daughters to her there could be trouble.

"There will be trouble while that woman is under this roof. She shall not stay here."

"But the young Prince is still dangerously ill."

"I have said I will not have her here and I mean it."

"Sir . . ."

"Let the child be removed to Kensington and his mother can go there to be with him."

"I will ask the doctors if he is well enough to be moved, Your Majesty."

"He is to be moved. They say the air at Kensington is good. Let him go there and his mother with him."

"It shall be so, sir."

*     *     *

The doctors came to see the King.

"Your Majesty, the child is too sick to be moved."

"I do not want his mother here."

"He has improved a little since her coming, sir."

"She makes trouble under this roof. I will not have her."

"We do not advise moving the child."

"Nonsense! They tell me the air at Kensington is better than here at St. James's."

"But at this time of year . . . the weather being so inclement . . . and the child so sick."

"Send him to Kensington or send his mother away."

The next day Caroline and her baby left St. James's for Kensington Palace.

\* \* \*

The child was dying. Caroline knew and so did the Prince who had joined her at Kensington.

They sat on either side of the small cradle and wept; and while they watched that small frail body seized by convulsions they were filled with a great hatred for the man whom they believed was responsible.

Henrietta who had accompanied them to Kensington came and stood at some little distance from the cradle. She knew before they did that the child was dead.

Eventually Caroline rose and went quietly from the apartment.

I shall hate him as long as we both live, she thought.

And when she rode back to Albemarle Street and the crowds were silent in their sympathy she felt a little comfort because she knew that they too hated the man who was their King.

## The Royal Quarrel

HER child dead, her children taken from her care, Caroline felt there was only one thing left to her. She would take her revenge on the man who had treated her so cruelly and by so doing lay the foundations of the power she was determined should be hers when she was Queen of England.

"Ve can't stay at Grantham's house," she told the Prince. "Ve must find a place of our own."

George Augustus, whose grief was superficial, agreed.

"Ve vill find a suitable residence," said Caroline, "and ven ve have found it vill ve build such a court as to make the King's look like a provincial country gentleman's house."

The Prince was delighted. His hatred of his father was far from superficial.

"Vell," said Caroline, "ve begin to look vithout delay."

It was not long before they discovered Leicester House, and as soon as Caroline saw it she knew that she wanted it.

It was on the north side of Leicester Fields and a courtyard stood between it and the public square. It had a pleasant Dutch garden at the back; and Caroline pointed out to the

Prince that if they bought the house which adjoined it they could have complete privacy. Although it had only two storeys, the reception rooms were very fine and there was a grand staircase. The neighbourhood was not all that might be desired; on either side of the house were rows of shops; but the main drawback was that Leicester Fields had a bad reputation, having been the resort of all kinds of undesirable characters in the past. Footpads had lurked in the Fields by night and confidence tricksters by day; many a duel had been fought in front of Leicester House, many a nose split by the terrifying Mohocks.

"Is this suitable for the Prince and Princess of Vales?" asked the Prince.

"Not now ... but it vill be. Ve vill make it so," replied his wife.

*　　*　　*

Caroline was right. As soon as she and the Prince settled in with their household the neighbourhood changed over night. In place of the footpads came the linkmen; the Fields were almost as safe by night as by day, crowded with the coaches of the rich and influential and the Sedan chairs of the great.

All those who were dissatisfied with the Government began to make their way to Leicester House; and not only those. There were astute statesmen who began to realize that the Princess of Wales, if not the Prince, was extremely clever; and although she suffered personally through the loss of her children, her popularity with the people had multiplied because of it. There was scarcely a mother in London and its surrounding villages who did not cry shame to the monster who could deprive a woman of her children.

Caroline mourning for them, deplored the fact that she had no say in their upbringing; but she made full use of the situation; and sought to forget her sorrowful resentment in building the rival court.

This she quickly succeeded in doing and so efficiently that some of the King's ministers advised him to seek an end of the quarrel. A house divided against itself was in danger, they pointed out; particularly when there was a Prince across the water whom many considered to be the real King.

George shrugged these warnings aside. He disliked his son; he deplored his conduct; and he did not trust the Princess of Wales, although he admired her as a woman. He would state his terms to his son and his son must accept them or content himself with exile.

Meanwhile the charm and beauty of Caroline's ladies-in-waiting brought the young bloods to Leicester House—men like the brilliant Lord Hervey whose verses were so clever and who was so good looking, but in a somewhat effeminate way so that he was at times like a handsome girl; but he was clever enough to be an ornament to any Court and Caroline encouraged him. Then there was clever young Lord Stanhope, Lord Chester-field's heir—so witty that he could not fail to amuse, although he was cruel with it. A strange young man, in looks as different from Hervey as he could be—with an enormous head which made him look stunted and almost dwarf like; and although he was only in his early twenties his teeth were already black. Unprepossessing though he was, he was continually boasting of his successes with women; and his wit was pungent and even more cruel than Hervey's. Another was Lord Peterborough, a tall cadaverous young man; he was amoral doubtless, but amusing. These young men fluttered round the maids of honour with many others; and the promise they gave of being the men of the future interested Caroline.

But her most welcome guests were the writers and for them there was always a ready welcome. Before she had been long at Leicester House Pope, Gay and Tickell were regular visitors; and she had expressed a wish that when Jonathan Swift was in London he would visit her. Isaac Newton was always welcome and since he lived in St. Martin's Lane not far from Leicester Fields, he enjoyed many conversations with Caroline.

This was what she had always wanted—not only a Court where politicians gathered, but one which should be the centre of the arts. Thus it had been in the days of her childhood when she had been so impressed by the court of Sophia Char-lotte; she had always dreamed of being the moving spirit in such a court; and now she could be. There was a difference between herself and Sophia Charlotte though—Sophia Charlotte had loved the arts only and had never sought to take a share in government. Caroline wanted both.

George Augustus had little time for the writers. He despised what he called "boetry". He even remonstrated with Lord Hervey for writing it.

"Vot for you vant to write this boetry?" he demanded. "That is for little Mr. Pope and his kind ... not for a noble lord."

But he indulged his wife. "If you like these men, my tear, then haf them ... but they are only boets and vill not help us fight my father?"

Caroline's reply was that she believed there was more strength in the pen than anything else; and these people delighted her with their clever use of words.

"You vere alvays von governess," said the Prince affectionately.

And the writers continued to come.

Caroline knew that in time it would be the turn of the important politicians.

\* \* \*

Caroline was not surprised when Sir Spencer Compton came to Leicester House with a message from the King, and she and the Prince received him in the latter's apartment.

His Majesty, explained Sir Spencer, deplored the differences which existed between him and his son.

George Augustus retorted that if that were so his father only had to behave like any rational father and he and the Princess would be happy to forget those differences.

"This," said Sir Spencer, "is exactly what His Majesty wishes to do, and if Your Highness will abide by certain rules this unfortunate trouble should be over."

"Can you tell me vat these rules are?"

"I can, for it is for the purpose of laying them before you that I have come here."

"Pray proceed."

"His Majesty requires you to pay for your children's households—that of your daughters in St. James's and your son in Hanover."

"If my father vill allow my son to come to England and be under my direction I shall have the greatest pleasure in paying for his establishment over here."

"It is the King's wish that he remains in Hanover."

George Augustus's face was purple with anger. "Then it shall be the King's privilege to provide for him there."

"Is that Your Highness's final answer on that point?"

The Prince rapped his fist on the table. "That is my final answer."

"And your daughters' household?"

"If the King vill have charge of them he must pay for them."

"Then I will continue with the conditions which the King has asked me to put before you. You are to fill no places in your household without the King's pleasure, and to retain in your service no one disagreeable to His Majesty."

"That vould doubtless mean ridding ourselves of some of those who are dearest to us," said Caroline quickly.

"It is a condition His Majesty has imposed."

Caroline looked at the Prince and shook her head; she had no need. He was growing angrier every minute.

"Vat else?" he asked.

"It would be necessary for you to sever relations with any whom the King declared was disagreeable to him and to treat the King's servants in a civil manner."

"I can scarcely believe that is all His Majesty demands!" said George Augustus with heavy sarcasm.

"And the children?" cried Caroline hastily. "If ve did these things should ve be allowed to have our children back?"

"There is one other condition, Your Highnesses."

"Yes?"

"You would be obliged to acquiesce in the King's right to the guardianship of his grandchildren."

"No," cried Caroline.

"No, no, *no!*" echoed the Prince.

Caroline smiled at him. "Ve are better as ve are. I know the Prince is too vise and shrewd and also too proud to give vay to such conditions."

"That is true," said the Prince.

So Sir Spencer Compton went away; and the quarrel persisted, as fierce as ever.

"He is the von who vill be sorry," Caroline told the Prince, though in her heart she would have been ready to agree to any condition which brought back her children to her, and the King knew it. It was for this reason that he had struck her in such a way that she should suffer most.

Very well. It was open warfare. If the King wanted battle between himself and his son and daughter-in-law, he should have it.

And she was strong enough to make her own the winning side.

And when Robert Walpole became a visitor to Leicester House she believed she was going to succeed.

* * *

The Prince had never despaired of winning Mary Bellenden, and sought every opportunity of making her aware of his intentions, although she continually evaded him, sometimes pretending that she did not understand what he meant.

Because he liked to share confidences he told Henrietta about his feelings. In fact Henrietta could not have been ignorant of them, as no one else at court was; but it did not occur to him to think it strange that he should confide his desire to make a woman his mistress to one who already was.

He was the Prince and above reproach; moreover being as virile as he would have everyone believe him to be, it was not to be suspected that he could be satisfied with one mistress and one wife.

"This girl vants to be chased," he told Henrietta. "She is enjoying this courtship, but it goes on too long. Vat can I do?"

The meek Henrietta said that he might tell her of his intentions outright.

"She never gives me the chance. She laughs too much. Then she vill pretend she cannot understand vat I say ... like that rascal Newcastle. Then she talks so fast that I cannot understand her. She is von naughty girl ... though very pretty. I think, Henrietta, that she is the prettiest girl in my tear wife's household."

"Either Mary or Molly Lepel is according to the poets," admitted Henrietta.

"Oh boets. Don't talk to me of boets. The Princess thinks so highly of them she believes all they say. Mary is prettier than Molly and I have long had this fancy for her. Invite her to your rooms tonight, Henrietta, and I vill speak to her."

Henrietta, always docile agreed to do so. For one thing she knew very well that Mary would not accept the Prince, and for another she knew that if she did, it would make no difference to her own position. For all his talk of being English the Prince was completely German—certainly in his attitude to women. He would be like his father who had been faithful to Ermengarda Schulemburg for more than twenty years, no matter how many mistresses he had in addition.

So Henrietta told Mary Bellenden that she was expected to attend her apartment that night on orders of the Prince.

Mary looked glum when she received the command.

"I can't come," she declared.

"The Prince's orders."

"You must say I'm ill."

"If you say that there'll be another time. You can't be ill forever."

"What am I to do?"

"Tell him the truth."

Mary turned away; but even she dared not disobey the Prince's command and at nine o'clock that evening she went along to Henrietta's apartment. Precisely at nine—not a second before and not one after, for the Prince prided himself on his respect for time—George Augustus arrived at Henrietta's apartment, beaming with pleasure at the joyful anticipation of Mary's surrender.

He found the girl there with Henrietta who, on the pleas of Mary, remained as chaperon.

Strangely enough George Augustus did not seem to object to her presence and sat down immediately next to Mary and drew a table towards him.

"You are von very pretty fräulein," he told her.

"Your Highness is gracious," Mary replied uneasily.

"I vould be very gracious . . . if you are von sensible girl."

"*I* think I am sensible, Your Highness," replied Mary who could never resist a certain pertness.

"Ven vat are ve vaiting for?"

"Your Highness wished a game of cards perhaps? Mrs. Howard will doubtless summon others to join us."

"Not that game," said the Prince. "Our game shall be a game for two."

"I don't know that game, Your Highness, so you must excuse me."

She had half risen but he put out a hand to detain her.

"Von moment. You are a pretty girl. You spend much money, eh? On pretty clothes perhaps . . . on powder and patches, on ribbons and laces?"

"Alas, how Your Highness understands!"

"You vill find me most understanding. Vill she not, Henrietta?"

"I am sure if she is truthful to Your Highness she will find you most . . . accommodating."

"There, so you see."

He took out his purse and upset the contents on to the table. The guineas rolled over the surface and some fell on to the floor.

"Vot beautiful golden guineas! They vill buy much."

"I am sure they will," said Mary. She was flushing hotly for so many times he had shown her money. It would have been ludicrous if it had not been insulting, and suddenly, Mary, impulsive by nature, lost her temper and swept all the guineas on to the floor.

The Prince stared at her in dismay. "Vy you do that?"

"Because Your Highness I do not want your money. It makes no difference to me how many guineas you have in your purse. If you show me them again I . . . I shall run away. I don't want to see them."

"You don't vant guineas?"

"No, Your Highness."

"But they buy such pretty things."

"They can't buy me."

Mary had stood up, her eyes blazing; the Prince had risen too; Henrietta was looking on in dismay. Had Mary gone mad? Didn't she know that one didn't speak to the Prince of Wales like that?

Henrietta spoke softly: "I'm sure Mrs. Bellenden is over-wrought."

There was a short silence. Then Mary recovered herself and looked alarmed by what she had done; and seeing her thus the Prince knew how he could act. Henrietta's tact had saved his dignity.

Henrietta went on: "I think if Mrs. Bellenden told Your Highness what is in her mind ... you might understand how disturbed she is and forgive her."

The Prince turned to Mary who was looking down at the guineas.

"Vell," he said. "Let us sit down and you shall tell me vot is wrong."

Mary sat down. "I am in love," she blurted out. "I am going to be married."

"Who is this?" demanded the Prince.

"I would rather not say."

"She fears Your Highness's displeasure," suggested Henrietta.

"I am displeased," said the Prince looking like a boy deprived of a treat to which he has long looked forward.

"But Your Highness is gracious and will understand how it is with these young people."

"You may tell me," he said to Mary.

"I am in love Your Highness and for me there can be no other than the man I am going to marry."

"What is his name?"

"I cannot tell Your Highness."

The Prince looked at Henrietta.

"They have hoped to marry for a long time," she said, "perhaps before Mrs. Bellenden knew of Your Highness's interest she had already promised to be faithful and to marry." She lifted her shoulders.

"I do not like it," said the Prince.

"Mrs. Bellenden will wish to ask Your Highness's pardon."

"I ask Your Highness pardon," said Mary as though repeating a lesson.

"So you vill marry this man?"

"Yes, Your Highness."

"And that vill make you happy?"

"Yes, Your Highness."

"You must not marry without telling me. You understand that I vill vish to know."

Mary stood silent and Henrietta said: "His Highness will give you leave to go now, I daresay."

"Yes go," said the Prince.

When Mary had gone he sat down heavily and stared disconsolately at the table.

Henrietta silently picked up the guineas and put them into the purse.

"Vy did she not tell me before?" he cried suddenly banging his fist on the table.

"Doubtless she feared to."

"Am I such an ogre ... ?"

Henrietta smiled. "You are the Prince. None would care to displease you."

He laughed, but was serious suddenly. "And you, Henrietta, you vould not care to displease me?"

"I hope I never should, Your Highness."

"Henrietta," he said, "you are von good woman."

"I am glad Your Highness finds me so."

"I have enjoyed very much our ... friendship." He looked at his watch. "It is time we make love," he said.

\* \* \*

After she had left Henrietta Howard's apartment Mary went to find her lover. As he was in the Prince's household this was not difficult, but she was anxious that no one should see them together for as one of the reigning beauties of the court she was also a favourite subject for the lampooners and she was watched closely. She was anxious that no one should discover that the man to whom she had betrothed herself was John Campbell and write a verse about it. She met Sophie Howe who seeing her flushed cheeks and that she came from Henrietta Howard's apartment wanted to know what she had been doing.

"I've just done a bold thing," she said.

Sophie laughed. "I'm always doing bold things. Don't tell me you've taken Henrietta Howard's place with His Highness."

"How dare you say such a thing! As if I ever would!"

"Of course not. There's dear John, I know."

"Don't speak of it. If it got to his ears . . ."

"Who? His Royal Highness's? Oh he'd like as not be ready to give John a title and lands in exchange for his complaisance."

"Which John and I would not accept. Listen Sophie, there has just been such a *scene*. I knocked his guineas all over the floor."

"What! Did he offer those guineas again?"

"Yet again! And this time I was so angry . . . besides I was there alone with him and Henrietta Howard and it seemed so horrible. So I told him to leave me alone because I was in love."

"Oh, Mary Bellenden!"

"And now I'm afraid, and I want to see John and you must go and tell him."

"And why don't you go?"

"Because I don't want anyone to see us together and make a noise about it so that it gets to his ears. . . ."

"I see."

"Please Sophie."

"Very well. I'll go and see if I can find him."

"And bring him here . . . while we can talk in peace."

"And when I bring him would you like me to stay and chaperone you?"

"It won't be necessary."

"Guard your virtue, for what if you lost it? He might not be so eager to marry you if you do."

"Save such warnings for yourself. You need them more than I do. And if you ever say such a thing to me I'll never speak to you again."

"Well wait until I've brought him to you otherwise

M

you won't be able to tell me where I'm most likely to find him."

"In the Prince's apartments. Go now, Sophie."

Sophie was goodhearted and always ready for intrigue; she sped off and it was not long before John Campbell was with Mary.

"Sophie Howe said you wanted me ... urgently," he said as they embraced fondly.

"Always," she answered.

"And you know it is the same with me."

She nodded. "But I'm afraid."

When she recounted what had happened in Henrietta's apartment, John was grave.

"He'll not be prepared to give you up, I know it."

"He'll have to. But he may make trouble. If he attempts to I shall run away from court."

"If we were married..."

"Oh John, is it possible?"

"It would be in secret. Mary, would you?"

"Yes, John. I would."

"Then if he approached you again, you could tell the Princess."

"Do you think it wise, John?"

He laughed softly. "I've been trying to think of an excuse for a long time. This is it. Remember the Churchills. They married in secret. Why shouldn't we?"

"No one must know."

"No one shall know."

"Sophie may guess."

"Not she. She's about to embark on a new flirtation."

"How do you know?"

"When she came to find me I was with Nunty Lowther."

"I don't know him."

"Lord Lonsdale's young brother. They're rather taken with each other. I fancy that for a while Sophie's going to be too preoccupied with her own affairs to think about us."

The Prince of Wales left his mistress's apartments at precisely the same time as he always did and made his way to the royal quarters.

Henrietta was a good mistress. He would never desert her.

Meanwhile Mary and John Campbell had made their plans for their wedding which was to be kept a deadly secret.

* * *

Caroline, playing cards in the reception room which she had changed into a state apartment at Leicester House, was a little uneasy. She had just heard the latest story about Mary Bellenden and the guineas. The girl had been subdued lately and she guessed it was true. How she wished that George Augustus had a little more *sense*.

She was pregnant again. She thought often that her life was becoming a little like that of Queen Anne who had conceived regularly each year and as regularly lost the child she bore almost as soon as it made its appearance, with the exception of the little Duke of Gloucester who had not survived his boyhood. No, she was different from that. At least she had her dear Fritzchen and her girls. But somehow in the last years everything seemed to go wrong and she had now begun to think she would never again bear a healthy child.

She was afraid that again she would fail, that the King would never treat them properly and would live for years; meanwhile the conduct of the Prince made people titter at court and whisper behind their backs while the more fearless scribblers of the coffee houses made lampoons about him.

This was a passing phase, she assured herself ... a momentary depression. It was due to the fact that she longed for her children. If she could have them, she would be ready to face anything, and the cruelty of the King and the humiliating follies of the Prince would mean nothing to her.

She looked about the room, at the card players intent on their game; at handsome Lord Hervey talking to a group of her women; she caught sight of Molly Lepel's lovely face and Margaret Meadows was looking a little prim, no doubt shocked by something the brilliantly wicked Lord Hervey was saying. Henrietta Howard was in a party playing cards with the Prince. If only, thought Caroline, he would be content with Henrietta! She could trust that woman who never gave herself the slightest airs and was always so discreet. In fact her discretion had made much less of the guineas incident than might have been the case.

There was a temporary lull in the music and from a group of young men and women surrounding her a burst of laughter.

Young Lord Stanhope was being witty as usual, she supposed. She did not greatly care for the little man, who was almost a dwarf and so odd looking with his large head that seemed as though it would overbalance his body; he had a high falsetto voice which was as unattractive as the rest of him. But his tongue was poisonous.

"Vot is the joke?" asked Caroline.

"We were speaking of Madam Kielmansegge Your Highness," he told her.

"It was so amusing?"

"It is enough to look at that lady to be amused," replied Stanhope.

"Perhaps, my lord, you are more easily amused than most of us."

"Evidently not more than His Majesty who finds her so diverting."

It was the custom here to speak as slightingly as possible of the King and his affairs and Caroline always encouraged such talk for she believed there were few weapons as effective as ridicule.

Stanhope went on: "The standard of His Majesty's taste as exemplified in this mistress, makes all ladies who aspire to his favour and who are near the suitable age, strain and swell themselves, like the frogs in the fable, to rival the bulk and dignity of the ox. Some succeed. Others burst."

There was a shout of laughter led by Sophie Howe, whether because she was so amused or just enjoying the company of Anthony Lowther with whom she was exchanging affectionate glances. The others joined in and Caroline allowed herself to smile.

"At least," she said, "from her complexion she looks young —not more than eighteen or twenty."

"Oh yes, Madam," retorted Stanhope. "Eighteen to twenty stone."

Again the burst of laughter and eyes were turned their way.

It was always thus with Stanhope. Caroline looked across the room to handsome young Lord Hervey who was equally clever; and how much more attractive!

Still it was a successful evening and typical of many. She was hoping Robert Walpole and his brother-in-law Townsend would look in. They came occasionally and she always welcomed them; she knew of course that they were feeling their way. If they would come out openly against the King and for the Prince and Princess that would be a great step forward. With such men as her political friends and Gay, Pope, Newton to represent art and science she could make a brilliant court worthy to compare with any which had gone before; and in such a court she would build the foundations of her power.

She looked across at the Prince. Life was full of consolations. If she did not have a stupid husband could she have won the respect which she was fast winning? Could she have been the leader of the rival court which all, except the Prince, knew she was?

She must not be impatient. She must not take those miscarriages too much to heart. The day would come when she would have her children back; when everything that she longed for would be hers.

In the meantime there was the waiting.

The Prince rose abruptly from the card table. He looked at his watch. The game was over; he would go to his apartments to prepare for his visit to Henrietta. Since Mary Bellenden had made it clear that she was determined to reject his advances he visited Henrietta every evening. His preciseness was becoming something of a joke.

"The Prince," said the jokers, "does everything to time: eating, drinking, walking and making love." This was giving the opportunity for much ribaldry and Caroline feared ridicule.

If only he would not do this ... or that....

It was becoming a constant thought with her; yet she never dared show one hint of criticism.

The Prince retired and she with him. He would be ready fully ten minutes before nine o'clock and would pace the apartment, his watch in hand, watching the seconds go back, so that he might enter his mistress's apartment exactly on the point of nine.

Caroline shrugged her shoulders. There was nothing she could do. Only young girls and fools complained about their husband's mistresses. The Electress Sophia had taught her that.

Her women helped her undress; she was determined to be careful and bring this pregnancy to a satisfactory climax. Therefore she must guard her health and not allow herself to be distressed or even ruffled by anything the King—or the Prince—might do.

One of her women was hovering; clearly she wished to say something in secret.

Caroline dismissed the others and asked her to remain. She had scarcely noticed her before but now she saw that she was very pretty.

"Vell?" said Caroline. "Vat is it you have to say?"

"Your Highness, I have been thinking about whether I should tell you ... but I feel it is my duty to do so...."

Caroline was alert. "Yes, vat is it?"

"The Prince..."

"The Prince!"

"Yes, Madam. The Prince has made certain suggestions to me ... suggestions which alarm me. I have been brought up to be virtuous and ... Well, I thought Your Highness should know."

"That is enough," said Caroline. "You may go now."

"Your Highness, if I have offended..."

"You may go," said Caroline coolly.

She sat for a long time looking into her mirror. So this was what she would have to endure! She had detected a certain complacence about the girl—an injured virtue. Mary Bellenden was not going to be the only one who had had the honour of rejecting the Prince.

A clever woman accepted her husband's mistresses, of course. But there might be occasions when she did not have to do so.

She lay on her bed; she was very tired; and the most important thing at the moment was to keep the child she carried.

\* \* \*

"Henrietta," said Caroline the next day when they were alone together, "one of the new women said something to me which I found rather distasteful."

Henrietta looked alarmed.

"I don't know her name. The new one."

"I know to whom Your Highness refers. Perhaps she is a little new to court ways...."

"She made a suggestion about the Prince."

"The Prince, Madam?"

"She hinted that he was making advances which were repugnant to her virtue."

"These girls have strange fancies."

"So I thought. They twitter. They gossip. I do not think she is exactly suitable."

"No, Madam."

"So I will leave her to you, Henrietta."

"Your Highness may safely do so."

That day the new lady-in-waiting left Leicester House, and her going was scarcely noticed; so discreetly was it managed by Mrs. Howard, that even the Prince was unaware of it.

*    *    *

With the coming of summer Caroline felt that it would be unwise to stay at Leicester House. In view of her condition she needed the country air; and it was the custom of a court to retire to the country for the warm months. The King's Court was moving to Hampton.

"I am thankful," said Caroline to the Prince, "that ve shall not have to be there this year. But vere can ve go?"

"Ve must look about for a suitable place, my tear."

"On the river ... but not Hampton," said the Princess. "I have always loved Richmond."

"Richmond," cried the Prince, his face pink with pleasure. "It is von beautiful spot. There is the Lodge."

It was true. Caroline knew it slightly but she had been struck by its charm. For the last hundred years the old palace had been almost a ruin but the Lodge had been preserved and embellished and would make a delightful country house.

"It is in the keeping of Grantham," said Caroline. "I am sure he vould be delighted for us to have it."

"Vy, it was Grantham who put his house in Albemarle Street at our disposal ven ve vere so callously turned out by that vicked old scoundrel. He vill be happy, I know, for us to take Richmond Lodge. He is von goot man."

"Ve must speak to him as soon as possible," said Caroline. "I vant to be in the country as soon as it can be arranged."

"Leave this to me, my tear. You shall be at Richmond in the next week or so."

\* \* \*

But it was not so easily arranged as they had thought it would be for the King had his spies at the Prince's Court and it came to his ears that the Prince and Princess planned to spend their summers at Richmond Lodge.

This was by no means as grand as Hampton Court, but George had been irritated by the stories he had heard, of the rival court and he so hated his son and daughter-in-law that he determined to spoil their pleasure whenever he could.

He sent for the Earl of Grantham, who owned the Lodge, and told him that if he either lent or sold it to the Prince and Princess of Wales he would have to forfeit it.

Grantham was stunned and went at once to the Princess to tell her of the King's order.

When she heard it Caroline almost lost her control.

"Is it not enough," she cried, "that he takes my children from me? Does he have to stop us living vere ve vill?"

Grantham declared that he was as grieved as the Princess but he dared not disobey the King's wishes. Indeed, of what use would it be, for as soon as he attempted to hand over the Lodge it would not be in his power to do so.

"That man is an insensitive monster," declared Caroline.

\* \* \*

There was nothing to do but look for a new country residence, but Caroline's heart had been set on Richmond. Moreover, would the King prevent them going anywhere else they decided on?

Caroline was feeling the strains of pregnancy and this made her more resentful than usual; but when Sir Robert Walpole came to Leicester House she was excited and delighted to be able to have a few words with him, because she recognized in him one of the ablest statesmen of the day. He was very cautious; and she knew that she could not at this stage rely on his loyalty to her, but she did imagine that he was feeling his way with her as she was with him.

Friendship between Walpole and the Prince and Princess of Wales would disturb the King and his friends more than anything else; and for that reason alone she would welcome it. But Walpole made it clear that he was not concerned politically at the moment. He had resigned from the government when his brother-in-law was dismissed and had retired to his country house at Houghton in Norfolk where he had grand plans for rebuilding it. He now talked to Caroline of Houghton and how he intended to enlarge it and fill it with works of art which he loved.

Caroline was very interested and they discussed painting of which she discovered Walpole to be a connoisseur.

"I envy you," said Caroline. "You have doubtless heard that the Prince and I planned to spend the summer at Richmond Lodge and this has been denied us."

"Most churlishly, Madam."

"And so it seems as though ve are doomed to spend the hot weather in this place."

"Surely not, Madam."

"Vere then should ve spend it?"

"Why not at Richmond Lodge?"

"But the King has this forbidden. He has threatened to confiscate it if Grantham sells it to us ... or even lends it."

"Has Your Highness considered whether it is in His Majesty's power to do this?"

"I do not you *comprendre* ..." said Caroline.

"This is a constitutional monarchy, Madam. I doubt very much whether the King has the power to forbid a man to sell or lend what is his."

"You mean he may not?"

"I mean, Madam, that if I were so treated I should find out what my position was with regard to the law."

"And you, Sir Robert..."

He smiled at her wryly. "Oh, I am a man in retirement, Your Highness. I merely offer advice."

"Thank you, Sir Robert," said Caroline.

I was right, she thought, to cultivate this man. He is for us and against the King, but he is too shrewd, too wily at this time when we are in decline and all the power is the King's, to say so.

Not a loyal friend? But he had never said he was a friend. He was a shrewd politician seeking his own advantage. Well, that was how Caroline would prefer him to be. He was the kind of man she would have about them when the time came.

The King at Hampton was angry. In spite of his wishes the Prince and Princess were installed in Richmond Lodge. His objections had been overruled. He had no power to prevent Grantham letting them have the house. In a constitutional monarchy such as this the law must prevail against the King's pleasure.

Caroline was delighted. Not only was this a victory over the dour old King but they had this lovely house. The town of Richmond enchanted her; on either side of the river were meadows and here and there a charming country house. On one side of the house were the gardens which ran down to the river and on the other an avenue of trees which led to the little town, about half a mile distance.

It was near enough to London to make travel to and fro convenient and yet was in the country. It was true the roads were unsafe, but then so were all roads; and travellers should always endeavour to go back and forth by daylight.

Those first weeks at Richmond were delightful. So was everyone, including the country people who had heard the story and were amused because the Prince and Princess had outwitted the King and secured the house which he had tried to deny them.

There were cheers whenever any members of the Prince and

Princess's court sailed along the river. This river had now become gay with all the fashionable people who came to Richmond Lodge; and everyone who possessed a boat took it on to the river to hear the music from the Lodge which sounded very sweet and tuneful.

The Prince and the Princess were so much more gay than the King; and the people were on their side.

If I could have the children with me, now, thought Caroline, I would ask nothing more.

\*      \*      \*

The day had been sultry and Caroline had felt so listless that she was in no mood for her usual walk.

This, she thought, is how one feels when one's time is not far off—particularly after two recent miscarriages.

Yesterday had been a trying day. During the evening Bridget Carteret had ridden in in a state of hysteria. The whole of the Lodge, including herself and the Prince had heard the girl screaming. Her coach had been stopped by highwaymen and all her jewels had been taken from her.

Bridget had had to be put to bed and comforted. The other girls had gathered in her room while she went over and over her adventure, remembering more and more terrifying moments and unnerving even the most practical of them.

They were now declaring that never never would they take the dangerous road between Richmond and London after dusk.

Caroline called to Henrietta. What a comfort that creature was!

Henrietta was cool, efficient, pleasant-looking but not disturbingly beautiful. Between us, thought Caroline, we know exactly how to manage George Augustus. If he will stop pestering my silly girls we can conduct our lives in a dignified manner.

"This Bridget Carteret affair, Henrietta," she said. "I suppose I must compensate her for her loss."

"There is no reason why Your Highness should, although, of course the girl would be delighted."

Yes, thought Caroline, poor Bridget would. And it gave her great pleasure to look after her women.

"There is a necklace ... the one with the single diamond stone on a gold chain."

"I know the one, Madam."

"Bring it to me ... and the gold watch you vill find there."

Henrietta brought them and put them into Caroline's hands.

"They would be very handsome compensation," said Henrietta.

"Vell, poor child she was very frightened."

"We shall have all of them seeking adventures with highwaymen."

"Oh I don't think so. They vouldn't risk their lives for the sake of a few trinkets which after all might not adequately replace vat they had lost."

"The fact that they are given by Your Highness enhances their value."

"You flatter, Henrietta. Send for the little Carteret and afterwards bring my shoes and clock. I vill go for a valk. I must make the most of the Richmond air."

"It is very overcast, Your Highness."

"I vill keep close to the Lodge."

Bridget Carteret was delighted with the gifts and gave Caroline a graphic description of her adventure. While she was doing so it had become almost as dark as night outside, and the first raindrops had begun to fall.

"This is going to be a bad storm, I fancy," said Caroline going to the window and at that moment a flash of lightning lit up the room. The immediate crack of thunder showed it to be right overhead.

"Your Highness should come away from the window," said Bridget. "I've heard ..."

Caroline turned to smile at her lady-in-waiting.

"It's only a passing storm," she said.

"In your condition, Madam..." began Henrietta; and at that moment a flash more vivid than the last made Caroline step back from the window; but just at that moment one of the elm trees came crashing down and there was sound of breaking glass mingling with the roar of thunder.

Caroline cried out in alarm, stepped back hastily and tripped.

She was aware of the branches of the tree coming through the broken window, of the scream of Bridget Carteret, and Henrietta bending over her before she lost consciousness.

\* \* \*

She was lying in bed. The Prince was seated at her bedside, fussily attentive.

"Vot have happened?"

"You're all right, my tear. The doctors haf assured me...."

He held her hand. "I haf been so anxious. You are tearer to me than my life. But it is all right. They have me told."

"The child...."

"There vill be children. You vill not be upset now. You vill soon be vell ... and that is my only concern."

So she had lost the child!

Was there some curse on her? The children she had were taken from her; and it seemed that fate had decided she was not to bear another.

\* \* \*

In time the Princess recovered from her disappointment. There would be another child, for George Augustus was as regular in his attentions to her as he was to his mistress. I cannot go on being so unfortunate she told herself. And she must be grateful for her good health which helped her to recover from these disappointments more readily than most.

She fretted constantly for the children. She heard that Fritzchen was drinking too much, and was getting a taste for gambling; she heard too that he was not very strong. He was subject to fever; his back was weak so he was obliged to wear whalebone stays—not steel, which would have pressed uncomfortably on his nerves. He had glandular trouble. His doctors ordered a diet of asses' milk. What was happening to Fritzchen? How unnatural that all these years should be allowed to pass and a mother not be permitted to see her son!

And the little girls? She heard that they had danced for

their grandfather at Hampton; that they were treated with respect by ambassadors—different from the way in which that unnatural man insisted his son and daughter-in-law should be treated! They did meet occasionally; but how difficult it was when George Augustus was not allowed to visit Hampton and they were surrounded by spies. The girls were growing up and one could not expect them to be unaffected by the conflict in the family.

How different was this summer from that glorious one at Hampton!

In Hampton George tried to forget that he had a son and daughter-in-law! He regarded Frederick Lewis his grandson in Hanover as his heir; and although he had no tenderness for his grandchildren he liked to see them now and then to remind himself of their existence and the power he had to take them from their parents.

From time to time he heard how the Princess grieved for them and that gave him a grim pleasure. The woman had flouted him; she was far too clever, luring men to her court and winning the affection of the people. She should pay for that as anyone who offended him had to pay.

He had no intention of trying to make Hampton like Richmond. His Court would be as he liked it. Some might say it was dull but what did he care. His Duchesses of Kendal and Darlington—in other words Schulemburg and Kielmansegge—pleased him, particularly the former without whom he never liked to go far. Ermengarda was to him as a wife—a good placid wife who never stood in the way of anything he wanted. In his youth his hobbies had been war and women; now he was getting too old for war so it was merely women. But although he liked occasional variety he went back and back again to Ermengarda. She was a rich woman in her own right now, for since she had been to England she had developed an unsuspected talent for amassing money, but that made no difference to their relationship. She was still his placid Ermengarda, always ready to obey.

There was one thing he did enjoy in England and that was the theatre.

He therefore had the great hall at Hampton fitted up as a

theatre and sent to Colley Cibber and his company to come down to entertain him.

Cibber played Henry VIII and other Shakespearian plays, of which the King was especially fond; Cibber provided German translations which the King read beforehand that he might follow the action on the stage and so delighted the King; and the King delighted Cibber.

This to the King was a pleasant existence: to see the play, with the Duchess of Kendal and Darlington on either side of him—the three of them had long formed a habit of going about together—and then to retire with one of them, or a fancy of the moment, to what he called a seasonable bedtime.

So passed the summer months.

\* \* \*

To see the King going to Drury Lane was a sight which amused the people of London. His Sedan chair would be carried from St. James's Palace preceded by his beefeaters and guards. Immediately behind would be two other chairs, and if the people were lucky they would catch a glimpse of the red and black wigs above what they considered to be two of the most grotesquely ugly faces in the kingdom.

George cared nothing for the jeers of his subjects. Nor did his two mistresses, who in any case had grown accustomed to them.

And when he reached the theatre and was welcomed by the manager he would refuse the royal box and ask for one where he could not be so easily seen.

Then he would sit at the back of this, a Duchess on either side of him and prepare to enjoy the play.

One evening that autumn as his chair came out of the palace a young man leaped out of the crowd and ran towards the chair. If one of the guards had not seen him, he would have shot the King; as it was the bullet merely grazed the top of the chair.

The young man was seized and dragged away. The King went on to the theatre.

\* \* \*

In the cart the young man was being taken to Tyburn. His name was James Shepherd and he was only eighteen years old.

He shouted to the crowd: "There is only one true King of England. He is James III. Down with the German!"

"Down with the German!" echoed many in the crowd.

"He's young to die," said others. "The King should have shown mercy."

The Jacobites watched sullenly and said the King was a monster. His own wife, the Queen of England, was languishing in prison; he had quarrelled with his son; his daughter-in-law was deprived of her children. They hadn't a King on the throne. They had a monster.

Some remembered that the Princess of Wales had pleaded for the boy. He was young, she said; he was doubtless led astray. Let him be punished in some slight way and cautioned.

But the King had ignored the pleas of the Princess of Wales, and James Shepherd was taken to Tyburn and the rope was placed about his neck.

Even the staunchest Hanoverians said as they watched that young body hanging there: "He is young to die."

\*      \*      \*

The King was aware of the murmurs against him. It was not often that he cared about public opinion. It had always been his comment that if the English didn't want him here he would willingly go back to Hanover.

But he was angry that even out of such an incident as an attempt on his life and the—to him—perfectly just punishment of such an act, the Princess should squeeze a little popularity.

She was kind, they were saying now. She was humane. She had pleaded with the King to spare the life of the young man who had attempted to kill him. Of course she did! Doubtless she thought the fellow some sort of hero.

And the people admired her for it.

He was in this mood of resentment when Henry Howard, the husband of the Prince's mistress, who was one of the grooms of his bedchamber, caught his eyes and he summoned him to him.

"Is it not a rule," he said, "that the wives of men in my service should leave that of the Prince and Princess of Wales if they happen to be with them?"

"Yes, Your Majesty."

"And what of your wife?"

"She has refused, Your Majesty."

The King knew of this and he had not insisted at the time because he had thought it would plague Caroline, and do George Augustus no good in the eyes of the people, to keep his mistress.

But the affair seemed to be accepted and Caroline no doubt saw that it was conducted with decorum.

The King nodded. He saw the chance of making trouble with a little scandal.

"It is your duty to insist that your wife leaves Leicester House and comes to you here."

Henry Howard bowed and said he would obey the King's orders.

\* \* \*

When Henrietta received a letter from her husband demanding that she return to him and leave the household of the Prince and Princess of Wales, she did not take the matter seriously. She knew that Henry was drinking heavily, that he did not want her and was in fact glad to be rid of her; so she ignored the letter and forgot about it. But a few nights later there was a disturbance at the gates of Leicester House. Next morning everyone was talking about it and when Henrietta went into the apartment where the maids-of-honour were noisily discussing it, there was a silence.

"What is it?" she asked.

"Did you hear the noise last night?" asked Molly Lepel.

"Yes. What was it?"

"A ... a man ... the worse for drink. The doorman turned him away but he was shouting for a long time."

Mary Bellenden said gravely: "It was your husband, Mrs. Howard. He was asking for you. He said he wanted to take you away with him."

Henrietta turned pale and said: "There is some mistake."

No one answered; and Henrietta went to Caroline's apartment to tell her what she had heard.

Caroline listened gravely. "Do you think he really vants you to return to him, Henrietta?"

"No." Henrietta was shivering with apprehension and Caroline had never seen her so before.

"You're frightened, Henrietta."

"I could not live with him, Madam. He is a drunkard. He's a brute. He ill treated me before. I have never been so happy as I am here with you ... and the Prince."

And the Prince! thought Caroline. How much does he mean to her? Can she really care for him? Surely not! She wanted peace and comfort; she did not seek power or great riches, but this life suited her and she was in terror of losing it.

"It is strange that he should come here. There must be some meaning behind it."

Caroline did not say that she suspected the King, for poor Henrietta was in such a state of anxiety to which this could only add.

"Don't fret," said Caroline ."I shall not let you go. If I send this brute avay ... avay he must go. Do not fret, Henrietta. Here shall you stay."

Henrietta was comforted; but she was uneasy. So was Caroline. Could the man force his wife to live with him? And if he took this matter to court and if the court decided that a husband had rights over his wife, must Henrietta go? And then would George Augustus be seeking a new mistress ... or mistresses? Young girls of the bedchamber who lacked the tact of Henrietta, who might have to be taught that familiarity with the Prince did not mean that liberties could be taken with the Princess?

A few days later Caroline received a letter from the Archbishop of Canterbury.

Marriage was a sacrament, he pointed out. The Princess would do well to bear this in mind. She must bear in mind the privileges of a husband and the duty a wife owed to him. She must therefore command a certain woman of her household to return to her husband and remember that although she was a Princess she had a duty to God.

Caroline read the letter thoughtfully.

Why had the Archbishop written to her? Would Henry Howard have gone to him and drunkenly suggested that he should do so?

Of course not. She saw the hand of the King in this.

Slowly she tore up the Archbishop's letter.

\*　　\*　　\*

Caroline was resting. It had been a heavy dinner and she followed the Hanoverian custom of retiring afterwards. In his apartments George Augustus would be sleeping heavily; and afterwards he would come to her apartments and they would take a walk together.

She was thinking of Henrietta and what steps the King might take to force her to send the woman away. What an implacable enemy he was, and how he hated them! Not content with striking the worst blow any man could give any woman by taking her children from her, he must think of these little pinpricks to torment her.

She heard a scuffle at her door and rising from her bed she threw a robe about her.

"I will see her," cried a voice. "I insist. You can't keep me away."

The door was flung open and a man with bloodshot eyes, his coat bedraggled, his wig awry, burst into the room.

"Who..." began the Princess.

"I'm Henry Howard," he cried. "And I've come for my wife."

"How dare you. Go away at once. You vill hear more of this."

"And so will you, Madam, if you hide my wife. Where is she? In the Prince's bed? I tell you I'll have her out of that. I'll have her where she belongs."

"This is very unseemly," said Caroline, and wondered how she remained so cool; for she had heard Henrietta say that her husband was half mad and when he had been drinking entirely so. Certainly he had been drinking now.

"Do not think that I shan't have my wife. If I have to pull her out of your coach, I'll get her."

He stood before her, hands on his hips, his bloodshot eyes leering. The window was behind them and for one moment Caroline thought that he was going to pick her up and throw her out of it.

She was aware of the open door and one of the footmen standing there, mouth agape. She managed to move swiftly from the window and as she stood with her back to the footman facing the window, she felt safer.

Her moment of complete panic had passed.

"I assure you no one vould dare take any servant of mine from my coach."

He was aware of the footman and the open door for he lost a little of his truculence. Caroline was quick to seize the advantage.

"Your wife shall certainly not be forced to go vith you. It is a matter she herself vill decide. If she vishes to go vith you that is her affair."

"Madam, I warn you I shall take my case to the King."

"Do so if you vish. The King has nothing to do vith my servants. And if you do not leave my presence immediately you vill be thrown out."

Henry Howard gaped at her for a few moments; then he muttered something, bowed and went out.

Caroline shut the door quickly and leaned against it.

This had gone farther than she had thought. Henry Howard would never have dared break into her apartment, he would never have spoken to her as he had if he had not had the support of the King behind him.

Henrietta came running into the apartment, her hair hanging in disorder, her eyes wide with terror.

She threw herself at Caroline's feet and embraced her knees.

"Oh, Madam, Madam ... he has been here. He will drag me away. What shall I do?"

"Be calm, Henrietta. This is the King's doing."

"The King!"

"Ve must face the truth. He only vants to cause more trouble, more scandal for us."

"Madam. You don't want me to go away?"

Caroline's face hardened. "Vat! And play right into their

hands. No. Ve must fight them. If they take this to a court ve must let them know what sort of a man your husband is. Ve'll prove him the cruel half-insane creature he is. That von't look so vell for one of the King's servants, vill it?"

"But he can take me away . . . Oh Madam. . . ."

The Prince burst into the apartment, his face pink, the veins knotted at his temples, his eyes blazing.

"Vot the devil. . . ."

"Mrs. Howard's husband has been here demanding her return."

"She shall not go. I vill not it allow."

"No, ve vill not allow it," said Caroline.

"Got damn him," cried the Prince and taking off his wig started to kick it round the apartment.

Caroline caught it as it came her way. She picked it up and gently replaced it on his head.

"It is not goot to disturb ourselves," she said gently, "ve vill this matter settle."

Henrietta raised her eyes to Caroline's face and her look was almost trustful; the Prince was undoubtedly soothed.

Even in this, thought Caroline, they look to me; and the thought gave her a grain of comfort.

\* \* \*

The King lost interest suddenly; he had achieved his purpose; everyone knew that Henry Howard had broken into the Princess's apartment and drunkenly demanded she give up her husband's mistress and that she had refused to do so. It made an amusingly ribald story and the lampooners were busy with it.

This could bring little credit to Leicester House, thought the King.

Henry Howard however did not see why he should abandon a project which could be profitable and decided to take the matter to court. Everyone concerned knew that the law could force a wife to return to her husband and all sides were in a panic—Henry Howard because he did not want his wife back and Henrietta, the Prince and Princess because they feared she would have to go.

It was an absurd situation. Howard's advisers suggested he ask for a reasonable settlement from the Prince on receipt of which he would be prepared to let the matter drop.

Negotiations went on through the winter and when the Prince and Princess of Wales moved to Richmond for the summer, Henrietta left disguised with the Duke of Argyll and his brother Lord Islay—two of the Prince's greatest friends—and arrived at Richmond earlier than the royal party.

Eventually the matter was settled. Henry Howard would allow his wife to remain in the Princess's service for an annual payment of £1,200 a year.

He believed he had come out of the affair very nicely. As for the Prince, Princess and Henrietta, they could only be delighted that the affair was over; and Caroline began to wonder whether the quarrel might be mended, for while this unhappy state of affairs continued they could expect such unpleasantness from the King. Moreover the longing to have her children with her was becoming too acute to be endured.

Time was passing. They were growing away from her. Should she seek some compromise?

She was beginning to think that she would agree to almost anything if she could have her children back.

She was turning over in her mind whether Sir Robert Walpole might have some suggestion to make.

## The Reconciliation

It was Walpole himself who suggested the reconciliation.

The King unable to stay away for long from his beloved Hanover had paid another visit and had left a Council of Regency, consisting of thirteen Lord Justices to govern during his absence, in which this Prince of Wales had no part.

Caroline had realized then that she and the Prince had everything to lose from the continuance of this quarrel. Walpole during his visits to Leicester House had made her aware of the situation in Spain where the all powerful Cardinal Alberoni ruled for weak Philip V. As a guest at this Court was James Stuart, known there as James III of England, and the Spanish were ready to help him drive out the Hanoverians.

"They believe," Walpole had explained, "that the people are weary of Hanoverians and that they long for the return of the Stuart."

"Do *you* believe this to be true?" asked Caroline. "I want a truthful answer please."

Walpole had looked her straight into her face and said: "Madam, anything but the truth between us would be both pointless and dangerous. I do not believe the people of England are tired of your family; but I do believe they are tired of your family quarrels."

"Then let us end them," she cried passionately. "I would be prepared to immediately."

"There would doubtless be conditions on both sides."

"There is only one condition I should insist on: The return of my children."

"There is the Prince," Walpole reminded her.

"I would do anything . . . and persuade the Prince to . . . if I could have my children back."

Walpole smiled slowly. "It must be arranged," he said.

And her hopes were higher than they had ever been. There was a strength about Walpole. She trusted him.

*   *   *

George Augustus was not easy to control. He deeply resented the fact that he had been left out of the Regency. He talked slightingly of his father and Caroline was anxious because she knew that the King's spies were everywhere and that they would report every word that was said.

"My father thinks he has the better of me," boasted George Augustus. "But time vill tell. He is getting old and can't live forever. Then it vill be my turn. Things vill be different then."

Caroline shivered. The last thing any man—King or commoner—wanted to hear was how much better his successor would carry out his tasks when he was dead.

George came back from Hanover. The Spanish attempt to put James back on the English throne had failed but there were Jacobite rumblings all over the country.

Furious with his son, having heard that he had boasted of what he would do when he was King, George tried to pass the Peerage Bill through the Commons and Lords. This proposed to limit the House of Lords so that when the Prince became King he would be unable to create any new peers.

This bill almost became law but Walpole made such a brilliant speech against it that it was rejected. Stanhope and his ministers had long been trying to persuade Walpole to come back into the Government but he had held back and had professed himself content with the rebuilding of Houghton and the collection of pictures, content now and then to take his seat in parliament and play the part of an ordinary member.

This was not true, of course. He was an ambitious man; he loved the country life it was true; he liked to drink with congenial companions; but he was well aware that he was a master of politics and he longed for power.

He pointed out to Stanhope that this quarrel in the royal family was undermining the country's prestige abroad. Time which should have been given to serious matters was taken up in petty spite and pinpricks.

"If there is a reconciliation between the King and the Prince I should come back into the government ... not otherwise," he declared. And when Stanhope asked if he could bring about that reconciliation, he said he would try to.

"So you will approach the Prince?"

Walpole laughed. "Oh no," he replied. "The Princess."

\*　　\*　　\*

Lady Cowper grumbled to Mrs. Clayton that that fellow Walpole monopolized the Princess. "At every gathering," she complained, "he's at her side. Everyone is noticing it."

"They know, of course," replied Mrs. Clayton, "that he is trying to bring about a reconciliation. If anyone can do it ... he can."

"I don't trust him. Out for himself is Master Walpole."

But Caroline trusted him; and now her great desire was to have her children back. Every time she saw them it was becoming increasingly hard to say goodbye. They noticed her sadness and told her that although they were separated from her they thought of her every day and longed for the next meeting as much as she did.

But they never saw their father. That was forbidden.

And what were they hearing of him? wondered Caroline. She knew that at St. James's and Hampton they could not be unaware of the criticism ... no, it was worse than that ... ridicule.

And how easy it was to ridicule the Prince!

She was deeply touched when they gathered a basket of cherries which they sent to him.

"Tell Papa that we gathered these ourselves."

She had told them he would be so delighted that he would want to keep them for ever.

"That," replied Anne, "would not be a very clever thing to do for they would soon be unfit for anything."

What do they hear of him? wondered Caroline. I must have them back. This is the time when we should all be living a happy family life.

She told Walpole: "I must have the children back. I know this stupid quarrel is no good to us ... no good to the family. But give me my children back and I shall accept anything the King likes to impose on us."

"Madam, would you approach the Prince? Will you discover whether he would be willing to write a conciliatory note to His Majesty? If he would do this ... we might begin negotiations."

"I vill talk to the Prince," promised Caroline.

\* \* \*

It was not easy.

"A letter to that old rascal! This I vill not do. It is that von who should send me a letter."

"It is the only vay. If ve are to have the children ..."

"He is von scoundrel. To take our children ..."

"And ve must get them back. It is a matter on vich ve agree. If he vill give them back to us ..."

"Yes, he must give them back. But he must pay my debts too and all my servants I vill vant.... And to be kept from the royal palaces ... that is von scandal."

"But to have our children back ... living under the same roof ... that is the first thing. Ve agree on that."

"That ve must have," said the Prince.

\* \* \*

The King said: "It is not for him to make conditions. He has behaved atrociously. He wants a reconciliation, but I am not sure that I am prepared to give it."

Walpole reminded him that the quarrel was having bad effects on foreign policy.

"The Prince is of no account," said the King. "He has no effect whatsoever."

"The stories of the quarrel are exaggerated by our enemies, sir. I think the Spanish would not have attempted to help the Stuart if they did not think we were a house divided against itself. The quarrel is ridiculed by our writers. There are lampoons and ballads distributed all over the country."

"And so my son is a buffoon to amuse the people! They like to be amused."

"They like to be amused. yes, sir. But they ridicule the royal family and this is never good. There will be trouble if a reconciliation does not occur soon."

"And you are on the side of the Prince?"

"I am on the side of the House of Hanover and my country."

George looked shrewdly at Walpole. This was a good man; he had been sorry when he had left his government. It was men such as this one that they needed.

He grudgingly admitted that he would consider the matter.

*　　*　　*

Walpole brought a letter he had drafted to Caroline.

"The Prince should copy this and send it to the King," he said. "The first move must come from him."

"And if he signs it?"

"The King will then be prepared for a reconciliation."

"And my children?"

Walpole hesitated. The Princess was obsessed by one thing. He was not at all certain that the King would relinquish the little girls but he knew that Caroline would not move until she had an assurance that he would.

Walpole was a politician and politicians sometimes had to take risks.

"Let the Prince sign this and you will have your children."

Caroline took the paper, and went away to begin the difficult task of persuading the Prince to humble his pride.

*　　*　　*

George said: No. He would not give up the little girls. It gave him pleasure to have them in the palace. They amused him. It was true he did not see a great deal of them; but they were his grandchildren and he was the King. It was fitting that he should have control of them and keep them living under his roof.

Walpole pointed out that their mother would be prepared to accept anything if they could but be returned to her.

"It is not for the Princess to make terms," said the King coldly.

Here was trouble, thought Walpole. The King was ready to return the Prince's guards to him; to allow him to live in the royal palaces and take back the honours due to the Prince of Wales. There was only one condition he would not accept and that was the return of the children.

It was difficult to face the Princess and tell her this. She would immediately tell the Prince that they must not give way, and as the Prince would as usual be made to see her point, the reconciliation would not take place; the quarrel would continue, probably more bitter than before; and Walpole would have failed. The last was inconceivable. But how get the King to relent? How get Caroline to forego her children? The King was the most obstinate and vindictive man on earth; and Caroline was a woman crying out for her children.

He would try first to persuade the King; and if that failed he did not know what he would do, but of course he would find a way.

\* \* \*

He presented himself to Caroline.

"The King is not prepared to part with the children ... yet," he began cautiously.

Her face grew stony. "Then the quarrel goes on."

"It should not go on. If it does there will be more Jacobite risings. They might not always fail."

"I vant my children," she said stubbornly.

"It has occurred to me the Duchess of Kendal might help."

"That ... woman!"

"She has a good heart. She also has a daughter of her own."

"Whom she calls her niece and whom we all know is the King's daughter."

"She would understand a mother's feelings perhaps, and might be on your side in this matter."

"Vat do you suggest?"

"That you speak to her ... explain...."

"That I humble myself to the King's harlot?"

"He regards the Duchess as his wife. They have been together for nearly thirty years. She is a kind woman...."

"You think it might help?" asked Caroline piteously.

"I do, Madam."

\* \* \*

So she went to Ermengarda, Duchess of Kendal, told her how she longed for her children and asked her to imagine what it meant to be separated from three little girls whom she was only allowed to see now and then, as though she were a stranger.

The Duchess wept with her.

"It is very sad," she said.

"The King does not seem to understand."

"So many state matters occupy his mind," said the Duchess.

"If you could explain to him...."

"I!" The Duchess was alarmed.

"I know of your devotion to each other."

"But I would never presume to advise the King."

Caroline looked at her sadly and thought No, I suppose that is why you have held your place so long.

She had humbled herself unnecessarily.

\* \* \*

Walpole was in a quandary. The King would not give up his guardianship of his granddaughters. He would grant concessions, yes; but the grandchildren should remain under his roof.

The Princess was in despair.

"It's no jesting matter to me," she told Walpole. "I shall not give in. I shall continue to complain until I have my children."

Yet the reconciliation must be made. He had determined on it. His own reputation depended on its success for he had sworn that he would bring it about. Moreover it was creating bad feeling abroad. Not only Walpole but England needed it.

The Prince was his hope. George Augustus had debts to the amount of about one hundred thousand pounds. He needed money badly. The Prince, Walpole believed, would be ready to give way if he received in return certain honours and money. The King would not be prepared to pay his debts but Walpole knew of a way of making money through the South Seas venture and if he could do this for the Prince, if he could bring him those concessions which his vanity craved, George Augustus would be ready to give in.

It was only Caroline who insisted on having the children.

*       *       *

As Walpole had predicted the Prince was delighted to have money; he wanted his beefeaters and his guards; he wanted to be treated as the Prince of Wales.

For this he would write the letter, the draft of which Walpole had sent him; and having received it the King, for he must take the advice of his ministers, would, if a little ungraciously, receive the Prince.

Therefore the matter could be concluded without the Princess.

Walpole regretted this for he respected the Princess and was eager for her goodwill; but when she insisted on having her children back under her care she was clinging to the one condition to which the King would not agree.

*       *       *

News came from the Palace of St. James's both for the Prince and Princess. To the Prince came a command from his father. For the first time since the quarrel he was prepared to see him. For the Princess was a letter from Lady Portland who wrote that Anne was sick and the smallpox was feared.

The Prince had reached St. James's by the time Caroline's

letter was brought to her. There the King received his son with some embarrassment.

George Augustus knew that he had to be humble. Walpole had made that clear; and for the sake of the bribe and the glory of having guards again and being treated as Prince of Wales he was ready to be so.

"I have come to express my grief in causing Your Majesty displeasure," he said, "and with all my heart I thank you for giving me leave to wait upon you. It is my sincere hope that during the rest of my life I shall give Your Majesty nothing of which to complain."

The King muttered that it was his son's conduct.... "Your conduct..." he repeated.

Little more was said but the King made it clear that if the Prince was ready to behave in a seemly manner he would be treated as the Prince of Wales.

When he left the King—and they were only five minutes together—he went to see his children. Anne was well enough to see him and he was told that she was not as sick as had been feared.

News of the interview had crept out and people were congregating outside the palace to see the Prince emerge from the Palace. As his chair was carried through the streets it was accompanied by guards and beefeaters and although he had arrived like a private person in a Sedan chair he made the return journey like a Prince.

Cheers filled the air. Everyone was tired of the quarrel which had been so diverting in the first place.

En route he met the Princess in her chair on her way to the Palace to see Anne.

When Caroline saw his chair she called to her chairmen to halt. For a few terrible seconds she thought that he had been summoned to the Palace because Anne was worse.

She alighted; so did the Prince.

"All's vell," he cried. "The King and I are friends again."

"And Anne...."

"I have seen her. I have seen the children. They are vell ... and Anne is not so ill as they thought. All is vell now, my tear."

He embraced her to the cheers of the people.

* * *

The following day Caroline went along to St. James's to make her peace with the King and was granted an interview. Before seeing the King she went to Anne who was well enough to be overjoyed by her mother's presence.

"Good news, my darling," said Caroline. "Your father and the King are now friends and we are all to be together again."

Anne clung to her mother's hand and her expression betrayed how happy she was.

After that Caroline went to Amelia and Caroline and taking Caroline on to her lap while she held Amelia in the crook of her arm she explained to them that the trouble was over, their father and grandfather were now good friends, and as a result they would live together under one roof and as one family.

"Now," said Amelia, "we shall no longer live like charity girls."

Caroline kissed them tenderly; and went along to the King's apartments for the promised interview.

George received her coldly—but she had not expected anything else.

He told her that he was glad George Augustus had come to his senses and that he would never have had any quarrel with her if she had not supported her husband.

"I am sure Your Majesty would not have expected anything else from a good wife."

"No, but I expect a good subject to obey her King."

"So would I do in all things," she answered, "but in disobeying the wishes of my husband."

George grunted.

"Well now you can please us both, for your husband repents of his conduct and has regained his status."

"I rejoice in Your Majesty's good favour."

He grunted again.

"I have told the children," she said. "They love you but they will naturally be pleased to be back with their parents."

The King looked startled. "That matter remains as before."

Caroline was astounded. "I do not understand, Your Majesty."

He looked at her grimly. "There is to be no change," he said. "My grandchildren stay under my care."

"No..." she began.

He had turned away but she saw the triumph in his eyes and the grim determination of his lips.

"Frederick is to remain in Hanover," she began indignantly. "The girls..."

"Frederick to remain in Hanover," he said, "and the girls will continue as before."

"I understood..."

"You misunderstood," said the King.

She was crying; she could not stop the tears, crying with frustration, rage and an infinite sorrow.

She had been cheated. The Prince and Walpole had gone behind her back. They had settled without her; and the one condition she had insisted on had been thrust aside.

There was no victory. The King, the Prince ... and Walpole had outwitted her.

## The Bubble

THE King was away on yet another visit to Hanover when panic struck London.

All through the year people of all kinds—the nobility and the poorest in the land—had been excited by the South Sea Trading Company, through which it was believed fortunes could be made in a few days. So busy was the Stock Exchange that desks had to be set up for clerks in the street to cope with all the business, for anyone who had any money was eager to invest it. People dreamed of riches, talked of riches, and many became rich.

It was there for everyone to see; those who had never dreamed of owning a carriage now had three or four. Humble merchants became millionaires. It was not only humble merchants; it was cabinet ministers, members of the nobility, the King's German mistresses—the Prince himself. Everyone was determined to grow rich through the exploitation of the South Seas. It was as though a fever was raging through the country—a fever of excitement, and to become rich quickly was the aim of every man and woman.

Stock worth one hundred today could be worth a thousand tomorrow so great was the demand for it.

So popular was the South Seas company that many other companies were floated. No project was too absurd to float a company; and still people rushed into them, eager to invest the guinea that they were convinced would miraculously turn to ten within the space of a few weeks.

Such a state of affairs must come to an end. The South Sea Company, knowing that its methods were being imitated by companies which had nothing at all to offer, decided to expose them; this it did and no sooner had the enquiries begun than fraud was exposed and the panic began to set in. The dream was evaporating; but in uncovering the fraudulent dealings of others the South Sea Company had exposed its own vulnerability.

It was a genuine trading company, but so far on no sound financial basis, and as soon as the panic stricken investors began to back out the company itself collapsed. Shares consequently tumbled in price and investors saw not only their dreams disappearing but their original investments.

The scenes on the stock exchange were such as were never seen before. Ruined men gathered on the streets; they were too bewildered at first to understand what had happened to them. Then they began to cry out that they had been the victims of a hoax. There were no big fortunes to be made. Instead of being millionaires they were paupers.

And who was to blame? The Government, the King, the Prince, the King's mistresses, the Cabinet ministers who had known all along that the South Sea Company was not the rich enterprise it had been made out to be, but merely an empty name to provide a gamble at which they could grow rich at the expense of the ignorant?

\*     \*     \*

Caroline, still mourning the manner in which she had been outwitted, came out of her listlessness to listen aghast to the news.

People were massing in the streets. Riots could break out at any moment. And these people who had been ruined through what they were calling the South Sea Bubble, were looking for a scapegoat.

Why not the Germans whom they hated? The Prince was involved in this. He had been advised by Walpole how to gamble through the South Sea Company on the stock exchange and had made large sums of money. What some had gained others had lost. It was a frightening situation.

Henrietta came to her in panic and told her that it was being said that the royal family should leave England. They had never been so unpopular. They should get away while they had a chance.

"It will pass," said Caroline.

Walpole came to see her. She had been cool to him since the reconciliation and had told him that she understood how she had been duped.

He had been deeply concerned, assuring her that he had done everything in his power to restore her children to her. All the same she had made it clear to him that he was out of favour with her.

He had done something to regain her esteem by showing how her dissatisfaction disturbed him and using every effort to win back her approval.

She saw him differently now; to her he was a man of unattractive appearance; he was too bulky in figure, too coarse in his habits; and she had heard he drank heavily and lived an immoral life. Even so, she made excuses for him. His married life was not happy; his wife went her own way as he did, and took lovers while he took mistresses. He had a daughter who was a chronic invalid and her sufferings distressed him deeply. And in spite of all this he was the most brilliant statesman of his day.

She was aware of this and wanted him to be on her side. He knew that she was a clever woman married to a foolish husband who would one day be King. They both respected each other and would continue to do so whatever the differences between them.

Now it was as though his fearful disaster had brought them a little closer. She confided in him what she had heard and he replied that there was some feeling against the royal family, but it would be folly to run away. The trouble would pass although he believed it would mean the fall of Stanhope.

"But that, Madam," he said his eyes twinkling, "need be no great concern of yours. Stanhope was scarcely your friend."

"They are blaming him?"

"He's one of the culprits. Sunderland too. They'll have to resign."

"And then?"

Walpole smiled. "I was warning people, you know, before the crash. I advised them not to buy."

"And you yourself?"

"I sold out at the highest price."

"This will not be held against you?"

"Why should it? I warned others to sell. I was ignored."

"And now you are able to go ahead with your building plans."

"Yes, Madam. I hope one day to have the honour of entertaining you and the Prince at Houghton. I will show you the pictures I am collecting. I am sure they will enchant you."

"You will not retire to Houghton again?"

"I doubt it, Madam. I doubt it now."

*       *       *

He was right, of course. Stanhope, rising in Parliament to defend himself, dropped to the floor unconscious, and the next day died. The strain was too much for him. Sunderland, as Walpole had predicted, was forced to resign.

This was the opportunity for which Walpole had been waiting. He was ready.

Sir Robert Walpole became Prime Minister.

## The Double Wedding Plan

CAROLINE had adjusted herself to her new role. Now she was the first lady of the Court. The King showed no objection to this for he had always had quite an affection for her. If she had had the character of his Duchess of Kendal, if she had not been his son's wife ... he admitted to himself he might have looked for a warmer relationship. But he was not one to seek a complicated life. All the same he was not displeased to have her back in her place. He liked to listen to her conversation when she spoke French and German. He could even understand her English better than that of his English ministers, interspersed as it was with French and German words and all pronounced with a decided German accent. Yes, his daughter-in-law was a fine woman, yet, as he had always known, one who would have to be watched.

He was content enough with the Duchess of Kendal and Darlington and other mistresses whom he picked up and dropped from time to time.

Dangers came and went. The affair of the South Sea Bubble

had subsided and it had brought him Walpole, who, he knew very well, was the shrewdest minister in both England and Germany.

James across the water was a menace and always would be. Particularly now that he had married and produced a son, Charles Edward—so that now the line would continue and this boy could well grow up to harry them, though doubtless that would be in the days of George Augustus, his foolish son.

Well, at least he would have a clever wife to help him.

She hated her father-in-law of course. She'd never forgive him for keeping Frederick at Hanover and the girls under his control.

Well, she was pregnant again; and he would put no restrictions on this child. If it lived she should keep this one. That might make her a little more affectionate towards her father-in-law.

\* \* \*

Mary Bellenden had given little attention to what was happening, being absorbed by her own affairs. She was wondering what would happen when she betrayed her secret; and she would have to sooner or later. The Prince still eyed her lasciviously although he had taken several mistresses recently.

He had changed—everybody was changing.

We're growing older, thought Mary. It was true; she was no longer the frivolous young girl she had been; nor was Molly Lepel; not even Sophie.

That reminded her. She had meant to speak to Molly about Sophie who had changed more than any of them. A short while ago she had been so frivolous that they had all scolded her. She seemed not to have a serious thought in her head. Lately she had been very quiet. What was on *her* mind?

She found Molly Lepel putting the Princess's clothes away.

"I should be helping you," said Mary. "I quite forgot."

Molly murmured something; and that was not like her usual talkative self.

"Is anything wrong?"

"Well ... hardly that. Mary ... I'm married."

"You ... too!"

"You mean ..."

Mary nodded; and they both began to laugh.

"I might have known," said Molly at length. "How long...."

"Too long to keep it secret. I thought we'd better when the Prince was getting more of a nuisance than ever. And you?"

"Lord Hervey."

"Lord Hervey! Molly! Who would have thought ..."

"That he would have a wife?"

Mary was silent. Molly and Hervey! It was incredible. What a handsome pair they would be and yet ... She could not imagine Hervey as a husband. Still, Molly looked happy.

"I want to retire to the country. I'm tired of Court life," said Molly. "And you?"

"John has to stay at Court so I shall, too. One in the Prince's household, one in that of the Princess. You must admit it's convenient. I wonder if Sophie's married too and that's why she's been so quiet lately."

"We must find out," said Molly.

"I know she has been meeting Anthony Lowther lately."

"We'll ask at the first opportunity. After all if we tell her our secret, she should tell us hers."

The opportunity came a few days later.

The three girls were alone together in the Princess's robing chamber when Mary said: "We want to tell you something, Sophie. Molly and I are married."

Sophie did not answer and as she lowered her head and her lip trembled Mary and Molly began to understand.

"Is it Tony Lowther?" asked Mary.

Sophie nodded.

"How long?"

"Three months."

"You will have to be married ... secretly as we were."

"But ..."

"You mean he won't."

Sophie nodded. "What am I going to do?" she asked.

"Tony Lowther will have to marry you. That's the only answer."

But Sophie only shook her head.

The two girls did what they could to comfort her; but there was no comforting Sophie.

\*     \*     \*

Caroline was sorry for the girl. Poor silly little Sophie! She was an example of the folly of acting without thought. It was no use speaking to Lowther; he had left court knowing that pressure might be brought to bear on him; and would it be wise to force marriage on him? Even Sophie did not wish that.

Margaret Meadows went about with lips pursed and an air of 'I told you so'.

Poor heartbroken little Sophie!

Caroline sent for the girl.

"My poor child," she said, "I think you should leave the Court and go home."

"Yes, Your Highness."

"There at least you vill be far from gossip. I vill write to your family and tell them to be kind to you."

"Your Highness is good."

"I vish I could help you more. I suppose he promised to marry you?"

"Yes, Madam."

"You are not the first to be deceived by empty promises. Your ... indiscretion vill be a lesson to you. Take it to heart but try to make a new life for yourself. Profit from your misfortune, my tear, and try to be happy in the new life you vill surely make for yourself."

Sophie sank to her knees and kissed the Princess's hand.

A few days later she left court; and it was not long afterwards when Molly Lepel, her marriage no longer a secret, left the Princess's service to start a new life in the country.

My Court will not be the same without them, thought Caroline. And even Mary Bellenden has emerged as a married woman.

But she soon ceased to think about the affairs of her maids of honour for the time came for her child to be born and this time to her great joy it was a healthy boy whom she called William Augustus; and when she held him in her arms she believed that her ill luck had changed. This child would be her very own and no one would attempt to take him from her.

\*     \*     \*

She was right. From the time of the child's birth she was happier. She would have more children and then it would seem as though she had another little family all her own. The King showed that he did not find her company distasteful. He would often sit dourly listening when she talked, but he seemed to enjoy her conversation as much as he enjoyed any.

When she heard from Lady Mary Wortley Montague that in Turkey smallpox was rendered harmless by making a small wound and infecting it with pus from a smallpox sore she was very interested. Lady Mary wrote that she had allowed her own son to be inoculated; and when her doctor, Charles Maitland, came to England Caroline sent for him and asked him to tell her more.

There was an outcry, for nothing the Princess did could pass unnoticed. Lady Mary was counted an unnatural mother; the doctors decried the practice as against God's Will.

Caroline pondered the matter. She was constantly afraid of the smallpox which had killed her mother; every other person in the street was marked by it; she herself had escaped lightly, through great good fortune; she learned that seventy-two people out of every thousand died of it.

She longed to make her own children secure against it but dared not take any risk.

She tried to talk to the Prince about it, but he was not really interested.

"Imagine," she said, "the benefit to the nation ... if ve could vipe out this terrible scourge."

"It vould be goot ... very goot. ..."

He thinks of nothing but his own vanities, she thought a little contemptuously, a little indulgently. Strangely enough as the years passed she was discovering that she would not have had him otherwise.

At the King's reception one evening she had an opportunity

of speaking to the King. George was there. The Duchesses of Kendal and Darlington inevitably were in attendance, listening to music while some played cards.

Mary Bellenden was present with her husband and as they came in the Prince scowled at her and shook his finger; then he turned his back. It might have been comic but he was really angry with her for preferring his bedchamber groom to himself. Caroline was glad though that he had not dismissed John Campbell and confined his display of pique to a shake of the finger and a turn of the back.

Caroline took her place next to the King and talked awhile to the Duchess of Kendal who, she secretly thought, grew uglier every day.

Then she broached the subject of inoculation and told the King of Mary Wortley Montague's experiences. The Prince scowled when he heard the name of Mary Wortley Montague because she had attracted him and refused to become his mistress. It was bad enough to have the beautiful Bellenden there with her husband, but to hear Caroline refer to another who had refused him was most irritating. He was surprised that Caroline should be so inconsiderate; she was not usually so. Then he realized that she was on her old hobby horse inoculation, so he ceased to be interested.

"If I were sure," she was saying to the King, "I should like to have the children innoculated."

George nodded.

"There would have to be more experiments first. I have talked to Maitland."

"Who is this Maitland?"

"The doctor who inoculated Lady Mary's son."

The King nodded.

"I think we should try these experiments. Suppose we took prisoners from Newgate ... those condemned to die in any case. Would Your Majesty agree that might be a good idea?"

The King nodded. "It is a good idea," he said.

That was all she needed.

The next day she summoned Maitland and the experiment began.

To Caroline's delight it was entirely successful.

"But we must be sure," she told Maitland, and six charity children were inoculated with equal success.

Caroline summoned Sir Hans Sloane for discussions with Maitland. As he was favourably impressed she allowed Amelia and Caroline to be inoculated.

When this was successful, many hurried to be inoculated . It became the fashion to be so treated.

Caroline was delighted. The battle against the deadly killer had begun.

\*       \*       \*

Little more than a year after the birth of William Augustus, Caroline's daughter Mary was born. This was great happiness. She now had two healthy children and the fact that the older ones were not entirely hers gave her less anguish. She had a second little family which was a consolation.

Occasionally she was uneasy about her daughters whom she was sure lacked the training she would have given them. Anne was very haughty and she believed very ambitious; Amelia showed signs of beauty and was more amiable than her sister; Caroline, her namesake and favourite, was quiet and delicate, her health a constant source of anxiety. They need their mother, thought the Princess uneasily and often. But there was nothing more to be done. As for Frederick—little Fritzchen— he was now nearly seventeen, a man who kept a mistress. It was so long since she had seen him and although she had pined for him in those first years of separation, now she hardly ever gave him a thought.

How grateful she was therefore to have her dear little William Augustus and Mary—her own, entirely her own.

She was able to invite to her court those men of letters who interested her; she was able to read their works and discuss them with their authors. That was a great pleasure. She enjoyed both Pope's *Iliad* and Defoe's *Robinson Crusoe*, and when she read *Gulliver's Travels* with its allusions to the political figures of the day—the Prince not excepted—she declared she must meet the author as soon as he arrived in London.

Life had certainly taken a happier turn.

The King even condescended to tell her of the marriage project which his daughter, Sophia Dorothea, longed to put into practice: her daughter for Frederick, her son for Amelia. She admitted that the crown of Prussia would be a good proposition for Amelia and she had no objection to Frederick's marrying his cousin.

She thought of Sophia Dorothea, the gay young sister-in-law whom she had known during the first months of her marriage, and who had determined to marry the King of Prussia's heir ... her own beloved Sophia Charlotte's son. It had been a strange marriage for the King of Prussia had turned out to be a violent man; but Sophia Dorothea had spirit and in spite of the fact that there was violence between them, they had a lasting affection for each other.

She, Caroline, would, of course, have no say in the marriage of her children; the King would decide and she and George Augustus would accept his decision; but it was pleasant that he should condescend to discuss the matter with her.

\*     \*     \*

She talked to the Prince about the proposal. His face grew purple at the thought of it.

"This I vill not haf," he said. "They are mad, that family. Their father is mad. I hate him."

"But their mother is your own sister."

"Vot is that? She have von husband who is a madman."

"His manners are strange, yes...."

"And this I vill not haf."

"If the King decides we must accept."

"I vill not. She is my daughter. Frederick is my son. This double vedding I vill not haf. I hate the King of Prussia. Vonce he tried to marry you."

"That came to nothing."

"How happy I am that it did not." His blue eyes filled with tears. "Vot should I haf done vithout my Caroline, eh?"

"Doubtless they vould have found another von for you."

"That I vould not haf. It has been a happy marriage. I vould never love another as I love my Caroline."

She thought of him, waiting outside Henrietta's apartments watch in hand. She thought of his attempts with Mary

Bellenden and Mary Wortley Montague. They were two unsuccessful ones; there had been many others which had succeeded.

"They are but mistresses," he would say. "You are the Princess and my vife."

He was like a child in so many ways; and the reason why he was so much against the double wedding was because at one time there had been a possibility of the King of Prussia's being a suitor for Caroline.

\* \* \*

The Duchess of Darlington was pensive. She had heard that Wilhelmina, the daughter of the King of Prussia was a very clever and forceful woman. If she married Frederick he would come to England, for then he could no longer be kept away. Another clever woman at the Court! That would be too much. The cleverness of the Princess Caroline was a hindrance to so many of her plans; and although the King was supposed to be on bad terms with the Prince and Princess it was clear that even he was impressed by this cleverness.

No, definitely the Duchess did not want another clever woman at Court.

"I have heard," she told the King, "that Wilhelmina is so ugly that she is quite frightful to look at; and violent with it—so much so that she has epileptic fits."

The King was horrified. This was gossip, of course; but very often there was truth in rumour. They wanted no epilepsy in the family.

\* \* \*

The Duchess of Kendal had been aloof from the matter until she had been offered money to support the scheme. She rarely interfered with matters of state knowing she owed her hold on the King to this very quality; but money could tempt her.

She did not try to persuade the King or even show any interest to him. She had become wiser over the years but she did write to the Queen of Prussia telling her of the rumours and suggesting she invite the King to Berlin so that he might see the Princess Wilhelmina for himself and prove them false.

This advice was taken by the Queen and as a result the King decided he would pay another visit to his beloved Hanover and call at Berlin on route.

*    *    *

George arrived in due course at Lützenburg which had been renamed Charlottenburg after Sophia Charlotte and there was greeted by his daughter and son-in-law.

Almost immediately he wished that he had stayed away. Sophia Dorothea had grown so like her mother that it was a shock to come face to face with her after all this time. However, he was not one to betray his feelings and his dour expression scarcely changed.

Sophia Dorothea was excited; there was so much she wanted to know about George Augustus and Caroline. She had heard such stories of the quarrel and how Caroline had managed to become popular in England. But it was hopeless to expect interesting gossip from her father. All she could do was welcome him as well as she could manage; but even that wasn't easy for the King of Prussia was miserly in the extreme and grudged spending money on anything but his armies.

What a life I lead! thought Sophia Dorothea and inwardly grimaced; for in fact she did not hate it as much as it might have seemed natural for her to do. Frederick William was so violent at times that she thought he was verging on madness; her son and daughter were terrified of him; and so was she ... in a way, a rather exciting fear, like a child who begs for stories of horror even though she knows they will bring nightmares. Oh yes, life was certainly not dull with Frederick William—neither for her nor the children. They were used to their father's ungovernable rages and the punishment he seemed to enjoy giving them; they thought nothing of it when he kicked them or beat them with his own hands; he liked to lock them in their apartments and starve them and then he would gloat over the amount of money he was saving by not feeding them.

He never attempted to beat her, although at one time he had tried; he contented himself with swearing at her, calling her abusive names and spitting in her food, especially if it was a dish she particularly enjoyed.

She was by no means meek; she would retaliate by telling him he was a brute, that he was a madman and ought to be put into a cage. Then he would laugh and there might follow a reconciliation—on the other hand there might not. One could never be sure with Frederick William. That was the joy of living with him.

What a dull life Caroline and George Augustus must lead! And her mother too ... her poor mother to whom she wrote from time to time and had tried to bring out of her prison ... what a misery her life was!

No, Sophia Dorothea, oddly enough, regretted nothing and would not have changed her life if she could. Now she assured herself she was about to see realized her most cherished plan: the Double Wedding; her son married to her brother's daughter; her brother's son married to her daughter. What an excellent plan! Her Wilhelmina would be Queen of England and George Augustus's daughter Queen of Prussia.

Thus, she had promised herself, we keep the crowns in the family.

And her enemies had tried to prevent it by spreading lies about Wilhelmina. Epileptic indeed! They should see her daughter who was clever and good looking enough to please anyone—even the English.

"Your Majesty will wish to see your granddaughter, I am sure," she told her father. "She is all eagerness for the honour."

Wilhelmina stepped forward, and knelt before the King. He saw a tall girl who appeared to be sound, but one could never tell with epilepsy.

He did not smile but merely stared at her.

"She's tall," he said.

Then his daughter gave him her hand and led him to her apartments whither the King of Prussia and Wilhelmina followed with some of their attendants. No sooner had they reached the apartment than the King demanded a candle and when it was brought to him summoned his granddaughter to stand before. When she did so he held the candle so close to her that she thought he would catch her hair alight, and examined her as though she were a horse or cow.

Wilhelmina felt very agitated and was relieved when her grandfather told her mother that he wished to speak with her alone.

Poor Wilhelmina knew that she was under discussion and felt embarrassed until some of the King's English suite began to talk to her, although she was sure that they too were trying to put her to the test, but when they told her that she had the manners and bearing of an Englishwoman she smiled wryly knowing they were trying to be complimentary.

She thought her grandfather terrifying. He never smiled; he seemed melancholy; and his only interest in her was whether she would make a suitable wife for his grandson of whom in any case he saw very little. She would be glad when he left; and almost preferred her violent father to this dour man.

That evening there was a banquet to honour the King of England. He was seated beside the Queen who talked to him as though she were not in the least in awe of him. Wilhelmina who now and then stole glances at him noticed that he had his eyes closed.

Lord Townsend was whispering to her. "I think His Majesty is unwell. Could you sign to your mother to prepare to leave the table. I am sure the King should be in his bed."

Wilhelmina rose from her chair and went to her mother and whispered what Lord Townsend had suggested.

The Queen gave her father a startled look and said: "I see Your Majesty is a little tired. We will now retire."

"I am not tired," said the King gruffly. "Pray be seated, and go on talking."

But Sophia Dorothea thought there was something strange about him and insisted that she was now going to give the sign for all to leave the table.

As she spoke she stood up. The King rose too, but even as he stood on his feet, he swayed ... and in a few seconds had collapsed on to the floor where he lay unconscious.

There was pandemonium in the hall. The King of Prussia gave orders that cushions should be brought with blankets to cover the King of England who lay still unaware of what was happening.

"He has had a paralytic seizure," said the Queen. "That this should have happened here! My poor father. Send for the physicians at once."

But before the physicians arrived the King had recovered. Almost immediately he seemed to know where he was and reaching for his wig which had fallen off, put it on his head.

"It is nothing," he said. "Here! Help me to my feet."

With the aid of the King of Prussia and Lord Townsend he stood up.

"I will conduct you to your apartments," he told his daughter.

"Your Majesty . . ."

"I will conduct you to your apartments," he repeated.

The assembly looked on in amazement while he did so.

Then he returned to his own apartments. There was no sign of paralysis.

"It is nothing," was the verdict. "The King merely fainted."

And after that, since it was his wish, no mention was made of the incident.

He was not inclined however to complete the negotiations for the double wedding.

"I shall come back to Hanover," he told his daughter. "The children are young yet . . . too young for marriage."

"I hear Frederick already has a mistress in Hanover," pointed out Sophia Dorothea.

"They are too young yet," said the King obstinately.

And that was all the satisfaction she could get.

## The Ghost of the Old Leine Schloss

In spite of the fact that the King had wished to keep the news of his collapse secret he was unable to do so, and accounts of it reached England.

The Prince received them exultantly, Caroline inwardly so, but outwardly she was more restrained than her husband.

George Augustus strode up and down his wife's apartment, his wig awry, his blue eyes brilliant.

"This is the end of him," he declared. "A paralytic seizure at his age!"

"They are saying that he appears to be as vell as he vas on the day he left England."

"Impossible. I tell you this, my tear. It is my turn now. King of Englandt! How you like that, eh? King George II!"

"It sounds very vell, but let us vait a bit and be careful."

He came to the chair on which she was sitting and pinched her cheek. "Oh, you are the cautious von, alvays, my Caroline. Ve shall soon be planning our coronation."

"Let us not talk so ... even in private." She glanced over her shoulder. But he only laughed the louder. He was so sure of himself, standing on tiptoe, seeing himself in the mirror, a crown instead of the wig on his head.

Caroline was alarmed, imagining the King's spies carrying tales of his son's unseemly behaviour; would it be possible for him to have George Augustus passed over in favour of Frederick? Who knew what vindictive scheme that man might invent. And Frederick thought Caroline, what do I know of Frederick? My son is a stranger to me. We must be careful ... more so now than ever.

But how make the exuberant George Augustus understand this?

\*     \*     \*

The King had returned to England. Before she saw him Caroline heard that he showed no ill effects; but she could not believe that. He was advancing into his sixties. How could a man of that age collapse mysteriously at dinner and it have no significance?

When he received her he was attended as usual by the Duchesses of Kendal and Darlington, and Caroline was immediately aware of their anxious looks. But the King had not changed at all. There was no sign of illness in his dour unwelcoming face.

Did he look at her a little sardonically? He would know of course how their hopes had soared. Was he saying: Not yet, my dear. It is not the turn of that booby of a husband of yours yet. Oh, no you have to wait, my dear.

"I have brought you a present," he told Caroline.

She was surprised and pleased for it was the first time he had brought a gift for her.

"You Majesty is gracious to me."

His lips turned up at the corners; it was as near as he could get to a smile. Was she visualizing some magnificent piece of jewellery, wondered the King. She was going to have yet another surprise and he wondered whether this one would be as unpalatable as the first, for when she had come to him she had expected to see him disabled from his so-called seizure.

He signed to one of his attendants and said that the Princess's gift was to be brought to her.

The man disappeared and when he returned there was an astonished silence throughout the apartment, for he led by a chain attached to the creature's neck what might have been a boy or a monkey. The creature stooped slightly and loped while it looked about it at the assembled company with something between fear and defiance. It was dressed in a bright blue suit lined with red, and red stockings. "It is a wild boy," said the King. "We found him in the forest; he ran on all fours then, but he can stand up already. He lived on grass, moss, nuts and whatever he could find. I thought he would amuse Your Highness."

Caroline said, without showing her distaste or surprise: "Your Majesty is gracious."

She took the chain which was offered her and led the creature from the King's presence.

\*     \*     \*

Everyone was talking of the Wild Boy and wondered what lay behind the King's motive in presenting him to the Princess. Was it because she had introduced the fashion for innoculation? Was the King hinting that as she appeared to be interested in medical science, here was an opportunity to try a further experiment?

Caroline, however, had given no sign of her dismay; the first thing she did on reaching her apartments was to send for her good friend Dr. Arbuthnot.

She showed him the boy who glared at them both from under his bushy eyebrows and Caroline asked the doctor if he thought by gentle treatment and teaching he might become normal.

"It would be interesting," she said, "to discover whether this is possible."

The doctor agreed and said he would take the wild boy away and see what could be done with him.

"Poor boy," said Caroline. "I wonder what *his* history is. He doubtless lost his parents in some way or was abandoned. But he must certainly have fended for himself for some ten or twelve years."

"That we may discover ... if we can reach him to speak."

"Then teach him. I know you will be kind to him. I fancy he needs kindness. He looks at us so suspiciously. I think he is rather frightened. You must bring him to visit me from time to time; and he should have a name. We will call him Peter."

So Dr. Arbuthnot took Peter away and tried to teach him; and very soon the wild boy was forgotten except by Caroline who had many interviews with Dr. Arbuthnot, who could report little progress; and she continued to wonder why the King had given her such a present.

\* \* \*

Soon after the King's return from Hanover Caroline's daughter Louisa was born. Caroline now had a little family of three and to these she devoted herself; she was able to visit Anne, Amelia and Caroline more frequently than she had before the reconciliation, but she still felt resentful because she had no control of them.

The Court was less gay than it had been in the old days. Molly Lepel was rarely there although Lord Hervey was a frequent visitor and Caroline was always delighted to see him. Mary Bellenden remained but she had become quieter in her contentment. Poor Sophie Howe would never return. She was heartbroken and had fallen into such a decline that it was not expected she would live more than a few more months.

It was a saddening thought. Henrietta, Mrs. Clayton and Lady Cowper retained their posts but they had never been the gay spirits of the Court. Yes, the Court had lost its earlier sparkle.

Walpole was a frequent visitor; but she told herself she could not forgive him for deceiving her at the time of the reconciliation; and she still talked continually of her desire to have her older children back under her roof. The King was devoted to Walpole and for that reason—and because his debts had not been paid as Walpole had promised they would—the Prince disliked him.

Yet in spite of this Caroline was fascinated by the man. He was wily and had even succeeded in ousting the Germans from the King's favour and holding first position there himself.

Walpole must be watched, she thought, so that when the great day came his services could be called upon.

If George Augustus hated Walpole he did not hate Walpole's wife. Rumour was that she was for a time his mistress and as she was notorious for the fact that she took lover after lover while her husband went his own way, it seemed possible.

And so a few years slipped by and although the King grew older he remained in excellent health and when Anne Brett, a very handsome, dark-haired young woman came to court he showed marked interest in her.

Caroline, aware of this, wondered whether the King could live for another ten or fifteen years. Would her children ever be returned to her? Was Frederick going to be kept in Hanover for the rest of the King's life? Would the crown never be her husband's? Would she never know the power for which ever since her marriage she had been preparing herself?

The King was approaching his sixty-sixth year. Was he going to outlive them all?

\*　　\*　　\*

George was pleased with life. He had become reconciled to England; he was devoted to his two German mistresses, particularly the Duchess of Kendal; she was constantly with him and was to him as a wife. At the same time Anne Brett excited him and he would enjoy his association with her as wholeheartedly as he had indulged in such affairs at the age of eighteen.

He too had begun to think he was immortal.

Anne was no Ermengarda. She made demands; but she was so young and he was perhaps ready nowadays to do a little more courting than he had been in his youth.

She amused him; she delighted him; she was as beautiful as the Countess von Platen and that made a pleasant change from the Duchesses of Kendal and Darlington.

Then his content was disturbed—and for the strangest reason. He should have been pleased if anything—at least indifferent, but he was surprised to find he was not.

A messenger arrived from Hanover with news that his wife Sophia Dorothea had died in her prison at Ahlden after thirty two years of that captivity to which her husband had condemned her.

George shut himself in his apartment. Why should he care? She deserved it, he said. She betrayed me with Königsmarck.

And for some strange reason the past became clear again; he remembered the quarrels when she had accused him of infidelity. Ermengarda had been the cause of the quarrel, and she was still with him, his dear Duchess of Kendal.

Then Sophia Dorothea had taken her lover, been discovered, her lover mysteriously murdered, herself made a prisoner for life ... the prisoner of her husband.

How she must have hated him, living out her lonely life in Ahlden, calling herself Queen of England, a country she would never see—for he had condemned her to life imprisonment!

She had died cursing him. He did not want to know more. It was better not.

He made up his mind there should be a brief announcement —that was all. And life should go on as though nothing had happened.

Nor had it. She had been nothing to him for years. And now she was dead.

\*     \*     \*

"My mother is dead," said George Augustus.

Caroline thought of Sophia Dorothea of whom she had heard so much during her first years in Hanover, although she had never seen her. She remembered the shadow which had seemed to hang over the old Leine Schloss; she recalled vividly the spot where it was said Königsmarck, creeping from his mistress's rooms, had been set upon and murdered.

Poor Sophia Dorothea, the victim of the King's vindictiveness even as she was!

"The Court must go into mourning," she said.

\*     \*     \*

The King came into her apartment, his eyes bulging, his jaw trembling. Never before had she seen him moved in this way.

"What is this I hear?" he demanded. "The Court in mourning! Why?"

"For the death of the Prince's mother."

"She is . . . nothing. There will be no mourning. Do you hear me. I said no mourning."

"If it is Your Majesty's command. . . ."

"It is an order. No mourning, I say. No mourning."

She bowed her head. "There shall be no mourning."

He left her. No, certainly she had never seen him so disturbed.

He looked ten years older than he had before the news had come.

\*     \*     \*

That night the King went to the theatre, with more pomp than usual. On one side of him was the Duchess of Kendal, on the other the Duchess of Darlington.

He gave an impression of enjoying the show more than usual.

Caroline, who had been ordered to go to the theatre with the Prince at the same time, watched him more than the play.

He is too eager, she thought. And he has aged. Can it really be that he suffers remorse, or is it that he is more afraid of the dead than of the living?

\*     \*     \*

George could not shut himself away from rumour. Sophia Dorothea had cursed him when she was dying. Those who had been at her bedside had heard it distinctly. She had been half conscious but she had talked of him. He would not survive her a year, she had prophesied; he would be called to face her at the judgement seat when he would have to answer for what he had done to her.

The King heard the prophecies and laughed at them. Anne Brett had become his mistress after he had given her fine apartments in St. James's Palace and a good pension, but she wanted a title too.

He had explained that that was a matter which took some time to arrange but it should be hers in due course.

The young woman strutted about the Court giving herself airs as none of the other mistresses had dared do. The Duchess of Kendal was annoyed that another woman should take up so much of the King's time, and some said that to placate her the King married her—but there was no proof of this. However, in spite of his infatuation for Anne Brett, he still did not waver in his devotion to Ermengarda. Perhaps when they were alone together they talked of those early days when his devotion to her had called forth the protests of his wife—for that had been the beginning of the trouble. Ermengarda had had no hand in the condemnation of Sophia Dorothea but because she was in some way involved he found even greater comfort in her company.

But this, of course, he would not admit. Sophia Dorothea was dead—and that was the end of an episode which over the years had become insignificant.

And the time came for him to pay another visit to Hanover. He was going to remonstrate with his daughter, the Queen of Prussia, because she had ordered the deepest mourning at her court for her mother. If she wanted the double marriage this was not the way to get it.

He must go to Hanover; he must show the world—and perhaps himself—that he cared nothing for the death-bed prophecies of the woman whose life he had ruined when he had condemned her to life imprisonment.

It was on a June day, about seven months after the death of Sophia Dorothea, that he set out on his journey.

\* \* \*

The crossing was a bad one and Ermengarda always had suffered from sea sickeness.

"You must rest for a day or so at the Hague," said the King. "You can follow me when you have recovered."

She agreed that she must do this and he went on alone with his escort, which included Lord Townsend, and on the borders of Holland and Germany stopped at the mansion of a Count Twittle who was waiting to receive the royal party. Supper was waiting for them, a meal which the King thoroughly enjoyed.

The Count said that his mansion was at the King's disposal for as long as he should need it and Townsend suggested that they should rest there at Delden for a few days which would enable the King to recover from the journey and the Duchess of Kendal to join them.

But the King would not wait; he would not even stay the night. The horses must be saddled, he said, and they would continue their journey to Osnabrück where his brother would be waiting to welcome him.

As the King stepped into his coach he saw a letter lying on the seat. He picked it up; he did not know the handwriting and yet there was something familiar about it.

"Ride on," he ordered; and as his coach rattled out of Delden he read the letter.

His hands began to shake so that he could scarcely hold the letter. As soon as he began to read it he knew why the handwriting had seemed familiar. He had not seen it for years because it was hers.

She was ill, she wrote; she would soon die. But he need not think that he would live much longer than she had. He had ruined her life; he had condemned her to lonely exile. What life did he think she had had ... she who should have shared the throne of England, she who was the true Queen? But his time would come. He should not live long to survive her. As soon as he heard of her death ... he should prepare for his own.

The King lay back in his seat; his heart was beating so fast that it shocked him; a red mist swam before his eyes.

Townsend beside him spoke but the King could not hear his voice clearly.

"Your Majesty..."

"Drive to Osnabrück," he whispered. "I must get to Osnabrück."

"Your Majesty is ill. We will drive back to Delden...."

"To Osnabrück," said the King.

"I am afraid for His Majesty..." began Townsend. "We need doctors..."

"To Osnabrück ..." muttered George.

"You had better do as the King commands," said Townsend. "Drive with all speed to Osnabrück."

George lay back in the coach. His eyes were glazed; but his lips moved now and then. "To Osnabrück. To Osnabrück," he whispered.

And by the time his coach reached Osnabrück King George I was dead.

## The End of Waiting

IN the palace of St. James Anne Brett was giving orders to the workmen.

"I want this door taken away and a new staircase made," she was explaining. "You need have no fear. I have the King's authority to do as I wish."

They hesitated but she was an imperious young woman and they knew how she commanded the King.

But the Princess Anne, almost eighteen years old, was as imperious as Anne Brett and she was supported by a dignity which being born granddaughter of a King had come to her naturally.

"What is being done here?" she demanded.

And when she was told she said: "This door remains and there shall be no new staircase."

Anne Brett came out to face the Princess Anne.

"I have given orders . . ." said Mistress Brett.

"And I have countermanded them."

"I want that door taken away."

"But I want it to remain."

"We shall see. When I tell the King..."

"Being the King's whore does not entitle you to rule us all, Madam."

"You will see ... when the King comes home...."

"Until then, pray remember without him you are nothing but a common whore and as such should remember your place."

"You are insolent."

"You are mistaken. It is you who are insolent. Have you forgotten that I am a Princess."

Anne swept haughtily away; but the workmen dared not continue the work.

Anne Brett went to her room to rage and await the return of the King.

\*     \*     \*

When the Duchess of Kendal heard the news she refused to believe it; she tore at her wig, pulled her bodice to shreds and threw herself on to her bed where she wailed in her misery.

For so many years they had been together. It wasn't true. It couldn't be true. She could not live without him.

Her friends tried to soothe her, but they could not; and they feared for her reason.

\*     \*     \*

In Richmond the Prince was enjoying his after dinner nap. The weather was warm and he had eaten with his usual gusto.

Caroline in her apartments had just risen when she heard the clatter of horses hoofs in the courtyard. She went to the window and saw Sir Robert Walpole.

He looked excited. Something important had happened for him to come riding to Richmond in the hot afternoon.

She went to the Prince's bedroom to tell him that Walpole was below and just as she had awakened him the minister burst into the apartment.

The Prince sat up in bed. Walpole was on his knees.

Caroline heard him say: "Your Majesty..."

And she knew the moment had come. The waiting was over. She was Queen of England.

*    *    *

There was change everywhere.

Caroline went to her daughters.

"We are all together now," she told them, embracing them in tears.

Frederick would come home from Hanover.

The whole family would be reunited.

Anne Brett made a hasty retreat from the Palace. She had nothing to hope for now, so even if she had succeeded in getting the alterations she wanted of what use would they have been to her?

The only one who truly mourned the King was Ermengarda, who went into deep mourning and was melancholy for the rest of her life. After a stay at Brunswick she came back to her house in Isleworth and her only comfort was a raven whom she dressed in sable because she believed it was the King come back to her, as he had promised to do if it were possible.

George Augustus strutted happily about the court. None dared cross him now. The tyrant was dead; and now there was George II to reign over England.

Caroline was beside him, and wise men knew who would be the true ruler. It would not be King George but Queen Caroline.